THE TOWN

The Town is the second novel in William Faulkner's trilogy devoted to the origin, rise and dominance of the Snopes family. Its predecessor is *The Hamlet*.

The Town gives us a record of the town of Jefferson—the intrigues, the laziness, the violence, the myth-making—over a period of years when the rapacious Snopes' were spreading their tentacles over this Southern community. Against all odds—and these include his beautiful and amoral wife, Eula, and Gavin Stevens the lawyer—Flem Snopes gradually wins the power which is all he wants, or understands, in life. Packed with incident, full of broad comedy, *The Town* is a novel soaked in the very essence of the life it springs from.

By William Faulkner

*

Soldier's Pay
Sartoris
The Sound and the Fury
The Wild Palms
As I Lay Dying
Sanctuary
Light in August
Pylon
Absalom, Absalom!
The Unvanquished
The Hamlet
Go Down, Moses
Intruder in the Dust
Knight's Gambit
Requiem for a Nun
A Fable
The Town

Short Stories

Uncle Willy & Other Stories
These Thirteen
Dr Martino & Other Stories
Collected Stories
Faulkner's County
A Green Bough (Poems)

THE TOWN

William Faulkner

1958

CHATTO AND WINDUS

LONDON

PUBLISHED BY
CHATTO AND WINDUS LTD
42 WILLIAM IV STREET
LONDON W.C.2

TO PHIL STONE

He did the laughing for thirty years

I

CHARLES MALLISON

I WASN'T born yet, so it was Cousin Gowan who was there and big enough to see and remember and tell me afterward when I was big enough for it to make sense. That is, it was Cousin Gowan plus Uncle Gavin or maybe Uncle Gavin rather plus Cousin Gowan. He—Cousin Gowan—was thirteen. His grandfather was Grandfather's brother, so by the time it got down to us, he and I didn't know what cousin to each other we were. So he just called all of us except Grandfather "cousin" and all of us except Grandfather called him "cousin" and let it go at that.

They lived in Washington, where his father worked for the State Department, and all of a sudden the State Department sent his father to China or India or some far place, to be gone two years; and his mother was going too, so they sent Gowan down to stay with us and go to school in Jefferson until they got back. "Us" was Grandfather and Mother and Father and Uncle Gavin then. So this is what Gowan knew about it until I got born and big enough to know about it too. So when I say "we" and "we thought" what I mean is Jefferson and what Jefferson thought.

At first we thought that the water tank was only Flem Snopes's monument. We didn't know any better then. It wasn't until afterward that we realised that that object low on the sky above Jefferson, Mississippi, wasn't a monument at all. It was a footprint.

One day one summer he drove up the south-east road into town in a two-mule wagon containing his wife and baby and a small assortment of house-furnishings. The next day he was behind the counter of a small back-alley restaurant which belonged to V. K. Ratliff. That is, Ratliff owned it with a partner, since he—Ratliff —had to spend most of his time in his buckboard (this was before he owned the Model T Ford) about the county with his demonstrator sewing machine for which he was the agent. That is, we thought Ratliff was still the other partner until we saw the stranger in the other greasy apron behind the counter—a squat uncommunicative man with a neat minute bow tie and opaque eyes and a sudden little hooked nose like the beak of a small hawk; a week after that, Snopes had set up a canvas tent behind the restaurant and he and his wife and baby were living in it. And that was when Ratliff told Uncle Gavin:

"Just give him time. Give him six months and he'll have Grover Cleveland" (Grover Cleveland Winbush was the partner) "out of that café too."

That was the first summer, the first Summer of the Snopeses, Uncle Gavin called it. He was in Harvard now, working for his M.A. After that he was going to the University of Mississippi law school to get ready to be Grandfather's partner. But already he was spending the vacations helping Grandfather be City Attorney; he had barely seen Mrs Snopes yet, so he not only didn't know he would ever go to Germany to enter Heidelberg University; he didn't even know yet that he would ever want to: only to talk about going there some day as a nice idea to keep in mind or to talk about.

He and Ratliff talked together a lot. Because although Ratliff had never been to school anywhere much and spent his time travelling about our country selling sewing machines (or selling or swapping or trading anything else for that matter), he and Uncle Gavin were both interested in people—or so Uncle Gavin said. Because what I always thought they were mainly interested in was curiosity. Until this time, that is. Because this time it had already gone a good deal further than just curiosity. This time it was alarm.

Ratliff was how we first began to learn about Snopes. Or rather, Snopeses. No, that's wrong: there had been a Snopes in Colonel Sartoris's cavalry command in 1864—in that part of it whose occupation had been raiding Yankee picket-lines for horses. Only this time it was a Confederate picket which caught him—that Snopes—raiding a Confederate horse-line and, it was believed, hung him. Which was evidently wrong too, since (Ratliff told Uncle Gavin) about ten years ago Flem and an old man who seemed to be his father appeared suddenly from nowhere one day and rented a little farm from Mr Will Varner who just about owned the whole settlement and district called Frenchman's Bend, about twenty miles from Jefferson. It was a farm so poor and small and already worn out that only the most trifling farmers would undertake it, and even they stayed only one year. Yet Ab and Flem rented it and evidently (this is Ratliff) he or Flem or both of them together found it—

"Found what?" Uncle Gavin said.

"I don't know," Ratliff said. "Whatever it was Uncle Billy and Jody had buried out there and thought was safe"—because that winter Flem was the clerk in Uncle Billy's store. And what they found on that farm must have been a good one, or maybe they didn't even need it any more; maybe Flem found something else the Varners thought was hidden and safe under the counter of the store itself. Because in another year old Ab had moved into Frenchman's Bend to live with his son and another Snopes had appeared from somewhere to take over the rented farm; and in two years more still another Snopes was the official smith in Mr Varner's blacksmith shop. So there were as many Snopeses in Frenchman's Bend as there were Varners; and five years after that, which was the year Flem moved to Jefferson, there were even more Snopeses than Varners because one Varner was married to a Snopes and was nursing another small Snopes at her breast.

Because what Flem found that last time was inside Uncle Billy's house. She was his only daughter and youngest child, not just a local belle but a belle throughout that whole section. Nor was it just because of old Will's land and money. Because I saw her too and I knew what it was too, even if she was grown and married and with a child older than I was and I only eleven and twelve and thirteen. ("Oh ay," Uncle Gavin said. "Even at twelve don't think you are the first man ever chewed his bitter thumbs for a reason such as her.") She wasn't too big, heroic, what they call Junoesque. It was that there was just too much of what she was for any one human female package to contain, and hold: too much of white, too much of female, too much of maybe just glory, I don't know: so that at first sight of her you felt a kind of shock of gratitude just for being alive and being male at the same instant with her in space and time, and then in the next second and forever after a kind of despair because you knew that there never would be enough of any one male to match and hold and deserve her; grief forever after, because forever after nothing less would ever do.

That was what he found this time. One day, according to Ratliff, Frenchman's Bend learned that Flem Snopes and Eula Varner had driven across the line into the next county the night

before and bought a licence and got married; the same day, still
according to Ratliff, Frenchman's Bend learned that three young
men, three of Eula's old suitors, had left the country suddenly by
night too, for Texas it was said, or anyway west, far enough west to
be farther than Uncle Billy or Jody Varner could have reached if
they had needed to try. Then a month later Flem and Eula also
departed for Texas (that borne, Uncle Gavin said, in our time for
the implicated, the insolvent or the merely hopeful), to return the
next summer with a girl baby a little larger than you would have
expected at only three months—

"And the horses," Uncle Gavin said. Because we did know
about that, mainly because Flem Snopes had not been the first to
import them. Every year or so someone brought into the county
a string of wild unbroken plains ponies from somewhere in the
west and auctioned them off. This time the ponies arrived, in the
charge of a man who was obviously from Texas, at the same time
that Mr and Mrs Snopes returned home from that state. This
string, however, seemed to be uncommonly wild, since the result-
ant scattering of the untamed and untamable calico-splotched
animals covered not just Frenchman's Bend but the whole east
half of the county too. Though even to the last, no one ever
definitely connected Snopes with their ownership. "No, no,"
Uncle Gavin said. "You were not one of the three that ran from
the smell of Will Varner's shotgun. And don't tell me Flem Snopes
traded you one of those horses for your half of that restaurant
because I won't believe it. What was it?"

Ratliff sat there with his bland brown smoothly shaven face
and his neat tieless blue shirt and his shrewd intelligent gentle
eyes not quite looking at Uncle Gavin. "It was that old house,"
he said. Uncle Gavin waited. "The Old Frenchman place."
Uncle Gavin waited. "That buried money." Then Uncle Gavin
understood: not an old pre-Civil War plantation house in all
Mississippi or the South either but had its legend of the money and
plate buried in the flower garden from Yankee raiders—in this
particular case, the ruined mansion which in the old time had
dominated and bequeathed its name to the whole section known
as Frenchman's Bend, which the Varners now owned. "It was
Henry Armstid's fault, trying to get even with Flem for that horse
that Texas man sold him that broke his leg. No," Ratliff said, "it

was me too as much as anybody else, as any of us. To figger out what Flem was doing owning that old place that anybody could see wasn't worth nothing. I don't mean why Flem bought it. I mean, why he even taken it when Uncle Billy give it to him and Eula for a wedding gift. So when Henry taken to following and watching Flem and finally caught him that night digging in that old flower garden, I don't reckon Henry had to persuade me very hard to go back the next night and watch Flem digging myself."

"So when Flem finally quit digging and went away, you and Henry crawled out of the bushes and dug too," Uncle Gavin said. "And found it. Some of it. Enough of it. Just exactly barely enough of it for you to hardly wait for daylight to swap Flem Snopes your half of that restaurant for your half of the Old Frenchman place. How much longer did you and Henry dig before you quit?"

"I quit after the second night," Ratliff said. "That was when I finally thought to look at the money."

"All right," Uncle Gavin said. "The money."

"They was silver dollars me and Henry dug up. Some of them was pretty old. One of Henry's was minted almost thirty years ago."

"A salted gold mine," Uncle Gavin said. "One of the oldest tricks in the world, yet you fell for it. Not Henry Armstid: you."

"Yes," Ratliff said. "Almost as old as that handkerchief Eula Varner dropped. Almost as old as Uncle Billy Varner's shotgun." That was what he said then. Because another year had passed when he stopped Uncle Gavin on the street and said, "With the court's permission, Lawyer, I would like to take a exception. I want to change that-ere to 'still'."

"Change what-ere to 'still'?" Uncle Gavin said.

"Last year I said 'That handkerchief Miz Flem Snopes dropped.' I want to change that 'dropped' to 'still dropping'. They's one feller I know still following it."

Because in six months Snopes had not only eliminated the partner from the restaurant, Snopes himself was out of it, replaced behind the greasy counter and in the canvas tent too by another Snopes accreted in from Frenchman's Bend into the vacuum behind the first one's next advancement by that same sort of osmosis by which, according to Ratliff, they had covered Frenchman's

Bend, the chain unbroken, every Snopes in Frenchman's Bend
moving up one step, leaving that last slot at the bottom open for
the next Snopes to appear from nowhere and fill, which without
doubt he had already done though Ratliff had not yet had time to
go out there and see.

And now Flem and his wife lived in a small rented house in a
back street near the edge of town, and Flem was now superintendent of the town power-plant which pumped the water and produced the electricity. Our outrage was primarily shock; shock not
that Flem had the job, we had not got that far yet, but shock that
we had not known until now that the job existed; that there was
such a position in Jefferson as superintendent of the power-plant.
Because the plant—the boilers and the engines which ran the
pump and dynamo—was operated by an old saw-mill engineer
named Harker, and the dynamos and the electric wiring which
covered the town were cared for by a private electrician who
worked on a retainer from the town—a condition which had been
completely satisfactory ever since running water and electricity
first came to Jefferson. Yet suddenly and without warning, we
needed a superintendent for it. And as suddenly and simultaneously and with that same absence of warning, a country man
who had not been in town two years now, and (we assumed) had
probably never seen an electric light until that first night two
years go when he drove in, was that superintendent.

That was the only shock. It wasn't that the country man was
Flem Snopes. Because we had all seen Mrs Snopes by now, what
few times we did see her which was usually behind the counter
in the restaurant in another greasy apron, frying the hamburgers
and eggs and ham and the tough pieces of steak on the grease-
crusted kerosene griddle, or maybe once a week on the Square,
always alone; not, as far as we knew, going anywhere: just moving,
walking in that aura of decorum and modesty and solitariness ten
times more immodest and a hundred times more disturbing than
one of the bathing-suits young women would begin to wear about
1920 or so, as if in the second just before you looked, her garments
had managed in one last frantic pell-mell scurry to overtake and
cover her. Though only for a moment, because in the next one,
if only you followed long enough, they would wilt and fail from
that mere plain and simple striding which would shred them

away like the wheel of a constellation through a wisp and cling of trivial scud.

And we had known the mayor, Major de Spain, longer than that. Jefferson, Mississippi, the whole South for that matter, was still full at that time of men called General or Colonel or Major because their fathers or grandfathers had been generals or colonels or majors or maybe just privates in Confederate armies, or who had contributed to the campaign funds of successful state governors. But Major de Spain's father had been a real major of Confederate cavalry, and De Spain himself was a West Pointer who had gone to Cuba as a second lieutenant with troops and came home with a wound—a long scar running from his hair through his left ear and down his jaw, which could have been left by the sabre or gun-rammer we naturally assumed some embattled Spaniard had hit him with, or by the axe which political tactics during the race for mayor claimed a sergeant in a dice game had hit him with.

Because he had not been long at home and out of his blue Yankee coat before we realised that he and Jefferson were incorrigibly and invincibly awry to one another, and that one of them was going to have to give. And that it would not be him: that he would neither flee Jefferson nor try to alter himself to fit Jefferson, but instead would try to wrench Jefferson until the town fitted him, and—the young people hoped—would succeed.

Until then, Jefferson was like all the other little Southern towns: nothing had happened in it since the last carpet-bagger had given up and gone home or been assimilated into another unregenerate Mississippian. We had the usual mayor and board of aldermen who seemed to the young people to have been in perpetuity since the Ark, or certainly since the last Chickasaw departed for Oklahoma in 1820, as old then as now and even now no older: old Mr Adams the mayor with a long patriarchal white beard, who probably seemed to young people like Cousin Gowan older than God Himself, until he might actually have been the first man; Uncle Gavin said there were more than just boys of twelve and thirteen like Cousin Gowan that referred to him by name, leaving off the last s, and to his old fat wife as "Miss Eve Adam", fat old Eve long since free of the danger of inciting a snake or anything else to tempt her.

So we were wondering just what axe Lieutenant de Spain would use to chop the corners off Jefferson and make it fit him. One day he found it. The city electrician (the one who kept the town's generators and dynamos and transformers working) was a genius. One afternoon in 1904 he drove out of his back yard into the street in the first automobile we had ever seen, made by hand completely, engine and all, from magneto coil to radius rod, and drove into the Square at the moment when Colonel Sartoris the banker's surrey and blooded matched team were crossing it on the way home. Although Colonel Sartoris and his driver were not hurt and the horses when caught had no scratch on them and the electrician offered to repair the surrey (it was said he even offered to put a gasoline engine in it this time), Colonel Sartoris appeared in person before the next meeting of the board of aldermen, who passed an edict that no gasoline-propelled vehicle should ever operate on the streets of Jefferson.

That was De Spain's chance. It was more than just his. It was the opportunity which that whole contemporary generation of young people had been waiting for, not just in Jefferson but everywhere, who had seen in that stinking noisy little home-made self-propelled buggy which Mr Buffaloe (the electrician) had made out of odds and ends in his back yard in his spare time, not just a phenomenon but an augury, a promise of the destiny which would belong to the United States. He—De Spain—didn't even need to campaign for mayor: all he needed was to announce. And the old dug-in city fathers saw that too, which was why they spooked to the desperate expedient of creating or exhuming or repeating (whichever it was) the story of the Cuban dice game and the sergeant's axe. And De Spain settled that once and for all not even as a politician; Caesar himself couldn't have done it any neater.

It was one morning at mail-time. Mayor Adams and his youngest son Theron who was not as old as De Spain and not even very much bigger either, mainly just taller, were coming out of the post office when De Spain met them. That is, he was already standing there with a good crowd watching, his finger already touching the scar when Mr Adams saw him. "Good-morning, Mister Mayor," he said. "What's this I hear about a dice game with an axe in it?"

"That's what the voters of the city of Jefferson would like to ask you, sir," Mr Adams said. "If you know of any proof to the contrary nearer than Cuba, I would advise you to produce it."

"I know a quicker way than that," De Spain said. "Your Honour's a little too old for it, but Theron there's a good-sized boy now. Let him and me step over to McCaslin's hardware store and get a couple of axes and find out right now if you are right."

"Aw now, Lieutenant," Theron said.

"That's all right," De Spain said. "I'll pay for both of them."

"Gentlemen," Theron said. And that was all of that. In June De Spain was elected mayor. It was a landslide because more than just he had won, been elected. The new age had entered Jefferson; he was merely its champion, the Godfrey de Bouillon, the Tancred, the Jefferson Richard Lion-heart of the twentieth century.

He wore that mantle well. No: it wasn't a mantle: it was a banner, a flag, and he was carrying it, already out in front before Jefferson knew we were even ready for it. He made Mr Buffaloe City Electrician with a monthly salary, though his first official act was about Colonel Sartoris's edict against automobiles. We thought of course that he and his new aldermen would have repealed it for no other reason than that one old mossback like Colonel Sartoris had told another old mossback like Mayor Adams to pass it, and the second old mossback did. But they didn't do that. Like I said, it was a landslide that elected him; it was like that axe business with old Mayor Adams and Theron in front of the post office that morning had turned on a light for all the other young people in Jefferson. I mean, the ones who were not yet store- and gin-owners and already settled lawyers and doctors, but were only the clerks and bookkeepers in the stores and gins and offices, trying to save enough to get married on, who all went to work to get De Spain elected mayor. And not only did that, but more: before they knew it or even intended it, they had displaced the old dug-in aldermen and themselves rode into office as the city fathers on Manfred de Spain's coat-tails or anyway axe. So you would have thought the first thing they would have done would be to throw out forever that automobile law. Instead, they had it copied out on a piece of parchment like a diploma or a citation and framed and hung on the wall in a lighted glass case in the hall of the Courthouse, where pretty soon people were coming in automobiles from as far away as Chicago to laugh at it. Because Uncle Gavin said this was still that fabulous and legendary time when there was still no paradox between an automobile and mirth, before the time when every American had to have one and they were killing more people than wars did.

He—De Spain—did even more than that. He himself had brought into town the first real automobile—a red E.M.F. roadster, and sold the horses out of the livery stable his father had left him and tore out the stalls and cribs and tack-rooms and established the first garage and automobile agency in Jefferson, so that now all his aldermen and all the other young people to whom neither of the banks would lend one cent to buy a motor vehicle with, no matter how solvent they were, could own them too. Oh yes, the motor age had reached Jefferson, and De Spain led it in that red roadster: that vehicle alien and debonair, as invincibly and irrevocably polygamous and bachelor as De Spain himself. And would ever be, living alone in his late father's big wooden house with a cook and a houseman in a white coat; he led the yearly cotillion and was first on the list of the ladies' german; if café society—not the Social Register nor the Four Hundred: Café Society—had been invented yet and any of it had come to Jefferson, he would have led it; born a generation too soon, he would have been by acclamation ordained a high priest in that new national religious cult of Cheesecake as it translated still alive the Harlows and Grables and Monroes into the hierarchy of American cherubim.

So when we first saw Mrs Snopes walking in the Square giving off that terrifying impression that in another second her flesh itself would burn her garments off, leaving not even a veil of ashes between her and the light of day, it seemed to us that we were watching Fate, a fate of which both she and Mayor de Spain were victims. We didn't know when they met, laid eyes for the first time on each other. We didn't need to. In a way, we didn't want to. We assumed of course that he was slipping her into his house by some devious means or method at night, but we didn't know that either. With any else but them, some of us—some boy or boys or youths—would have lain in ambush just to find out. But not with him. On the contrary, we were on his side. We didn't want to know. We were his allies, his confederates; our whole town was accessory to that cuckolding—that cuckolding which for any proof we had we had invented ourselves out of whole cloth; that same cuckoldry in which we would watch De Spain and Snopes walking amicably together while (though we didn't know it yet) De Spain was creating, planning how to create, that office of power-plant superintendent which we didn't even know we didn't have, let alone needed, and then get Mr Snopes into it. It was not because we were against Mr Snopes; we had not yet read the signs and portents which should have warned, alerted, sprung us into frantic concord to defend our town from him. Nor were we really in favour of adultery, sin: we were simply in favour of De Spain and Eula Snopes, for what Uncle Gavin called the divinity of simple unadulterated uninhibited immortal lust which they represented; for the two people in each of whom the other had found his single ordained fate; each to have found out of all the earth that one match for his mettle; ours the pride that Jefferson would supply their battleground.

Even Uncle Gavin; Uncle Gavin also. He said to Ratliff: "This town ain't that big. Why hasn't Flem caught them?"

"He don't want to," Ratliff said. "He don't need to yet."

Then we learned that the town—the mayor, the board of aldermen, whoever and however it was done—had created the office of power-plant superintendent, and appointed Flem Snopes to fill it.

At night Mr Harker, the veteran saw-mill engineer, ran the power-plant, with Tomey's Turl Beauchamp, the Negro fireman, to fire the boilers as long as Mr Harker was there to watch the pressure gauges, which Tomey's Turl either could not or would not do, apparently simply declining to take seriously any connection between the firebox below the boiler and the little dirty clock-face which didn't even tell the hour, on top of it. During the day the other Negro fireman, Tom Tom Bird, ran the plant alone, with Mr Buffaloe to look in now and then, though as a matter of routine since Tom Tom not only fired the boilers, he was as competent to read the gauges and keep the bearings of the steam engine and the dynamos cleaned and oiled as Mr Buffaloe and Mr Harker were: a completely satisfactory arrangement since Mr Harker was old enough not to mind or possibly even prefer the night shift, and Tom Tom—a big bull of a man weighing two hundred pounds and sixty years old but looking about forty and married about two years ago to his fourth wife: a young woman whom he kept with the strict jealous seclusion of a Turk in a cabin about two miles down the railroad track from the plant —declined to consider anything but the day one. Though by the time Cousin Gowan joined Mr Harker's night shift, Mr Snopes had learned to read the gauges and even fill the oil cups too.

This was about two years after he became superintendent. Gowan had decided to go out for the football team that fall, and he got the idea, I don't reckon even he knew where, that a job shovelling coal on a power-plant night shift would be the exact perfect training for dodging or crashing over enemy tacklers. Mother and Father didn't think so until Uncle Gavin took a hand. (He had his Harvard M.A. now and had finished the University of Mississippi law school and passed his bar and Grandfather had begun to retire and now Uncle Gavin really was the city attorney; it had been a whole year now—this was in June, he had just got home from the University and he hadn't seen Mrs Snopes yet this summer—since he had even talked of Heidelberg as a pleasant idea for conversation.)

"Why not?" he said. "Gowan's going on thirteen now: it's time for him to begin to stay out all night. And what better place can he find than down there at the plant where Mr Harker and the fireman can keep him awake?"

So Gowan got the job as Tomey's Turl's helper and at once Mr Harker began to keep him awake talking about Mr Snopes, talking about him with the kind of amoral amazement with which you would recount having witnessed the collision of a planet. According to Mr Harker, it began last year. One afternoon Tom Tom had finished cleaning his fires and was now sitting in the gangway smoking his pipe, pressure up and the safety-valve on the middle boiler blowing off, when Mr Snopes came in and stood there for a while, chewing tobacco and looking up at the whistling valve.

"How much does that whistle weigh?" he said.

"If you talking about that valve, about ten pounds," Tom Tom said.

"Solid brass?" Mr Snopes said.

"All except that little hole it's what you call whistling through," Tom Tom said. And that was all then, Mr Harker said; it was two months later when he, Mr Harker, came on duty one evening and found the three safety-valves gone from the boilers and the vents stopped with one-inch steel screw plugs capable of a pressure of a thousand pounds and Tomey's Turl still shovelling coal into the fireboxes because he hadn't heard one of them blow off yet.

"And them three boiler heads you could poke a hole through with a sody straw," Mr Harker said. "When I seen the gauge on the first boiler I never believed I would live to reach the injector.

"So when I finally got it into Turl's head that that 100 on that dial meant where Turl wouldn't only lose his job, he would lose it so good wouldn't nobody never find the job nor him again neither, I finally got settled down enough to inquire where them safety-valves had went to.

" 'Mr Snopes took um off,' he says.

" 'What in hell for?'

" 'I don't know. I just telling you what Tom Tom told me. He say Mr Snopes say the shut-off float in the water tank ain't heavy enough. Say that tank start leaking some day, so he going to fasten them three safety-valves on the float and weight it heavier.'

" 'You mean,' I says. That's as far as I could get. 'You mean—'

" 'That's what Tom Tom say. I don't know nothing about it.'

"Anyhow they was gone; whether they was in the water tank or not, was too late to find out now. Until then, me and Turl had been taking it pretty easy after the load went off and things got kind of quiet. But you can bet we never dozed none that night. Me and him spent the whole of it time about on the coal pile, where we could watch them three gauges all at once. And from midnight on, after the load went off, we never had enough steam in all them three boilers put together to run a peanut parcher. And even when I was home in bed, I couldn't go to sleep. Time I shut my eyes I would begin to see a steam gauge about the size of a washtub, with a red needle big as a coal scoop moving up toward a hundred pounds, and I would wake myself up hollering and sweating.

"So come daylight enough to see; and I never sent Turl neither: I clumb up there myself and looked at that float. And there wasn't no safety-valves weighting it neither and maybe he hadn't aimed for them to be fastened to it where the first feller that looked in could a reached them. And even if that tank is forty-two foot deep I still could a opened the cock and dreened it. Only I just work there, Mr Snopes was the superintendent, and it was the day shift now and Tom Tom could answer whatever questions Joe Buffaloe would want to know in case he happened in and seen them thousand-pound screw plugs where safety-valves was supposed to been.

"So I went on home and that next night I couldn't hardly get Turl to run them gauge needles up high enough to turn the low-pressure piston, let alone move the dynamos; and the next night, and the next one, until about ten days when the express delivered a box; Tom Tom had waited and me and him opened the box (it was marked C.O.D. in big black paint but the tag itself had been wrenched off and gone temporarily. 'I know where he throwed it,' Tom Tom said) and taken them screw plugs out of the vents and put the three new safety-valves back on; and sho enough Tom Tom did have the crumpled-up tag: Mister Flem Snopes Power-plant Jefferson Miss C.O.D. twenty-three dollars and eighty-one cents."

And now there was some of it which Mr Harker himself didn't know until Uncle Gavin told him after Tom Tom told Uncle Gavin: how one afternoon Tom Tom was smoking his pipe on the coal pile when Mr Snopes came in carrying in his hand what Tom Tom thought at first was a number-three mule shoe until Mr Snopes took it into a corner behind the boilers where a pile of discarded fittings—valves, rods, bolts and such—had been accumulating probably since the first light was turned on in Jefferson; and, kneeling (Mr Snopes), tested every piece one by one into two separate piles in the gangway behind him. Then Tom Tom watched him test with the magnet every loose piece of metal in the whole boiler room, sorting the mere iron from the brass. Then Snopes ordered Tom Tom to gather up the separated brass and bring it to the office.

Tom Tom gathered the brass into a box. Snopes was waiting in the office, chewing tobacco. Tom Tom said he never stopped chewing even to spit. "How do you and Turl get along?" he said.

"I tend to my business," Tom Tom said. "What Turl does with his ain't none of mine."

"That ain't what Turl thinks," Mr Snopes said. "He wants me to give him your day shift. He claims he's tired of firing at night."

"Let him fire as long as I is, and he can have it," Tom Tom said.

"Turl don't aim to wait that long," Mr Snopes said. Then he told Tom Tom: how Turl was planning to steal iron from the plant and lay it on Tom Tom and get him fired. That's right. That's what Tom Tom told Uncle Gavin Mr Snopes called it: iron. Maybe Mr Snopes hadn't heard of a magnet himself until just yesterday and so he thought that Tom Tom had never heard of one and so didn't know what he was doing. I mean, not of magnets nor brass either and couldn't tell brass from iron. Or maybe he just thought that Tom Tom, being a Negro, wouldn't care. Or maybe that, being a Negro, whether he knew or not or cared or not, he wouldn't have any part of what a white man was mixed up in. Only we had to imagine this part of it of course. Not that it was hard to do: Tom Tom standing there about the size and shape and colour (disposition too) of a Black Angus bull, looking down at the white man. Turl on the contrary was the colour of a saddle and even with a scoop full of coal he barely touched a hundred and fifty pounds. "That's what he's up to," Mr Snopes said. "So I want you to take this stuff out to your house and hide it and don't breathe a word to nobody. And soon as I get enough evidence on Turl, I'm going to fire him."

"I knows a better way than that," Tom Tom said.

"What way?" Snopes said. Then he said: "No no, that won't do. You have any trouble with Turl and I'll fire you both. You do like I say. Unless you are tired of your job and want Turl to have it. Are you?"

"Ain't no man complained about my pressure yet," Tom Tom said.

"Then you do like I tell you," Snopes said. "You take that stuff home with you tonight. Don't let nobody see you, even your wife. And if you don't want to do it, just say so. I reckon I can find somebody that will."

So Tom Tom did. And each time the pile of discarded fittings accumulated again, he would watch Snopes test out another batch of brass with his magnet for Tom Tom to take home and hide. Because Tom Tom had been firing boilers for forty years now, ever since he became a man, and these three for the twenty they had been there, since it was he who built the first fires beneath them. At first he had fired one boiler and he had got five dollars a month for it. Now he had the three and got sixty dollars a month, and now he was sixty and he owned his little cabin and a little piece of corn land and a mule and wagon to ride to church in twice each Sunday, with a gold watch and the young wife who was the last new young wife he would probably have too.

Though all Mr Harker knew at this time was that the junked metal would accumulate slowly in the corner behind the boilers, then suddenly disappear overnight; now it became his nightly joke to enter the plant with his busy bustling air and say to Turl: "Well, I notice that-ere little engine is still running. There's a right smart of brass in them bushings and wrist-pins, but I reckon they're moving too fast to hold that magnet against. But I reckon we're lucky, at that. I reckon he'd sell them boilers too if he knowed any way you and Tom Tom could keep up steam without them."

Though he—Mr Harker—did tell what came next, which was at the first of the year, when the town was audited: "They come down here, two of them in spectacles. They went over the books and poked around ever where, counting ever thing in sight and writing it down. Then they went back to the office and they was still there at six o'clock when I come on. It seems there was something a little out; it seems there was some old brass fittings wrote down in the books, except that that brass seemed to be missing or something. It was on the books all right, and the new valves and truck that had replaced it was there. But be durn if they could find a one of them old fittings except one busted bib that had done got mislaid beyond magnet range you might say under a work bench some way or other. It was right strange. So I went back with them and held the light while they looked again in all the corners, getting a right smart of sut and grease and coal-dust on them white shirts. But that brass just naturally seemed to be plumb gone. So they went away.

"And the next morning they come back. They had the city

clerk with them this time and they beat Mr Snopes down here and so they had to wait until he come in in his check cap and his chew of tobacco, chewing and looking at them while they hemmed and hawed until they told him. They was right sorry; they hemmed and hawed a right smart being sorry, but there wasn't nothing else they could do except come back on him being as he was the superintendent; and did he want me and Turl and Tom Tom arrested right now or would tomorrow do? And him standing there chewing, with his eyes looking like two gobs of cup grease on a hunk of raw dough, and them still telling him how sorry they was.

" 'How much does it come to?'' he says.

" 'Two hundred and eighteen dollars and fifty-two cents, Mr Snopes.'

" 'Is that the full amount?'

" 'We checked our figgers twice, Mr Snopes.'

" 'All right,' he says. And he reaches down and hauls out the money and pays the two hundred and eighteen dollars and fifty-two cents in cash and asks for a receipt."

Only by the next summer Gowan was Turl's student fireman, so now Gowan saw and heard it from Turl at first hand; it was evening when Mr Snopes stood suddenly in the door to the boiler room and crooked his finger at Turl, and so this time it was Turl and Snopes facing one another in the office.

"What's this trouble about you and Tom Tom?" he said.

"Me and which?" Turl said. "If Tom Tom depending on me for his trouble, he done quit firing and turned waiter. It takes two folks to have trouble and Tom Tom ain't but one, I don't care how big he is."

"Tom Tom thinks you want to fire the day shift," Mr Snopes said.

Turl was looking at everything now without looking at anything. "I can handle as much coal as Tom Tom," he said.

"Tom Tom knows that too," Mr Snopes said. "He knows he's getting old. But he knows there ain't nobody else can crowd him for his job but you." Then Mr Snopes told him how for two years now Tom Tom had been stealing brass from the plant and laying it on Turl to get him fired; how only that day Tom Tom had told him, Mr Snopes, that Turl was the thief.

"That's a lie," Turl said. "Can't no nigger accuse me of stealing something I ain't, I don't care how big he is."

"Sho," Mr Snopes said. "So the thing to do is to get that brass back."

"Not me," Turl said. "That's what they pays Mr Buck Connor for." Buck Connors was the town marshal.

"Then you'll go to jail sho enough," Snopes said. "Tom Tom will say he never even knowed it was there. You'll be the only one that knew that. So what you reckon Mr Connor'll think? You'll be the one that knowed where it was hid at, and Buck Connor'll know that even a fool has got more sense than to steal something and hide it in his own corn crib. The only thing you can do is, get that brass back. Go out there in the daytime, while Tom Tom is here at work, and get that brass and bring it to me and I'll put it away to use as evidence on Tom Tom. Or maybe you don't want that day shift. Say so, if you don't. I can find somebody else."

Because Turl hadn't fired any boilers forty years. He hadn't done anything at all that long, since he was only thirty. And if he were a hundred, nobody could accuse him of having done anything that would aggregate forty years net. "Unless tomcatting at night would add up that much," Mr Harker said. "If Turl ever is unlucky enough to get married he would still have to climb in his own back window or he wouldn't even know what he come after. Ain't that right, Turl?"

So, as Mr Harker said, it was not Turl's fault so much as Snopes's mistake. "Which was," Mr Harker said, "when Mr Snopes forgot to remember in time about that young light-coloured new wife of Tom Tom's. To think how he picked Turl out of all the Negroes in Jefferson, that's prowled at least once—or tried to—every gal within ten miles of town, to go out there to Tom Tom's house knowing all the time how Tom Tom is right here under Mr Snopes's eye wrastling coal until six o'clock a.m. and then with two miles to walk down the railroad home, and expect Turl to spend his time out there" (Gowan was doing nearly all the night firing now. He had to; Turl had to get some sleep, on the coal pile in the bunker after midnight. He was losing weight too, which he could afford even less than sleep) "hunting anything that ain't hid in Tom Tom's bed. And when I think about Tom Tom in here wrastling them boilers in that-ere same amical

cuckolry like what your uncle says Miz Snopes and Mayor de
Spain walks around in, stealing brass so he can keep Turl from
getting his job away from him, and all the time Turl is out yonder
tending by daylight to Tom Tom's night homework, sometimes I
think I will jest die."

He was spared that; we all knew it couldn't last much longer.
The question was, which would happen first: if Tom Tom would
catch Turl, or if Mr Snopes would catch Turl, or if Mr Harker
really would burst a blood vessel. Mr Snopes won. He was standing in the office door that evening when Mr Harker, Turl and
Gowan came on duty; once more he crooked his finger at Turl and
once more they stood facing each other in the office. "Did you
find it this time?" Mr Snopes said.

"Find it which time?" Turl said.

"Just before dark tonight," Mr Snopes said. "I was standing at
the corner of the crib when you crawled out of that corn patch and
climbed in that back window." And now indeed Turl was looking
everywhere fast at nothing. "Maybe you are still looking in the
wrong place," Mr Snopes said. "If Tom Tom had hid that iron
in his bed, you ought to found it three weeks ago. You take one
more look. If you don't find it this time, maybe I better tell Tom
Tom to help you." Turl was looking fast at nothing now.

"I'm gonter have to have three or four extra hours off tomorrow night," he said. "And Tom Tom gonter have to be held
right here unto I gets back."

"I'll see to it," Snopes said.

"I mean held right here unto I walks in and touches him,"
Turl said. "I don't care how late it is."

"I'll see to that," Snopes said.

Except that it had already quit lasting any longer at all;
Gowan and Mr Harker had barely reached the plant the next
evening when Mr Harker took one quick glance around. But
before he could even speak Mr Snopes was standing in the office
door, saying, "Where's Tom Tom?" Because it wasn't Tom Tom
waiting to turn over to the night crew: it was Tom Tom's substitute, who fired the boilers on Sunday while Tom Tom was
taking his new young wife to church; Gowan said Mr Harker said,
"Hell fire," already moving, running past Mr Snopes into the
office and scrabbling at the telephone. Then he was out of the

office again, not even stopping while he hollered at Gowan:
"All right, Otis"—his nephew or cousin or something who had
inherited the saw-mill, who would come in and take over when
Mr Harker wanted a night off—"Otis'll be here in fifteen minutes.
Jest do the best you can until then."

"Hold up," Gowan said. "I'm going too."

"Durn that," Mr Harker said, still running, "I seen it first:" on
out the back where the spur track for the coal cars led back to the
main line where Tom Tom would walk every morning and
evening between his home and his job, running (Mr Harker) in
the moonlight now because the moon was almost full. In fact, the
whole thing was full of moonlight when Mr Harker and Turl
appeared peacefully at the regular hour to relieve Tom Tom's
substitute the next evening:

"Yes sir," Mr Harker told Gowan, "I was jest in time. It was
Turl's desperation, you see. This would be his last go-round. This
time he was going to have to find that brass or come back and tell
Mr Snopes he couldn't; in either case that country picnic was
going to be over. So I was jest in time to see him creep up out of
that corn patch and cross the moonlight to that back window and
tomcat through it; jest exactly time enough for him to creep across
the room to the bed and likely fling the quilt back and lay his
hand on meat and say, 'Honeybunch, lay calm. Papa's done
arrived.' " And Gowan said how even twenty-four hours afterward he partook for the instant of Turl's horrid surprise, who
believed that at that moment Tom Tom was two miles away at
the power-plant waiting for him (Turl) to appear and relieve him
of the coal scoop—Tom Tom lying fully dressed beneath the quilt
with a naked butcher knife in his hand when Turl flung it back.

"Jest exactly time enough," Mr Harker said. "Jest exactly as on
time as two engines switching freight cars. Tom Tom must a made
his jump jest exactly when Turl whirled to run, Turl jumping out
of the house into the moonlight again with Tom Tom and the
butcher knife riding on his back so that they looked jest like—
what do you call them double-jointed half-horse fellers in the old
picture books?"

"Centaur," Gowan said.

"—looking jest like a centawyer running on its hind legs and
trying to ketch up with itself with a butcher knife about a yard

long in one of its extry front hoofs until they ran out of the moon-light again into the woods. Yes sir, Turl ain't even half as big as Tom Tom, but he sho toted him. If you'd a ever bobbled once, that butcher knife would a caught you whether Tom Tom did or not, wouldn't it?"

"Tom Tom a big buck man," Turl said. "Make three of me. But I toted him. I had to. And whenever I would fling my eye back and see the moon shining on that butcher knife I could a picked up two more like him without even slowing down." Turl said how at first he just ran; it was only after he found himself—or themself—among the trees that he thought about trying to rake Tom Tom off against the trunk of one. "But he helt on so tight with that one arm that whenever I tried to bust him against a tree I busted myself too. Then we'd bounce off and I'd catch another flash of moonlight on that nekkid blade and all I could do was just run.

" 'Bout then was when Tom Tom started squalling to let him down. He was holding on with both hands now, so I knowed I had done outrun that butcher knife anyway. But I was good started then; my feets never paid Tom Tom no more mind when he started squalling to stop and let him off than they done me. Then he grabbed my head with both hands and started to wrench-ing it around like I was a runaway bareback mule, and then I seed the ditch too. It was about forty foot deep and it looked a solid mile across but it was too late then. My feets never even slowed up. They ran as far as from here to that coal pile yonder out into nekkid air before we even begun to fall. And they was still clawing moonlight when me and Tom Tom hit the bottom."

The first thing Gowan wanted to know was, what Tom Tom had used in lieu of the dropped butcher knife. Turl told that. Nothing. He and Tom Tom just sat in the moonlight on the floor of the ditch and talked. And Uncle Gavin explained that: a sanctuary, a rationality of perspective, which animals, humans too, not merely reach but earn by passing through unbearable emotional states like furious rage or furious fear, the two of them sitting there not only in Uncle Gavin's amicable cuckoldry but in mutual and complete federation too: Tom Tom's home violated not by Tomey's Turl but by Flem Snopes; Turl's life and limbs put into frantic jeopardy not by Tom Tom but by Flem Snopes.

"That was where I come in," Mr Harker said.

"You?" Gowan said.

"He holp us," Turl said.

"Be durn if that's so," Mr Harker said. "Have you and Tom Tom both already forgot what I told you right there in that ditch last night? I never knowed nothing and I don't aim to know nothing, I don't give a durn how hard either one of you try to make me."

"All right," Gowan said. "Then what?" Turl told that: how he and Tom Tom went back to the house and Tom Tom untied his wife where he had tied her to a chair in the kitchen and the three of them hitched the mule to the wagon and got the brass out of the corn crib and loaded it to haul it away. There was near a half-ton of it; it took them the rest of the night to finish moving it.

"Move it where?" Gowan said. Only he said he decided to let Mr Snopes himself ask that; it was nearing daylight now and soon Tom Tom would come up the spur track from the main line, carrying his lunch pail to take over for the day shift; and presently there he was, with his little high hard round intractable cannon-ball head, when they all turned and there was Mr Snopes too standing in the boiler-room door. And Gowan said that even Mr Snopes seemed to know he would just be wasting his time crooking his finger at anybody this time; he just said right out to Turl:

"Why didn't you find it?"

"Because it wasn't there," Turl said.

"How do you know it wasn't there?" Mr Snopes said.

"Because Tom Tom said it wasn't," Turl said.

Because the time for wasting time was over now. Mr Snopes just looked at Tom Tom a minute. Then he said: "What did you do with it?"

"We put it where you said you wanted it," Tom Tom said.

"We?" Mr Snopes said.

"Me and Turl," Tom Tom said. And now Mr Snopes looked at Tom Tom for another minute. Then he said:

"Where I said I wanted it when?"

"When you told me what you aimed to do with them safety-valves," Tom Tom said.

Though by the time the water in the tank would begin to taste brassy enough for somebody to think about draining the tank to clean it, it wouldn't be Mr Snopes. Because he was no longer superintendent now, having resigned, as Mr de Spain would have said when he was still Lieutenant de Spain, "for the good of the service." So he could sit all day now on the gallery of his little back-street rented house and look at the shape of the tank standing against the sky above the Jefferson roof-line—looking at his own monument, some might have thought. Except that it was not a monument: it was a footprint. A monument only says *At least I got this far* while a footprint says *This is where I was when I moved again.*

"Not even now?" Uncle Gavin said to Ratliff.

"Not even now," Ratliff said. "Not catching his wife with Manfred de Spain yet is like that twenty-dollar gold piece pinned to your undershirt on your first maiden trip to what you hope is going to be a Memphis whorehouse. He don't need to unpin it yet."

2

GAVIN STEVENS

H E hadn't unpinned it yet. So we all wondered what he was using to live on, for money, sitting (apparently) all day long day after day through the rest of that summer on the flimsy porch of that little rented house, looking at his water tank. Nor would we ever know, until the town would decide to drain the tank and clean it and so rid the water of the brassy taste, exactly how much brass he had used one of the Negro firemen to blackmail the other into stealing for him and which the two Negroes, confederating for simple mutual preservation, had put into the tank where he could never, would never dare, recover it.

And even now we don't know whether or not that brass was all. We will never know exactly how much he might have stolen and sold privately (I mean before he thought of drafting Tom Tom or Turl to help him) either before or after someone—Buffaloe probably, since if old Harker had ever noticed those discarded fittings enough to miss any of them he would probably have beat Snopes to the market; very likely, for all his pretence of simple spectator enjoyment, his real feeling was rage at his own blindness—notified somebody at the city hall and had the auditors in. All we knew was that one day the three safety-valves were missing from the boilers; we had to assume, imagine, what happened next: Manfred de Spain—it would be Manfred—sending for him and saying, "Well, Bud," or Doc or Buster or whatever Manfred would call his . . . you might say foster husband; who knows? maybe even Superintendent: "Well, Superintendent, this twenty-three dollars and eighty-one cents' worth of brass"—naturally he would have looked in the catalogue before he sent for him—"was missing during your regime, which you naturally wish to keep spotless as Caesar's wife: which a simple C.O.D. tag addressed to you will do." And that, according to Harker, the two auditors hemmed and hawed around the plant for two days before they got up nerve enough to tell Snopes what amount of brass they thought to the best of their knowledge was missing, and that Snopes took the cash out of his pocket and paid them.

That is, disregarding his salary of fifty dollars a month, the job cost Snopes two hundred and forty-two dollars and thirty-three cents out of his own pocket or actual cash money you might say. And even if he had saved every penny of his salary, less that two-hundred-plus-dollar loss, and assuming there had been two hundred dollars more of brass for him to have stolen successfully during that time, that was still not enough for him to support his family on very long. Yet for two years now he had been sitting on that little front gallery, looking (as far as we knew) at that water tank. So I asked Ratliff.

"He's farming," Ratliff said. "Farming?" I said (all right, cried if you like). "Farming what? Sitting there on that gallery from sunup to sundown watching that water tank?"

Farming Snopeses, Ratliff said. Farming Snopeses: the whole rigid hierarchy moving intact upward one step as he vacated ahead of it except that one who had inherited into the restaurant was not a Snopes. Indubitably and indefensibly not a Snopes; even to impugn him so was indefensible and outrageous and forever beyond all pale of pardon, whose mother, like her incredible sister-by-marriage a generation later, had, must have, as the old bucolic poet said, cast a leglin girth herself before she married whatever Snopes was Eck's titular father.

That was his name: Eck. The one with the broken neck; he brought it to town when he moved in as Flem's immediate successor, rigid in a steel brace and leather harness. Never in the world a Snopes. Ratliff told it; it happened at the saw-mill. (You see, even his family—Flem—knew he was not a Snopes: sending, disposing of him into a saw-mill where even the owner must be a financial genius to avoid bankruptcy and there is nothing for a rogue at all since all to steal is lumber, and to embezzle a wagonload of planks is about like embezzling an iron safe or a—yes: that dammed water tank itself.)

So Flem sent Eck to Uncle Billy Varner's saw-mill (it was that, I suppose, or chloroform or shoot him as you do a sick dog or a wornout mule) and Ratliff told about it: one day Eck made the proposition that for a dollar each he and one of the Negro hands (one of the larger ones and of course the more imbecilic) would pick up a tremendous cypress log and set it on to the saw-carriage. And they did (didn't I just say that one was not even a Snopes and the other already imbecile), had the log almost safely on, when the Negro slipped, something, anyway went down; whereupon all Eck had to do was let go his end and leap out from under. But not he: no Snopes nor no damned thing else, bracing his shoulder under and holding his end up and even taking the shock when the Negro's end fell to the ground, still braced under it until it occurred to someone to drag the Negro out.

And still without sense enough to jump, let alone Snopes enough, not even knowing yet that even Jody Varner wasn't going to pay him anything for saving even a Varner Negro: just standing there holding that whole damned log up, with a little blood already beginning to run out of his mouth, until it finally occurred again to them to shim the log up with another one and pull him from under too, where he could sit hunkered over under a tree, spitting blood and complaining of a headache. ("Don't tell me they gave him the dollar," I said—all right: cried—to Ratliff. "Don't tell me that!")

Never in this world a Snopes: himself and his wife and son living in the tent behind the restaurant and Eck in his turn in the greasy apron and the steel-and-leather neck harness (behind the counter, frying on the crusted grill the eggs and meat which, because of the rigid brace, he couldn't even see to gauge the doneness, cooking, as the blind pianist plays, by simple ear), having less business here than even in the saw-mill, since at the saw-mill all he could do was break his own bones where here he was a threat to his whole family's long tradition of slow and invincible rapacity because of that same incredible and innocent assumption that all people practise courage and honesty for the simple reason that if they didn't everybody would be frightened and confused; saying one day, not even privately but right out loud where half a dozen strangers not even kin by marriage to Snopeses heard him: "Ain't we supposed to be selling beef in these here hamburgers? I don't know jest what this is yet, but it ain't no beef."

So of course they—when I say "they" I mean Snopeses; when you say "Snopeses" in Jefferson you mean Flem Snopes—fired him. They had to; he was intolerable there. Only of course the question rose immediately: where in Jefferson, not in the Jefferson economy but in the Snopes (oh yes, when you say Snopes in Jefferson you mean Flem Snopes) economy would he not be intolerable, would Snopeses be safe from him? Ratliff knew that too. I mean, everybody in Jefferson knew because within twenty-four hours everybody in Jefferson had heard about that hamburger remark and naturally knew that something would have to be done about Eck Snopes and done quick and so of course (being interested) as soon as possible, almost as soon in fact as Flem himself knew, what and where. I mean, it was Ratliff who told me. No: I mean it had to be Ratliff who told me: Ratliff with his damned smooth face and his damned shrewd bland innocent intelligent eyes, too damned innocent, too damned intelligent:

"He's night watchman now down at Renfrow's oil tank at the deepo. Where it won't be no strain on his neck like having to look down to see what that was he jest smelled burning. He won't need to look up to see whether the tank's still there or not, he can jest walk up and feel the bottom of it. Or even set there in his chair in the door and send that boy to look. That horse boy," Ratliff said.

"That what boy?" I said, cried.

"That horse boy," Ratliff said. "Eck's boy. Wallstreet Panic. The day that Texas feller arctioned off them wild Snopes ponies, I was out there. It was jest dust-dark and we had done et supper at Miz Littlejohn's and I was jest undressing in my room to go to bed when Henry Armstid and Eck and that boy of hisn went in the lot to ketch their horses; Eck had two: the one the Texas feller give him to get the arction started off, and the one Eck felt he had to at least bid on after having been give one for nothing, and won it. So when Henry Armstid left the gate open and the whole herd stampeded over him and out of it, I reckon the hardest instantaneous decision Eck ever had to make in his life was to decide which one of them horses to chase: the one the Texas man give him, which represented the most net profit if he caught it, or the one that he already had five or six dollars of his own money invested in; that is, was a hundred-plus per cent of a free horse worth more than just a hundred per cent of a six-dollar horse? That is, jest how far can you risk losing a horse that no matter what you get for him you still have to subtract six dollars from it, to jest catch one that will be all net profit?

B

"Or maybe he decided him and that boy better split up after both of them while he figgered it out. Anyway, the first I knowed, I had done took off my britches and was jest leaning out of the window in my shirt-tail trying to see what was going on, when I heerd a kind of sound behind me and looked over my shoulder and there was one of them horses standing in the door looking at me and standing in the hall behind him with a piece of plough-line was that boy of Eck's. I reckon we both moved at the same moment: me out of the window in my shirt-tail and the horse swirling to run on down the hall, me realising I never had no britches on and running around the house toward the front steps jest about the time the horse met Miz Littlejohn coming on to the back gallery with a armful of washing in one hand and the wash-board in the other; they claimed she said 'git out of here you son of a bitch' and split the washboard down the centre of its face and throwed the two pieces at it without even changing hands, it swirling again to run back up the hall jest as I ran up the front steps, and jumped clean over that boy still standing in the hall with his plough-line without touching a hair, on to the front gallery again and seen me and never even stopped: jest swirled and run to the end of the gallery and jumped the railing and back into the lot again, looking jest like a big circus-coloured hawk, sailing out into the moonlight and across the lot again in about two jumps and out the gate that still hadn't nobody thought to close yet; I heerd him once more when he hit the wooden bridge jest this side of Bookright's turn-off. Then that boy come out of the house, still toting the plough-line. 'Howdy, Mr Ratliff,' he says. 'Which way did he go?'—Except you're wrong."

Horse boy, dog boy, cat boy, monkey boy, elephant boy: any-thing but Snopes boy. And then suppose, just suppose; suppose and tremble: one generation more removed from Eck Snopes and his innocence; one generation more until that innocent and outrageous belief that courage and honour are practical has had time to fade and cool so that merely the habit of courage and honour remain; add to that then that generation's natural heritage of cold rapacity as instinctive as breathing, and tremble at that prospect: the habit of courage and honour compounded by rapacity or rapacity raised to the absolute nth by courage and honour: not horse boy but a lion or tiger boy: Genghis Khan or Tamerlane or Attila in the defenceless midst of indefensible Jefferson. Then Ratliff was looking at me. I mean, he always was. I mean, I discovered with a kind of terror that for a second I had forgot it. "What?" I said. "What did you say?"

"That you're wrong. About Eck's night watchman job at the oil tank. It wasn't Manfred de Spain this time. It was the Masons."

"What?" I said, cried.

"That's right. Eck was one of the biggest ones of Uncle Billy Varner's Frenchman's Bend Masons. It was Uncle Billy sent word in to the Masons in Jefferson to find Eck a good light broke-neck job."

"That bad?" I said. "That bad? The next one in the progression so outrageous and portentous and terrifying that Will Varner himself had to use influence twenty-two miles away to save Frenchman's Bend?" Because the next one after Eck behind the restaurant counter was I.O., the blacksmith-cum-schoolmaster-cum-bigamist, or multiplied by bigamy—a thin undersize voluble weasel-faced man talking constantly in a steady stream of worn saws and proverbs usually having no connection with one another nor application to anything else, who even with the hammer would not have weighed as much as the anvil he abrogated and dispossessed; who (Ratliff of course, Ratliff always) entered Frenchman's Bend already talking, or rather appeared one morning already talking in Varner's blacksmith shop which an old man named Trumbull had run man and boy for fifty years.

But no blacksmith, I.O. He merely held the living. It was the other one, our Eck, his cousin (whatever the relationship was, unless simply being both Snopes was enough until one proved himself unworthy, as Eck was to do, like two Masons from that moment to apostasy like Eck's, forever sworn to show a common front to life), who did the actual work. Until one day, one morning, perhaps the curate, Eck, was not there or perhaps it simply occurred to the vicar, the high priest, for the first time that his actually was the right and the authority to hold a communion service and nobody could really prevent him: that morning, Zack Houston with his gaited stallion until Snopes quicked it with the first nail; whereupon Houston picked Snopes up and threw him hammer and all into the cooling tub and managed somehow to hold the plunging horse and wrench the shoe off and the nail out

at the same time, and led the horse outside and tied it and came
back and threw Snopes back into the cooling tub again.

And no schoolmaster either. He didn't merely usurp that as a
position among strangers, he actually stole it as a vocation from
his own kin. Though Frenchman's Bend didn't know that yet.
They knew only that he was hardly out of the blacksmith shop (or
dried again out of the cooling tub where Houston had flung him)
when he was installed as teacher ("Professor," the teacher was
called in Frenchman's Bend, provided of course he wore trousers)
in the one-room schoolhouse which was an integer of old Varner's
princedom—an integer not because old Varner or anyone else in
Frenchman's Bend considered that juvenile education filled any
actual communal lack or need, but simply because his settlement
had to have a going schoolhouse to be complete as a freight train
has to have a caboose to be complete.

So I.O. Snopes was now the schoolmaster; shortly afterward he
was married to a Frenchman's Bend belle and within a year he
was pushing a home-made perambulator about the village and
his wife was already pregnant again; here, you would have said,
was a man not merely settled but doomed to immobilisation,
until one day in the third year a vast grey-coloured though still
young woman, accompanied by a vast grey-coloured five-year-
old boy, drove up to Varner's store in a buggy—

"It was his wife," Ratliff said.

"His wife?" I said, cried. "But I thought—"

"So did we," Ratliff said. "Pushing that-ere home-made buggy
with two of them in it this time, twins, already named Bilbo and
Vardaman, besides the first one, Clarence. Yes sir, three chaps
already while he was waiting for his other wife with that one to
catch up with him—a little dried-up feller not much bigger than
a crawfish, and that other wife—no, I mean the one he had now
in Frenchman's Bend when that-ere number-one one druv up—
wasn't a big girl neither—Miz Vernon Tull's sister's niece by
marriage she was—yet he got on to her too them same big grey-
coloured kind of chaps like the one in the buggy with his ma
driving up to the store and saying to whoever was setting on the
gallery at the moment: 'I hear I.O. inside.' (He was. We could
all hear him.) 'Kindly step in and tell him his wife's come.'

"That was all. It was enough. When he come to the Bend that

day three years ago he had a big carpet-bag, and in them three
years he had probably accumulated some more stuff; I mean
besides them three new chaps. But he never stopped for none of it.
He jest stepped right out of the back door of the store. And Flem
had done long since already sold old man Trumbull back to
Varner for the blacksmith, but now they was needing a new professor too or anyhow they would as soon as I.O. could get around
the first corner out of sight where he could cut across country.
Which he evidently done; never nobody reported any dust-cloud
travelling fast along a road nowhere. They said he even stopped
talking, though I doubt that. You got to draw the line somewhere,
ain't you?"

You have indeed. Though I.O. didn't. That is, he was already
talking when he appeared in his turn behind the restaurant
counter in the greasy apron, taking your order and cooking it
wrong or cooking the wrong thing not because he worked so fast
but simply because he never stopped talking long enough for you
to correct or check him, babbling that steady stream of confused
and garbled proverbs and metaphors attached to nothing and
going nowhere.

And the wife, I mean the number-one wife, what might be
called the original wife, who was number one in the cast even
though she was number two on the stage. The other one, the
number two in the cast even though she was number one on the
stage, the Tull's wife's sister's niece wife, who foaled the second
set of what Ratliff called grey-coloured chaps, Clarence and the
twins Vardaman and Bilbo, remained in Frenchman's Bend. It
was the original one, who appeared in Frenchman's Bend sitting
in the buggy and left Frenchman's Bend in the buggy, still sitting,
and appeared in Jefferson five years later still sitting, translated,
we knew not how, and with no interval between from the buggy
where Ratliff had seen her twenty-two miles away that day five
years ago, to the rocking-chair on the front gallery of the boarding-house where we saw her now, still at that same right angle
enclosing her lap as if she had no movable hinge at the hips at all
—a woman who gave an impression of specific density and immobility like lead or uranium, so that whatever force had moved
her from the buggy to that chair had not been merely human, not
even ten I.O.s.

Because Snopes was moving his echelons up fast now. That one
—I.O. and the vast grey-coloured sitting wife and that vast grey-
coloured boy (his name was Montgomery Ward)—did not even
pause at the tent behind the restaurant where Eck and his wife
and two sons now ("Why not?" Ratliff said. "There's a heap of
more things beside frying a hamburger you don't really have to
look down for") were still living. They—the I.O.s—by-passed it
completely, the wife already sitting in the rocking-chair on the
boarding-house's front gallery—a big more-or-less unpainted
square building just off the Square where itinerant cattle-drovers
and horse- and mule-traders stopped and where were incarcer-
ated, boarded and fed, juries and important witnesses during
court term, where she would sit rocking steadily—not doing anything, not reading, not particularly watching who passed in or
out of the door or along the street: just rocking—for the next five
years while and then after the place changed from a boarding-
house to a warren, with nailed to one of the front veranda posts a
pine board lettered terrifically by hand, with both S's reversed:

Snopes Hotel

And now Eck, whose innocence or honesty or both had long
since eliminated him from the restaurant into his night watchman's chair beside the depot oil tank, had vacated his wife and
sons (Wallstreet Panic: oh yes, I was like Ratliff: I couldn't believe that one either, though the younger one, Admiral Dewey,
we both could) from the tent behind it. In fact, the restaurant was
not sold lock stock barrel and goodwill, but gutted, moved intact
even to the customers and without even a single whole day's
closure, into the new boarding-house where Mrs Eck was now the
landlady; moved intact past the rocking figure on the gallery
which continued to rock there through mere legend and into
landmark like the effigy signs before the old-time English public
houses, so that country men coming into town and inquiring for
the Snopes hotel were told simply to walk in that direction until
they came to a woman rocking, and that was it.

And now there entered that one, not whose vocation but at
least the designation of whose vocation, I.O. Snopes had usurped.
This was the actual Snopes schoolmaster. No: he looked like a
schoolmaster. No: he looked like John Brown with an ineradicable

and unhidable flaw: a tall gaunt man in a soiled frock-coat and string tie and a wide politician's hat, with cold furious eyes and the long chin of a talker: not that verbal diarrhoea of his cousin (whatever kin I.O. was; they none of them seemed to bear any specific kinship to one another; they were just Snopeses, like colonies of rats or termites are just rats and termites) but a kind of unerring gift for a base and evil ratiocination in argument, and for correctly reading the people with whom he dealt: a dema-gogue's capacity for using people to serve his own appetites, all clouded over with a veneer of culture and religion; the very names of his two sons, Byron and Virgil, were not only instances but warnings.

And no schoolmaster himself either. That is, unlike his cousin, he was not even with us long enough to have to prove he was not. Or maybe, coming to us in the summer and then gone before the summer was, he was merely between assignments. Or maybe taking a busman's holiday from a busman's holiday. Or maybe in and about the boarding-house and the Square in the mere brief intervals from his true bucolic vocation whose stage and scene were the scattered country churches and creeks and horse-ponds where during the hot summer Sundays revival services and baptisings took place: himself (he had a good baritone voice and probably the last working pitch-pipe in north Mississippi) setting the tune and lining out the words, until one day a posse of en-raged fathers caught him and a fourteen-year-old girl in an empty cotton house and tarred and feathered him out of the country. There had been talk of castration also, though some timid con-servative dissuaded them into holding that as a promise against his return.

So of him there remained only the two sons, Byron and Virgil. Nor was Byron with us long either, gone to Memphis now to attend business college. To learn book-keeping; we learned with incredulity that Colonel Sartoris himself was behind that: Colonel Sartoris himself in the back room of the bank which was his office—an incredulity which demanded, compelled inquiry while we remembered what some of us, the older ones, my father among them, had not forgot: the original Ab Snopes, the (depend-ing on where you stand) patriot horse raider or simple horse thief who had been hanged (not by a Federal provost-marshal but

by a Confederate one, the old story was) while a member of
the cavalry command of old Colonel Sartoris, the real colonel,
father of our present banker-honorary colonel who had been only
an uncommissioned A.D.C. on his father's staff back in that
desperate twilight of 1864-65 when more people than men named
Snopes had to choose not survival with honour but simply between
empty honour and almost as empty survival.

The horse which came home to roost. Oh yes, we all said that,
all us wits: we would not have missed that chance. Not that we
believed it or even disbelieved it, but simply to defend the old
Colonel's memory by being first to say aloud among ourselves
what we believed the whole Snopes tribe was long since chortling
over to one another. Indeed, no Confederate provost-marshal
changed that first Ab Snopes, but Snopeses themselves had immolated him in that skeleton, to put, as the saying is, that monkey
on the back of Ab's commander's descendant as soon as the
lineage produced a back profitable to the monkey; in this case, the
new bank which our Colonel Sartoris established about five years
ago.

Not that we really believed that, of course. I mean, our
Colonel Sartoris did not need to be blackmailed with a skeleton.
Because we all in our country, even half a century after, senti-
mentalise the heroes of our gallant lost irrevocable unreconstructible debacle, and those heroes were indeed ours because
they were our fathers and grandfathers and uncles and great-
uncles when Colonel Sartoris raised the command right here in
our contiguous counties. And who with more right to senti-
mentalise them than our Colonel Sartoris, whose father had been
the Colonel Sartoris who had raised and trained the command
and saved its individual lives when he could in battle and even
defended them or at least extricated them from their own simple
human lusts and vices while idle between engagements; Byron
Snopes was not the first descendant of those old company and
battalion and regimental names who knew our Colonel Sartoris's
bounty.

But the horse which at last came home to roost sounded better.
Not witty, but rather an immediate unified irrevocably scornful
front to what the word Snopes was to mean to us, and to all
others, no matter who, whom simple juxtaposition to the word

irrevocably smirched and contaminated. Anyway, he (it: the horse come to roost) appeared in good time, armed and girded with his business-college diploma; we would see him through, beyond, inside the grillework which guarded our money and the complex records of it whose custodian Colonel Sartoris was, bowed (he, Snopes, Byron) over the book-keeper's desk in an attitude not really of prayer, obeisance; not really of humility before the shine, the blind glare of the blind money, but rather of a sort of respectful unhumble insistence, a deferent invincible curiosity and inquiry into the mechanics of its recording; he had not entered crawling into the glare of a mystery so much as, without attracting any attention to himself, he was trying to lift a corner of its skirt.

Using, since he was the low last man in that hierarchy, a long cane fishing-pole until he could accrete close enough for the hand to reach; using, to really mix, really confuse our metaphor, an humble cane out of that same quiver which had contained that power-plant superintendency, since Colonel Sartoris had been of that original group of old Major de Spain's bear and deer hunters when Major de Spain established his annual hunting camp in the Big Bottom shortly after the war; and when Colonel Sartoris started his bank five years ago, Manfred de Spain used his father's money to become one of the first stockholders and directors.

Oh yes: the horse home at last and stabled. And in time of course (we had only to wait, never to know how of course even though we watched it, but at least to know more or less when) to own the stable, Colonel Sartoris dis-stabled of his byre and rick in his turn as Ratliff and Grover Cleveland Winbush had been dis-restauranted in theirs. We not to know how of course since that was none of our business; indeed, who to say but there was not one among us but did not want to know: who, already realising that we would never defend Jefferson from Snopeses, let us then give, relinquish Jefferson to Snopeses, banker mayor aldermen church and all, so that, in defending themselves from Snopeses, Snopeses must of necessity defend and shield us, their vassals and chattels, too.

The quiver borne on Manfred de Spain's back, but the arrows drawn in turn by that hand, that damned incredible woman, that

Frenchman's Bend Helen, Semiramis—no: not Helen nor
Semiramis: Lilith: the one before Eve herself whom earth's
Creator had perforce in desperate and amazed alarm in person to
efface, remove, obliterate, that Adam might create a progeny to
populate it; and we were in my office now where I had not sent
for him nor even invited him: he had just followed, entered, to sit
across the desk in his neat faded tieless blue shirt and the brown
smooth bland face and the eyes watching me too damned shrewd,
too damned intelligent.

"You used to laugh at them too," he said.

"Why not?" I said. "What else are we going to do about them?
Of course you've got the best joke: you don't have to fry hamburgers any more. But give them time; maybe they have got one
taking a correspondence-school law course. Then I won't have to
be acting city attorney any more either."

"I said 'too'," Ratliff said.

"What?" I said.

"At first you laughed at them too," he said. "Or maybe I'm
wrong, and this here is still laughing?"—looking at me, watching
me, too damned shrewd, too damned intelligent. "Why don't
you say it?"

"Say what?" I said.

" 'Get out of my office, Ratliff,' " he said.

"Get out of my office, Ratliff," I said.

3

CHARLES MALLISON

MAYBE it was because Mother and Uncle Gavin were twins, that Mother knew what Uncle Gavin's trouble was just about as soon as Ratliff did.

We were all living with Grandfather then. I mean Grandfather was still alive then and he and Uncle Gavin had one side of the house, Grandfather in his bedroom and what we all called the office downstairs, and Uncle Gavin on the same side upstairs, where he had built an outside stairway so that he could go and come from the side yard, and Mother and Father and Cousin Gowan on the other side while Gowan was going to the Jefferson high school while he was waiting to enter the prep school in Washington to get ready for the University of Virginia.

So Mother would sit at the end of the table where Grandmother used to sit, and Grandfather opposite at the other end, and Father on one side and Uncle Gavin and Gowan (I wasn't born then, and even if I had been I would have been eating in the kitchen with Aleck Sander yet) on the other and, Gowan said, Uncle Gavin not even pretending any more to eat: just sitting there talking about Snopeses like he had been doing now through every meal for the last two weeks. It was almost like he was talking to himself, like something wound up that couldn't even run down, let alone stop, like there wasn't anybody or anything that wished he would stop more than he did. It wasn't snarling. Gowan didn't know what it was. It was like something Uncle Gavin had to tell, but it was so funny that his main job in telling it was to keep it from being as funny as it really was, because if he ever let it be as funny as it really was, everybody and himself too would be laughing so hard they couldn't hear him. And Mother not eating either now: just sitting there perfectly still, watching Uncle Gavin, until at last Grandfather took his napkin out of his collar and stood up and Father and Uncle Gavin and Gowan stood up too and Grandfather said to Mother like he did every time:

"Thank you for the meal, Margaret," and put the napkin on the table, and Gowan went and stood by the door while he went

out like I was going to have to do after I got born and got big
enough. And Gowan would have stood there while Mother and
Father and Uncle Gavin went out too. But not this time. Mother
hadn't even moved, still sitting there and watching Uncle Gavin;
she was still watching Uncle Gavin when she said to Father:

"Don't you and Gowan want to be excused too?"

"Nome," Gowan said. Because he had been in the office that
day when Ratliff came in and said,

"Evening, Lawyer. I just dropped in to hear the latest Snopes
news," and Uncle Gavin said:

"What news?" and Ratliff said:

"Or do you jest mean what Snopes?" and sat there too looking
at Uncle Gavin, until at last he said, "Why don't you go on and
say it?" and Uncle Gavin said,

"Say what?" and Ratliff said,

"'Get out of my office, Ratliff.'" So Gowan said,
"Nome."

"Then maybe you'll excuse me," Uncle Gavin said, putting his
napkin down. But still Mother didn't move.

"Would you like me to call on her?" she said.

"Call on who?" Uncle Gavin said. And even to Gowan he said
it too quick. Because even Father caught on then. Though I don't
know about that. Even if I had been there and no older than
Gowan was, I would have known that if I had been about twenty-
one or maybe even less when Mrs Snopes first walked through the
Square, I not only would have known what was going on, I might
even have been Uncle Gavin myself. But Gowan said Father
sounded like he had just caught on. He said to Uncle Gavin:

"I'll be damned. So that's what's been eating you for the past
two weeks." Then he said to Mother: "No, by Jupiter. My wife
call on that—"

"That what?" Uncle Gavin said, hard and quick. And still
Mother hadn't moved: just sitting there between them while they
stood over her.

"'Sir,'" she said.

"What?" Uncle Gavin said.

"'That what, sir?'" she said. "Or maybe just 'sir' with an in-
flection."

"You name it then," Father said to Uncle Gavin. "You know

what. What this whole town is calling her. What this whole town knows about her and Manfred de Spain."

"What whole town?" Uncle Gavin said. "Besides you? you and who else? The same ones that probably rake Maggie here over the coals too without knowing any more than you do?"

"Are you talking about my wife?" Father said.

"No," Uncle Gavin said. "I'm talking about my sister and Mrs Snopes."

"Boys, boys, boys," Mother said "At least spare my nephew." She said to Gowan: "Gowan, don't you really want to be excused?"

"Nome," Gowan said.

"Damn your nephew," Father said. "I'm not going to have his aunt—"

"Are you still talking about your wife?" Uncle Gavin said. This time Mother stood up too, between them, while they both leaned a little forward, glaring at each other across the table.

"That really will be all now," Mother said. "Both of you apologise to me." They did. "Now apologise to Gowan." Gowan said they did that too.

"But I'll still be damned if I'm going to let—" Father said.

"Just the apology, please," Mother said. "Even if Mrs Snopes is what you say she is, as long as I am what you and Gavin both agree I am since at least you agree on that, how can I run any risk sitting for ten minutes in her parlour? The trouble with both of you is, you know nothing about women. Women are not interested in morals. They aren't even interested in unmorals. The ladies of Jefferson don't care what she does. What they will never forgive is the way she looks. No: the way the Jefferson gentlemen look at her."

"Speak for your brother," Father said. "I never looked at her in her life."

"Then so much the worse for me," Mother said, "with a mole for a husband. No: moles have warm blood; a Mammoth Cave fish—"

"Well, I *will* be damned," Father said. "That's what you want, is it? A husband that will spend every Saturday night in Memphis chasing back and forth between Gayoso and Mulberry Street—"

"Now I will excuse you whether you want to be or not," Mother said. So Uncle Gavin went out and on upstairs toward his room and Mother rang the bell for Guster, and Gowan stood at the door again for Mother and Father and then Mother and Gowan went out to the front gallery (it was October, still warm enough to sit outside at noon) and she took up the sewing-basket again and Father came out with his hat on and said,

"Flem Snopes's wife, riding into Jefferson society on Judge Lemuel Stevens's daughter's coat-tail," and went on to town to the store; and then Uncle Gavin came out and said:

"You'll do it, then?"

"Of course," Mother said. "Is it that bad?"

"I intend to try to not let it be," Uncle Gavin said. "Even if you aren't anything but just a woman, you must have seen her. You must have."

"Anyway, I have watched men seeing her," Mother said.

"Yes," Uncle Gavin said. It didn't sound like an out-breathe, like talking. It sounded like an in-breathe: "Yes."

"You're going to save her," Mother said, not looking at Uncle Gavin now: just watching the sock she was darning.

"Yes!" Uncle Gavin said, fast, quick: no in-breathe this time, so quick he almost said the rest of it before he could stop himself, so that all Mother had to do was say it for him:

"—from Manfred de Spain."

But Uncle Gavin had caught himself by now; his voice was just harsh now. "You too," he said. "You and your husband too. The best people, the pure, the unimpugnable. Charles who by his own affirmation has never even looked at her; you by that same affirmation not only Judge Stevens's daughter, but Caesar's wife."

"Just what—" Mother said, then Gowan said she stopped and looked at him. "Don't you really want to be excused a little while? As a personal favour?" she said.

"Nome," Gowan said.

"You can't help it either, can you?" she said. "You've got to be a man too, haven't you?" She just talked to Uncle Gavin then: "Just what is it about this that you can't stand? That Mrs Snopes may not be chaste, or that it looks like she picked Manfred de Spain out to be unchaste with?"

"Yes!" Uncle Gavin said. "I mean no! It's all lies—gossip. It's all—"

"Yes," Mother said. "You're right. It's probably all just that. Saturday's not a very good afternoon to get in the barbershop, but you might think about it when you pass."

"Thanks," Uncle Gavin said. "But if I'm to go on this crusade with any hope of success, the least I can do is look wild and shaggy enough to be believed. You'll do it, then?"

"Of course," Mother said.

"Thank you," Uncle Gavin said. Then he was gone.

"I suppose I could be excused now," Gowan said.

"What for now?" Mother said. She was still watching Uncle Gavin, down the walk and into the street now. "He should have married Melisandre Backus," she said. Melisandre Backus lived on a plantation about six miles from town with her father and a bottle of whisky. I don't mean he was a drunkard. He was a good farmer. He just spent the rest of his time sitting on the gallery in summer and in the library in winter with the bottle, reading Latin poetry. Miss Melisandre and Mother had been in school together, at high school and the Seminary both. That is, Miss Melisandre was always four years behind Mother. "At one time I thought he might; I didn't know any better then."

"Cousin Gavin?" Gowan said. "Him married?"

"Oh yes," Mother said. "He's just too young yet. He's the sort of man doomed to marry a widow with grown children."

"He could still marry Miss Melisandre," Gowan said.

"It's too late," Mother said. "He didn't know she was there."

"He sees her every day she comes in to town," Gowan said.

"You can see things without looking at them, just like you can hear things without listening," Mother said.

"He sure didn't just do that when he saw Mrs Snopes that day," Gowan said. "Maybe he's waiting for her to have another child besides Linda and for them to grow up?"

"No no," Mother said. "You don't marry Semiramis: you just commit some form of suicide for her. Only gentlemen with as little to lose as Mr Flem Snopes can risk marrying Semiramis.—It's too bad you are so old too. A few years ago I could have made you come with me to call on her. Now you'll have to admit openly that you want to come; you may even have to say 'Please'."

But Gowan didn't. It was Saturday afternoon and there was a football game, and though he hadn't made the regular team yet

you never could tell when somebody that had might break a leg
or have a stroke or even a simple condition in arithmetic. Besides,
he said Mother didn't need his help anyway, having the whole
town's help in place of it; he said they hadn't even reached the
Square the next morning on the way to church when the first
lady they met said brightly:

"What's this I hear about yesterday afternoon?" and Mother
said just as brightly:

"Indeed?" and the second lady they met said (she belonged to
the Byron Society and the Cotillion Club too):

"I always say we'd all be much happier to believe nothing we
don't see with our own eyes, and only half of that," and Mother
said still just as brightly:

"Indeed?" They—the Byron Society and the Cotillion Club,
both when possible of course though either alone in a pinch—
seemed to be the measure. Now Uncle Gavin stopped talking
about Snopeses. I mean, Gowan said he stopped talking at all.
It was like he didn't have time any more to concentrate on talk in
order to raise it to conversation, art, like he believed was everybody's duty. It was like he didn't have time to do anything but
wait, to get something done that the only way he knew to get it
done was waiting. More than that, than just waiting: not only
never missing a chance to do things for Mother, he even invented
little things to do for her, so that even when he would talk a little,
it was like he was killing two birds with the same stone.

Because when he talked now, in sudden spells and bursts of it
that sometimes never had any connection at all with what Father
and Mother and Grandfather might have been talking about the
minute before, it wouldn't even be what he called BB-gun conversation. It would be the most outrageous praise, praise so outrageous that even Gowan at just thirteen years old could tell that.
It would be of Jefferson ladies that he and Mother had known all
their lives, so that whatever ideas either one of them must have
had about them, the other must have known it a long time by
now. Yet all of a sudden every few days during the next month
Uncle Gavin would stop chewing fast over his plate and drag a
fresh one of them by the hair you might say into the middle of
whatever Grandfather and Mother and Father had been talking
about, talking not to Grandfather or Father or Gowan, but telling

Mother how good or pretty or intelligent or witty somebody was that Mother had grown up with or anyway known all her life.

Oh yes, members of the Byron Society and the Cotillion Club or maybe just one of them (probably only Mother knew it was the Cotillion Club he was working for) at a pinch, so that each time they would know that another new one had called on Mrs Flem Snopes. Until Gowan would wonder how Uncle Gavin would always know when the next one had called, how to scratch her off the list that hadn't or add her on to the score that had or whatever it was he kept. So Gowan decided that maybe Uncle Gavin watched Mrs Snopes's house. And it was November now, good fine hunting weather, and since Gowan had finally given up on the football team, by rights he and Top (Top was Aleck Sander's older brother except that Aleck Sander wasn't born yet either. I mean, he was Guster's boy and his father was named Top too so they called him Big Top and Top Little Top) would have spent every afternoon after school with the beagles Uncle Gavin gave them after rabbits. But instead, Gowan spent every afternoon for almost a week in the big ditch behind Mr Snopes's house, not watching the house but to see if Uncle Gavin was hid somewhere in the ditch too watching to see who called on Mrs Snopes next. Because Gowan was only thirteen then; he was just watching for Uncle Gavin; it wasn't until later that he said how he realised that if he had tried harder or longer, he might have caught Mr de Spain climbing in or out of the back window like most of Jefferson was convinced he was doing, and then he really would have had something he could have sold for a dollar or two to a lot of people in town.

But if Uncle Gavin was hid somewhere in that ditch too, Gowan never caught him. Better still, Uncle Gavin never caught Gowan in it. Because if Mother had ever found out Gowan was hiding in that ditch behind Mr Snopes's house because he thought Uncle Gavin was hidden in it too, Gowan didn't know what she might have done about Uncle Gavin but he sure knew what would have happened to him. And worse: if Mr Snopes had ever found out Gowan thought Uncle Gavin might be hiding in that ditch spying on his house. Or worse still: if the town ever found out Gowan was hiding in that ditch because he thought Uncle Gavin was.

Because when you are just thirteen you don't have sense enough to realise what you are doing and shudder. Because even now I can remember some of the things Aleck Sander and I did for instance and never think twice about it, and I wonder how any boys ever live long enough to grow up. I remember, I was just twelve; Uncle Gavin had just given me my shotgun; this was after (this is how Father put it) Mrs Snopes had sent him to Heidelberg to finish his education and he had been in the War and then come back home and got himself elected County Attorney in his own right; there were five of us; me and three other white boys and Aleck Sander, hunting rabbits one Saturday. It was cold, one of the coldest spells we ever had; when we came to Harrykin Creek it was frozen over solid and we begun talk about how much we would take to jump into it. Aleck Sander said he would do it if each one of us would give him a dollar, so we said we would, and sure enough, before we could have stopped him, Aleck Sander hauled off and jumped into the creek, right through the ice, clothes and all.

So we got him out and built a fire while he stripped off and wrapped up in our hunting-coats while we tried to dry his clothes before they froze solid too and got him dressed again at last and then he said, "All right. Now pay me my money."

We hadn't thought about that. Back then, no Jefferson, Mississippi, boy or anywhere else in Mississipi that I know of, ever had a whole dollar at one time very often, let alone four at the same time. So we had to trade with him. Buck Connors and Aleck Sander traded first: if Buck jumped through the ice, Aleck Sander would let him off his dollar. So Buck did, and while we dried him off I said,

"If that's what we got to do, let's all jump in at once and get it over with," and we even started for the creek when Aleck Sander said No, that we were all white boys taking advantage of him because he was a Negro by asking him to let us do the same thing he did. So we had to trade again. Ashley Holcomb was next. He climbed up a tree until Aleck Sander said he was high enough and shut his eyes and jumped out of it, and Aleck Sander let him off his dollar. Then I was next, and somebody said how, because Aleck Sander's mother was our cook and Aleck Sander and I had more or less lived together ever since we were born, that Aleck Sander would probably let me off light. But Aleck Sander said No, he had thought of that himself and for that very reason he was going to have to be harder on me than on Ashley and so the tree I would jump out of would be over a brier patch. And I did; it was like jumping into cold fire streaking my hands and face and tearing my britches though my hunting-coat was brand new almost (Uncle Gavin had mailed it to me from Germany the day he got Mother's cable that I was born; it was the best hunting-coat in Jefferson everybody said when I finally got big enough to wear it) so it didn't tear except for one pocket.

So that left only John Wesley Roebuck, and maybe all of a sudden Aleck Sander realised that here was his last dollar going because John Wesley suggested everything but Aleck Sander still said No. Finally John Wesley offered to do all of them: jump through the ice then out of Ashley's tree and then out of mine, but Aleck Sander still said No. So this is how they finally traded though in a way that still wasn't fair to Aleck Sander because old man Ab Snopes had already shot John Wesley in the back once about two years ago and so John Wesley was used to it, which may have been one of the reasons why he agreed to the trade. This was it. John Wesley borrowed my hunting-coat to put on top of his because we had already proved that mine was the toughest, and he borrowed Ashley's sweater to wrap around his head and neck, and we counted off twenty-five steps for him and Aleck Sander put one shell in his gun and somebody, maybe me, counted One Two Three slow and when whoever it was said One John Wesley broke and ran and when whoever it was said Three Aleck Sander shot John Wesley in the back and John Wesley gave me and Ashley back the sweater and my hunting-coat and (it was late by then) we went home. Except that I had to run all the way (it was cold, the coldest spell I ever remember) because we had to burn up my hunting-coat because it would be easier to explain no hunting-coat at all than one with the back full of Number Six shot.

Then we found out how Uncle Gavin would find out which one called next. It was Father did the scoring for him. I don't mean Father was Uncle Gavin's spy. The last thing Father was trying to do was to help Uncle Gavin, ease Uncle Gavin's mind. If anything, he was harder against Uncle Gavin even than he had thought he was that first day against Mother going to call on Mrs

Snopes; it was like he was trying to take revenge on Mother and Uncle Gavin both: on Uncle Gavin for even wanting Mother to call on Mrs Snopes, and on Mother for saying right out loud in front of Uncle Gavin and Gowan both that she not only was going to do it, she didn't see any harm in it. In fact, Gowan said it was Father's mind that Mrs Snopes seemed to stay on now, more than on Uncle Gavin's. Almost any time now Father would walk in rubbing his hands and saying "oh you kid" or "twenty-three skiddoo" and they knew that he had just seen Mrs Snopes again on the street or had just heard that another Cotillion or Byron Society member had called on her; if they had invented wolf whistles then, Father would have been giving one.

Then it was December; Mother had just told how the Cotillion Club had finally voted to send Mr and Mrs Snopes an invitation to the Christmas Ball and Grandfather had got up and put his napkin down and said, "Thank you for the meal, Margaret," and Gowan went and held the door for him to go out, then Father said:

"Dance? Suppose she don't know how?" and Gowan said,

"Does she have to?" and now they all stopped; he said they all stopped at exactly the same time and looked at him and he said that even if Mother and Uncle Gavin were brother and sister one was a woman and the other was a man and Father wasn't any kin to either one of them. Yet he said they all three looked at him with exactly the same expression on their faces. Then Father said to Mother:

"Hold him while I look at his teeth again. You told me he wasn't but thirteen."

"What have I said?" Gowan said.

"Yes," Father said. "What were we saying? Oh yes, dancing, the Christmas Cotillion." He was talking to Uncle Gavin now. "Well, by godfrey, that puts you one up on Manfred de Spain, don't it? He's a lone orphan; he hasn't got a wife or a twin sister who was one of the original founders of Jefferson literary and snobbery clubs; all he can do to Flem Snopes's wife is—" Gowan said how until now Mother was always between Father and Uncle Gavin, with one hand on each of their chests to hold them apart. He said that now Mother and Uncle Gavin were both at Father, with Mother holding one hand on Father's mouth and reaching for his, Gowan's, ears with the other, and she and Uncle Gavin both saying the same thing, only Uncle Gavin was just using another set of words for it:

"Don't you dare!"

"Go on. Say it."

So Father didn't. But even he didn't anticipate what Uncle Gavin would do next: try to persuade Mother to make the Cotillion committee not invite Mr de Spain to the ball at all. "Hell fire," Father said. "You can't do that."

"Why can't we?" Mother said.

"He's the mayor!" Father said.

"The mayor of a town is a servant," Mother said. "He's the head servant, of course: the butler. You don't invite a butler to a party because he's a butler. You invite him in spite of it."

But Mayor de Spain got his invitation too. Maybe the reason Mother didn't stop it like Uncle Gavin wanted her to, was simply for that reason she had already given, explained, described; that she and the Cotillion Club didn't have to invite him because he was Mayor, and so they invited him just to show it, prove it. Only Father didn't think that was the reason. "No sir," he said. "You damned gals ain't fooling me or anybody else. You want trouble. You want something to happen. You like it. You want two red-combed roosters strutting at one another, provided one of you hens is the reason for it. And if there's anything else you can think of to shove them in to where one of them will have to draw blood in self-defence, you'll do that too because every drop of that blood or every black eye or every public-torn collar or split or muddy britches is another item of revenge on that race of menfolks that holds you ladies thralled all day long day after day with nothing to do between meals but swap gossip over the telephone. By godfrey," he said, "if there wasn't any club to give a Christmas dance two weeks from now, you all would probably organise one just to invite Mrs Snopes and Gavin and Manfred de Spain to it. Except you are wasting your time and money this trip. Gavin don't know how to make trouble."

"Gavin's a gentleman," Mother said.

"Sure," Father said. "That's what I said: it ain't that he don't want to make trouble: he just don't know how. Oh, I don't mean he won't try. He'll do the best he knows. But he just don't know how to make the kind of trouble that a man like Manfred de Spain will take seriously."

But Mr de Spain did the best he could to teach Uncle Gavin how. He began the day the invitations were sent out and he got his after all. When he bought that red E.M.F. the first thing he did was to have a cut-out put on it and until he got elected mayor the first time you could hear him all the way to the Square the moment he left home. And soon after that Lucius Hogganbeck got somebody (it was Mr Roth Edmonds and maybe Mr de Spain too since Lucius's father, old Boon Hogganbeck, had been Mr Roth's father's, Mr McCaslin Edmonds, and his uncle's, Uncle Ike McCaslin, and old Major de Spain's huntsman-doghandler-man-Friday back in the time of Major de Spain's old hunting-camp) to sign a note for him to buy a Model T Ford and set up in the jitney passenger-hauling business, and he had a cut-out too and on Sunday afternoons half the men in Jefferson would slip off from their wives and go out to a straight stretch of road about two miles from town (even two miles back in town you could hear them when the wind was right) and Mr de Spain and Lucius would race each other. Lucius would charge his passengers a nickel a head to ride in the race, though Mr de Spain carried his free.

Though the first thing Mr de Spain did after he got to be mayor was to have an ordinance passed that no cut-out could be opened inside the town limits. So it had been years now since we had heard one. Then one morning we did. I mean we—Grandfather and Mother and Father and Uncle Gavin and Gowan—did, because it was right in front of our house. It was just about the time everybody would be going to school or to work and Gowan knew which car it was even before he got to the window because Lucius's Ford made a different sound, and besides nobody but the mayor would have risked that cut-out with the cut-out law in force. It was him: the red car just going out of sight and the cut-out off again as soon as he had passed the house; and Uncle Gavin still sitting at the table finishing his breakfast just as if there hadn't been any new noise at all.

And as Gowan reached the corner on the way home from school at noon, he heard it again; Mr de Spain had driven blocks out of his way to rip past our house again in second gear with the cut-out wide open; and again while Mother and Father and Grandfather and Uncle Gavin and he were still sitting at the table finishing dinner, with Mother sitting right still and not looking at anything and Father looking at Uncle Gavin and Uncle Gavin sitting there stirring his coffee like there wasn't a sound anywhere in the world except maybe his spoon in the cup.

And again about half-past five, about dark, when the storekeepers and doctors and lawyers and mayors and such as that would be going home at the end of the day to eat supper all quiet and peaceful, without having to go back to town until tomorrow morning; and this time Gowan could even see Uncle Gavin listening to the cut-out when it passed the house. I mean, this time Uncle Gavin didn't mind them seeing that he heard it, looking up from the paper a little and holding the paper in front of him until the sound went on and then quit off when Mr de Spain passed the end of our yard and picked up his foot; Uncle Gavin and Grandfather both looking up while it passed though all Grandfather did yet was just to frown a little and Uncle Gavin not even doing that: just waiting, almost peaceful, so that Gowan could almost hear him saying *That's all at last. He had to make the fourth run past to get back home.*

And it was all, through supper and afterward when they went to the office where Mother would sit in the rocking-chair always sewing something though it seemed to be mostly darning socks and Gowan's stockings and Grandfather and Father would sit across the desk from one another playing checkers and sometimes Uncle Gavin would come in too with his book when he wouldn't feel like trying again to teach Mother to play chess until I got born next year and finally got big enough so he could begin to try to teach me. And now it was already past the time when the ones going to the picture show would have gone to it, and the men just going back to town after supper to loaf in Christian's drugstore or to talk with the drummers in the Holston House lobby or drink some more coffee in the café, and anybody would have thought he was safe. Only this time it wasn't even Father. It was Grandfather himself jerking his head up and saying:

"What the devil's that? That's the second time today."

"It's the fifth time today," Father said. "His foot slipped."

"What?" Grandfather said.

"He was trying to mash on the brake to go quiet past the house,"

Father said. "Only his foot slipped and mashed on the cut-out instead."

"Telephone Connors," Grandfather said. That was Mr Buck Connors. "I won't have it."

"That's Gavin's job," Father said. "He's the acting City Attorney when you're in a checker game. He's the one to speak to the marshal. Or better still, the mayor. Ain't that right, Gavin?" And Gowan said they all looked at Uncle Gavin, and that he himself was ashamed, not of Uncle Gavin: of us, the rest of them. He said it was like watching somebody's britches falling down while he's got to use both hands trying to hold up the roof: you are sorry it is funny, ashamed you had to be there watching Uncle Gavin when he never even had any warning he would need to try to hide his face's nakedness when that cut-out went on and the car ripped slow in second gear past the house again after you would have thought that anybody would have had the right to believe that other time before supper would be the last one at least until to-morrow, the cut-out ripping past and sounding just like laughing, still sounding like laughing even after the car had reached the corner where Mr de Spain would always lift his foot off the cut-out. Because he was laughing: it was Father sitting at his side of the checker board, looking at Uncle Gavin and laughing.

"Charley!" Mother said. "Stop it!" But it was already too late. Uncle Gavin had already got up, quick, going toward the door like he couldn't quite see it, and on out.

"What the devil's this?" Grandfather said.

"He rushed out to telephone Buck Connors," Father said. "Since this was the fifth time today, he must have decided that fellow's foot never slipped at all." Now Mother was standing right over Father with the stocking and the darning egg in one hand and the needle in the other like a dagger.

"Will you please hush, dearest?" she said. "Will you please shut your gee dee mouth?—I'm sorry, Papa," she said to Grandfather. "But he—" Then she was at Father again: "Will you? Will you now?"

"Sure, kid," Father said. "I'm all for peace and quiet too." Then Mother was gone too and then it was bedtime and then Gowan told how he saw Uncle Gavin sitting in the dark parlour with no light except through the hall door, so that he couldn't read if he tried. Which Gowan said he wasn't: just sitting there in the half-dark, until Mother came down the stairs in her dressing gown and her hair down and said,

"Why don't you go to bed? Go on now. Go on," and Gowan said,

"Yessum," and she went on into the parlour and stood beside Uncle Gavin's chair and said,

"I'm going to telephone him," and Uncle Gavin said,

"Telephone who?" and Mother came back and said,

"Come on now. This minute," and waited until Gowan went up the stairs in front of her. When he was in bed with the light off, she came to the door and said good-night, and all they would have to do now would be just to wait. Because even if five was an odd number and it would take an even number to make the night whole for Uncle Gavin, it couldn't possibly be very long because the drugstore closed as soon as the picture show was out, and anybody still sitting in the Holston House lobby after the drummers had all gone to bed would have to explain it to Jefferson some time or other, no matter how much of a bachelor he was. And Gowan said he thought how at least Uncle Gavin and he had their nice warm comfortable familiar home to wait in, even if Uncle Gavin was having to sit up in the dark parlour by himself, instead of having to use the drugstore or the hotel to put off finally having to go home as long as possible.

And this time Gowan said Mr de Spain opened the cut-out as soon as he left the Square; he could hear it all the way getting louder and louder as it turned the two corners into our street, the ripping loud and jeering but at least not in second gear this time, going fast past the house and the dark parlour where Uncle Gavin was sitting, and on around the other two corners he would have to turn to get back into the street he belonged in, dying away at last until all you could hear was just the night and then Uncle Gavin's feet coming quiet up the stairs. Then the hall light went out, and that was all.

All for that night, that day I mean. Because even Uncle Gavin didn't expect it to be completely all. In fact, the rest of them found out pretty quick that Uncle Gavin didn't aim for it to be all; the next morning at breakfast it was Uncle Gavin himself that raised his head first and said: "There goes Manfred back to our salt-mine," and then to Gowan: "Mr de Spain has almost as much fun with his automobile as you're going to have with one as soon as your Cousin Charley buys it, doesn't he?" Whenever that would be, because Father said almost before Uncle Gavin could finish getting the words out:

"Me own one of those stinking noisy things? I wouldn't dare. Too many of my customers use horses and mules for a living." But Gowan said that if Father ever did buy one while he was there, he would find something better to do with it besides running back and forth in front of the house with the cut-out open.

And again while he was on the way home at noon to eat dinner, and again while they were sitting at the table. Nor was it just Gowan who found out Uncle Gavin didn't aim for that to be all because Mother caught Gowan almost before Uncle Gavin turned his back. Gowan didn't know how she did it. Aleck Sander always said that his mother could see and hear through a wall (when he got bigger he said Guster could smell his breath over the telephone), so maybe all women that were already mothers or just acting like mothers like Mother had to while Gowan lived with us, could do that too and that was how Mother did it: stepping out of the parlour just as Gowan put his hand in his pocket.

"Where is it?" Mother said. "What Gavin just gave you. It was a box of tacks; wasn't it a box of tacks? To scatter out there in the street where he will run over them? Wasn't it? Acting just like a high-school sophomore. He should marry Melisandre Backus before he ruins the whole family."

"I thought you said it's too late for that," Gowan said. "That the one that marries Cousin Gavin will have to be a widow with four children."

"Maybe I meant too early," Mother said. "Melisandre hasn't even got a husband yet." Then she wasn't seeing Gowan. "Which is exactly what Manfred de Spain is acting like," she said. "A high school sophomore." Gowan said she was looking right at him but she wasn't seeing him at all, and all of a sudden he said she was pretty, looking just like a girl. "No: exactly what we are all acting like," and now she was seeing him again. "But don't you dare let me see you doing it, do you hear? Don't you dare!"

"Yessum," Gowan said. It was no trouble. All he and Top had to do after school was just divide the tacks into their hands and

kind of fool around out in the middle of the street like they were
trying to decide what to do next while the tacks dribbled down
across the tracks of the automobile; Mr de Spain had made nine
trips by now, so Gowan said he almost had two ruts. Only he and
Top had to stay out in the cold now because they wanted to see it.
Top said that when the wheels blew up, they would blow the
whole automobile up. Gowan didn't think so, but he didn't know
either and Top might be partly right, enough right anyway to
be worth watching.

So they had to stand behind the big jasmine bush and it began
to get dark and it got colder and colder and Guster opened the
kitchen door and begun to holler for Top, then after awhile she
came to the front door and hollered for both of them; it was full
dark and good and cold now when at last they saw the lights
coming, they reached the corner of the yard and the cut-out went
on and the car ripped slow and loud past and they listened and
watched both but nothing happened, nothing at all, it just went
on and even the cut-out went back off; Gowan said how maybe it
would take a little time for the tacks to finally work in and blow
the wheels up and they waited for that too but nothing happened.
And now it had been long enough for him to be home.

And after supper, all of them in the office again, but not anything at all this time, not even anything passed the house so
Gowan thought maybe it hadn't blown up until after he was home
and now Uncle Gavin never would know when it would be safe
to come out of the dark parlour and go upstairs to bed; so that he,
Gowan, made a chance to whisper to Uncle Gavin: "Do you
want me to go up to his house and look?" Only Father said,

"What? What're you whispering about?" so that didn't do any
good either. And the next morning nothing happened either, the
cut-out ripping slow past the house like next time it was coming
right through the dining-room itself. And twice more at noon and
that afternoon when Gowan got home from school Top jerked his
head at him and they went to the cellar; Top had an old rake-
head with a little of the handle still in it, so they built a fire behind
the stable and burned the handle out and when it was dark enough
Gowan watched up and down the street while Top scraped a
trench across the tire-rut and set the rake teeth-up in it and scattered some leaves over to hide it and they watched from behind

the jasmine bush again while the car ripped past. And nothing happened though when the car was gone they went and saw for themselves where the wheels had mashed right across the rake.

"We'll try it once more," Gowan said. And they did: the next morning: and nothing. And that afternoon Top worked on the rake a while with an old file and then Gowan worked on it a while even after they both knew they would still be working on it that way when the Cotillion Club would be planning next year's Christmas Ball. "We need a grindstone," Gowan said.

"Unk Noon," Top said.

"We'll take the gun like we are going rabbit hunting," Gowan said. So they did: as far as Uncle Noon Gatewood's blacksmith shop on the edge of town. Uncle Noon was big and yellow; he had a warped knee that just seemed to fit exactly into the break of a horse's forearm and pastern; he would pick up a horse's hind leg and set the foot inside the knee and reach out with one hand and take hold of the nearest post, and if the post held, the horse could jerk and plunge all it wanted to and Uncle Noon and the horse might sway back and forth but the foot wouldn't move. He let Gowan and Top use his rock while Top turned and tilted the water-can Gowan held the teeth one by one to the stone until they would have gone through almost anything that mashed against them, let alone an automobile.

And Gowan said they sure did have to wait for dark this time. For dark and late too, when they knew nobody would see them. Because if the sharpened rake worked, the car might not blow up so bad that Mr de Spain wouldn't have time to wonder what caused it and start looking around and find the rake. And at first it looked like it was going to be a good thing it was a long December night, too, because the ground was frozen so hard that they had to dig the trench through, not just a short trench like before to set the rake in but one long enough so they could tie a string to the rake and then snatch the rake back into the yard between the time the wheel blew up and Mr de Spain could begin to hunt for what caused it. But Gowan said at least tomorrow was Saturday so they would have all day to fix the rake so they could be behind the jasmine bush and see it by daylight.

So they were: already behind the bush with the rake-head fixed and the end of the string in Gowan's hand when they heard it coming and then saw it, then the cut-out came on and it came ripping past with the cut-out like it was saying HAhaHAhaHAha until they were already thinking they had missed this time too when the wheel said BANG and Gowan said he didn't have time to snatch the string because the string did the snatching, out of his hand and around the jasmine bush like the tail of a snake, the car saying HAhaHAhaclankHAhaHAhaclank every time the rake that seemed to be stuck to the wheel would wham against the mudguard again, until Mr de Spain finally stopped it. Then Gowan said the parlour window behind them opened, with Mother and Father standing in it until Mother said:

"You and Top go out and help him so you both will learn something about automobiles when your Cousin Charley buys one."

"Me buy one of those noisy stinking things?" Father said. "Why, I'd lose every horse and mule customer I've got—"

"Nonsense," Mother said. "You'd buy one today if you thought Papa would stand for it.—No," she said to Gowan. "Just you help Mr de Spain. I want Top in the house."

So Top went into the house and Gowan went out to the car, where Mr de Spain was standing beside the crumpled wheel holding the rake-head in his hand and looking down at it with his lips poked out like he was kind of whistling a tune to himself, Gowan said. Then he looked around at Gowan and took out his knife and cut the string loose and put the rake-head into his overcoat pocket and begun to roll the string up, watching the string where it came jerking out of our yard, his mouth still pursed out like he was whistling to himself. Then Top came up. He was wearing the white jacket he wore when Mother would try to teach him to wait on the table, carrying a tray with a cup of coffee and the cream and sugar bowl. "Miss Maggie say would you care for a cup of coffee while you resting in the cold?" he said.

"Much obliged," Mr de Spain said. He finished rolling the string up and took the tray from Top and set it on the mudguard of the car and then handed the rolled-up string to Top. "Here's a good fish-line for you," he said.

"It ain't none of mine," Top said.

"It is now," Mr de Spain said. "I just gave it to you." So Top took the string. Then Mr de Spain told him to take off that clean white coat first and then he opened the back of the automobile

and showed Gowan and Top the jack and tire tool and then he
drank the coffee while Top crawled under the car and set the jack
in place and he and Gowan wound up the wheel. Then Mr de
Spain put down the empty cup and took off his overcoat and
hunkered down by the crumpled wheel with the tire tool. Except
that from then on Gowan said all he and Top learned was some
curse-words they never had heard before, until Mr de Spain stood
up and threw the tire tool at the wheel and said, to Gowan this
time: "Run in the house and telephone Buck Connors to bring
Jabbo here double quick." Only Father was there by that time.

"Maybe you've got too many experts," he said. "Come on in
and have a drink. I know it's too early in the morning, but this
is Christmas."

So they all went into the house and Father telephoned Mr
Connors to bring Jabbo. Jabbo was Uncle Noon Gatewood's son.
He was going to be a blacksmith too until Mr de Spain brought
that first red automobile to town and, as Uncle Noon said, "ruint
him". Though Gowan said that never made much sense to him
because Jabbo used to get drunk and wind up in jail three or four
times a year while he was still only a blacksmith, while now, since
automobiles had come to Jefferson, Jabbo was the best mechanic
in the county and although he still got drunk and into jail as much
as ever, he never stayed longer than just overnight any more
because somebody with an automobile always needed him enough
to pay his fine by morning.

They then went into the dining-room, where Mother already
had the decanter and glasses set out. "Wait," Father said. "I'll
call Gavin."

"He's already gone," Mother said right quick. "Sit down now
and have your toddy."

"Maybe he hasn't," Father said, going out anyway.

"Please don't wait on them," Mother said to Mr de Spain.

"I don't mind waiting," Mr de Spain said. "It's too early in
the morning to start drinking for the next few minutes." Then
Father came back.

"Gavin says to please excuse him," Father said. "He seems to
have heartburn these days."

"Tell him salt is good for heartburn," Mr de Spain said.

"What?" Father said.

"Tell him to come on," Mr de Spain said. "Tell him Maggie will set a salt-cellar between us." And that was all then. Mr Connors came with a shotgun and Jabbo in handcuffs, and they all went out to the car while Mr Connors handed the shotgun to Jabbo to hold while he got out the key and unlocked the handcuffs and took the shotgun back. Then Jabbo picked up the tire tool and had the tire off in no time.

"Why don't you," Father said, "if you could just kind of embalm Jabbo a little—you know: so he wouldn't get cold or hungry —tie him on the back of the car like he was an extra wheel or engine, then every time you had a puncture or it wouldn't start, all you'd have to do would be to untie Jabbo and stand him up and unbalm him—is that the word? Unbalm?"

"When you get it patched," Mr de Spain said to Jabbo, "bring it on to my office."

"Yes sir," Jabbo said. "Mr Buck can bring the fining paper along with us."

"Thank your aunt for the coffee," Mr de Spain said to Gowan.

"She's my cousin," Gowan said. "And the toddy."

"I'll walk to town with you," Father said to Mr de Spain. That was Saturday. The Cotillion Ball would be Wednesday. On Monday and Tuesday and Wednesday Jefferson had the biggest run on flowers the town ever had, even when old General Compson died, who had not only been a Confederate brigadier, but for two days he had been Governor of Mississippi too. It wasn't through any of us that Mr de Spain found out what Uncle Gavin was planning to do, and decided that he—Mr de Spain—had better do it too. And it would be nice to think that the same notion occurred to Uncle Gavin and Mr de Spain at the same time. But that was too much to expect either.

So it was Mrs Rouncewell. She ran the flower shop; not, Uncle Gavin said, because she loved flowers nor even because she loved money, but because she loved funerals; she had buried two husbands herself and took the second one's insurance and opened the flower shop and furnished the flowers for every funeral in Jefferson since; she would be the one that told Mr de Spain how Uncle Gavin had wanted to send Mrs Snopes a corsage to wear to the ball until Mother told him that Mrs Snopes already had a husband and he couldn't send one to her alone and Uncle Gavin

said All right, did Mother want him to send one to Mr Snopes
too? And Mother said he knew what she meant and Uncle Gavin
said All right, he would send one to each one of the Cotillion
ladies. Until Mr de Spain had to do the same thing, so that not
just Mrs Snopes but all the ladies of the Cotillion club were going
to get two corsages apiece.

Not to mention the rest of the town: not just the husbands and
beaus of the ladies in the Club, but the husbands and beaus of all
the other ladies who were invited; especially the husbands who
were already married because they wouldn't have had to send
their wives a corsage at all because their wives wouldn't have
expected one except for Uncle Gavin and Mr de Spain. But
mainly Uncle Gavin, since he started the whole thing; to listen
to them around the barbershop getting their hair cut for the
dance, and in Mr Kneeland's tailor shop renting the dress
suits you would have thought they were going to lynch Uncle
Gavin.

And one was more than just cussing Uncle Gavin: Mr Grenier
Weddel and Mrs Maurice Priest. But all that came out later; we
didn't hear about that until the day after the Ball. All we knew
about now was the corsage-run on Mrs Rouncewell, what Father
called the Rouncewell panic. ("I had to make that one myself,"
Father said. "It was Gavin's by right; he should have done it, but
right now he ain't even as faintly close to humour as that one was."
Because he was cussing Uncle Gavin too, since now he would
have to send Mother a corsage that he hadn't figured on doing,
since Uncle Gavin was, which would make three she would get—
that is, if the rest of the men aiming to attend the Ball didn't panic
too and decide they would all have to send the members a separate
corsage.) Because by Monday night Mrs Rouncewell had run
clean out of flowers; by the time the northbound train ran Tuesday afternoon, all the towns up and down the road from Jefferson
had been milked dry too; and early Wednesday morning a special
hired automobile made a night emergency run from Memphis
with enough flowers to make out so Mrs Rouncewell could begin
to deliver the corsages, using her own delivery boy and Lucius
Hogganbeck's jitney and even renting Miss Eunice Habersham's
home-made truck that she peddled vegetables from to finish the
deliveries in time, delivering five of them at our house which they

all thought were for Mother until she read the names on the boxes and said:

"This one's not for me. It's for Gavin." And they all stood watching Uncle Gavin while he stood right still looking down at the box, his hand already raised toward the box and then his hand stopped too in midair. Until at last he broke the string and lifted the lid and moved the tissue paper aside and then—Gowan said it was all of a sudden yet it wasn't fast either—moved the tissue paper back and put the lid back on and picked up the box. "Aren't you going to let us see it?" Mother said.

"No," Uncle Gavin said. But Gowan had already seen. It was the rake-head, with two flowers like a bouquet, all bound together with a band or strip of something that Gowan knew was thin rubber, but it was another year or two until he was a good deal bigger and older that he knew what the thing was; and at the same time he realised what it was, he said he knew it had already been used; and at the same time he knew at least how Uncle Gavin was supposed to believe it had been used, which was the reason Mr de Spain sent it to him: that whether Uncle Gavin was right or not about how it had been used, he would never be sure and so forever afterward would have no peace about it.

And Gowan was just thirteen then; until that one, he wouldn't have thought that anybody could have paid him or even dragged him to a Cotillion Ball. But he said he had already had to see too much by now; he had to be there if there was going to be anything else, any more to it, even if he couldn't imagine what else there could be after this, what more could happen at just a dance. So he put on his blue Sunday suit and watched Mother with her hair all primped and Grandmother's diamond earrings trying to make Father say which one of her four corsages to carry: the one he gave her or to agree with the one of the other three that she thought went best with her dress; then he went across to Uncle Gavin's room where Uncle Gavin got out another white bow tie like his and put it on Gowan and a flower for his buttonhole too and they all went downstairs, the hack was waiting and they drove through the cold to the Square and the Opera House, where the other hacks and now and then a car were pulling up for the other guests to get out crimped and frizzed in scarves and earrings and perfume and long white gloves like Mother or in

C

claw-hammer coats and boiled shirts and white ties and yesterday's haircuts like Father and Uncle Gavin and (the white tie at least) Gowan, with the loafers, Negro and white boys too, hanging around the door to hear the music after the band started to play.

It was Professor Handy, from Beale Street in Memphis. His band played at all the balls in north Mississippi, and Gowan said how the hall was all decorated for Christmas and the Cotillion Club ladies and their escorts all lined up to receive the guests; he said you could smell all the corsages even before you began to climb the stairs and that when you got inside the ballroom it looked like you should have been able to see the smell from them too like mist in a swamp on a cold morning. And he said how Mr Snopes was there too, in a rented dress suit, and Jefferson probably thought at first that that rented dress suit was just the second foot-print made on it, until they had time to realise that it wasn't any more than just a footprint than that water tank was a monument: it was a red flag. No: it was that sign at the railroad crossing that says Look Out for the Locomotive.

And Gowan said how, since Mother was President of the Club that year, everybody (once Mrs Rouncewell finally realised that floral gold-mine she had fallen into, there wasn't anybody in Jefferson in the dark any longer about Mr de Spain and Uncle Gavin and Mrs Snopes) expected her to give Uncle Gavin the first dance with Mrs Snopes. But she didn't. She sent Grenier Weddel; he was a bachelor too. And even after that she still kept the dances equal between Uncle Gavin and Mr de Spain until Mr de Spain ruined it. Because he was a bachelor. I mean, like Uncle Gavin said: that there are some men who are incorrigibly and invincibly bachelor no matter how often they marry, just as some men are doomed and emasculate husbands if they never find a woman to take them. And Mr de Spain was one of them. I mean the first kind: incorrigibly and invincibly bachelor and threat no matter what happened to him because Uncle Gavin said things, circumstance and conditions, didn't happen to people like Mr de Spain: people like him happened to circumstances and conditions.

This time he had help. I wasn't there to see it, and I know now that Gowan didn't know what he was seeing either. Because after a while I got born and then big enough to see Mrs Snopes myself, and after a while more I was old enough to feel what Uncle Gavin

and Mr de Spain (and all the other men in Jefferson, and Frenchman's Bend and everywhere else that ever saw her I reckon, the
little cautious men who were not as brave and unlucky as Uncle
Gavin and brave and lucky as Mr de Spain, though they probably
called it being more sensible) felt just looking at her. And after a
while more still and she was dead and Mr de Spain had left town
wearing public mourning for her as if she had been his wife and
Jefferson finally quit talking about her, my bet is there was more
than me in Jefferson that even just remembering her could feel
it still and grieve. I mean, grieve because her daughter didn't
have whatever it was that she had; until you realised that what
you grieved for wasn't that the daughter didn't have it too;
grieved not that we didn't have it any more, but that we couldn't
have it any more: that even a whole Jefferson full of little weak
puny frightened men couldn't have stood more than one Mrs
Snopes inside of just one one-hundred years. And I reckon there was
a second or two at first when even Mr de Spain had time to be
afraid. I reckon there was a second when even he said Hold on
here; have I maybe blundered into something not just purer than
me but even braver than me, braver and tougher than me because
it is purer than me, cleaner than me? Because that was what it was.

Gowan said it was the way Mrs Snopes and Mr de Spain began
to dance together. That is, the way that Mr de Spain all of a
sudden began to dance with Mrs Snopes. Up to that time, Gowan
said, Uncle Gavin and Mr de Spain and the other men Mother
sent to write their names on Mrs Snopes's programme had been
taking turns all calm and peaceful. Then all of a sudden Gowan
said everybody else stopped dancing and kind of fell back and he
said he saw Mrs Snopes and Mr de Spain dancing together alone
in a kind of aghast circle of people. And when I was old enough,
fourteen or sixteen, I knew what Gowan had seen without knowing what he was seeing: that second when Mr de Spain felt
astonishment, amazement and unbelief and terror too at himself
because of what he found himself doing without even knowing
he was going to—dancing like that with Mrs Snopes to take
revenge on Uncle Gavin for having frightened him, Mr de Spain,
enough to make him play the sophomore tricks like the cut-out
and the rake-head and the used rubber thing in a corsage;
frightened at himself at finding out that he couldn't possibly be

only what he had thought for all those years he was, if he could find himself in a condition capable of playing tricks like that; while Mrs Snopes was dancing that way, letting Mr de Spain get her into dancing that way in public, simply because she was alive and not ashamed of it like maybe right now or even for the last two weeks Mr de Spain and Uncle Gavin had been ashamed; was what she was and looked the way she looked and wasn't ashamed of it and not afraid or ashamed of being glad of it, nor even of doing this to prove it, since this appeared to be the only way of proving it, not being afraid or ashamed, that the little puny people fallen back speechless and aghast in a shocked circle around them, could understand; all the other little doomed mean cowardly married and unmarried husbands looking aghast and outraged in order to keep one another from seeing that what they really wanted to do was cry, weep because they were not that brave, each one knowing that even if there was no other man on earth, let alone in that ballroom, they still could not have survived, let alone matched or coped with, that splendour, that splendid unshame.

It should have been Mr Snopes of course, because he was the husband, the squire, the protector in the formal ritual. But it was Uncle Gavin and he wasn't any husband or squire or knight or defender or protector either except simply and quickly his own: who didn't really care even how badly Mrs Snopes got battered and bruised in the business provided there was enough of her left when he finally got the last spark of life trampled out of Mr de Spain. Gowan said how he stepped in and grabbed Mr de Spain by the shoulder and jerked, and now a kind of sound went up and then he said all the men were streaming across the floor toward the back stairs that led down into the back alley and now the ladies were screaming good, only Gowan said that a lot of them were streaking after the men too so that he had to kind of burrow along among skirts and legs, down the back stairs; he said he could see Uncle Gavin through the legs just getting up from the alley and he, Gowan, pushed on through to the front and saw Uncle Gavin just getting up from the alley again with his face all bloody and two men helping him or anyway trying to, because he flung them off and ran at Mr de Spain again: and when I was older I knew that too: that Uncle Gavin wasn't trying any more to destroy or even hurt Mr de Spain because he had already found out by that time that he couldn't. Because now Uncle Gavin was himself again. What he was doing was simply defending forever with his blood the principle that chastity and virtue in women shall be defended whether they exist or not.

"Damn it," Mr de Spain said, "hold him, some of you fellows, and let me get out of here." So Father held Uncle Gavin and somebody brought Mr de Spain's hat and coat and he left; and Gowan said this was the time he expected to hear that cut-out again for sure. But he didn't. There was nothing: just Uncle Gavin standing there wiping the blood from his face on his handkerchief then on Father's.

"You fool," Father said. "Don't you know you can't fight? You don't know how."

"Can you suggest a better way to learn than the one I just tried?" Uncle Gavin said.

And at home too, in his bathroom, where he could take off his vest and collar and tie and shirt and hold a wet towel against the bleeding, when Mother came in. She had a flower in her hand, a red rose from one of the corsages. "Here," she said. "She sent it to you."

"You lie," Uncle Gavin said. "You did it."

"Lie yourself!" Mother said. "She sent it!"

"No," Uncle Gavin said.

"Then she should have!" Mother said; and now Gowan said she was crying, half way holding to Uncle Gavin and half way beating him with both fists, crying: "You fool! You fool! They don't deserve you! They aren't good enough for you! None of them are, no matter how much they look and act like a—like a—like a god damn whorehouse! None of them! None of them!"

Only Mr Snopes left more footprints than them on Jefferson that night; he left another bloody nose and two black eyes. That fourth corsage Mother got that night was from Grenier Weddel. He was a bachelor like Mr de Spain. I mean, he was the kind of bachelor that Uncle Gavin said would still be one no matter how many times who married him. Maybe that was why Sally Hampton turned him down. Anyway, she sent his ring back and married

Maurice Priest instead and so when Uncle Gavin and Mr de Spain started what Father called the Mrs Rouncewell panic that day, Grenier saw his chance too and sent Mrs Priest not just what Father called a standard panic-size corsage, but a triple one. Maybe that was why she didn't wear it to the ball that night; it was too big to carry. Anyway she didn't, but anyway after Uncle Gavin and Mr de Spain got through with the alley, Grenier and Maurice Priest went back there and Grenier came out with one of the black eyes and Maurice went home with the bloody nose and the next morning when Sally Priest came to town she had the other black eye. And maybe she didn't wear the corsage in public but she sure did that eye. She was not only around town all that morning, she came back that afternoon so everybody in Jefferson would have a chance to see it or at least hear about it. Gowan said you would even have thought she was proud of it.

4

V. K. RATLIFF

SHE was. His aunt (not his two uncles nor his grandpaw, but any of his womenfolks) could have told him why: proud she still had a husband that could and would black her eye; proud her husband had a wife that could still make him need to.

And Flem wasn't the first Snopes in Jefferson neither. The first one was Mink, that spent two and a half months in the Jefferson jail on his way to his permanent residence in the penitentiary at Parchman for killing Zack Houston. And he spent them two and a half months labouring under a mistake.

I don't mean a mistake in killing Houston. He knowed what he aimed to do then. Zack was a proud man to begin with, and he had just lost his young wife that he had had a considerable trouble persuading her folks to let her marry him—she was old man Cal Bookright's youngest child, a school teacher, and although Zack owned his place and was a good farmer, that's all he was: just a farmer without no special schooling, besides being a hard liver when he was a young man and even right up to when he got serious about Letty Bookright and found out that old Cal was serious too. Then when he, or both of them together I reckon, finally beat old Cal down and they was married, he never even had her a whole year before he lost her. And even then he had to lose her hard, the hardest way: that same blood stallion killed her with his feet in the stall one day that Mink shot Houston off of that morning—and that made him a little extra morose because he was unhappy. So between being proud to begin with and then unhappy on top of that, he was a little overbearing. But since most of the folks around Frenchman's Bend knowed he was proud and knowed how hard he had to work to persuade old Cal to let Letty marry him, he would still a been all right if he hadn't tangled with Mink Snopes.

Because Mink Snopes was mean. He was the only out-and-out mean Snopes we ever experienced. There was mad short-tempered barn-burners like old Ab, and there was the mild innocent ones like Eck that not only wasn't no Snopes, no matter what his maw

said, he never had no more business being born into a Snopes
nest than a sparrow would have in a hawk's nest; and there was
the one pure out-and-out fool like I.O. But we never had run into
one before that was just mean without no profit consideration or
hope at all.

Maybe that was why he was the only mean Snopes: there wasn't
no sign of any profit in it. Only he was bound or anyway must
a had a little of his cousin I.O.'s foolishness too or he wouldn't
have made his mistake. I mean, the mistake not of shooting
Houston but of when he picked out to do it; picking out the time
to do it while Flem was still off on his Texas honeymoon. Sholy
he knowed that Flem hadn't got back yet. Or maybe the night
before he had got the Snopes grapevine word that he had been
waiting for, that Flem would reach Frenchman's Bend tomorrow,
and it was only then that he had taken that old wore-out ten-gauge
britch-loader and hid in that thicket and bush-whacked Houston
off the horse when he rid past. But then I don't know. Maybe by
that time nothing else mattered to him but seeing Houston over
the end of them barrels then feeling that stock jolt back against
his shoulder.

Anyhow, that's what he done. And likely it wasn't until
Houston was laying in the mud in the road and that skeered
stallion with the loose reins and the empty saddle and flapping
stirrups already tearing on to Varner's store to spread the news,
that he realised with whatever horror it was, that he had done
too soon something it was long since too late to undo. Which was
why he tried to hide the body and then dropped the gun into that
slough and come on to the store, hanging around the store ever
day while the sheriff was still hunting for Houston, not to keep up
with whether the sheriff was getting warm or not but waiting for
Flem to get back from Texas and save him; right up to the time
when Houston's hound led them to the body and some fish-
grabblers even found the gun in the slough that ever body knowed
was hisn because wouldn't nobody else own it.

And that was when the rage and the outrage and the injustice
and the betrayal must a got unbearable to him, when he decided
or realised or whatever it was, that Flem by now must a heard
about the killing and was deliberately keeping away from Frenchman's Bend or maybe even all Mississippi so he wouldn't have

to help him, get him out of it. Not even despair: just simple anger
and outrage: to show Flem Snopes that he never give a durn
about him neither: handcuffed now and in the sheriff's surrey on
the way in to the jail when he seen his chance right quick and
wedged his neck tight into the V of the top stanchion and tried
to fling his legs and body over the side until they caught him back.

But it was just the initial outrage and hurt and disappointment;
it couldn't last. Which likely his good sense told him it wouldn't
and probably he was glad in a way he had got shut of it so calm
good sense could come back. Which it did, since now all he had
to do was just to be as comfortable as he could in jail and wait
until Flem did get home since even Flem Snopes couldn't stay
forever even on a honeymoon even in Texas.

So that's what he done. Up there on the top floor of the jail
(since he was a authentic top-class murderer, he wouldn't have
to go out and work on the streets like just a Negro crap-shooter),
not even impatient for a long time: just standing there with his
hands laying in the crossbars where he could watch the street
and the sidewalk that Flem would come walking up from the
Square; not impatient during all that first month and not even
bad worried in the second one after the Grand Jury indicted him:
just hollering down now and then to somebody passing if Flem
Snopes was in town yet; not even until the end of the second
month that he begun to think that maybe Flem hadn't got back
yet and he would holler down to folks to send word out to Frenchman's Bend for Will Varner to come in and see him.

So it wasn't until just them two last weeks before Court and no
Will Varner nor nobody else had come in to see him that he
probably found out he simply could not believe that Flem Snopes
hadn't got back to Frenchman's Bend; he just could not believe
that; he dassent to believe that: only that the grown folks he had
been hollering down to hadn't never delivered his message, not
sleeping much at night now so that (that-ere top floor behind
the barred window would be dark and with the street light shining
on it you could see the white blob of his face and the two blobs
of his hands gripping the bars) he had plenty of time to stand there
all night if necessary waiting for somebody to pass that he could
trust would deliver his message: boys, a boy like that Stevens
boy, Lawyer Stevens's visiting nephew, that hadn't been spoiled

c*

and corrupted yet by the world of growed-up men into being his
enemies, whispering down to them until they would stop and look
up at him; still whispering down at them even after they had done
broke and run: "Boys! Fellers! You, there. You want ten dollars?
Get word out to Frenchman's Bend, tell Flem Snopes his cousin
Mink Snopes says to hurry in here, hurry—"

And right up to that morning in court. As soon as they brung
him in the door, handcuffed, he started to craning his neck, looking at all the faces, still craning his neck around at the folks still
crowding in long after they had run out of anything to set on and
still at it while they was choosing the jury, even trying to stand
up on a chair to see better until they would shove him down; still
craning and darting his head while the clerk read the indictment
and then said, "Guilty or not guilty?" Only this time he had
already stood up before they could stop him, looking out over the
crowd toward the last faces at the clean back of the room and says:
"Flem!"

And now the Judge was banging his little mallet and the lawyer
the Court had appointed was up too and the bailiff hollering,
"Order! Order in the court!"

And Mink says again, "Flem! Flem Snopes!" Only this time the
Judge his-self leaned down toward him across the Bench and says,

"You there! Snopes!" until Mink finally turned and looked at
him. "Are you guilty or not guilty?"

"What?" Mink says.

"Did you kill Zack Houston or didn't you?" the Judge says.

"Don't bother me now," Mink says. "Can't you see I'm busy?"
turning his head again toward the faces come to see if maybe they
wouldn't hang him anyhow, no matter who said he was crazy,
since that was what he seemed to want his-self, having already
tried it once and so the Law wouldn't be doing no more than just
accommodating him, saying: "Somebody there! Anybody with a
car. To run out to Varner's store quick and get Flem Snopes. He
will pay you, whatever you charge and whatever extry—ten
dollars extry—twenty extry—"

Last summer Lawyer had to do something, he didn't know
what. Now he had to do something, he didn't care what. I don't

even think he especially hunted around for something. I think he just reached his hand and snatched something, the first nearest thing, and it just happened to be that old quick-vanishing power-plant brass that ever body in Jefferson, including Flem Snopes— sholy including Flem Snopes—had been trying out of pure and simple politeness to forget about.

When as acting City Attorney he drawed up the suit against Mayor de Spain's bonding company, charging malfeasance in office and criminal connivance or however they put it, naturally ever body thought all he aimed to do then was to walk in and lay the papers on Manfred de Spain's desk. But they was wrong; he never no more wanted to buy anything from De Spain than he did that night in the alley behind that Christmas Ball, when his brother-in-law told him he couldn't fight because he never knowed how—a piece of information already in Lawyer's possession, having already lived with his-self for more or less twenty-two or may-be twenty-three years. He didn't want nothing from De Spain because the only thing De Spain had that he wanted, Lawyer didn't know his-self that was what he wanted until his paw told him that last afternoon.

So Lawyer filed the suit. And the first thing was the pleasant young feller from the bonding company in his nice city suit getting off the morning train with his nice city suitcase, saying, "Now, fellers, let's all have a drink of this-here nice city whiskey and see if we can jest all get together on this thing," then spending one quick horrified day, mostly on the long-distance telephone be-tween talking with them two Negro firemen, Tom Tom Bird and Tomey's Turl Beauchamp, while waiting for Flem to get back from where he had went suddenly on a visit into the next county.

So on the third day the one come from the bonding company that was big enough in it to have the grey hair and come in a Pull-man in striped britches and a gold watch chain big enough to boom logs with and gold eyeglasses and even a gold toothpick and the pigeon-tailed coat and the plug hat until by nightfall you couldn't even a got a glass of water in the Holston Hotel for ever porter and waiter hanging around his door to wait on him and he could a owned ever other Negro in Jefferson too by to-morrow if he had had anything he could a done with them, saying "Gentlemen. Gentlemen. Gentlemen." And the mayor coming in where they was all setting around the table, to stand there laughing at them for a while and then saying,

"You'll have to excuse me. Even the mayor of just Jefferson, Mississippi, has got to do a little work now and then." And Lawyer Stevens setting there calm and white in the face and looking exactly like he done that night when he told his brother-in-law: "Can you suh-jest a better way for me to learn how to fight than the one I just tried?"

And Flem Snopes hadn't got back yet and in fact they couldn't even locate him, like he had evidently went on a camping trip in the woods where there wasn't no telephone; and the big boss one, the one with the white vest and the gold toothpick, says: "I'm sure Mr de Spain would resign. Why don't we jest let him resign and forget all this here unhappiness?" and Lawyer Stevens says, "He's a good mayor. We don't want him to resign," and the white vest says, "Then what do you want? You will have to prove our client's representative stole any brass, and all you have is the word of them two nigras because Mr Snopes his-self has went out of town."

"That water tank ain't went out of town," Lawyer says. "We can drain that water tank."

So what they called was a special meeting of the board of aldermen. What they got was like one of them mass carcasses to vote between two beauty queens, the court-house bell beginning to ring about eight o'clock like it actively was some kind of a night session of court, and the folks coming up the streets and gathering in the Square, laughing and making jokes back and forth, until they decided right quick that the mayor's office wouldn't hold even the start of it, so they moved into the courtroom upstairs like it was Court.

Because this was just January; that Christmas Ball wasn't barely three weeks old yet. Even when they chose sides it was still jest fun, because most of them had jest come to watch and listen anyhow, even after somebody beat the Judge's mallet on the table until they quit laughing and joking and hushed and one of the aldermen said, "I don't know how much it will cost to drain that tank, but I for one will be damned—"

"I do," Lawyer Stevens says. "I already asked. It will cost three hundred and eighty dollars to rig a auxiliary tank long enough to drain and then fill the other one up again and then dismantle the auxiliary and get shut of it. It won't cost nothing to send somebody down inside of it to look because I'll do that myself."

"All right," the alderman says. "Then I will still be damned—"

"All right," Lawyer says. "Then I will pay for it myself," and the old bonding feller, the white-vest one, saying "Gentlemen. Gentlemen. Gentlemen." And the young one, the first one, standing up now and hollering:

"Don't you see, Mr Stevens? Don't you see, Mr Stevens? If you find brass in the tank, there won't be no crime because the brass already belongs to the city?"

"I already thought of that too," Lawyer says. "The brass still belongs to the city even if we don't drain the tank. Only, where is it at?" and the little bonding feller saying:

"Wait! Wait! That ain't what I meant. I mean if the brass ain't missing there ain't no crime because it wasn't never stole."

"Tom Tom Bird and Tomey's Turl Beauchamp says it was because they stole it," Lawyer says. Now they was two aldermen talking at once, saying,

"Hold up here; hold up here," until finally the loudest one, Henry Best, won:

"Then who are you charging, Gavin? Are them nigras under Manfred's bond too?"

"But there ain't no crime! We know the brass is in that tank because that's where the nigras said they put it." The little bonding feller was hollering, and all this time the big one, the white-vest one, still saying "Gentlemen. Gentlemen. Gentlemen," like a big bass drum a far piece off that never nobody paid any attention to nohow; until Henry Best hollered,

"Wait, god damn it," so loud that they did hush and Henry said: "Them nigras confessed they stole that brass, but there ain't no evidence of theft until we drain that tank. So right now, they didn't steal no brass. And if we drain that damn tank and find brass in it, they did steal brass and are guilty of theft. Only, as soon as we find brass in that tank, they never stole any brass because the brass is not just once more in the possession of the city: it ain't never been out of it. God damn it, Gavin, is that what you are trying to tell us? Then what the hell do you want? What in hell do you want?"

And Lawyer Stevens setting there calm and still, with his face still white and still as paper. And maybe he hadn't learned how to fight yet neither. But he still hadn't heard about no rule against trying. "That's right," he says. "If there is brass in that tank—valuable property of the city unlawfully constrained into that tank by the connivance and condonance of a employee of the city, a crime has been committed. If we find brass in that tank —valuable property belonging to the city unlawfully constrained into that tank with the connivance or condonance of a employee of the city, even if it is recovered, a attempt at a crime has been condoned by a employee of the city. But that tank *per se* and what brass may or may not *per se* be in it, is beside the point. What we have engaged the attention of this honourable bonding company about is, jest which malfeasance did our honourable mayor commit? Jest which crime, by who, did our chief servant of our city condone?" Because he didn't know either what he wanted. And even when next day his paw told him what his behaviour looked like he wanted and for a minute Lawyer even agreed, that still wasn't it.

Because that was all they got then, which wasn't nothing to be settled jest off-hand by a passel of amateurs like a alderman board. It was something for a professional, a sho-enough active judge; whether they aimed to or not, they had done got themselves now to where they would have to have a court. Though I didn't know Judge Dukinfield was in the crowd until Henry Best stood up and looked out at us and hollered: "Judge Dukinfield, is Judge Dukinfield still here?" and Judge Dukinfield stood up in the back and says,

"Yes, Henry?"

"I reckon we'll have to have help, Judge," Henry says. "I reckon you heard as much of this as we done, and we all hope you made more sense out of it than we done—"

"Yes; all right," Judge Dukinfield says. "We will hold the hearing here in chambers tomorrow morning at nine. I don't believe either plaintiff or defendant will need more counsel than are represented tonight, but they are welcome to bring juniors if they like—or should we say seconds?"

Then we all got up to leave, still laughing and talking and joking back and forth, still not taking no sides but jest mainly en-

joying it, jest being in principle on whichever other side from
them two foreign bonding fellers for the simple reason that they
was foreigners, not even paying no attention to Lawyer's twin
sister standing there by him now until you could almost hear her
telling Henry Best: "Now you're satisfied; maybe you can let him
alone now"; not even paying no attention when a boy—I didn't
recognise who he was—come burrowing through and up to the
table and handed Lawyer something and Lawyer taken it; not
realising until tomorrow that something had happened between
that meeting that night and the next morning that we never
knowed about and it's my opinion we ain't going to, just going on
home or about our business until the Square was empty except
for that one light in his and his paw's office over the hardware
store where he was setting alone—provided it was him of course
and providing he was alone—how does the feller say it? inviting
his soul?

5

GAVIN STEVENS

THE poets are wrong of course. According to them I should have known the note was on the way, let alone who it was from. As it was, I didn't even know who it was from after I read it. But then, poets are almost always wrong about facts. That's because they are not really interested in facts: only in truth: which is why the truth they speak is so true that even those who hate poets by simple natural instinct are exalted and terrified by it.

No: that's wrong. It's because you don't dare to hope, you are afraid to hope. Not afraid of the extent of hope of which you are capable, but that you—the frail web of bone and flesh snaring that fragile temeritous boundless aspirant sleepless with dream and hope—cannot match it; as Ratliff would say, Knowing always you won't never be man enough to do the harm and damage you would do if you were just man enough—and, he might add, or maybe I do it for him, thank God for it. Ay, thank God for it or thank anything else for it that will give you any peace after it's too late; peace in which to coddle that frail web and its unsleeping ensnared anguish both on your knee and whisper to it: There, there, it's all right; I know you are brave.

The first thing I did on entering the office was to turn on all the lights; if it hadn't been January and the thermometer in the low thirties I would have propped the door to stand open too for that much more of a Mississippi gentleman's tender circumspection toward her good name. The second thing I did was to think *My God all the lights on for the whole town to see* because now I would have Grover Winbush (the night marshal) up the stairs as surely as if I had sent for him, since with the usual single desk-lamp on he would have thought I was merely working and would let me alone, where with all of them burning like this he would come up certainly, not to surprise the intruder but to participate in the conversation.

So I should have leaped to turn them off again, knowing that once I moved, turned loose the chair arms I would probably bolt, flee, run home to Maggie, who has tried to be my mother ever since ours died and some day may succeed. So I just sat there thinking how if there were only time and means to communicate, suggest, project on to her wherever she might be at this moment between her home and here, the rubber soles for silence and the dark enveloping night-blending cloak and scarf for invisibility; then in the next second thinking how the simple suggestion of secret shoes and concealing cloak would forever abrogate and render null all need for either since although I might still be I, she must forever be some lesser and baser other to be vulnerable to the base insult of secrecy and fearfulness and silence.

So when I heard her feet on the stairs I didn't even think *For God's sake take off your shoes or at least tiptoe.* What I thought was How can you move and make that little noise, with only the sound of trivial human feet: who should have moved like Wagner: not with but *in* the sonorous sweep of thunder or brass music, even the very limbs moving in tune with the striding other in a sound of tuned wind and storm and mighty harps. I thought *Since making this more or less secret date to meet me here at this hour of night is her idea, at least she will have to look at me.* Which she had never done yet. If she had ever even seen me yet while I was too busy playing the fool because of her to notice, buffoon for her, playing with tacks in the street like a vicious boy, using not even honest bribery but my own delayed vicious juvenility to play on the natural and normal savagery (plus curiosity; don't forget that) of an authentic juvenile—to gain what? for what? what did I want, what was I trying for: like the child striking matches in a hay-stack yet at the same time trembling with terror lest he does see holocaust.

You see? terror. I hadn't taken time to wonder what in hell she wanted with me: only the terror after the boy put the note in my hand and I found privacy to open and read it and still (the terror) in the courage, desperation, despair—call it whatever you like and whatever it was and wherever I found it—to cross to the door and open it and think as I always had each time I was that near, either to dance with her or merely to challenge and give twenty or thirty pounds to an impugner of her honour: *Why, she can't possibly be this small, this little,* apparently standing only inches short of my own six feet, yet small, little; too small to have displaced enough of my peace to contain this much unsleep, to have disarranged this much of what I had at least thought was peace. In fact I might have said she stood almost eye to eye with me if she had looked at me that long, which she did not: that one quick unhasting blue (they were dark blue) envelopment and then no more; no more needing to look—if she ever had—at me, but rather instead one single complete perception to which that adjective complete were as trivial as the adjective dampness to the blue sea itself; that one single glance to add me up and then subtract and then dispense as if that calm unhasting blueness had picked me up whole and palped me over front and back and sides and set me down again. But she didn't sit down herself. She didn't even move yet. Then I realised suddenly that she was simply examining the office as women examine a room they have never seen before.

"Won't you sit down?" I said.

"All right," she said. And, sitting in that ordinary chair across the desk, she was still too small to hold, compass without one bursting seam all that unslumber, all that chewed anguish of the poet's bitter thumbs which were not just my thumbs but all male Jefferson's or actually all male earth's by proxy, that thumb being all men's fate who had earned or deserved the right to call themselves men; too small, too little to contain, bear those . . . I had, must have, seen her at least five years ago though it was only last summer that I must have looked at her; say only since last summer, since until then I had been too busy passing bar examinations to have had time to prone and supine myself for proper relinquishment; call it two hundred for round numbers from June to January with some (not much) out for sleeping— two hundred nights of fevered projection of my brother's mantle to defend and save her honour from its ravisher.

You see? It still had not once occurred to me to ask her what she wanted. I was not even waiting for her to tell me. I was simply waiting for those two hundred nights to culminate as I had spent at least some of them or some small part of them expecting when this moment came, if it did, would, was fated: I to be swept up as into storm or hurricane or tornado itself and tossed and wrung and wrenched and consumed, the light last final spent insentient husk to float slowing and weightless, for a moment longer during the long vacant rest of life, and then no more.

Only it didn't happen, no consumption to wrench, wring and consume me down to the utlimate last proud indestructible grateful husk, but rather simply to destroy me as the embalmer destroys with very intactness what was still life, was still life even though it was only the living worm's. Because she was not examining the office again because I realised now that she had never stopped doing it, examining it rapidly once more with that comprehensive female glance.

"I thought it would be all right here," she said. "Better here."

"Here?" I said.

"Do it here. In your office. You can lock the door and I don't imagine there'll be anybody high enough up this late at night to see in the window. Or maybe—" Because she was already up and probably for a moment I couldn't have moved, just watching as she went to the window and had already begun to pull down the shade.

"Here?" I said again, like a parrot. "Here? In here?" Now she was looking at me over her shoulder. That's right. She didn't even turn: just her head, her face to look back at me across her shoulder, her hands still drawing the shade down across the window in little final tucking tugs against the sill. No: not again. She never had looked at me but that once as she entered. She simply confronted me across her shoulder with that blue envelopment like the sea, not questioning nor waiting, as the sea itself doesn't need to question or wait but simply to be the sea. "Oh," I said. "And be quick, hurry too maybe since you haven't got much time, since you really ought to be in bed this minute with your husband, or is this one of Manfred's nights?" and she still watching me, though turned now, standing, perhaps leaning a little against the window-sill behind her, watching me quite grave, just a little curious. "But of course," I said. "Naturally it's one of Manfred's nights since it's Manfred you're saving: not Flem.—No, wait," I said. "Maybe I'm wrong; maybe it is both of them; maybe they both sent you: both of them that scared, that desperate; their mutual crisis and fear so critical as to justify even this last desperate gambit of your woman's—their mutual woman's—all?" And still she just watched me: the calm unfathomable serenely waiting blue, waiting not on me but simply on time. "I didn't mean that," I said. "You know I didn't. I know it's Manfred. And I know he didn't send you. Least of all, he." Now I could get up. "Say you forgive me first," I said.

"All right," she said. Then I went and opened the door. "Good-night," I said.

"You mean you don't want to?" she said.

Now I could laugh too.

"I thought that was what you wanted," she said. And now she was looking at me. "What did you do it for?" Oh yes, I could laugh, with the door open in my hand and the cold dark leaning into the room like an invisible cloud, and if Grover Winbush were anywhere on the Square now (which he would not be in this cold since he was not a fool about everything) he would not need merely to see all the lights. Oh yes, she was looking at me now: the sea which in a moment more would destroy me, not with any deliberate and calculated sentient wave but simply because I stood there in its insentient way. No: that was wrong too. Because she began to move.

"Shut the door," she said. "It's cold"—walking toward me, not fast. "Was that what you thought I came here for? Because of Manfred?"

"Didn't you?" I said.

"Maybe I did." She came toward me, not fast. "Maybe at first. But that doesn't matter. I mean, to Manfred. I mean that brass. He doesn't mind it. He likes it. He's enjoying himself. Shut the door before it gets so cold." I shut it and turned quickly, stepping back a little.

"Don't touch me," I said.

"All right," she said. "Because you can't. . . ." Because even she stopped then; even the insentient sea compassionate too, but then I could bear that too; I could even say it for her:

"Manfred wouldn't really mind because just I can't hurt him, harm him, do any harm; not Manfred, not just me, no matter what I do. That he would really just as soon resign as not and the only reason he doesn't is just to show me I can't make him. All right. Agreed. Then why don't you go home? What do you want here?"

"Because you are unhappy," she said. "I don't like unhappy people. They're a nuisance. Especially when it can—"

"Yes," I said, cried, "this easy, at no more cost than this.

When nobody will even miss it, least of all Manfred since we both agree that Gavin Stevens can't possibly hurt Manfred de Spain even by cuckolding him on his mistress. So you came just from compassion, pity: not even from honest fear or even just decent respect. Just compassion. Just pity." Then I saw all of it. "Not just to prove to me that having what I think I want won't make me happy, but to show me that what I thought I wanted is not even worth being unhappy over. Does it mean that little to you? I don't mean with Flem: even with Manfred?" I said, cried: "Don't tell me next that this is why Manfred sent you: to abate a nuisance!"

But she just stood there looking at me with that blue serene terrible envelopment. "You spend too much time expecting," she said. "Don't expect. You just are, and you need, and you must, and so you do. That's all. Don't waste time expecting," moving again toward me where I was trapped not just by the door but by the corner of the desk too.

"Don't touch me!" I said. "So if I had only had sense enough to have stopped expecting, or better still, never expected at all, never hoped at all, dreamed at all; if I had just had sense enough to say *I am, I want, I will and so here goes*—If I had just done that, it might have been me instead of Manfred? But don't you see? Can't you see? I wouldn't have been me then?" No: she wasn't even listening: just looking at me: the unbearable and unfathomable blue, speculative and serene.

"Maybe it's because you're a gentleman, and I never knew one before."

"So is Manfred!" I said. "And that other one, that first one— your child's father—" *the only other one* I thought because, yes, oh yes, I knew now: Snopes himself was impotent. I even said it: "The only other one besides Manfred. Back there in Frenchman's Bend, that Ratliff told me about, that fought off the five or six men who tried to ambush you in the buggy that night, fought them off with the buggy whip and one hand because he had to use the other to shield you with, whipped them all off even with one arm broken where I couldn't even finish the fight I started myself with just one opponent?" And still not moving: just standing there facing me so that what I smelled was not even just woman but that terrible, that drowning envelopment. "Both

alike," I said. "But not like me. All three gentlemen but only
two were men."

"Lock the door," she said. "I've already drawn the shade.
Stop being afraid of things," she said. "Why are you afraid?"

"No," I said, cried. I might—would—have struck her with my
out-flung arm, but there was room: out of the trap now and even
around her until I could reach the door knob and open it. Oh yes,
I knew now. "I might buy Manfred from you, but I won't buy
Flem," I said. "Because it is Flem, isn't it? Isn't it?" But there was
only the blue envelopment and the fading Wagner, trumpet and
storm rich brasses diminuendo toward the fading arm and hand
and the rainbow-fading ring. "You told me not to expect: why
don't you try it yourself? We've all bought Snopeses here, whether
we wanted to or not; you of all people should certainly know that.
I don't know why we bought them. I mean, why we had to: what
coin and when and where we so recklessly and improvidently spent
that we had to have Snopeses too. But we do. But nothing can hurt
you if you refuse it, not even a brass-stealing Snopes. And nothing
is of value that costs nothing so maybe you will value this refusal
at what I value it cost me." She moved then, and only then did I
notice that she had evidently brought nothing with her: none of
the scatter of gloves, bags, veils, this and that which women bring
into a room with them so that the first minute of their quitting it
is a problem resembling scavenging. "Don't worry about your
husband," I said. "Just say I represent Jefferson and so Flem
Snopes is my burden too. You see, the least I can do is to match
you: to value him as highly as your coming here proves you do.
Good-night."

"Good-night," she said. The cold invisible cloud leaned in
again. Again I closed it.

6

V. K. RATLIFF

So next morning first thing we heard was that Judge Dukinfield had recused his-self and designated Judge Stevens, Lawyer's paw, to preside in his stead. And they ought to rung the courthouse bell this time sholy, because whether or not it was a matter of communal interest and urgency last night, it was now. But it was to be in chambers this time, and what Judge Dukinfield called his chamber wouldn't a helt us. So all we done this time was just to happen to be somewhere about the Square, in the store doors or jest looking by chance and accident out of the upstairs doctors' and suches' windows while old man Job, that had been Judge Dukinfield's janitor for longer than anybody in Jefferson, including Job and Judge Dukinfield too, knowed, in a old cast-off tailcoat of Judge Dukinfield's that he wore on Sundays, bustled in and out of the little brick house back of the courthouse that Judge Dukinfield called his chambers, sweeping and dusting it until it suited him enough to let folks in it.

Then we watched Judge Stevens cross the Square from his office and go through the door and then we watched the two bonding fellers come out of the hotel and cross the Square with their little lawyers' grips, the young one toting his own grip but Samson, the hotel porter, walking behind the white-vest one toting his, and Samson's least boy walking behind Samson toting what I reckon was the folded Memphis paper the white-vest one had been reading while they et breakfast and they, except Samson and his boy, went in too. Then Lawyer come up by his-self and went in, and sho enough before extra long we heard the car and then Mayor de Spain druv up and parked and got out and says,

"Morning, gentlemen. Any of you fellers looking for me? Excuse me a minute while I step inside and pass good-morning with our out-of-town guests and I'll be right with you." Then he went in too and that was about all: Judge Stevens setting behind the desk with his glasses on and the paper open in his hand, and the two bonding fellers setting quiet and polite and anxious across

from him, and Lawyer setting at one end of the table and Manfred
de Spain that hadn't even set down: jest leaning against the wall
with his hands in his pockets and that-ere dont-give-a-durn face
of his already full of laughing even though it hadn't moved yet.
Until Judge Stevens folded the paper up slow and deliberate and
laid it to one side and taken off his glasses and folded them too and
then laid his hands one in the other on the desk in front of him
and says:

"The plaintiff in this suit has of this date withdrawn his charge
and his bill of particulars. The suit—if it was a suit—no longer
exists. The litigants—plaintiff, defendant and prisoner—if there
was a prisoner—are discharged. With the Court's apologies to the
gentlemen from Saint Louis that their stay among us was marred,
and its hope and trust that their next one will not be, Court is
adjourned. Good-morning, gentlemen," and the two bonding
fellers got up and begun to thank Judge Stevens for a little spell,
until they stopped and taken up their grips and kind of tip-toed
out; and now there wasn't nobody but just Lawyer still setting
with his paper-coloured face bent a little and Judge Stevens still
setting there not looking at nothing in particular yet and Manfred
de Spain still leaning with his feet crossed against the wall and
his face still full of that laughing that was still jest waiting for a
spell too. Then Judge Stevens was looking at him.

"Manfred," he says, "Do you want to resign?"

"Certainly, sir," De Spain says. "I'll be glad to. But not for the
city: for Gavin. I want to do it for Gavin. All he's got to do is say
Please."

And still Lawyer didn't move: jest setting there with that still
paper-coloured face like it was froze stiff and his hands too laying
on the table in front of him: not clenched one inside the other like
his paw's: jest laying there. Then Manfred begun to laugh, not
loud, not even in no hurry: jest standing there laughing with his
feet still crossed and his hands still in his pockets, jest laughing
even while he turned and went across to the door and opened it
and went out and closed it behind him. Which jest left Lawyer
and his paw and that was when Lawyer said it.

"So you don't want him not to be mayor," Judge Stevens says.
"Then what is it you do want? For him not to be alive? Is that
it?"

That was when Lawyer said it: "What must I do now, Papa? Papa, what can I do now?"

So something happened somewhere between that board of aldermen meeting last night and that special court session this morning. Except that if we ever knowed what it was, it wasn't going to be Lawyer's fault. I mean, we might a knowed or anyway had a good idea what happened and where while them lights was burning in that upstairs office long after ever body else in Jefferson had done went home to bed; some day Lawyer hisself might tell it, probably would, would have to tell it to somebody jest to get some rest from it. What we wouldn't know would be jest how it happened. Because when Lawyer come to tell it, he wouldn't be having to tell what happened: he would be having to tell, to say, it wouldn't much matter what, to somebody, anybody listening, it wouldn't much matter who.

The only one of the whole three of them that understood her was Flem. Because needing or expecting to understand one another hadn't never occurred between her and Manfred de Spain. All the understanding one another they needed was you might say for both of them to agree on when and where next and jest how long away it would have to be. But apart from that, they never no more needed to waste time understanding one another than sun and water did to make rain. They never no more needed to be drawed together than sun and water needed to be. In fact, most of Manfred's work had already been done for him by that boy back in Frenchman's Bend—McCarron, who except that he come first, could a been Manfred's younger brother; who never even lived in Frenchman's Bend and nobody in Frenchman's Bend ever seen or heard of him before that summer, like he had been sent through Frenchman's Bend at the one exact moment to see her, like you might say Manfred de Spain had been sent through Jefferson at the one exact moment to see her.

And a heap of McCarron's work already done for him too because she done it: that night when them five Frenchman's Bend boys laid for them and bushwacked them in the buggy to drag him out of it and maybe beat him up or anyhow skeer him out of Frenchman's Bend. And gradually the tale come out how, even with one arm broke, he fought them all off and got the buggy turned around and got her back home all safe except for a natural maiden swoon. Which ain't quite right. Because them five boys (I knowed two of them) never told it, which you might say is proof. That after they broke his arm it was her that taken the loaded end of the buggy-whip and finished the last one or maybe two, and her that turned the buggy around in the road and got it away from there. Jest far enough; not back home yet: jest far enough; to as the feller says crown the triumph on the still-hot field of the triumph; right there on the ground in the middle of the dark road because somebody had to still hold that skeered horse, with the horse standing over them and her likely having to help hold him up too off of that broke arm; not jest her first time but the time she got that baby. Which folks says ain't likely to happen jest the first time but between what did happen and what ought to happened, I don't never have trouble picking ought.

But Lawyer Stevens never understood her and never would: that he never had jest Manfred de Spain to have to cope with, he was faced with a simple natural force repeating itself under the name of De Spain or McCarron or whatever into ever gap or vacancy in her breathing as long as she breathed; and that wouldn't never none of them be him. And he never did realise that she understood him because she never had no way of telling him because she didn't know herself how she done it. Since women learn at about two or three years old and then forget it, the knowledge about their-selves that a man stumbles on by accident forty-odd years later with the same kind of startled amazement of finding a twenty-five-cent piece in a old pair of britches you had started to throw away. No, they don't forget it: they jest put it away until ten or twenty or forty years later the need for it comes up and they reach around and pick it out and use it and then hang it up again without no more remembering jest which one it was than she could remember today which finger it was she scratched with yesterday: only that tomorrow maybe she will itch again but she will find something to scratch that one with too.

Or I don't know, maybe he did understand all that and maybe he did get what he wanted. I mean, not what he wanted but what he knew he could have, the next-best, like anything is better

than nothing, even if that anything is jest a next-best anything.
Because there was more folks among the Helens and Juliets and
Isoldes and Guineveres than jest the Launcelots and Tristrams
and Romeos and Parises. There was them others that never got
their names in the poetry books, the next-best ones that sweated
and panted too. And being the next-best to Paris is jest a next-best
too, but it ain't no bad next-best to be. Not ever body had Helen,
but then not ever body lost her neither.

So I kind of happened to be at the deepo that day when Lucius
Hogganbeck's jitney drove up and Lawyer got out with his grips
and trunk and his ticket to Mottstown junction to catch the
express from Memphis to New York and get on the boat that
would take him to that German university he had been talking
for two years now about what a good idea it would be to go to it
providing you happened to want to go to a university in Germany
like that one; until that morning yesterday or maybe it was the
day before when he told his paw: "What must I do now, Papa?
Papa, what can I do now?" It was still cold, so he taken his sister
on into the waiting room and then he come back out where I was.

"Good," he says, brisk and chipper as you could want. "I was
hoping to see you before I left, to pass the torch on into your
active hand. You'll have to hold the fort now. You'll have to tote
the load."

"What fort?" I says. "What load?"

"Jefferson," he says. "Snopeses. Think you can handle them
till I get back?"

"Not me nor a hundred of me," I says. "The only thing to do
is get completely shut of them, abolish them."

"No no," he says, "Say a herd of tigers suddenly appears in
Yoknapatawpha County; wouldn't it be a heap better to have
them shut up in a mule-pen where we could at least watch them,
keep up with them, even if you do lose a arm or a leg ever time
you get within ten feet of the wire, than to have them roaming
and strolling loose all over ever where in the entire country? No,
we got them now; they're ourn now; I don't know jest what
Jefferson could a committed back there whenever it was, to have
won this punishment, gained this right, earned this privilege. But
we did. So it's for us to cope, to resist; us to endure, and (if we
can) survive."

"But why me?" I says. "Why out of all Jefferson pick on me?"

"Because you're the only one in Jefferson I can trust," Lawyer says.

Except that that one don't really ever lose Helen, because for the rest of her life she don't never actively get rid of him. Likely it's because she don't want to.

7

CHARLES MALLISON

I REMEMBER how Ratliff once said that the world's Helens never really lose forever the men who once loved and lost them; probably because they—the Helens—don't want to.

I still wasn't born when Uncle Gavin left for Heidelberg, so as far as I know his hair had already begun to turn white when I saw him. Because although I was born by then, I couldn't remember him when he came home from Europe in the middle of the war, to get ready to go back to it. He said that at first, right up to the last minute, he believed that as soon as he finished his Ph.D. he was going as a stretcher-bearer with the German army; almost up to the last second before he admitted to himself that the Germany he could have loved that well had died somewhere between the Liège and Namur forts and the year 1848. Or rather, the Germany which had emerged between 1848 and the Belgian forts he did not love since it was no longer the Germany of Goethe and Bach and Beethoven and Schiller. This is what he said hurt, was hard to admit, to admit even after he reached Amsterdam and could begin to really ask about the American Field Service of which he had heard.

But he said how we—America—were not used yet to European wars and still took them seriously; and there was the fact that he had been for two years a student in a German university. But the French were different: to whom another Germanic war was just the same old chronic nuisance; a nation of practical and practising pessimists who were willing to let anyone regardless of his politics, who wanted to, do anything—particularly one who was willing to do it free. So he—Uncle Gavin—spent those five months with his stretcher just behind Verdun and presently was himself in a bed in an American hospital until he got over the pneumonia and could come home, in Jefferson again, waiting, he said, until we were in it, which would not be long.

And he was right: the Sartoris boys, Colonel Sartoris's twin grandsons, had already gone to England into the Royal Flying Corps and then it was April and then Uncle Gavin had his appointment as a Y.M.C.A. secretary, to go back to France with the first American troops; when suddenly there was Montgomery Ward Snopes, the first of what Ratliff called "them big grey-coloured chaps of I.O.'s," the one whose mama was still rocking in the chair in the front window of the Snopes Hotel because it was still too cold yet to move back on to the front gallery. And Jackson McLendon had organised his Jefferson company and had been elected captain of it and Montgomery Ward could have joined them. But instead he came to Uncle Gavin, to go to France with Uncle Gavin in the Y.M.C.A.; and that was when Ratliff said what he did about sometimes the men that loved and lost Helen of Troy just thought they had lost her. Only he could have added, All her kinfolks too. Because Uncle Gavin did it. I mean, took Montgomery Ward.

"Confound it, Lawyer," Ratliff said. "It's a Snopes."

"Certainly," Uncle Gavin said. "Can you suggest a better place for a Snopes today than north-western France? As far west of Amiens and Verdun as you can get him?"

"But why?" Ratliff said.

"I thought of that too," Uncle Gavin said. "If he had said he wanted to go in order to defend his country, I would have had Hub Hampton handcuff him hand and foot in jail and sit on him while I telephoned Washington. But what he said was, 'They're going to pass a law soon to draft us all anyhow, and if I go with you like you're going, I figger I'll get there first and have time to look around.' "

"To look around," Ratliff said. He and Uncle Gavin looked at one another. Ratliff blinked two or three times.

"Yes," Uncle Gavin said. Ratliff blinked two or three times again.

"To look around," he said.

"Yes," Uncle Gavin said. And Uncle Gavin took Montgomery Ward Snopes with him, and that was the exact time when Ratliff said about the folks that thought they had finally lost Helen of Troy. But Gowan was still living with us; maybe because of the war in Europe the State Department still hadn't let his mother and father come back from China or wherever it was yet; at least once every week on the way home across the Square he would meet Ratliff, almost like Ratliff was waiting for him, and

Gowan would tell Ratliff the news from Uncle Gavin and Ratliff would say:

"Tell him to watch close. Tell him I'm doing the best I can here."

"The best you can what?" Gowan said.

"Holding and toting," Ratliff said.

"Holding and toting what?" Gowan said. That was when Gowan said he first noticed that you didn't notice Ratliff hardly at all, until suddenly you did or anyway Gowan did. And after that, he began to look for him. Because the next time, Ratliff said:

"How old are you?"

"Seventeen," Gowan said.

"Then of course your aunt lets you drink coffee," Ratliff said. "What do you say—"

"She's not my aunt, she's my cousin," Gowan said. "Sure. I drink coffee. I don't specially like it. Why?"

"I like a occasional ice-cream cone myself," Ratliff said.

"What's wrong with that?" Gowan said.

"What say me and you step in the drugstore here and have a ice-cream cone?" Ratliff said. So they did. Gowan said Ratliff always had strawberry when they had it, and that he could expect Ratliff almost any afternoon now, and now Gowan said he was in for it, he would have to eat the cone whether he wanted it or not, he and Ratliff now standing treat about, until finally Ratliff said, already holding the pink-topped cone in his brown hand:

"This here is jest about as pleasant a invention as any I know about. It's so pleasant a feller jest don't dare risk getting burnt-out on it. I can't imagine no tragedy worse than being burnt-out on strawberry ice cream. So what you say we jest make this a once-a-week habit and the rest of the time jest swapping news?"

So Gowan said all right and after that they would just meet in passing and Gowan would give Ratliff Uncle Gavin's last message: "He says to tell you he's doing the best he can too but that you were right: just one ain't enough. One what?" Gowan said. "Ain't enough for what?" But then Gowan was seventeen; he had a few other things to do, whether grown people believed it or not, though he didn't object to delivering the messages Mother said Uncle Gavin sent in his letters to Ratliff, when he happened to see Ratliff, or that is when Ratliff saw, caught him, which

seemed to be almost every day so that he wondered just when
Ratliff found time to earn a living. But he didn't always listen to
all Ratliff would be saying at those times, so that afterward he
couldn't even say just how it was or when that Ratliff put it into
his mind and he even got interested in it like a game, a contest
or even a battle, a war, that Snopeses had to be watched constantly like an invasion of snakes or wildcats and that Uncle
Gavin and Ratliff were doing it or trying to because nobody else
in Jefferson seemed to recognise the danger. So that winter when
the draft finally came and got Byron Snopes out of Colonel
Sartoris's bank, Gowan knew exactly what Ratliff was talking
about when he said:

"I don't know how he will do it, but I will lay a million to one
he don't never leave the United States; I will lay a hundred to one
he won't get further away from Mississippi than that first fort over
in Arkansas where they first sends them; and if you will give me
ten dollars I will give you eleven if he ain't back here in Jefferson
in three weeks." Gowan didn't do it, but he said later he wished
he had because Ratliff would have lost by two days and so Byron
was back in the bank again. But we didn't know how, and even
Ratliff never found out how he did it until after he had robbed
the bank and escaped to Mexico, because Ratliff said the reason
Snopeses were successful was that they had all federated unani-
mously to remove being a Snopes from just a zoological category
into a condition composed of success by means of the single rule
and regulation and sacred oath of never to tell anybody how. The
way Byron did it was to go to bed every night with a fresh plug of
chewing tobacco taped into his left armpit until it ran his heart
up to where the army doctors finally discharged him and sent him
home.

So at least there was some fresh Snopes news to send Uncle
Gavin, which was when Ratliff noticed that it had been months
since Uncle Gavin had mentioned Montgomery Ward Snopes.
Though by the time Uncle Gavin's letter got back saying *Don't
mention that name to me again. I won't discuss it. I will not* we had some
fresh Snopes news of our own to send him.

This time it was Eck. "Your uncle was right," Ratliff said.

"He's my cousin, I tell you," Gowan said.

"All right, all right," Ratliff said. "Eck wasn't a Snopes. That's

why he had to die. Like there wasn't no true authentic room for
Snopeses in the world and they made theirselves one by that pure
and simple mutual federation, and the first time one slips or
falters or fails in being Snopes, it don't even need the rest of the
pack like wolves to finish him: simple environment jest watched
its chance and taken it."

Eck was the one with the steel brace where a log broke his
neck one time, the night watchman of the oil company's storage
tank at the depot; I knew about this myself because I was almost
four years old now. It was just dust-dark; we were at supper when
there came a tremendous explosion, the loudest sound at one
time that Jefferson ever heard, so loud that we all knew it couldn't
be anything else but that German bomb come at last that we—
Mayor de Spain—had been looking for ever since the Germans
sank the *Lusitania* and we finally had to get into the war too. That
is, Mayor de Spain had gone to West Point and had been a
lieutenant in Cuba, and when this one started he wanted to get
into it too. But he couldn't maybe, so he tried to organise a Home
Guard company, except that nobody but him took it very
seriously. But at least he had an alarm system to ring the courthouse bell when a German attack came.

So when that tremendous big sound went off and the bell began
to ring, we all knew what it was and we were all waiting for the
next one to fall, until the people running out into the street
hollering "Which way was it?" finally located it down toward the
depot. It was the oil storage tank. It was a big round tank, about
thirty feet long and ten feet deep, sitting on brick trestles. That is,
it had been there, because there wasn't anything there now, not
even the trestles. Then about that time they finally got Mrs
Nunnery to hush long enough to tell what happened.

She was Cedric Nunnery's mamma. He was about five years
old. They lived in a little house just up the hill from the depot and
finally they made her sit down and somebody gave her a drink of
whiskey and she quit screaming and told how about five o'clock
she couldn't find Cedric anywhere and she came down to where
Mr Snopes was sitting in his chair in front of the little house about
the size of a privy that he called the office where he night-watched
the tank, to ask him if he had seen Cedric. He hadn't, but he got
up right away to help her hunt, in all the box cars on the side track

D

and in the freight warehouse and everywhere, hollering Cedric's name all around; only Mrs Nunnery didn't remember which of them thought of the oil tank first. Likely it was Mr Snopes, since he was the one that knew it was empty, though probably Mrs Nunnery had seen the ladder too still leaning against it where Mr Snopes had climbed up to open the manhole in the top to let fresh air come in and drive the gas out.

And likely Mr Snopes thought all the gas was out by now, though they probably both must have figured there would still be enough left to fix Cedric when he climbed down inside. Because Mrs Nunnery said that's where they both thought Cedric was and that he was dead; she said she was so sure that she couldn't even bear to wait and see, she was already running—not running anywhere: just running—when Mr Snopes came out of his little office with the lighted lantern and still running while he was climbing up the ladder and still running when he swung the lantern over into the manhole; that is she said she was still running when the explosion (she said she never even heard it, she never heard anything, or she would have stopped) knocked her down and the air all around her whizzing with pieces of the tank like a swarm of bumblebees. And Mr Harker from the power-plant that got there first and found her, said she begun to try to run again as soon as he picked her up, shrieking and screaming and thrashing around while they held her, until she sat down and drank the whiskey and the rest of them walked and hunted around among the scattered bricks from the trestles, still trying to find some trace of Cedric and Mr Snopes, until Cedric came at a dead run up the track from where he had been playing in a culvert about a half a mile away when he heard the explosion.

But they never did find Mr Snopes until the next morning when Tom Tom Bird, the day fireman at the powerplant, on his way in to work from where he lived about two miles down the track, saw something hanging in the telegraph wires about two hundred yards from where the tank had been and got a long pole and punched it down and when he showed it to Mr Harker at the plant, it was Mr Snopes's steel neck-brace, though none of the leather was left.

But they never did find anything of Mr Snopes, who was a good man, everybody liked him, sitting in his chair beside the office door where he could watch the tank or walking around the tank when he would let the coal oil run into the cans and drums and delivery tanks, with his neck and head stiff in the steel brace so he couldn't turn his head at all: he would have to turn all of himself like turning a wooden post. All the boys in town knew him because pretty soon they all found out that he kept a meal sack full of raw peanuts from the country and would holler to any of them that passed and give them a handful.

Besides, he was a Mason too. He had been a Mason such a long time that he was a good one even if he wasn't very high up in it. So they buried the neck-brace anyway, in a coffin all regular, with the Masons in charge of the funeral, and more people than you would have thought sent flowers, even the oil company too, although Mr Snopes had ruined their tank for nothing because Cedric Nunnery wasn't even in it.

So they buried what they did have of him; there was the Baptist preacher too, and the Masons in their aprons dropping a pinch of dirt into the grave and saying "Alas my brother," and covered the raw red dirt with the flowers (one of the flower pieces had the Mason signs worked into it); and the tank was insured so when the oil company got through cussing Mr Snopes for being a grown man with no more sense than that, they even gave Mrs Snopes a thousand dollars to show they were sorry for her even if she had married a fool. That is, they gave the money to Mrs Snopes because their oldest boy, Wallstreet, wasn't but sixteen then. But he was the one that used it.

But that came later. All that happened now was that Mayor de Spain finally got to be a commanding officer long enough to ring his alarm bell at least, and we had some more fresh Snopes news to send Uncle Gavin. By "we" I mean me now. Gowan's mother and father had finally got home from China or wherever it was and now Gowan was in Washington (it was fall) for the last year anyway at the prep school getting ready for the University of Virginia next year, and one afternoon Mother sent for me, into the parlour, and there was Ratliff in his neat faded blue tieless shirt and his smooth brown face, in the parlour like company (there was a tea tray and Ratliff had a teacup and a cucumber sandwich and I know now there were a lot of people in Jefferson let alone in the county where Ratliff came from, that wouldn't have known what to do with a cup of tea at four o'clock in the afternoon and maybe Ratliff never saw one before then either but you couldn't have told it by watching him), and Mother said,

"Make your manners to Mister Ratliff, bub. He's come to call on us," and Ratliff said,

"Is that what you call him?" and Mother said,

"No, we just call him whatever is handy yet," and Ratliff said,

"Sometimes fellers named Charles gets called Chick when they gets to school." Then he said to me: "Do you like strawberry ice-cream cones?" and I said,

"I like any kind of ice-cream cones," and Ratliff said:

"Then maybe your cousin—" and stopped and said to Mother: "Excuse me, Miz Mallison; I done been corrected so many times that it looks like it may take me a spell yet." So after that it was me and Ratliff instead of Gowan and Ratliff, only instead of two cones it cost Ratliff three now because when I went to town without Mother, Aleck Sander was with me. And I don't know how Ratliff did it and of course I can't remember when because I wasn't even five yet. But he had put into my mind too, just like into Gowan's, that idea of Snopeses covering Jefferson like an influx of snakes or varmints from the woods and he and Uncle Gavin were the only ones to recognise the danger and the threat and now he was having to tote the whole load by himself until they would finally stop the war and Uncle Gavin could get back home and help. "So you might just as well start listening now," he said, "whether you ain't but five or not. You're going to have to hear a heap of it before you get old enough or big enough to resist."

It was November. Then that day, the courthouse bell rang again and all the church bells too this time, wild and frantic too in the middle of the week from the Sunday steeples and a few shotguns and pistols too like the old veterans that were still alive when they unveiled the Confederate monument that day except that the ones this time hadn't been to a war yet, so maybe what they were celebrating this time was that this one finally got over before they had to go to it. So now Uncle Gavin could come home where Ratliff himself could ask him what Montgomery Ward Snopes had done that his name must not be mentioned or discussed. That was when Ratliff told me, "You might as well get used to hearing it even if you ain't but five." That was when he said: "What do you reckon it was he done? Your cousin has been watching Snopeses for going on ten years now; he even taken one all the way to France with him to keep his-self abreast and up to date. What you reckon a Snopes could a done after ten years to shock and startle him so much he couldn't bear even to discuss it?"

Or this was when he meant it because when Uncle Gavin came home it was for only two weeks. He was out of the uniform, the army, the Y.M.C.A. now, but as soon as he was out they put him into some kind of board or committee or bureau for war re-habilitation in Europe because he had lived in Europe all that time, especially the two years as a student in Germany. And possibly the only reason he came home at all was that Grand-father had died during the last year of the war and he came home to see us as people do in bereavement. Though I believed then that the reason he came was to tell Ratliff what it was about Montgomery Ward Snopes that was too bad to write on paper. Which was when Ratliff said about all the listening I would have to do, meaning that with him, Ratliff, alone again to tote the load, anyway I could do that much.

It was one day; sometimes Mother let me go to town by myself now. I mean, when she wasn't noticing enough to say Come back here. No: I mean, when she found out I had now she didn't jump on me too hard—it was one day, Ratliff's voice said, "Come here." He had traded off his buckboard and team and now he had a Model T, with the little painted house with the sewing machine in it fastened to the back in place of a back seat; what they call pickup trucks now though Ratliff and Uncle Noon Gatewood had made this one. He was sitting in it with the door already open and I got in and he shut the door and we drove right slow along the back streets around the edge of town. "How old did you say you was?" he said. I told him again: five. "Well, we can't help that, can we?"

"Can't help what?" I said. "Why?"

"Come to think of it, maybe you're right at that," he said. "So all we got to do now is jest take a short ride. So what happened to Montgomery Ward Snopes was, he quit the fighting army and went into business."

"What business?" I said.

"The . . . canteen business. Yes, the canteen business. That's what he done while he was with your cousin. They was at a town named Châlons, only your cousin had to stay in town to run the office, so he give Montgomery Ward, since he had the most spare time, the job of running the canteen at another little town not far away that would be more convenient for the soldiers—a kind of a shack with counters like a store where soldiers could buy the candy bars and sody pop and hand-knitted socks like your cousin told us about that time last week when they wasn't busy fighting, you remember? Except that after a while Montgomery Ward's canteen got to be just about the most popular canteen the army or even the Y.M.C.A. either ever had in France or anywhere else; it got so popular that finally your cousin went his-self and looked at it and found that Montgomery Ward had cut off the back end and fixed it up as a new fresh entertainment room with a door in the back and a young French lady he happened to know in it, so that any time a soldier got tired of jest buying socks or eating chocolate bars he could buy a ticket from Montgomery Ward and go around through the back door and get his-self entertained.

"That was what your cousin found out. Only the army and the Y.M.C.A. had some kind of a rule against entertainment; they figgered that a soldier ought to be satisfied jest buying socks and sody pop in a canteen. Or maybe it was your cousin; likely it was him. Because if the army and the Y.M.C.A. had found out about that back room, they would a fired Montgomery Ward so hard he would likely a come back to Jefferson in handcuffs—providing he never stopped off at Leavenworth, Kansas, first. Which reminds me of something I may have said to your other cousin Gowan once when likely you wasn't present: about how some of the folks that lost Helen of Troy might some day wish they hadn't found her to begin with."

"Why?" I said. "Where was I if I wasn't there then?"

"It was your cousin. Montgomery Ward might have even saved enough out of the back-room entertainment tickets to bought his-self out of it. But he never needed to. He had your cousin. He was the hair-shirt of your cousin's lost love and devotion, whether he knowed it or not or cared or not. Or maybe

it was Jefferson. Maybe your cousin couldn't bear the idea of
Jefferson being represented in Leavenworth prison even for the
reward of one Snopes less in Jefferson itself. So likely it was him,
and afterwards saying, 'But don't never let me see your face again
in France.'

"That is, don't never bring your face to me again. Because
Montgomery Ward was the hair-shirt; likely your cousin taken
the same kind of proud abject triumphant submissive horror in
keeping up with his doings that them old hermits setting on rocks
out in the hot sun in the desert use to take watching their blood
dry up and their legs swivelling, keeping up from a distance while
Montgomery Ward added more and more entertaining ladies to
that-ere new canteen he set up in Paris—"

"They have chocolate bars and soda pop in canteens," I said.
"Uncle Gavin said so. Chewing gum too."

"That was the American army," Ratliff said. "They had been
in the war such a short time that likely they hadn't got used to it
yet. This new canteen of Montgomery Ward's was you might say
a French canteen, with only private American military connections. The French have been in enough wars long enough to find
out that the best way to get shut of one is not to pay too much
attention to it. In fact the French probably thought the kind of
canteen Montgomery Ward was running this time was just about
the most solvent and economical and you might say self-per-
petuating kind he could a picked out, since, no matter how much
money you swap for ice cream and chocolate candy and sody pop,
even though the money still exists, that candy and ice cream and
sody pop don't any more because it has been consumed and will
cost some of that money to produce and replenish, where in jest
strict entertainment there ain't no destructive consumption at
all that's got to be replenished at a definite production labour
cost: only a normal natural general overall depreciation which
would have took place anyhow."

"Maybe Montgomery Ward won't come back to Jefferson,"
I said.

"If I was him, I wouldn't," Ratliff said.

"Unless he can bring the canteen with him," I said.

"In that case I sholy wouldn't," Ratliff said.

"Is it Uncle Gavin you keep on talking about?" I said.

"I'm sorry," Ratliff said.

"Then why don't you say so?" I said.

"I'm sorry," Ratliff said. "Your uncle. It was your cousin Gowan (I'm right this time, ain't I?) got me mixed up, but I'll remember now. I promise it."

Montgomery Ward didn't come home for two years. Though I had to be older than that before I understood what Ratliff meant when he said Montgomery Ward had done the best he knew to bring an acceptable Mississippi version of his Paris canteen back home with him. He was the last Yoknapatawpha soldier to return. One of Captain McLendon's company was wounded in the first battle in which American troops were engaged and was back in uniform with his wound stripe in 1918. Then early in 1919 the rest of the company, except two dead from flu and a few in the hospital, were all home again to wear their uniforms too around the Square for a little while. Then in May one of Colonel Sartoris's twin grandsons (the other one had been shot down in July last year) got home from the British Air Force though he didn't have on a uniform at all: just a big low-slung racing car that made the little red E.M.F. that Mayor de Spain used to own look like a toy, driving it fast around town between the times when Mr Connors would have to arrest him for speeding, but mostly about once a week back and forth to Memphis while he was getting settled down again. That is, that's what Mother said he was trying to do.

Only he couldn't seem to either, like the war had been too much for him too. I mean, Montgomery Ward Snopes couldn't seem to settle down enough from it to come back home, and Bayard Sartoris came home all right but he couldn't settle down, driving the car so fast between Sartoris Station and Jefferson that finally Colonel Sartoris, who hated automobiles almost as much as Grandfather did, who wouldn't even lend the bank's money to a man who was going to buy one, gave up the carriage and the matched team, to ride back and forth into town with Bayard in the car, in hopes that maybe that would make Bayard slow it down before he killed himself or somebody else.

So when Bayard finally did kill somebody, as we (all Yoknapatawpha County grown folks) all expected he would, it was his grandfather. Because we didn't know that either: that Colonel

Sartoris had a heart condition; Doctor Peabody had told him that
three years ago, and that he had no business in an automobile at
all. But Colonel Sartoris hadn't told anybody else, not even his
sister, Mrs Du Pre, that kept house for him: just riding in that
car back and forth to town every day to keep Bayard slowed down
(they even managed somehow to persuade Miss Narcissa Benbow
to marry him in hopes maybe that would settle him down) until
that morning they came over a hill at about fifty miles an hour
and there was a Negro family in a wagon in the road and Bayard
said, "Hold on, Grandfather," and turned the car off into the
ditch; it didn't turn over or even wreck very bad: just stopped
in the ditch with Colonel Sartoris still sitting in it with his eyes
still open.

So now his bank didn't have a president any more. Then we
found out just who owned the stock in it: that Colonel Sartoris
and Major de Spain, Mayor de Spain's father until he died, had
owned two of the three biggest blocks, and old man Will Varner
out in Frenchman's Bend owned the other one. So we thought
that maybe it wasn't just Colonel Sartoris's father's cavalry
command that got Byron Snopes his job in the bank, but maybe
old Will Varner had something to do with it too. Except that we
never really believed that since we knew Colonel Sartoris well
enough to know that any single one of those old cavalry raids or
even just one night around a bivouac fire would have been enough.

Of course there was more of it, that much again and even more
scattered around in a dozen families like the Compsons and
Benbows and Peabodys and Miss Eunice Habersham and us and
a hundred others that were farmers around in the county.
Though it wasn't until Mayor de Spain got elected president of it
to succeed Colonel Sartoris (in fact, because of that) that we
found out that Mr Flem Snopes had been buying the stock in lots
anywhere from one to ten shares for several years; this, added to
Mr Varner's and Mayor de Spain's own that he had inherited
from his father, would have been enough to elect him up from
vice-president to president (there was so much going on that we
didn't even notice that when the dust finally settled Mr Flem
Snopes would be vice-president of it too) even if Mrs Du Pre and
Bayard's wife (Bayard had finally got himself killed testing an
aeroplane at an Ohio testing-field that they said nobody else

D*

would fly and that Baynard himself didn't have any business in) hadn't voted theirs for him.

Because Mayor de Spain resigned from being mayor and sold his automobile agency and became president of the bank just in time. Colonel Sartoris's bank was a national bank because Ratliff said likely Colonel Sartoris knew that would sound safer to country folks with maybe an extra ten dollars to risk in a bank, let alone the female widows and orphans, since females never had much confidence in menfolks' doings about anything, let alone money, even when they were not widows too. So with a change of presidents like that, Ratliff said the government would have to send somebody to inspect the books even if the regular inspection wasn't about due; the two auditors waiting in front of the bank at eight o'clock that morning for somebody to unlock the door and let them in, which would have been Byron Snopes except that he didn't show up. So they had to wait for the next one with a key: which was Mr de Spain.

And by fifteen minutes after eight, which was about thirteen minutes after the auditors decided to start on the books that Byron kept, Mr de Spain found out from the Snopes Hotel that nobody had seen Byron since the south-bound train at nine twenty-two last night, and by noon everybody knew that Byron was probably already in Texas though he probably wouldn't reach Mexico itself for another day yet. Though it was not until two days later that the head auditor was ready to commit himself roughly as to how much money was missing; by that time they had called a meeting of the bank's board of directors and even Mr Varner that Jefferson never saw once in twelve months had come in and listened to the head auditor for about a minute and then said, "Police hell. Send somebody out home for my pistol, then show me which way he went."

Which wasn't anything to the uproar Mr de Spain himself was making, with all this time all Jefferson watching and listening, until on the third day Ratliff said, though I didn't know what he meant then: "That's how much it was, was it? At least we know now jest how much Miz Flem Snopes is worth. Now your uncle won't need to worry about how much he lost when he gets home because now he can know exactly to the last decimal how much he saved." Because the bank itself was all right. It was a national bank, so whatever money Byron stole would be guaranteed whether they caught Byron or not. We were watching Mr de Spain. Since his father's money had helped Colonel Sartoris start it and Mr de Spain had himself been vice-president of it, even if he had not been promoted president of it just ahead of when the auditors decided to look at Byron Snopes's books, we believed he would still have insisted on making good every cent of the money. What we expected to hear was that he had mortgaged his home, and when we didn't hear that, we just thought that he had made money out of his automobile agency that was saved up and put away that we didn't know about. Because we never expected anything else of him; when the next day they called another sudden meeting of the board of directors and announced the day after that that the stolen money had been made good by the voluntary personal efforts of the president, we were not even surprised. As Ratliff said, we were so unsurprised in fact that it was two or three days before anybody seemed to notice how at the same time they announced that Mr Flem Snopes was now the new vice-president of it.

And now, it was another year, the last two Jefferson soldiers came home for good, or anyway temporarily for good: Uncle Gavin finally came back from rehabilitating war-torn Europe to get elected County Attorney, and a few months later, Montgomery Ward Snopes too except that he was just temporarily at home for good, like Bayard Sartoris. He wasn't in uniform either, but in a black suit and a black overcoat without any sleeves and a black thing on his head kind of drooping over one side like an empty cow's bladder made out of black velvet, and a long limp-ended bow tie; and his hair long and he had a beard and now there was another Snopes business in Jefferson. It had a name on the window that Ratliff didn't know either and when I went up to the office where Uncle Gavin was waiting for the first of the year to start being County Attorney and told him, he sat perfectly still for a good two seconds and then got up already walking. "Show me," he said.

So we went back to where Ratliff was waiting for us. It was a store on the corner by an alley, with a side door on the alley; the painter was just finishing the curlicue letters on the glass window that said

ATELIER MONTY

and inside, beyond the glass, Montgomery Ward still wearing the French cap (Uncle Gavin said it was a Basque beret) but in his shirtsleeves. Because we didn't go in then; Uncle Gavin said, "Come on now. Let him finish it first." Except Ratliff. He said, "Maybe I can help him." But Uncle Gavin took hold of my arm that time.

"If atelier means just a studio," I said, "why don't he call it that?"

"Yes," Uncle Gavin said. "That's what I want to know too." And even though Ratliff went in, he hadn't seen anything either. And he sounded just like me.

"Studio," he said. "I wonder why he don't just call it that?"

"Uncle Gavin didn't know either," I said.

"I know," Ratliff said. "I wasn't asking nobody yet. I was jest kind of looking around for a place to jump." He looked at me. He blinked two or three times. "Studio," he said. "That's right, you ain't even up that far yet. It's a photographing studio." He blinked again. "But why? His war record has done already showed he ain't a feller to be satisfied with no jest dull run-of-the-mill mediocrity like us stay-at-homes back here in Yoknapatawpha County has to get used to."

But that was all we knew then. Because the next day he had newspapers fastened on the window so you couldn't see inside and he kept the door locked, and all we ever saw would be the packages he would get out of the post office from Sears and Roebuck in Chicago and unlock the door long enough to take them inside.

Then on Thursday, when the *Clarion* came out, almost half of the front page was the announcement of the formal opening, saying *Ladies Especially Invited*, and at the bottom: *Tea*. "What?" I said. "I thought it was going to be a studio."

"It is," Uncle Gavin said. "You get a cup of tea with it. Only he's wasting his money. All the women in town and half the men will go once just to see why he kept the door locked." Because Mother had already said she was going.

"Of course you won't be there," she told Uncle Gavin.

"All right," he said. "Most of the men then." He was right. Montgomery Ward had to keep the opening running all day long to take care of the people that came. He would have had to run it in sections even with the store empty like he rented it. But now it wouldn't have held hardly a dozen at a time, it was so full of stuff, with black curtains hanging all the way to the floor on all the walls that when you drew them back with a king of pulley it would be like you were looking through a window at outdoors that he said one was the skyline of Paris and another was the Seine river bridges and ks, whatever they are, and another was the Eiffel Tower and another Notre Dame, and sofas with black pillows and tables with vases and cups and something burning in them that made a sweet kind of smell; until at first you didn't hardly notice the camera. But finally you did, and a door at the back, and Montgomery Ward said, he said it quick and he kind of moved quick, like he had already begun to move before he had time to decide that maybe he better not.

"That's the dark room. It's not open yet."

"I beg pardon?" Uncle Gavin said.

"That's the dark room," Montgomery Ward said. "It's not open yet."

"Are we expected to expect a dark room to be open to the public?" Uncle Gavin said. But Montgomery Ward was already giving Mrs Rouncewell another cup of tea. Oh yes, there was a vase of flowers too; in the *Clarion* announcement of the opening it said *Flowers by Rouncewell* and I said to Uncle Gavin, where else in Jefferson would anybody get flowers except from Mrs Rounce-well? and he said she probably paid for half the advertisement, plus a vase containing six overblown roses left over from another funeral, that she will probably take out in trade. Then he said he meant her trade and he hoped he was right. Now he looked at the door a minute, then he looked at Montgomery Ward filling Mrs Rouncewell's cup. "Beginning with tea," he said.

We left then. We had to, to make room. "How can he afford to keep on giving away tea?" I said.

"He won't after today," Uncle Gavin said. "That was just bait, ladies' bait. Now I'll ask you one: why did he have to need all the ladies in Jefferson to come in one time and look at his joint?" And now he sounded just like Ratliff; he kind of happened to be coming out of the hardware store when we passed. "Had your tea yet?" Uncle Gavin said.

"Tea," Ratliff said. He didn't ask it. He just said it. He blinked at Uncle Gavin.

"Yes," Uncle Gavin said. "So do we. The dark room ain't open yet."

"Ought it to be?" Ratliff said.

"Yes," Uncle Gavin said. "So did we."

"Maybe I can find out," Ratliff said.

"Do you even hope so?" Uncle Gavin said.

"Maybe I will hear about it," Ratliff said.

"Do you even hope so?" Uncle Gavin said.

"Maybe somebody else will find out about it and maybe I will be standing where I can hear him," Ratliff said.

And that was all. Montgomery Ward didn't give away any more cups of tea, but after a while photographs did begin to appear in the show window, faces that we knew—ladies with and without babies and high-school graduating classes and the prettiest girls in their graduation caps and gowns and now and then a couple just married from the country looking a little stiff and uncomfortable and just a little defiant and a narrow white line between his haircut and his sunburn; and now and then a couple that had been married fifty years that we had known all the time without really realising it until now how much alike they looked, not to mention being surprised, whether at being photographed or just being married that long.

And even when we begun to realise that not just the same faces but the same photographs of them had been in the same place in the window for over two years now, as if all of a sudden as soon as Montgomery Ward opened his atelier folks stopped graduating and getting married or staying married either, Montgomery Ward was still staying in business, either striking new pictures he didn't put in the window or maybe just selling copies of the old ones, to pay his rent and stay open. Because he was and maybe it was mostly dark-room work because it was now that we begun to realise that most of his business was at night like he did need darkness, his trade seeming to be mostly men now, the front room where he had had the opening dark now and the customers going and coming through the side door in the alley; and them the kind of men you wouldn't hardly think it had ever occurred to them they might ever need to have their picture struck. And his business was spreading too; in the second summer we begun to find out how people—men, the same kind of usually young men that his Jefferson customers were—were beginning to come from the next towns around us to leave or pick up their prints and negatives or whatever it was, by that alley door at night.

"No no," Uncle Gavin told Ratliff. "It can't be that. You simply just can't do that in Jefferson."

"There's folks would a said you couldn't a looted a bank in Jefferson too," Ratliff said.

"But she would have to eat," Uncle Gavin said. "He would have to bring her out now and then for simple air and exercise."

"Out where?" I said. "Bring who out?"

"It can't be liquor," Ratliff said. "At least that first suhjestion of yours would a been quiet, which you can't say about peddling whiskey."

"What first suggestion?" I said. "Bring who out?" Because it wasn't whiskey or gambling either; Grover Cleveland Winbush (the one that owned the other half of Ratliff's café until Mr Flem Snopes froze him out too. He was the night marshal now) had thought of that himself. He came to Uncle Gavin before Uncle Gavin had even thought of sending for him or Mr Buck Connors either, and told Uncle Gavin that he had been spending a good part of the nights examining and watching and checking on the studio and he was completely satisfied there wasn't any drinking or peddling whiskey or dice-shooting or card-playing going on in Montgomery Ward's dark room; that we were all proud of the good name of our town and we all aimed to keep it free of any taint of big-city corruption and misdemeanour and nobody more than him. Until for hours at night when he could have been sitting comfortably in his chair in the police station waiting for the time to make his next round, he would be hanging around that studio without once hearing any suspicion of dice or drinking or any one of Montgomery Ward's customers to come out smelling or even looking like he had had a drink. In fact, Grover Cleveland said, once during the daytime while it was not only his legal right but his duty to his job to be home in bed asleep, just like it was right now while he was giving up his rest to come back to town to make this report to Uncle Gavin as County Attorney, even though he had no warrant, not to mention the fact that by rights

this was a job that Buck Connors himself should have done, he
—Grover Cleveland—walked in the front door with the aim of
walking right on into the dark room even if he had to break the
door to do it since the reason the people of Jefferson appointed
him night marshal was to keep down big-city misdemeanour and
corruption like gambling and drinking, when to his surprise
Montgomery Ward not only didn't try to stop him, he didn't
even wait to be asked but instead opened the dark-room door
himself and told Grover Cleveland to walk right in and look
around.

So Grover Cleveland was satisfied, and he wanted the people
of Jefferson to be too, that there was no drinking or gambling or
any other corruption and misdemeanour going on in that back
room that would cause the Christian citizens of Jefferson to regret
their confidence in appointing him night marshal which was his
sworn duty to do even if he didn't take any more pride in Jefferson's good name than just an ordinary citizen, and any time he
could do anything else for Uncle Gavin in the line of his sworn
duty, for Uncle Gavin just to mention it. Then he went out,
pausing long enough in the door to say:

"Howdy, V.K.," before going on. Then Ratliff came the rest
of the way in.

"He come hipering across the Square and up the stairs like
maybe he had found something," Ratliff said. "But I reckon not.
I don't reckon Montgomery Ward Snopes would have no more
trouble easing him out of that studio than Flem Snopes done
easing him out of the rest of our café."

"No," Uncle Gavin said. He said: "What did Grover Cleveland
like for fun back then?"

"For fun?" Ratliff said. Then he said: "Oh. He liked excitement."

"What excitement?" Uncle Gavin said.

"The excitement of talking about it," Ratliff said.

"Of talking about what?" Uncle Gavin said.

"Of talking about excitement," Ratliff said. He didn't quite
look at me. No: he didn't quite not look at me. No, that's wrong
too, because even watching him you couldn't have said that he
had ever stopped looking at Uncle Gavin. He blinked twice.
"Female excitement," he said.

"All right," Uncle Gavin said. "How?"

"That's right," Ratliff said. "How?"

Because I was only eight now, going on nine, and if Uncle Gavin and Ratliff who were three times that and one of them had been all the way to Europe and back and the other had left at least one footprint in every back road and lane and turn-row too probably in Yoknapatawpha County didn't know what it was until somebody came and told them, it wasn't any wonder that I didn't.

There was another what Ratliff called Snopes industry in town now too, though Uncle Gavin refused to call it that because he still refused to believe that Eck was ever a Snopes. It was Eck's boy, Wallstreet Panic, and from the way he began to act as soon as he reached Jefferson and could look around and I reckon find out for the first time in his life that you didn't actually have to act like a Snopes in order to breathe, whether his father was a Snopes or not he sure wasn't.

Because they said (he was about twelve when they moved in from Frenchman's Bend) how as soon as he got to town and found out about school, he not only made his folks let him go to it but he took his brother, Admiral Dewey, who wasn't but six, with him, the two of them starting out together in the kinder- garten where the mothers brought the little children who were not big enough yet to stay in one place more than just half a day, with Wallstreet Panic sticking up out of the middle of them like a horse in a duck-pond.

Because he wasn't ashamed to enter the kindergarten: he was just ashamed to stay in it, not staying in it himself much longer than a half a day because in a week he was in the first grade and by Christmas he was in the second and now Miss Vaiden Wyott who taught the second grade began to help him, telling him what Wallstreet Panic meant and that he didn't have to be named that, so that when she helped him pass the third grade by studying with her the next summer, when he entered the fourth grade that fall his name was just Wall Snopes because she told him that Wall was a good family name in Mississippi with even a general in it and that he didn't even need to keep the Street if he didn't want to. And he said from that first day and he kept right on saying it when people asked him why he wanted to go to school so hard: "I want to learn how to count money," so that when he heard about it, Uncle Gavin said:

"You see? That proves what I said exactly: no Snopes wants to learn how to count money because he doesn't have to because you will do that for him—or you had damn well better."

He, I mean Wall, was going to need to learn to count it. Even during that first winter while he was making up two grades he had a job. The store next to the Snopes café that they lived behind in the tent was a grocery store about the same class as the Snopes café. Every morning Wall would get up before schooltime, as the days got shorter he would get up in the dark, to build a fire in the iron stove and sweep out the store, and as soon as he got back after school in the afternoon he would be the delivery boy too, using a wheelbarrow until finally the owner of the store bought him a second-hand bicycle and took the money out of his pay each week.

And on Saturdays and holidays he would clerk in the store too, and all that summer while Miss Wyott was helping him pass the third grade; and even that wasn't enough: he got enough recommendations around the Square to get the delivery route for one of the Memphis papers, only by that time he was so busy with his other affairs that he made his brother the paper boy. And the next fall, while he was in the fourth grade, he managed to get a Jackson paper too and now he had two more boys besides Admiral Dewey working for him, so that by that time any merchant or stock-trader or revival preacher or candidate that wanted handbills put out always went to Wall because he had an organisation already set up.

He could count money and save it too. So when he was sixteen and that empty oil tank blew his father away and the oil company gave Mrs Snopes the thousand dollars, about a month later we found out that Mrs Snopes had bought a half interest in the grocery store and Wall had graduated from high school by now and he was a partner in the store. Though he was still the one that got up before daylight on the winter mornings to start the fire and sweep. Then he was nineteen years old and his partner had sold the rest of the store to Mrs Snopes and retired, and even if because of Wall's age the store still couldn't be in his name, we knew who it really belonged to, with a hired boy of his own now to come before daylight on the winter mornings to build the fire and sweep.

And another one too, except that another Snopes industry wouldn't be the right word for this one, because there wasn't any profit in it. No, that's wrong; we worked at it too hard and Uncle Gavin says that anything people work at as hard as all of us did at this has a profit, is for profit whether you can convert that profit into dollars and cents or not or even want to.

The last Snopes they brought into Jefferson didn't quite make it. I mean, this one came just so far, right up to in sight of the town clock in fact, and then refused to go any farther; even, they said, threatening to go back to Frenchman's Bend, like an old cow or a mule that you finally get right up to the open gate of the pen, but not a step more.

He was the old one. Some folks said he was Mr Flem's father, but some said he was just his uncle: a short thick dirty old man with fierce eyes under a tangle of eyebrows and a neck that would begin to swell and turn red before, as Ratliff said, you had barely had time to cross the first word with him. So they bought a little house for him about a mile from town, where he lived with an old-maid daughter and the twin sons named Vardaman and Bilbo that belonged to I.O. Snopes's other wife, the one that Uncle Gavin called the number-two wife that was different from the number-one one that rocked all day long on the front gallery of the Snopes Hotel.

The house had a little piece of ground with it that old man Snopes made into a truck garden and watermelon patch. The watermelon patch was the industry. No, that's wrong. Maybe I mean the industry took place because of the watermelon patch. Because it was like the old man didn't really raise the water-melons to sell or even just to be eaten, but as a bait for the pleasure or sport or contest or maybe just getting that mad, of catching boys robbing it; planting and cultivating and growing watermelons just so he could sit ambushed with a loaded shotgun behind a morning-glory vine on his back gallery until he could hear sounds from the melon patch and then shooting at it.

Then one moonlight night he could see enough too and this time he actually shot John Wesley Roebuck with a load of squirrel shot, and the next morning Mr Hub Hampton, the sheriff, rode out there and told old Snopes that if he ever again let that shotgun off he would come back and take it away from him and throw him in jail to boot. So after that, old Snopes didn't dare use the gun. All he could do now was to stash away piles of rocks at different places along the fence, and just sit behind the vine with a heavy stick and a flashlight.

That was how the industry started. Mr Hampton had passed the word around town to all the mothers and fathers to tell their sons to stay out of that damned patch now; that any time they wanted a watermelon that bad, he, Mr Hampton, would buy them one, because if they kept on making old man Snopes that mad, some day he would burst a blood vessel and die and we would all be in jail. But old Snopes didn't know that, because Vardaman and Bilbo didn't tell him. They would wait until he was in the house, lying down maybe to take a nap after dinner, when they would run in and wake him, yelling, hollering that some boys were in the patch, and he would jump up yelling and cursing and grab up the oak cudgel and go tearing out to the patch, and nobody in it or near it except Vardaman and Bilbo behind a corner of the house dying laughing, then dodging and running and still laughing while the old man scrabbled up his piled rocks to throw at them.

Because he never would catch on. No, that's wrong too: he always caught on. The trouble was, he didn't dare risk doing nothing when they would run in hollering "Grampaw! Grampaw! Chaps in the melon patch!" because it might be true. He would have to jump up and grab the stick and run out, knowing beforehand he probably wouldn't find anybody there except Vardaman and Bilbo behind the corner of the house that he couldn't even catch, throwing the rocks and cursing them until he would give out of rocks and breath both, then standing there gasping and panting with his neck as red as a turkey gobbler's and without breath any more to curse louder than whispering. That's what we—all the boys in Jefferson between six and twelve years old and sometimes even older—would go out there to hide behind the fence and watch. We never had seen anybody bust a blood vessel and die, and we wanted to be there when it happened to see what it would look like.

This was after Uncle Gavin finally got home from rehabilitating Europe. We were crossing the Square when she passed us. I never could tell if she had looked at Uncle Gavin, though I know she never looked at me, let alone spoke when we passed. But then, that was all right; I didn't expect her either to or not to; sometimes she would speak to me but sometimes she never spoke to anybody and we were used to it. Like she did this time: just walking on past us exactly like a pointer dog walks just before it freezes on to the birds. Then I saw that Uncle Gavin had stopped and turned to look after her. But then I remembered he had been away since 1914 which was eight years ago now, so she was only about five or six when he saw her last.

"Who is that?" he said.

"Linda Snopes," I said. "You know: Mr Flem Snopes's girl." And I was still watching her too. "She walks like a pointer," I said. "I mean, a pointer that's just——"

"I know what you mean," Uncle Gavin said. "I know exactly what you mean."

8

GAVIN STEVENS

I KNEW exactly what he meant. She was walking steadily toward us, completely aware of us, yet not once had she looked at either of us, the eyes not hard and fixed so much as intent, oblivious; fixed and unblinking on something past us, beyond us, behind us, as a young pointer will walk over you if you don't move out of the way, during the last few yards before the actual point, since now it no longer needs depend on clumsy and fumbling scent because now it is actually looking at the huddled trigger-set covey. She went past us still walking, striding, like the young pointer bitch, the maiden bitch of course, the virgin bitch, immune now in virginity, not scorning the earth, spurning the earth, because she needed it to walk on in that immunity: just intent from earth and us too, not proud and not really oblivious : just immune in intensity and ignorance and innocence as the sleepwalker is for the moment immune from the anguishes and agonies of breath.

She would be thirteen, maybe fourteen now, and the reason I did not know her and would not have known her was not because I had possibly not seen her in eight years and human females change so drastically in the years between ten and fifteen. It was because of her mother. It was as though I—you too perhaps— could not have believed but that a woman like that must, could not other than, produce an exact replica of herself. That Eula Varner—You see? Eula *Varner*. Never Eula Snopes even though I had—had had to—watched them in bed together. Eula Snopes it could never be simply because it must not simply because I would decline to have it so—that Eula Varner owed that much at least to the simple male hunger which she blazed into anguish just by being, existing, breathing; having been born, becoming born, becoming a part of Motion—that hunger which she herself could never assuage since there was but one of her to match with all that hungering. And that single *one* doomed to fade; by the fact of that mortality doomed not to assuage nor even negate the hunger; doomed never to efface the anguish and the hunger from Motion even by her own act of quitting Motion and so fill with her own absence from it the aching void where once had glared that incandescent shape.

That's what you thought at first, of course: that she must of necessity repeat herself, duplicate herself if she reproduced at all. Because immediately afterward you realised that obviously she must not, must not suplicate: very Nature herself would not permit that to occur, permit two of them in a place no larger than Jefferson, Mississippi, in one century, let alone in overlapping succession, within the anguished scope of a single generation. Because even Nature, loving concupiscent uproar and excitement as even Nature loves it, insists that it at least be reproductive of fresh fodder for the uproar and the excitement. Which would take time, the time necessary to produce that new crop of fodder, since she —Eula Varner—had exhausted, consumed, burned up that one of hers. Whereupon I would remember what Maggie said once to Gowan back there in the dead long time ago when I was in the throes of my own apprenticeship to holocaust: "You don't marry Helen and Semiramis; you just commit suicide for her."

Because she—the child—didn't look at all like her mother. And then in that same second I knew exactly whom she did resemble. Back there in that time of my own clowning belated adolescence (none the less either for being both), I remember how I could never decide which of the two unbearables was the least unbearable; which (as the poet has it) of the two chewed bitter thumbs was the least bitter for chewing. That is, whether Manfred de Spain had seduced a chaste wife, or had simply been caught up in passing by a rotating nympholept. This was my anguish. If the first was right, what qualities of mere man did Manfred have that I didn't? If the second, what blind outrageous fortune's lightning-bolt was it that struck Manfred de Spain that mightn't, shouldn't, couldn't, anyway didn't, have blasted Gavin Stevens just as well? Or even also (oh yes, it was that bad once, that comical once) I would even have shared her if I had to, couldn't have had her any other way.

That was when (I mean the thinking why it hadn't been me in Manfred's place to check that glance's idle fateful swing that day whenever that moment had been) I would say that she must be chaste, a wife true and impeachless. I would think *It's that damned child, that damned baby*—that innocent infant which, simply by innocently being, breathing, existing, lacerated and scoriated and reft me of peace: if there had only been no question of the child's paternity; or better still, no child at all. Thus I would even get a little relief from my chewed thumbs since I would need both of them for the moment to count with. Ratliff had told me how they departed for Texas immediately after the wedding and when they returned twelve months later, the child was already walking. Which (the walking at least) I did not believe, not because of the anguish, the jealousy, the despair, but simply because of Ratliff. In fact, it was Ratliff who gave me that ease of hope—or if you like, ease from anguish; all right: tears too, peaceful tears but tears, which are the jewel-baubles of the belated adolescence's clown-comedian—to pant with. Because even if the child had been only one day old, Ratliff would have invented the walking, being Ratliff. In fact, if there had been no child at all yet, Ratliff would have invented one, invented one already walking for the simple sake of his own paradox and humour, secured as he was from checkable facts by this much miles and time between Frenchman's Bend and Jefferson two years later. That was when I would rather believe it was Flem's own child; rather defilement by Manfred de Spain than promiscuity by Eula Varner—whereupon I would need only to taste that thumb again to realise that any other thumb was less bitter, no matter which: let her accept the whole earth's Manfred de Spains and refuse Gavin Stevens, than to accept one Flem Snopes and still refuse him.

So you see how much effort a man will make and trouble he will invent to guard and defend himself from the boredom of peace of mind. Or rather perhaps the pervert who deliberately infests himself with lice, not just for the simple pleasure of being rid of them again, since even in the folly of youth we know that nothing lasts; but because even in that folly we are afraid that maybe Nothing will last, that maybe Nothing will last forever, and anything is better than Nothing, even lice. So now, as another poet sings, That Fancy passed me by And nothing will remain; which, praise the gods, is a damned lie since, praise, O gods! Nothing cannot remain anywhere since nothing is vacuum and vacuum is paradox and unbearable and we will have none of it even if we would, the damned-fool poet's Nothing steadily and perennially full of perennially new and perennially renewed anguishes for me to measure my stature against whenever I need reassure myself that I also am Motion.

Because the second premise was much better. If I was not to have her, then Flem Snopes shall never have. So instead of the poet's Fancy passes by And nothing remaining, it is Remaining which will always remain, never to be completely empty of that olden anguish. So no matter how much more the blood will slow and remembering grow more lascerant, the blood at least will always remember that once it was that capable, capable at least of anguish. So that girl-child was not Flem Snopes's at all, but mine; my child and my grandchild both, since the McCarron boy who begot her (oh yes, I can even believe Ratliff when it suits me) in that lost time, was Gavin Stevens in that lost time; and, since remaining must remain or quit being remaining, Gavin Stevens is fixed by his own child forever at that one age in that one moment. So since the son is father to the man, the McCarron fixed forever and timeless in that dead youth as Gavin Stevens is of necessity now the son of Gavin Stevens's age, and McCarron's child is Gavin Stevens's grandchild.

Whether Gavin Stevens intended to be that father-grandfather or not, of course. But then neither did he dream that that one idle glance of Eula Varner's eye which didn't even mark him in passing would confer on him foster-uncleship over every damned Snopes wanting to claim it out of that whole entire damned connection she married into. I mean foster-uncleship in the sense that simple enragement and outrage and obsession *per se* take care of their own just as simple *per se* poverty and (so they say) virtue do of theirs. But foster-uncleship only to *he*: never *she*. So this was not the first time I ever thought how apparently all Snopeses are male, as if the mere and simple incident of woman's divinity precluded Snopesishness and made it paradox. No: it was rather as if *Snopes* were some profound and incontrovertible hermaphroditic principle for the furtherance of a race, a species, the principle vested always physically in the male, any anonymous conceptive or gestative organ drawn into that radius to conceive and spawn, repeating that male principle and then vanishing; the Snopes female incapable of producing a Snopes and hence harmless like the malaria-bearing mosquito of whom only the female is armed and potent, turned upside down and backward. Or even more

than a mere natural principle: a divine one: the unsleeping hand
of God Himself, unflagging and constant, else before now they
would have owned the whole earth, let alone just Jefferson,
Mississippi.

Because now Flem Snopes was vice-president of what we still
called Colonel Sartoris's bank. Oh yes, our banks have vice-
presidents the same as anybody else's bank. Only nobody in Jefferson ever paid any attention to just the vice-president of a bank
before; he—a bank vice-president—was like someone who had
gained the privilege of calling himself major or colonel by having
contributed time or money or influence to getting a governor
elected, as compared to him who had rightfully inherited his
title from a father or grandfather who had actually ridden a horse
at a Yankee soldier, like Manfred de Spain or our Colonel Sartoris.

So Flem was the first actual living vice-president of a bank we
had ever seen to notice. We heard he had fallen heir to the vice-
presidency when Manfred de Spain moved up his notch, and we
knew why: Uncle Billy Varner's stock plus the odds and ends
which (we now learned) Flem himself had been picking up here
and there for some time, plus Manfred de Spain himself. Which
was all right; it was done now; too late to help; we were used to
our own Jefferson breed or strain of bank vice-presidents and we
expected no more of even a Snopes bank vice-president than
simple conformation to pattern.

Then to our surprise we saw that he was trying to be what he—
a Snopes or anyway a Flem Snopes—thought a bank vice-
president was or should be. He began to spend most of the day in
the bank. Not in the back office where Colonel Sartoris had used
to sit and where Manfred de Spain now sat, but in the lobby,
standing a little back from the window watching the clients coming and going to leave their money or draw it out, still in that little
cloth cap and the snap-on-behind bow tie he had come to town in
thirteen years ago and his jaw still moving faintly and steadily as
if he were chewing something though I anyway in my part of
those thirteen years had never seen him spit.

Then one day we saw him at his post in the lobby and we didn't
even know him. He was standing where he always stood, back
where he would be out of the actual path to the window but where
he could still watch it (watching how much money was going in

or how much was coming out, we didn't know which; whether perhaps what held him thralled there was the simply solvency of the bank which in a way—by deputy, by proxy—was now his bank, his pride: that no matter how much money people drew out of it, there was always that one who had just deposited that zero-plus-one dollar into it in time; or whether he actually did believe in an inevitable moment when De Spain or whoever the designated job would belong to, would come to the window from the inside and say "Sorry, folks, you can't draw out any more money because there ain't any more," and he—Flem—simply wanted to prove to himself that he was wrong).

But this time we didn't know him. He still wore the little bow tie and his jaw was still pulsing faintly and steadily, but now he wore a hat, a new one of the broad black felt kind which country preachers and politicians wore. And the next day he was actually inside the cage where the money actually was and where the steel door opened into the concrete vault where it stayed at night; and now we realised that he was not watching the money any longer; he had learned all there was to learn about that. Now he was watching the records of it, how they kept the books.

And now we—some of us, a few of us—believed that he was preparing himself to show his nephew or cousin Byron how to really loot a bank. But Ratliff (naturally it was Ratliff) stopped that quick. "No, no," he said, "he's jest trying to find out how anybody could think so light of money as to let a feller no brighter than Byron Snopes steal some of it. You boys have got Flem Snopes wrong. He's got too much respect and reverence not jest for money, but for sharpness too, to outrage and debase one of them by jest crude robbing and stealing the other one."

And as the days followed, he—Snopes—had his coat off too, in his galluses now like he actually worked there, was paid money every Saturday to stay inside the cage, except that he still wore the new hat, standing now right behind the book-keepers while he found out for himself how a bank was run. And now we heard how always when people came in to pay off notes or the interest on them, and sometimes when they came to borrow the money too (except the old short-tempered ones, old customers from back in Colonel Sartoris's time, who would run Flem out of the back room without waiting for De Spain to do it or even asking his—

De Spain's—leave) he would be there too, his jaw still faintly pulsing while he watched and learned; that was when Ratliff said that all he—Snopes—needed to learn now was how to write out a note so that the fellow borrowing the money couldn't even read when it was due, let alone the rate of interest, like Colonel Sartoris could write one (the tale, the legend was that once the colonel wrote out a note for a country-man customer, a farmer, who took the note and looked at it, then turned it upside down and looked at it, then handed it back to the colonel and said, "What does it say, Colonel? I can't read it," whereupon the colonel took it in his turn, looked at it, turned it upside down and looked at it, then tore it in two and threw it in the waste basket and said, "Be damned if I can either, Tom. We'll try another one"), then he—Snopes— would know all there was to learn about banking in Jefferson, and could graduate.

Evidently he learned that too. One day he was not in the bank any more, and the day after that, and the day after that. On the day the bank first opened about twenty years ago Mrs Jennie Du Pre, Colonel Sartoris's sister, had put a tremendous great rubber plant in the corner of the lobby. It was taller than a man, it took up as much room as a privy; it was in everybody's way and in summer they couldn't even open the front door all the way back because of it. But she wouldn't let the colonel nor the board of directors either remove it, since she belonged to that school which believed that any room inhabited by people had to have something green in it to absorb the poison from the air. Though why it had to be that monstrous rubber plant, nobody knew, unless perhaps she believed that nothing less than rubber and that much of it would be tough and durable and resilient enough to cope with air poisoned by the anxiety or exultation over as much money as her brother's, a Sartoris, old Colonel Sartoris's son's bank would naturally handle.

So when the days passed and Snopes was no longer to be seen taking up room in the lobby while he watched the borrowing and the lending and the paying in and the drawing out (or who did each, and how much of each, which according to Ratliff was the real reason he was there, was what he was really watching), it was as if Mrs De Pre's rubber tree had vanished from the lobby, abandoned it. And when still more days passed and we finally

realised he was not coming back any more, it was like hearing that
the rubber tree had been hauled away somewhere and burned,
destroyed forever. It was as if the single aim and purpose of that
long series of interlocked circumstances—the bank which a senti-
mentalist like Colonel Sartoris founded in order that, as Ratliff
said, a feller no brighter than Byron Snopes could steal from it,
the racing car which Bayard Sartoris drove too fast for our country
roads (the Jefferson ladies said because he was grieving so over
the death in battle of his twin brother that he too was seeking
death though in my opinion Bayard liked war and now that there
was no more war to go to, he was faced with the horrid prospect
of having to go to work) until his grandfather took to riding with
him in the hope that he would slow down: as a result of which, the
normal check-up of the bank for re-organisation revealed the fact
that Byron Snopes had been robbing it: as a result of which, to
save the good name of the bank which his father had helped to
found, Manfred de Spain had to allow Flem Snopes to become
vice-president of it—the single result of all this apparently was to
efface that checked cap from Flem Snopes and put that hot-
looking black politician-preacher's hat on him in its stead.

Because he still wore the hat. We saw that about the Square
every day. But never again in the bank, his bank, the one in which
he was not only a director but in whose hierarchy he had an
official designated place, second-in-command. Not even to deposit
his own money in it. Oh yes, we knew that; we had Ratliff's word
for that. Ratliff had to know a fact like that by now. After this
many years of working to establish and maintain himself as what
he uniquely was in Jefferson, Ratliff could not afford, he did
not dare, to walk the streets and not have the answer to any and
every situation which was not really any of his business. Ratliff
knew: that not only was Flem Snopes no longer a customer of the
bank of which he was vice-president, but that in the second year
he had transferred his account to the other, rival bank, the old
bank of Jefferson.

So we all knew the answer to that. I mean, we had been right
all along. All except Ratliff of course, who had dissuaded us before
against our mutually combined judgments. We had watched
Flem behind the grille of his bank while he taught himself the
intricacies of banking in order to plumb laboriously the crude and

awkward method by which his cousin or nephew Byron had made his petty and unambitious haul; we had seen him in and out of the vault itself while he learned the tide-cycle, the rise and fall of the actual cash against the moment when it would be most worth pillaging; we believed now that when that moment came, Flem would have already arranged himself for his profit to be one hundred per cent, that he himself was seeing to it in advance that he would not have to steal even one forgotten penny of his own money.

"No," Ratliff said. "No."

"In which case, he will defeat himself," I said. "What does he expect to happen when the other depositors, especially the ignorant ones that know too little about banks and the smart ones that know too much about Snopeses, begin to find out that the vice-president of the bank doesn't even keep his own loose change in it?"

"No, I tell you," Ratliff said. "You folks—"

"So he's hoping—wishing—dreaming of starting a run on his own bank, not to loot it but to empty it, abolish it. All right. Why? For revenge on Manfred de Spain because of his wife?"

"No no, I tell you!" Ratliff said. "I tell you, you got Flem all wrong, all of you have. I tell you, he ain't just got respect for money: he's got active" (he always said active for actual, though in this case I believe his choice was better than Webster's) "reverence for it. The last thing he would ever do is hurt that bank. Because any bank whether it's hisn or not stands for money, and the last thing he would ever do is to insult and degrade money by mishandling it. Likely the one and only thing in his life he is ashamed of is the one thing he won't never do again. That was that-ere power-plant brass that time. Likely he wakes up at night right now and writhes and squirms over it. Not because he lost by it because don't nobody know yet, nor never will, whether he actively lost or not because don't nobody know yet jest how much of that old brass he might a sold before he made the mistake of trying to do it wholesale by using Tom Tom Bird and Tomey Beauchamp. He's ashamed because when he made money that-a-way, he got his-self right down into the dirt with the folks that waste money because they stole it in the first place and ain't got nowhere to put it down where they can risk turning their backs on it."

"Then what is he up to?" I said. "What is he trying to do?"

"I don't know," Ratliff said. And now he not only didn't sound like Ratliff, answering he didn't know to any question, he didn't even look like Ratliff: the customary bland smooth quizzical inscrutable face not quite baffled, maybe but certainly questioning, certainly sober. "I jest don't know. We got to figger. That's why I come up here to see you: in case you did know. Hoping you knowed." Then he was Ratliff again, humorous, quizzical, invincibly . . . maybe the word I want is not optimism or courage or even hope, but rather of sanity or maybe even of innocence. "But naturally you don't know neither. Confound it, the trouble is we don't never know beforehand, to anticipate him. It's like a rabbit or maybe a bigger varmint, one with more poison or anyhow more teeth, in a patch or a brake: you can watch the bushes shaking but you can't see what it is or which-a-way it's going until it breaks out. But you can see it then, and usually it's in time. Of course, you got to move fast when he does break out, and he's got the advantage of you because he's already moving because he knows where he's going, and you ain't moving yet because you don't. But it's usually in time."

That was the first time the bushes shook. The next time was almost a year later; he came in, he said, "Good-morning, Lawyer," and he was Ratliff again, bland, smooth, courteous, a little too damned intelligent. "I figgered you might like to hear the latest news first, being as you're a member of the family too by simple bad luck and exposure, you might say. Being as so far don't nobody know about it except the directors of the Bank of Jefferson."

"The Bank of Jefferson?" I said.

"That's right. It's that non-Snopes boy of Eck's, that other non-Snopes that blowed his-self up in that empty oil tank back while you was away at the war, wasting his time jest hunting a lost child that wasn't even lost, jest his maw thought he was—"

"Yes," I said. "Wallstreet Panic." Because I already knew about that: the non-Snopes son of a non-Snopes who had had the good fortune to discover (or be discovered by) a good woman early in life: the second-grade teacher who, obviously recognising that un-Snopes anomaly, not only told him what Wallstreet Panic meant, but that he didn't really have to have it for his name if he didn't want to; but if he thought a too-violent change might be too much, then he could call himself simply Wall Snopes since

Wall was a good name, having been carried bravely by a brave Mississippi general at Chickamauga and Lookout Mountain, and though she didn't think that, being a non-Snopes, he would particularly need to remember courage, remembering courage never hurt anyone.

And how he had taken the indemnity money the oil company paid for his father's bizarre and needless and un-Snopesish death and bought into the little back-street grocery store where he had been the after-school-and-Saturday clerk and errand boy, and continued to save his money until, when the old owner died at last, he, Wallstreet, owned the store. And how he got married who was never a Snopes, never in this world a Snopes: doomed damned corrupted and self-convicted not merely of generosity but of taste; holding simple foolish innocent rewardless generosity, not to mention taste, even higher than his own repute when the town should learn he had actually proposed marriage to a woman ten years his senior.

That's what he did, not even waiting to graduate—the day, the moment when in the hot stiff brand-new serge suit, to walk sweating through the soundless agony of the cut flowers, across the high-school rostrum and receive his diploma from the hand of the principal—but only for the day when he knew he was done with the school, forever more beyond the range of its help or harm (he was nineteen. Seven years ago he and his six-year-old brother had entered the same kindergarten class. In this last year his grades had been such that they didn't even ask him to take the examinations)—to leave the store of which he was now actual even if not titular proprietor, just in time to be standing at the corner when the dismissal bell rang, standing there while the kindergarten then the first-grade children streamed past him, then the second grade, standing there while the Lilliputian flow divided around them like a brook around two herons, while without even attempting to touch her in this all juvenile Jefferson's sight, he proposed to the second-grade teacher and then saw her, as another teacher did from a distance, stare at him and partly raise one defending hand and then burst into tears, right then in plain view of the hundred children who at one time within the last three or four years had been second-graders too, to whom she had been mentor, authority, infallible.

Until he could lead her aside, on to the vacating playground, himself to screen her while she used his handkerchief to regain composure, then, against all the rules of the school and of respectable decorum too, back into the empty room itself smelling of chalk and anguished cerebration and the dry inflexibility of facts, she leading the way, not for the betrothing kiss, not to let him touch her even and least of all to remind him that she had already been twenty-two years old that day seven years ago and that twelve months from now he would discover that all Jefferson had been one year laughing at him. Who had been divinitive enough to see seven years beyond that Wallstreet Panic, but was more, much more than that: a lady, the tears effaced now and she once more the Miss Wyott, or rather the "Miss Vaiden" as Southern children called their teacher, telling him, feeding him none of those sorry reasons: saying simply that she was already engaged and some day she wanted him to know her fiancé because she knew they would be friends.

So that he would not know better until he was much older and had much more sense. Nor learning it then when it was too late because it was not too late, since didn't I just say that she was wise, more than just wise: divinitive? Also, remember her own people had come from the country (her own branch of it remained there where they had owned the nearest ford, crossing, ferry before even Jefferson even became Jefferson) so without doubt she even knew in advance the girl, which girl even, since she seems to have taken him directly there, within the week, almost as though she said "This is she. Marry her" and within the month he didn't even know probably that he had not remarked that Miss Vaiden Wyott had resigned from the Jefferson school where she had taught the second grade for a decade, to accept a position in a school in Bristol, Virginia, since when that fall day came he was two months husband to a tense fierce not quite plain-faced girl with an ambition equal to his and a will if anything even more furious against that morass, that swamp, that fetid seethe from which her husband (she naturally believed) had extricated himself by his own suspenders and boot straps, herself clerking in the store now so that the mother-in-law could now stay at home and do the cooking and housework; herself, although at that time she didn't weigh quite a hundred pounds, doing the apprentice

E

chores—sweeping, wrestling the barrels of flour and molasses, making the rounds of the town on the bicycle in which the telephone orders were delivered until they could afford to buy the second-hand Model T Ford—during the hours while the younger one, Admiral Dewey, was in school where it was she now, his sister-in-law, who made him go whether he would or not.

Yes, we all knew that; that was a part of our folklore, or Snopes-lore, if you like: how Flem himself was anyway the second one to see that here was a young man who was going to make money by simple honesty and industry, and tried to buy into the business or anyway lend Wallstreet money to expand it; and we all knew who had refused the offer. That is, we liked to believe, having come to know Wallstreet a little now, that he would have declined anyway. But since we had come to know his wife, we knew that he was going to decline. And how he had learned to be a clerk and a partner the hard way, and he would have to learn to be a proprietor the hard way too: and sure enough in time he over-bought his stock; and how he went to Colonel Sartoris's bank for help.

That was when we first realised that Flem Snopes actually was a member of the board of directors of a Jefferson bank. I mean, that a Flem Snopes actually could be. Oh, we had seen his name among the others on the annual bank report above the facsimile of Colonel Sartoris's illegible signature as president, but we merely drew the logical conclusion that that was simply old man Will Varner's voting proxy to save him a trip to town; all we thought was, "That means that Manfred de Spain will have Uncle Billy's stock too in case he ever wants anything."

And obviously we knew, believed, that Flem had tried again to buy into Wallstreet's business, save him with a personal private loan before he, as a director, blocked the loan from the bank. Because we thought we saw it all now; all we seemed to have missed was, what hold he could have had over the drummer to compel him to persuade Wallstreet to overbuy, and over the wholesale house in St Louis to persuade it to accept the sale—very likely the same sign or hoodoo-mark he planned to use on the other bank, the Bank of Jefferson, to prevent them lending Wall-street money after Colonel Sartoris's bank declined.

But there was never any question about which one of the Wallstreet Snopeses had turned Flem down. Anybody could have seen her that morning, running, thin, not so much tense as fierce, still weighing less than a hundred pounds, even after six months of marriage looking still not so much like a nymph as like a deer, not around the Square as pedestrians walked but across it, through it, darting among the automobiles and teams and wagons, toward and into the bank (and how she knew, divined so quickly that he had been refused the loan we didn't know either, though on second thought that was obvious too: that simple automatic fierce Snopes antipathy which had reacted as soon as common sense told her it should not have taken the bank that long to say Yes, and that Flem Snopes was on the board of directors of it)—darting into the lobby already crying: "Where is he? Where is Wall?" and out again when they told her Gone, not at all desperate: just fierce and hurried, on to the street where someone else told her he went that way: which was the street leading to the back street leading to the rented house where Flem lived, who had no office nor other place of business, running now until she overtook him, in time. And anyone there could have seen that too: clinging to him in broad daylight when even sweethearts didn't embrace on the street by daylight and no lady anywhere at any time said God damn in public, crying (weeping too but no tears, as if the fierce taut irreconcilable face blistered and evaporated tears away as fast as they emerged on to it): "Don't you dare! Them damn Snopes! God damn them! God damn them!"

So we thought of course that her father, a small though thrifty farmer, had found the money somehow. Because Wallstreet saved his business. And he had not only learned about solvency from that experience, he had learned something more about success too. In another year he had rented (then bought it) the store next door and converted it into a warehouse, stock room, so he could buy in larger wholesale lots for less money; another few years and he had rented what had been the last livery stable in Jefferson for his warehouse and knocked down the wall between the two stores and now he had in Jefferson the first self-service grocery store we had ever seen, built on the pattern which the big chain grocery stores were to make nationwide in the purveying of food; the street his store faced on made an L with the alley where the old Snopes restaurant had been so that the tent in which he had passed his

first night in Jefferson was directly behind his store too; he either
bought or rented that lot (there were more automobiles in Jefferson now) and made a parking lot and so taught the housewives of
Jefferson to come to town and seek his bargains and carry them
home themselves.

That is, we—or that is, I—thought that it was his father-in-law
who had found the money to save him, until now. "Well, I'll be
damned," I said. "So it was you."

"That's right," Ratliff said. "All I wanted was jest a note for
it. But he insisted on making me a partner. And I'll tell you something else we're fixing to do. We're fixing to open a wholesale."

"A what?" I said.

"A wholesale company like the big ones in St Louis, right here
in Jefferson, so that instead of either having to pay high freight
on a little shirt-tail full of stuff, or risk overloading on something
perishable to save freight, a merchant anywhere in the county
can buy jest what he needs at a decent price without having to
add no freight a-tall."

"Well I'll be damned," I said. "Why didn't you think of that
yourself years ago?"

"That's right," Ratliff said. "Why didn't you?"

"Well I'll be damned," I still said. Then I said: "Hell fire, are
you still selling stock? Can I get in?"

"Why not?" he said. "Long as your name ain't Snopes. Maybe
you could even buy some from him if your name wasn't jest Flem
Snopes. But you got to pass that-ere little gal first. His wife. You
ought to stop in there sometime and hear her say Them goddamn
Snopes once. Oh sho, all of us have thought that, and some of us
have even said it out loud. But she's different. She means it. And
she ain't going to never let him change neither."

"Yes," I said. "I've heard about that. I wonder why she never
changed their name."

"No, no," he said. "You don't understand. She don't want to
change it. She jest wants to live it down. She ain't trying to drag
him by the hair out of Snopes, to escape from Snopes. She's got
to purify Snopes itself. She's got to beat Snopes from the inside.
Stop in there and listen sometimes."

"A wholesale house," I said. "So that's why Flem—" But that
was foolish, as Ratliff himself saw even before I said it.

"—why Flem changed his account from his own bank to the other one? No no. We ain't using the banks here. We don't need them. Like Flem was the first feller in Jefferson to find out that. Wall's credit is too good with the big wholesalers and brokers we deal with. The way they figger, he ain't cutting into nobody's private business: he's helping all business. We don't need no bank. But we—he—still aims to keep it home-made. So you see him if you want to talk about stock."

"I will," I said. "But what is Flem himself up to? Why did he pull his money out of De Spain's bank as soon as he got to be vice-president of it? Because he's still that, so he still owns stock in it. But he doesn't keep his own money in it. Why?"

"Oh," he said, "is that what you're worried about? Why, we ain't sho yet. All we're doing now is watching the bushes shake." Between the voice and the face there were always two Ratliffs: the second one offering you a fair and open chance to divine what the first one really meant by what it was saying, provided you were smart enough. But this time that second Ratliff was trying to tell me something which for whatever reason the other could not say in words. "As long as that little gal lives, Flem ain't got no chance to ever get a finger-hold on Wall. So Eck Snopes is out. And I.O. Snopes never was in because I.O. never was worth nothing even to I.O., let alone for anybody else to take a cut of the profit. So that jest about exhausts all the Snopeses in reach that a earnest hard-working feller might make a forced share-crop on."

"There's that—" I said.

"All right," he said. "I'll say it for you. Montgomery Ward. The photograph gallery. If Flem ain't been in that thing all the time from the very first, he don't never aim to be. And the fact that there ain't been a new photograph in his show window in over a year now, let alone Jason Compson collecting his maw's rent prompt on time since the second month after Montgomery Ward opened up, is proof enough that Flem seen from the first day that there wasn't nothing there for him to waste his time on. So I can't think of but one Snopes object that he's got left."

"All right," I said. "I'll bite."

"That-ere twenty-dollar gold piece."

"What twenty-dollar gold piece?"

"Don't you remember what I said that day, about how when a country boy makes his first Sad-dy night trip to Memphis, that-ere twenty-dollar bill he wears pinned inside his undershirt so he can at least get back home?"

"Go on," I said. "You can't stop now."

"What's the one thing in Jefferson that Flem ain't got yet? The one thing he might want? That maybe he's been working at ever since they taken Colonel Sartoris out of that wrecked car and he voted Uncle Billy Varner's stock to make Manfred de Spain president of that bank?"

"To be president of it himself," I said. "No!" I said. "It can't be! It must not be!" But he was just watching me. "Nonsense," I said.

"Why nonsense?" he said.

"Because, to use what you call that twenty-dollar gold piece, he's got to use his wife too. Do you mean to tell me you believe for one moment that his wife will side with him against Manfred de Spain?" But still he just looked at me. "Don't you agree?" I said. "How can he hope for that?"

Yes, he was just looking at me. "That would jest be when he finally runs out of the bushes," he said. "Out to where we can see him. Into the clearing. What's that clearing?"

"Clearing?" I said.

"That he was working toward?—All right," he said. "That druv him to burrow through the bushes to get out of them?"

"Rapacity," I said. "Greed. Money. What else does he need? want? What else has ever driven him?"

But he just looked at me, and now I could actually watch that urgency fade until only the familiar face remained, bland, smooth, impenetrable and courteous. He drew out the dollar watch looped on a knotted shoelace between his button hole and his breast pocket. "I be dog if it ain't almost dinner time," he said. "Jest about time to walk to it."

9

V. K. RATLIFF

BECAUSE he missed it. He missed it completely.

10

CHARLES MALLISON

THEY finally caught Montgomery Ward Snopes. I mean, they caught Grover Cleveland Winbush. Like Ratliff said, anybody bootlegging anything that never had any more sense than to sell Grover Cleveland Winbush some of it deserved to be caught.

Except Uncle Gavin said that, even without Grover Cleveland, Montgomery Ward was bound to be caught sooner or later, since there simply wasn't any place in Jefferson, Mississippi, culture for a vocation or hobby or interest like the one Montgomery Ward had tried to establish among us. In Europe, yes; and maybe among the metropolitan rich or bohemians, yes too. But not in a land composed mainly of rural Baptists.

So they caught Grover Cleveland. It was one night, not very late. I mean, the stores were all closed but folks were still going home from the second running of the picture show; and some of them, I reckon anybody that passed and happened to look inside, saw the two fellows inside Uncle Willy Christian's drugstore working at the prescription case where Uncle Willy kept the medicines; and even though they were strangers—that is, nobody passing recognised them—the ones that looked in and saw them said the next day that they never thought anything of it, being that early and the lights on and Grover Cleveland not having anything to do as night marshal except to walk around the Square and look in the windows, that sooner or later he would have to see them if they never had any business there.

So it wasn't until the next morning when Uncle Willy opened up for business that he found out somebody had unlocked the store and not only unlocked the safe and took what money he had in it, they had broke open his pharmacy cabinet and stole all his morphine and sleeping pills. That's what caused the trouble. Ratliff said they could have taken the money or for that matter all the rest of the store too except that prescription case, including the alcohol, because Walter Christian, the Negro janitor, had been taking the alcohol, a drink at a time ever since he and Uncle Willy both were boys and first started in the store, and Uncle

Willy would have cussed and stomped around of course and even had the Law in, but that was all. But whoever touched that prescription cabinet with the morphine in it raised the devil himself. Uncle Willy was a bachelor, about sixty years old, and if you came in at the wrong time of day he even snarled at children too. But if you were careful to remember the right time of day he supplied the balls and bats for our baseball teams and after a game he would give the whole teams ice cream free whether they won or not. I mean, until one summer some of the church ladies decided to reform him. After that it was hard to tell when to speak to him or not. Then the ladies would give up for a while and it would be all right again.

Besides that, the federal drug inspectors had been nagging and worrying at him for years about keeping the morphine in that little flimsy wooden drawer that anybody with a screw-driver or a knife blade or maybe just a hair pin could prise open, even though it did have a key to it that Uncle Willy kept hidden under a gallon jug marked *Nux Vomica* on a dark shelf that nobody but him was even supposed to bother because it was so dark back there that even Walter never went back there since Uncle Willy couldn't have seen whether he had swept there or not even if he had; and each time Uncle Willy would have to promise the inspectors to lock the morphine up in the safe from now on.

So now he was going to have more trouble than ever explaining to the inspectors why he hadn't put the morphine in the safe like he promised; reminding them how, even if he had, the robbers would still have got it wasn't going to do any good now because, like Ratliff said, federal folks were not interested in whether anything worked or not, all they were interested in was that you did it exactly like their rules said to do it.

So Uncle Willy was the real cause of them catching Montgomery Ward Snopes. He was good and wild at first. He was so wild for a while that nobody could find out how much had been stolen or even what he was talking about, with more folks coming in from the street not so much to see where the robbery was but to watch Uncle Willy; until finally, it was Ratliff, of course, said: "Uncle Willy don't need no sheriff yet. What he needs first is Doc Peabody."

"Of course," Uncle Gavin said to Ratliff. "Why does it always

E*

have to be you?" He went back to where Skeets McGowan. Uncle Willy's clerk and soda-jerker, and two other boys were standing with their heads inside the open safe looking at where the money had been stolen from, and pulled Skeets out and told him to run upstairs quick and tell Doctor Peabody to hurry down. Then Uncle Gavin and the others kind of crowded Uncle Willy more or less quiet without actually holding him until Doctor Peabody came in with the needle already in his hand even and ran most of them out and rolled up Uncle Willy's sleeve then rolled it back down again and then Uncle Willy settled down into being just mad.

So he was the one responsible for catching Montgomery Ward. Or the two fellows that stole his morphine were. By this time we knew that several people passing from the picture show had seen the two fellows in the store, and now Uncle Willy wanted to know where Grover Cleveland Winbush was all that time. Yes sir, he wasn't wild now. He was just mad, as calm and steady and deadly about it as a horsefly. By that time, nine o'clock in the morning, Grover Cleveland would be at home in bed asleep. Somebody said they would telephone out and wake him up and tell him to get on back to the Square fast as he could.

"Hell," Uncle Willy said. "That'll take too long. I'll go out there myself. I'll wake him up and get him back to town. He won't need to worry about quick because I'll tend to that. Who's got a car?"

Only Mr Buck Connors, the marshal, the chief of police, was there by this time. "Hold up now, Uncle Willy," he said. "There's a right way and a wrong way to do things. We want to do this one the right way. These folks have probably done already trompled up most of the evidence. But at least we can make an investigation according to police procedure regulations. Besides, Grover Cleveland was up all last night on duty. He's to stay up again all night tonight. He's got to get his sleep."

"Exactly," Uncle Willy said. "Egg-zackly. Up all night, but not far enough up to see two damn scoundrels robbing my store in full view of the whole damn town. Robbed me of three hundred dollars' worth of valuable medicine, yet Grover Winbush—"

"How much cash did they get?" Mr Connors said.

"What?" Uncle Willy said.

"How much money was in the safe?"

"I don't know," Uncle Willy said. "I didn't count it.—Yet Grover Winbush that we pay a hundred and twenty-five a month just to wake up once an hour during the night and look around the Square, has got to get his sleep. If nobody's got a car here, get me a taxi. That son of a bitch has already cost me three hundred dollars; I ain't going to stop at just one more quarter."

But they still held him hemmed off while somebody telephoned Grover Cleveland. And at first we thought that whoever telephoned and woke him up had scared him good too, until we learned the rest of it and realised all he needed for his scare was to hear that anything had happened anywhere in Jefferson last night that he would have seen if he had been where he was supposed to be or where folks thought he was. Because it wasn't hardly any time before Ratliff said:

"There he was. I jest seen him."

"Where?" somebody said.

"He jest snatched his head back in the alley yonder," Ratliff said. We all watched the alley. It led from a side street on to the Square where Grover Cleveland could have cut across lots from his boarding-house. Then he stepped out of it, already walking fast. He didn't wear a uniform like Mr Connors; he wore ordinary clothes with usually his coat-tail hiked up over the handle of the pistol and the blackjack in his hip pocket, coming up the street fast, picking his feet up quick like a cat on a hot stove. And if you thought it would have been Mr Connors or even Mr Hampton, the sheriff, that did the investigating, you would have been wrong. It was Uncle Willy himself. At first Grover Cleveland tried to bluff. Then he fell back on lying. Then he just fell back.

"Howdy, son," Uncle Willy said. "Sorry to wake you up in the middle of the night like this, just to answer a few questions. The first one is, just where were you, roughly, more or less, at exactly half-past ten o'clock last night, more or less?"

"Who, me?" Grover Cleveland said. "Where I'm always at at that time of night: standing right across yonder in the station door, where if anybody after the last picture show might need anything, like maybe losing their car key or maybe they find out they got a flat tire—"

"Well, well," Uncle Willy said. "And yet you never saw a light on in my store, and them two damned scoundrels——"

"Wait," Grover Cleveland said. "I'm wrong. When I seen the last picture show beginning to let out, I noticed the time, half-past ten or maybe twenty-five to eleven, and I decided to go down and close up the Blue Goose and get that out of the way while I had time." The Blue Goose was a Negro café below the cotton gin. "I'm wrong," Grover Cleveland said. "That's where I was."

Uncle Willy never said anything. He just turned his head enough and hollered "Walter!" Walter came in. His grandfather had belonged to Uncle Willy's grandfather before the Surrender and he and Uncle Willy were about the same age and a good deal alike, except that instead of morphine Walter would go into the medicinal alcohol every time Uncle Willy put the key down and turned his back, and if anything Walter was a little more irascible and short-tempered. He came in from the back and said,

"Who calling me?"

"I am," Uncle Willy said. "Where were you at half-past ten last night?"

"Who, me?" Walter said, exactly like Grover Cleveland did, except he said it like Uncle Willy had asked him where he was when Dr Einstein first propounded his theory of relativity. "You talking about last night?" he said. "Where you reckon? At home in bed."

"You were at that damned Blue Goose café, where you are every night until Grover Winbush here comes in and runs all you niggers out and closes it up," Uncle Willy said.

"Then what you asking me, if you know so much?" Walter said.

"All right," Uncle Willy said. "What time last night did Mr Winbush close it?" Walter stood there, blinking. His eyes were always red. He made in an old-fashioned hand freezer the ice cream which Uncle Willy sold over his soda fountain. He made it in the cellar: a dark cool place with a single door opening on to the alley behind the store, sitting in the gloom and grinding the freezer, so that when you passed, about all you saw was his red eyes, looking not malevolent, not savage but just dangerous if you blundered out of your element and into his, like a dragon or a crocodile. He stood there, blinking. "What time did Grover Winbush close up the Blue Goose?" Uncle Willy said.

"I left before that," Walter said. Now suddenly, and we hadn't noticed him before, Mr Hampton was there, doing some of the looking too. He didn't blink like Walter. He was a big man with a big belly and little hard pale eyes that didn't seem to need to blink at all. They were looking at Grover Cleveland now.

"How do you know you did?" he said to Walter.

"Hell fire," Uncle Willy said. "He ain't never left that damned place before they turned the lights out since they first opened the door."

"I know that," Mr Hampton said. He was still looking at Grover Cleveland with his little hard pale unblinking eyes. "I've been marshal and sheriff both here a long time too." He said to Grover Cleveland: "Where were you last night when folks needed you?" But Grover Cleveland still tried; you'll have to give him that, even if now even he never believed in it:

"Oh, you mean them two fellers in Uncle Willy's store about half-past ten last night. Sure, I seen them. I naturally thought, taken for granted it was Uncle Willy and Skeets. So I . . ."

"So you what?" Mr Hampton said.

"I . . . stepped back inside and . . . taken up the evening paper," Grover Cleveland said. "Yes, that's where I was: setting right there in the station reading the Memphis evening paper. . . ."

"When Whit Rouncewell saw them two fellers in here, he went back to the station looking for you," Mr Hampton said. "He waited an hour. By that time the lights were off in here, but he never saw anybody come out the front door. And you never showed up. And Walter there says you never showed up at the Blue Goose either. Where were you last night, Grover?"

So now there wasn't anywhere for him to go. He just stood there with his coat-tail hiked up over the handle of his pistol and blackjack like a little boy's shirt-tail coming out. Maybe that's what it was: Grover Cleveland was too old to look like a boy. And Uncle Willy and Mr Hampton and all the rest of us looking at him until all of a sudden we were all ashamed to look at him any more, ashamed to have to find out what we were going to find out. Except that Mr Hampton wasn't ashamed to. Maybe it was being sheriff so long had made him that way, learned him it wasn't Grover Cleveland you had to be ashamed of: it was all of us.

"One night Doc Peabody was coming back from a case about one o'clock and he saw you coming out of that alley side door to what Montgomery Ward Snopes calls his studio. Another night I was going home late myself, about midnight, and I saw you going into it. What's going on in there, Grover?"

Grover Cleveland didn't move now either. It was almost a whisper: "It's a club."

Now Mr Hampton and Uncle Gavin were looking at each other. "Don't look at me," Uncle Gavin said. "You're the law." That was the funny thing: neither one of them paid any attention to Mr Connors, who was the marshal and ought to have been attending to this already. Maybe that was why.

"You're the County Attorney," Mr Hampton said. "You're the one to say what the law is before I can be it."

"What are we waiting for then?" Uncle Gavin said.

"Maybe Grover wants to tell us what it is and save time," Mr Hampton said.

"No, dammit," Uncle Gavin said. "Take your foot off him for a minute anyway." He said to Grover Cleveland: "You go on back to the station until we need you."

"You can read the rest of that Memphis paper," Mr Hampton said. "And we won't want you either," he said to Mr Connors.

"Like hell, Sheriff," Mr Connors said. "Your jurisdiction's just the county. What goes on in Jefferson is my jurisdiction. I got as much right—" He stopped then, but it was already too late. Mr Hampton looked at him with the little hard pale eyes that never seemed to need to blink at all.

"Go on," Mr Hampton said. "Got as much right to see what Montgomery Ward Snopes has got hid as me and Gavin have. Why didn't you persuade Grover to take you into that club then?" But Mr Connors could still blink. "Come on," Mr Hampton said to Uncle Gavin, turning. Uncle Gavin moved too.

"That means you too," he said to me.

"That means all of you," Mr Hampton said. "All of you get out of Uncle Willy's way now. He's got to make a list of what's missing for the narcotics folks and the insurance too."

So we stood on the street and watched Mr Hampton and Uncle Gavin go on toward Montgomery Ward's studio. "What?" I said to Ratliff.

"I don't know," he said. "That is, I reckon I know. We'll have to wait for Hub and your uncle to prove it."

"What do you reckon it is?" I said.

Now he looked at me. "Let's see," he said. "Even if you are nine going on ten, I reckon you still ain't outgrowed ice cream, have you. Come on. We won't bother Uncle Willy and Skeets now neither. We'll go to the Dixie Café." So we went to the Dixie Café and got two cones and stood on the street again.

"What?" I said.

"My guess is, it's a passel of French postcards Montgomery Ward brought back from the war in Paris. I reckon you don't know what that is, do you?"

"I don't know," I said.

"It's pictures of men and women together, experimenting with one another. Without no clothes on much." I don't know whether he was looking at me or not. "Do you know now?"

"I don't know," I said.

"But maybe you do?" he said.

That's what it was. Uncle Gavin said he had a big album of them, and that he had learned enough about photography to have made slides from some of them so he could throw them magnified on a sheet on the wall with a magic lantern in that back room. And he said how Montgomery Ward stood there laughing at him and Mr Hampton both. But he was talking mostly to Uncle Gavin.

"Oh, sure," he said. "I don't expect Hub here—"

"Call me Mister Hampton," Mr Hampton said.

"—to know any better—"

"Call me Mister Hampton, boy," Mr Hampton said.

"Mister Hampton," Montgomery Ward said. "—but you're a lawyer; you don't think I got into this without reading a little law first myself, do you? You can confiscate these—all you'll find here; I don't guess Mister Hampton will let a little thing like law stop him from that—"

That was when Mr Hampton slapped him. "Stop it, Hub!" Uncle Gavin said. "You damned fool!"

"Let him go ahead," Montgomery Ward said. "Suing his bondsmen is easier than running a magic lantern. Safer too. Where was I? Oh yes. Even if they had been sent through the mail, which they haven't, that would just be a federal charge, and I don't see any federal dicks around here. And even if you tried to cook up a charge that I've been making money out of them, where are your witnesses? All you got is Grover Winbush, and he don't dare testify, not because he will lose his job because he'll probably do that anyway, but because the God-fearing Christian holy citizens of Jefferson won't let him because they can't have it known that this is what their police do when they're supposed to be at work. Let alone the rest of my customers, not to mention any names scattered around in banks and stores and gins and filling stations and farms too two counties wide in either direction—sure; I just thought of this too: come on, put a fine on me and see how quick it will be paid . . ." and stopped and said with a kind of hushed amazement : "Sweet Christ." He was talking fast now: "Come on, lock me up, give me a thousand stamped envelopes and I'll make more money in three days than I made in the whole two years with that damned magic lantern." Now he was talking to Mr Hampton: "Maybe that's what you wanted, to begin with: not the postcards but the list of customers; retire from sheriff and spend all your time on the collections. Or no: keep the star to bring pressure on the slow payers—"

Only this time Uncle Gavin didn't have to say anything because this time Mr Hampton wasn't going to hit him. He just stood there with his little hard eyes shut until Montgomery Ward stopped. Then he said to Uncle Gavin:

"Is that right? We've got to have a federal officer? There's nothing on our books to touch him with? Come on, think. Nothing on the city books even?" Now it was Uncle Gavin who said By God.

"That automobile law," he said. "That Sartoris law," while Mr Hampton stood looking at him. "Hanging right there in that frame on the wall by our own office door? Didn't you ever look at it? That you can't drive an automobile on the streets of Jefferson—"

"What?" Montgomery Ward said.

"Louder," Uncle Gavin said. "Mr Hampton can't hear you."

"But that's just inside the city!" Montgomery Ward said. "Hampton's just County Sheriff; he can't make an arrest on just a city charge."

"So you say," Mr Hampton said; now he did put his hand on Montgomery Ward's shoulder; Uncle Gavin said if he had been Montgomery Ward, he'd just as soon Mr Hampton had slapped him again. "Tell your own lawyer, not ours."

"Wait!" Montgomery Ward said to Uncle Gavin. "You own a car too! So does Hampton!"

"We're doing this alphabetically," Uncle Gavin said. "We've passed the H's. We're in S now, and S-n comes before S-t. Take him on, Hub."

So Montgomery Ward didn't have anywhere to go then, he had run completely out; he just stood there now and Uncle Gavin watched Mr Hampton take his hand off Montgomery Ward and pick up the album of pictures and the envelopes that held the rest of them and carry them to the sink where Montgomery Ward really would develop a film now and then, and tumble them in and then start hunting among the bottles and cans of developer stuff on the shelf above it.

"What are you looking for?" Uncle Gavin said.

"Alcohol—coal oil—anything that'll burn," Mr Hampton said.

"Burn?" Montgomery Ward said. "Hell, man, those things are valuable. Look, I'll make a deal: give them back to me and I'll get to hell out of your damned town and it'll never see me again. —All right," he said. "I've got close to a hundred bucks in my pocket. I'll lay it on the table here and you and Stevens turn your backs and give me ten minutes—"

"Do you want to come back and hit him again?" Uncle Gavin said. "Don't mind me. Besides, he's already suggested we turn our backs so all you'll have to do is just swing your arm." But Mr Hampton just took another bottle down and took out the stopper and smelled. "You can't do that," Uncle Gavin said. "They're evidence."

"All we need is just one," Mr Hampton said.

"That depends," Uncle Gavin said. "Do you just want to convict him, or do you want to exterminate him?" Mr Hampton stopped, the bottle in one hand and the stopper in the other. "You know what Judge Long will do to the man that just owns one of these pictures." Judge Long was the Federal Judge of our district. "Think what he'll do to the man that owns a wheelbarrow full of them."

So Mr Hampton put the bottle back and after a while a deputy came with a suitcase and they put the album and the envelopes into it and locked it and Mr Hampton locked the suitcase in his safe to turn over to Mr Gombault, the U.S. marshal, when he got back to town, and they locked Montgomery Ward up in the county jail for operating an automobile contrary to law in the city of Jefferson, with Montgomery Ward cussing a while then threatening a while then trying again to bribe anybody connected with the jail or the town that would take the money. And we wondered how long it would be before he sent for Mr de Spain because of that connection. Because we knew that the last person on earth he would hope for help from would be his uncle or cousin Flem, who had already got shut of one Snopes through a murder charge so why should he balk at getting rid of another one with just a dirty postcard.

So even Uncle Gavin, that Ratliff said made a kind of religion of never letting Jefferson see that a Snopes had surprised him, didn't expect Mr Flem that afternoon when he walked into the office and laid his new black hat on the corner of the desk and sat there with the joints of his jaws working faint and steady like he was trying to chew without unclamping his teeth. You couldn't see behind Mr Hampton's eyes because they looked at you too hard; you couldn't pass them like you couldn't pass a horse in a lane that wasn't big enough for a horse and a man both but just for the horse. You couldn't see behind Mr Snopes's eyes because they were not really looking at you at all, like a pond of stagnant water is not looking at you. Uncle Gavin said that was why it took him a minute or two to realise that he and Mr Snopes were looking at exactly the same thing: it just wasn't with the same eye.

"I'm thinking of Jefferson," Mr Snopes said.

"So am I," Uncle Gavin said. "Of that damned Grover Winbush and every other arrested adolescent between fourteen and fifty-eight in half of north Mississippi with twenty-five cents to pay for one look inside that album."

"I forgot about Grover Winbush," Mr Snopes said. "He won't only lose his job, but when he does folks will want to know why and this whole business will come out." That was Mr Snopes's trouble. I mean, that was our trouble with Mr Snopes: there wasn't anything to see even when you thought he might be looking at you. "I don't know whether you know it or not. His ma lives out at Whiteleaf. He sends her a dollar's worth of furnish by the mail rider every Saturday morning."

"So to save one is to save both," Uncle Gavin said. "If Grover

Winbush's mother is to keep on getting that dollar's worth of fatback and molasses every Saturday morning, somebody will have to save your cousin, nephew—which is he, anyway?—too."

Like Ratliff said, Mr Snopes probably missed a lot folks said to him behind his back, but he never missed what folks didn't say to him to his face. Anyway, irony and sarcasm was not one of them. Or anyway it wasn't this time. "That's how I figgered it," he said. "But you're a lawyer. Your business is to know how to figger different."

Uncle Gavin didn't miss much of what wasn't quite said to his face either. "You've come to the wrong lawyer," he said. "This case is in federal court. Besides, I couldn't take it anyway; I draw a monthly salary to already be on the other side. Besides," he said (while he was just City Attorney he talked Harvard and Heidelberg. But after that summer he and I spent travelling about the county running for County Attorney, he began to talk like the people he would lean on fences or squat against the walls of country stores with, saying "drug" for "dragged" and "me and you" instead of "you and I" just like they did, even saying figgered just like Mr Snopes just said it), "let's you and me get together on this. I want him to go to the penitentiary."

And that's when Uncle Gavin found out that he and Mr Snopes were looking at exactly the same thing: they were just standing in different places, because Mr Snopes said, as quick and calm as Uncle Gavin himself: "So do I." Because Montgomery Ward was his rival just like Wallstreet was, both of them alike in that there just wasn't room in Jefferson for either one of them and Mr Snopes too. Because according to Ratliff, Uncle Gavin was missing it. "So do I," Mr Snopes said. "But not this way. I'm thinking of Jefferson."

"Then it's just too bad for Jefferson," Uncle Gavin said. "He will get Judge Long, and when Judge Long sees even one of those pictures, let alone a suitcase full of them, I will almost feel sorry even for Montgomery Ward. Have you forgotten about Wilbur Provine last year?"

Wilbur Provine lived in Frenchman's Bend too. Ratliff said he was really a Snopes; that when Providence realised that Eck Snopes was going to fail his lineage and tradition, it hunted around quick and produced Wilbur Provine to plug the gap. He ran a still in the creek bottom by a spring about a mile and a half from his house, with a path worn smooth as a ribbon and six inches deep from his back door to the spring where he had walked it twice a day for two years until they caught him and took him to federal court before Judge Long, looking as surprised and innocent as if he didn't even know what the word "still" meant while the lawyer questioned him, saying No, he never had any idea there was a still within ten miles, let alone a path leading from his back door to it because he himself hadn't been in that creek bottom in ten years, not even to hunt and fish since he was a Christian and he believed that no Christian should destroy God's creatures, and he had burned out on fish when he was eight years old and hadn't been able to eat it since.

Until Judge Long himself asked him how he accounted for that path, and Wilbur blinked at Judge Long once or twice and said he didn't have any idea, unless maybe his wife had worn it toting water from the spring; and Judge Long (he had the right name, he was six and a half feet tall and his nose looked almost a sixth of that) leaning down across the bench with his spectacles at the end of his nose, looking down at Wilbur for a while, until he said: "I'm going to send you to the penitentiary, not for making whiskey but for letting your wife carry water a mile and a half from that spring." That was who Montgomery Ward would get when he came up for trial and you would have thought that everybody in Yoknapatawpha County, let alone just Jefferson, had heard the story by now. But you would almost thought Mr Snopes hadn't. Because now even the hinges of his jaws had quit that little faint pumping.

"I heard Judge Long gave him five years," he said. "Maybe them extra four years was for the path."

"Maybe," Uncle Gavin said.

"It was five years, wasn't it?" Mr Snopes said.

"That's right," Uncle Gavin said.

"Send that boy out," Mr Snopes said.

"No," Uncle Gavin said.

Now the hinges of Mr Snopes's jaws were pumping again. "Send him out," he said.

"I'm thinking of Jefferson too," Uncle Gavin said. "You're vice-president of Colonel Sartoris's bank. I'm even thinking of you."

"Much obliged," Mr Snopes said. He wasn't looking at anything. He didn't waste any time, but he wasn't hurrying either: he just got up and took the new black hat from the desk and put it on and went to the door and opened it and didn't quite stop even then, just kind of changing feet to step around the opening door and said, not to anybody any more than he had ever been looking at anybody: "Good-day," and went out and closed the door behind him.

Then I said, "What—" and then stopped, Uncle Gavin and I both watching the door as it opened again, or began to, opening about a foot with no sound beyond it until we saw Ratliff's cheek and one of his eyes, then Ratliff came in, eased in, sidled in, still not making any sound.

"Am I too late, or jest too soon?" he said.

"Neither," Uncle Gavin said. "He stopped, decided not to. Something happened. The pattern went wrong. It started out all regular. You know: this is not just for me, and least of all for my kinsman. Do you know what he said?"

"How can I yet?" Ratliff said. "That's what I'm doing now."

"I said, 'You and I should get together. I want him to go to the penitentiary.' And he said, 'So do I.'"

"All right," Ratliff said. "Go on."

"'—not for me, my kinsman,'" Uncle Gavin said. "'For Jefferson.' So the next step should have been the threat. Only he didn't—"

"Why threat?" Ratliff said.

"The pattern," Uncle Gavin said. "First the soap, then the threat, then the bribe. As Montgomery Ward himself tried it."

"This ain't Montgomery Ward," Ratliff said. "If Montgomery Ward had been named Flem, them pictures wouldn't a never seen Jefferson, let alone vice versa. But we don't need to worry about Flem being smarter than Montgomery Ward; most anybody around here is that. What we got to worry about is, who else around here may not be as smart as him too. Then what?"

"He quit," Uncle Gavin said. "He came right up to it. He even asked me to send Chick out. And when I said No, he just picked up his hat and said Much obliged and went out as if he had just stopped in here to borrow a match."

Ratliff blinked at Uncle Gavin. "So he wants Montgomery

Ward to go to the penitentiary. Only he don't want him to go under the conditions he's on his way there now. Then he changed his mind."

"Because of Chick," Uncle Gavin said.

"Then he changed his mind," Ratliff said.

"You're right," Uncle Gavin said. "It was because he knew that by refusing to send Chick out I had already refused to be bribed."

"No," Ratliff said. "To Flem Snopes, there ain't a man breathing that can't be bought for something; all you need to do is jest to find it. Only, why did he change his mind?"

"All right," Uncle Gavin said. "Why?"

"What was the conversation about jest before he told you to send Chick out?"

"About the penitentiary," Uncle Gavin said. "I just told you."

"It was about Wilbur Provine," I said.

Ratliff looked at me. "Wilbur Provine?"

"His still," I said. "That path and Judge Long."

"Oh," Ratliff said. "Then what?"

"That's all," Uncle Gavin said. "He just said 'Send that boy out,' and I said—"

"That wasn't next," I said. "The next was what Mr Snopes said about the five years, that maybe the extra four years was for the path, and you said Maybe and Mr Snopes said again, 'It was five years, wasn't it?' and you said Yes and then he said to send me out."

"All right, all right," Uncle Gavin said. But he was looking at Ratliff. "Well?" he said.

"I don't know neither," Ratliff said. "All I know is, I'm glad I ain't Montgomery Ward Snopes."

"Yes," Uncle Gavin said. "When Judge Long sees that suitcase."

"Sho," Ratliff said. "That's jest Uncle Sam. It's his Uncle Flem that Montgomery Ward wants to worry about, even if he don't know it yet. And us too. As long as all he wanted was jest money, at least you knowed which way to guess even if you knowed you couldn't guess first. But this time—" He looked at us, blinking.

"All right," Uncle Gavin said. "How?"

"You mind that story about how the feller found his strayed dog? He jest set down and imagined where he would be if he was that dog and got up and went and got it and brung it home. All right. We're Flem Snopes. We got a chance to get shut of our—what's that old-timey word? unsavoury—unsavoury nephew into the penitentiary. Only we're vice-president of a bank now and we can't afford to have it knowed even a unsavoury nephew was running a peep show of French postcards. And the judge that will send him there is the same judge that told Wilbur Provine he was going to Parchman not for making whiskey but for letting his wife tote water a mile and a half." He blinked at Uncle Gavin. "You're right. The question ain't 'what' a-tall: it's jest 'how'. And since you wasn't interested in money, and he has got better sense than to offer it to Hub Hampton, we don't jest know what that 'how' is going to be. Unless maybe since he got to be a up-and-coming feller in the Baptist church, he is depending on Providence."

Maybe he was. Anyway, it worked. It was the next morning, about ten o'clock; Uncle Gavin and I were just leaving the office to drive up to Wyott's Crossing, where they were having some kind of a squabble over a drainage tax suit, when Mr Hampton came in. He was kind of blowing through his teeth, light and easy like he was whistling except that he wasn't making any noise and even less than that of tune. "Morning," he said. "Yesterday morning when we were in that studio and I was hunting through them bottles on that shelf for alcohol or something that would burn."

"All right," Uncle Gavin said.

"How many of them bottles and jugs did I draw the cork or unscrew the cap and smell? You were there. You were watching."

"I thought all of them," Uncle Gavin said. "Why?"

"So did I," Mr Hampton said. "I could be wrong." He looked at Uncle Gavin with his hard little eyes, making that soundless whistling between his teeth.

"You've prepared us," Uncle Gavin said. "Got us into the right state of nervous excitement. Now tell us."

"About six this morning, Jack Crenshaw telephoned me." (Mr Crenshaw was the Revenue field agent that did the moonshine still hunting in our district.) "He told me to come on to that studio as soon as I could. They were already inside, two of them. They had already searched it. Two of them gallon jugs on that shelf that I opened and smelled yesterday that never had nothing but developer in them, had raw corn whiskey in them this morning, though like I said I could have been wrong and missed them. Not to mention five gallons more of it in a oil can setting behind the heater, that I hadn't got around to smelling yesterday when you stopped me for the reason that I never seen it there when I looked behind the heater yesterday or I wouldn't been smelling at the bottles on that shelf for something to burn paper with. Though, as you say, I could be wrong."

"As *you* say," Uncle Gavin said.

"You may be right," Mr Hampton said. "After all, I've been having to snuff out moonshine whiskey in this country ever since I first got elected. And since 1919 I have been so in practice that now I don't even need to smell: I just kind of feel it the moment I get where some of it ain't supposed to be. Not to mention that five-gallon coal oil can full of it setting where you would have thought I would have fell over it reaching my hand to that shelf."

"All right," Uncle Gavin said. "Go on."

"That's all," Mr Hampton said.

"How did he get in?" Uncle Gavin said.

"He?" Mr Hampton said.

"All right," Uncle Gavin said. "Take 'they' if you like it better."

"I thought of that too," Mr Hampton said. "The key. I said *the* key because even that fool would have more sense than to have a key to that place anywhere except on a string around his neck."

"That one," Uncle Gavin said.

"Yep," Mr Hampton said. "I dropped it into the drawer where I usually keep such, handcuffs and a extra pistol. Anybody could have come in while me and Miss Elma" (she was the office deputy, widow of the sheriff Mr Hampton had succeeded last time) "was out, and taken it."

"Or the pistol either," Uncle Gavin said. "You really should start locking that place, Hub. Some day you'll leave your star in there and come back to find some little boy out on the street arresting people."

"Maybe I should," Mr Hampton said. "All right," he said. "Somebody took that key and planted that whiskey. It could have been any of them—any of the folks that that damned

Grover Winbush says was coming from four counties around to sweat over them damn pictures at night."

"Maybe it's lucky you at least had that suitcase locked up. I suppose you've still got that, since Mr Gombault hasn't got back yet?"

"That's right," Mr Hampton said.

"And Jack Crenshaw and his buddy are just interested in whiskey, not photography. Which means you haven't turned that suitcase over to anybody yet."

"That's right," Mr Hampton said.

"Are you going to?" Uncle Gavin said.

"What do you think?" Mr Hampton said.

"That's what I think too," Uncle Gavin said.

"After all, the whiskey is enough," Mr Hampton said. "And even if it ain't, all we got to do is show Judge Long just any one of them photographs right before he pronounces sentence. Damn it," he said. "it's Jefferson. We live here. Jefferson's got to come first, even before the pleasure of crucifying that damned—"

"Yes," Uncle Gavin said. "I've heard that sentiment." Then Mr Hampton left. And all we had to do was just to wait, and not long. You never had to wonder about how much Ratliff had heard because you knew in advance he had heard all of it. He closed the door and stood just inside it.

"Why didn't you tell him yesterday about Flem Snopes?" he said.

"Because he let Flem Snopes or whoever it was walk right in his office and steal that key. Hub's already got about all the felonious malfeasance he can afford to compound," Uncle Gavin said. He finished putting the papers into the briefcase and closed it and stood up.

"You leaving?" Ratliff said.

"Yes," Uncle Gavin said. "Wyott's Crossing."

"You ain't going to wait for Flem?"

"He won't come back here," Uncle Gavin said. "He won't dare. What he came here yesterday to try to bribe me to do is going to happen anyway without the bribe. But he don't dare come back here to find out. He will have to wait and see like anybody else. He knows that." But still Ratliff didn't move from the door.

"The trouble with us is, we don't never estimate Flem Snopes right. At first we made the mistake of not estimating him a-tall. Then we made the mistake of overestimating him. Now we're fixing to make the mistake of underestimating him again. When you jest want money, all you need to do to satisfy yourself is count it and put it where can't nobody get it, and forget about it. But this-here new thing he has done found out it's nice to have, is different. It's like keeping warm in winter or cool in summer, or peace or being free or contentment. You can't jest count it and lock it up somewhere safe and forget about it until you feel like looking at it again. You got to work at it steady, never to forget about it. It's got to be out in the open, where folks can see it, or there ain't no such thing."

"No such thing as what?" Uncle Gavin said.

"This-here new discovery he's jest made," Ratliff said. "Call it civic virtue."

"Why not?" Uncle Gavin said. "Were you going to call it something else?" Ratliff watched Uncle Gavin, curious, intent; it was as if he were waiting for something. "Go on," Uncle Gavin said. "You were saying."

Then it was gone, whatever it had been. "Oh yes," Ratliff said. "He'll be in to see you. He'll have to, to make sho you recognise it when you see it. He may kind of hang around until middle of the afternoon, to kind of give the dust a chance to settle. But he'll be back then, so a feller can at least see jest how much he missed heading him off."

So we didn't drive up to Wyott's then, and this time Ratliff was the one who underestimated. It wasn't a half an hour until we heard his feet on the stairs and the door opened and he came in. This time he didn't take off the black hat: he just said "Morning, gentlemen" and came on to the desk and dropped the key to Montgomery Ward's studio on it and was going back toward the door when Uncle Gavin said:

"Much obliged. I'll give it back to the sheriff. You're like me," he said. "You don't give a damn about truth either. What you are interested in is justice."

"I'm interested in Jefferson," Mr Snopes said, reaching for the door and opening it. "We got to live here. Morning, gentlemen."

11

V. K. RATLIFF

AND still he missed it, even set—sitting right there in his own office and actively watching Flem rid Jefferson of Montgomery Ward. And still I couldn't tell him.

12

CHARLES MALLISON

WHATEVER it was Ratliff thought Mr Snopes wanted, I don't reckon that what Uncle Gavin took up next helped it much either. And this time he didn't even have Miss Melisandre Backus for Mother to blame it on because Miss Melisandre herself was married now, to a man, a stranger, that everybody but Miss Melisandre (we never did know whether her father, sitting all day long out there on that front gallery with a glass of whiskey-and-water in one hand and Horace or Virgil in the other—a combination which Uncle Gavin said would have insulated from the reality of rural north Mississippi harder heads than his—knew or not) knew was a big rich New Orleans bootlegger. In fact, she still refused to believe it even when they brought him home with a bullet hole neatly plugged up in the middle of his forehead, in a bullet-proof hearse leading a cortege of Packards and Cadillac limousines that Hollywood itself, let alone Al Capone, wouldn't have been ashamed of.

No, that's wrong. We never did know whether she knew it or not too, even years after he was dead and she had all the money and the two children and the place which in her childhood had been just another Mississippi cotton farm but which he had changed with white fences and weather-vanes in the shape of horses so that it looked like a cross between a Kentucky country club and a Long Island race track, and plenty of friends who felt they owed it to her that she should know where all that money actually came from; and still, as soon as they approached the subject, she would change it—the slender dark girl still, even though she was a millionairess and the mother of two children, whose terrible power was that defencelessness and helplessness which conferred knighthood on any man who came within range, before he had a chance to turn and flee—changing the entire subject as if she had never heard her husband's name or, in fact, as though he had never lived.

I mean, this time Mother couldn't even say "If he would only marry Melisandre Backus, she would save him from all this," meaning Linda Snopes this time like she had meant Mrs Flem Snopes before. But at least she thought about saying it because almost at once she stopped worrying. "It's all right," she told Father. "It's the same thing again: don't you remember? He never was really interested in Melisandre. I mean . . . you know: really interested. Books and flowers. Picking my jonquils and narcissus as fast as they bloomed, to send out there where that whole two-acre front yard was full of jonquils, cutting my best roses to take out there and sit in that hammock reading poetry to her. He was just forming her mind: that's all he wanted. And Melisandre was only five years younger, where with this one he is twice her age, practically her grandfather. Of course that's all it is."

Then Father said: "Heh heh heh. Form is right, only it's on Gavin's mind, not hers. It would be on mine too if I wasn't already married and scared to look. Did you ever take a look at her? You're human even if you are a woman." Yes, I could remember a heap of times when Father had been born too soon, before they thought of wolf whistles.

"Stop it," Mother said.

"But after all," Father said, "maybe Gavin should be saved from those sixteen-year-old clutches. Suppose you speak to him; tell him I am willing to make a sacrifice of myself on the family altar—"

"Stop it! Stop it!" Mother said. "Can't you at least be funny?"

"I'm worse than that, I'm serious," Father said. "They were at a table in Christian's yesterday afternoon. Gavin just had a saucer of ice cream, but she was eating something in a dish that must have set him back twenty or thirty cents. So maybe Gavin knows what he's doing after all; she's got some looks of her own, but she still ain't quite up with her mother: you know—" using both hands to make a kind of undulating hourglass shape in the air in front of him while Mother stood watching him like a snake. "Maybe he's concentrating on just forming her form first you might say, without bothering too much yet about her mind. And who knows? Maybe some day she'll even look at him like she was looking at that banana split or whatever it was when Skeets McGowan set it down in front of her."

But by that time Mother was gone. And this time she sure needed somebody like Miss Melisandre, with all her friends (all Jefferson for that matter) on the watch to tell her whenever Uncle Gavin and Linda stopped in Christian's drugstore after school while Linda ate another banana split or ice-cream soda, with the last book of poetry Uncle Gavin had ordered for her lying in the melted ice cream or spilled Coca-Cola on the marble table-top. Because I reckon Jefferson was too small for a thirty-five-year-old bachelor, even a Harvard M.A. and a Ph.D. from Heidelberg and his hair already beginning to turn white even at just twenty-five, to eat ice cream and read poetry with a sixteen-year-old high-school girl. Though if it had to happen, maybe thirty-five was the best age for a bachelor to buy ice cream and poetry for a sixteen-year-old girl. I told Mother that. She didn't sound like a snake because snakes can't talk. But if dentist's drills could talk, she would have sounded just like one.

"There's no best or safe age for a bachelor anywhere between three and eighty to buy ice cream for a sixteen-year-old girl," she said. "Forming her mind," she said. But she sounded just like cream when she talked to Uncle Gavin. No: she didn't sound like anything because she didn't say anything. She waited for him to begin it. No: she just waited because she knew he would have to begin it. Because Jefferson was that small. No, I mean Uncle Gavin had lived in Jefferson or in little towns all his life, so he not only knew what Jefferson would be saying about him and Linda Snopes and those banana splits and ice-cream sodas and books of poetry by now, but that Mother had too many good friends to ever miss hearing about it.

So she just waited. It was Saturday. Uncle Gavin walked twice in and out of the office (we still called it that because Grandfather had, except when Mother could hear us. Though after a while even she stopped trying to call it the library) where Mother was sitting at the desk adding up something, maybe the laundry; he walked in and out twice, and she never moved. Then he said:

"I was thinking——" Because they were like that. I mean, I thought the reason they were like that was because they were twins. I mean, I assumed that because I didn't know any other twins to measure them against. She didn't even stop adding.

"Of course," she said. "Why not tomorrow?" So he could have

gone out then, since obviously both of them knew what the other was talking about. But he said:

"Thank you." Then he said to me: "Ain't Aleck Sander waiting for you outside?"

"Fiddlesticks," Mother said. "Anything he will learn about sixteen-year-old girls from you will probably be a good deal more innocent than what he will learn some day from sixteen-year-old girls. Shall I telephone her mother and ask her to let her come for dinner tomorrow, or do you want to?"

"Thank you," Uncle Gavin said. "Do you want me to tell you about it?"

"Do you want to?" Mother said.

"Maybe I'd better," Uncle Gavin said.

"Do you have to?" Mother said. This time Uncle Gavin didn't say anything. Then Mother said: "All right. We're listening." Again Uncle Gavin didn't say anything. But now he was Uncle Gavin again. I mean, until now he sounded a good deal like I sounded sometimes. But now he stood looking at the back of Mother's head, with his shock of white hair that always needed cutting and the stained bitt of the corncob pipe sticking out of his breast pocket and the eyes and the face that you never did quite know what they were going to say next except that when you heard it you realised it was always true, only a little cranksided that nobody else would have said it quite that way.

"Well, well," he said, "if that's what a mind with no more aptitude for gossip and dirt than yours is inventing and thinking, just imagine what the rest of Jefferson, the experts, have made of it by now. By Cicero, it makes me feel young already; when I go to town this morning I believe I will buy myself a red necktie." He looked at the back of Mother's head. "Thank you, Maggie," he said. "It will need all of us of good will. To save Jefferson from Snopeses is a crisis, an emergency, a duty. To save a Snopes from Snopeses is a privilege, an honour, a pride."

"Especially a sixteen-year-old female one," Mother said.

"Yes," Uncle Gavin said. "Do you deny it?"

"Have I tried to?" Mother said.

"Yes, you have tried." He moved quick and put his hand on the top of her head, still talking. "And bless you for it. Tried always to deny that damned female instinct for uxorious and

rigid respectability which is the backbone of any culture not yet
decadent, which remains strong and undecadent only so long
as it still produces an incorrigible unreconstructible with the
temerity to assail and affront and deny it—like you—" and for
a second both of us thought he was going to bend down and kiss
her; maybe all three of us thought it. Then he didn't, or anyway
Mother said:

"Stop it. Let me alone. Make up your mind: do you want me
to telephone her, or will you do it?"

"I'll do it," he said. He looked at me. "Two red ties: one for
you. I wish you were sixteen too. What she needs is a beau."

"Then if by being sixteen I'd have to be her beau, I'm glad
I'm not sixteen," I said. "She's already got a beau. Matt Levitt.
He won the Golden Gloves up in Ohio or somewhere last year.
He acts like he can still use them. Would like to, too. No, much
obliged," I said.

"What's that?" Mother said.

"Nothing," Uncle Gavin said.

"You never saw him box then," I said. "Or you wouldn't call
him nothing. I saw him once. With Preacher Birdsong."

"And just which of your sporting friends is Preacher Birdsong?" Mother said.

"He ain't sporting," I said. "He lives out in the country. He
learned to box in France in the war. He and Matt Levitt—"

"Let me," Uncle Gavin said. "He—"

"Which he?" Mother said. "Your rival?"

"—is from Ohio," Uncle Gavin said. "He graduated from that
new Ford mechanics' school and the company sent him here to
be a mechanic in the agency garage—"

"He's the one that owns that yellow cut-down racer," I said.

"And Linda rides in it?" Mother said.

"—and since Jefferson is not that large and he has two eyes,"
Uncle Gavin said, "sooner or later he saw Linda Snopes, probably somewhere between her home and the school house; being
male and about twenty-one, he naturally lost no time in making
her acquaintance; the Golden Gloves reputation which he either
really brought with him or invented somewhere en route has
apparently eliminated what rivals he might have expected—"

"Except you," Mother said.

"That's all," Uncle Gavin said.

"Except you," Mother said.

"He's maybe five years her senior," Uncle Gavin said. "I'm twice her age."

"Except you," Mother said. "I don't think you will live long enough to ever be twice any woman's age, I don't care what it is."

"All right," Uncle Gavin said. "What was it I just said? To save Jefferson from a Snopes is a duty; to save a Snopes from a Snopes is a privilege."

"An honour, you said," Mother said. "A pride."

"All right," Uncle Gavin said. "A joy then. Are you pleased now?" That was all then. After a while Father came home, but Mother didn't have much to tell him he didn't already know, so there wasn't anything for him to do except to keep on needing the wolf whistle that hadn't been invented yet; not until the next day after dinner in fact.

She arrived a little after twelve, just about when she could have got here after church if she had been to church. Which maybe she had, since she was wearing a hat. Or maybe it was her mother who made her wear the hat on account of Mother, coming up the street from the corner, running. Then I saw that the hat was a little awry on her head, as if something had pulled or jerked at it or it had caught on something in passing, and that she was holding one shoulder with the other hand. Then I saw that her face was mad. It was scared too, but right now it was mostly just mad as she turned in the gate, still holding her shoulder but not running now, just walking fast and hard, the mad look beginning to give way to the scared one. Then they both froze into something completely different because then the car passed, coming up fast from the corner—Matt Levitt's racer because there were other stripped-down racers around now, but his was the only one with that big double-barrel brass horn on the hood that played two notes when he pressed the button, going past fast; and suddenly it was like I had smelled something, caught a whiff of something for a second that even if I located it again I still wouldn't know whether I had ever smelled it before or not; the racer going on and Linda still walking rigid and fast with her hat on a little crooked and still holding her shoulder and still breathing a little fast even if what was on her face now was mostly being

F

scared, on to the gallery where Mother and Uncle Gavin were waiting.

"Good-morning, Linda," Mother said. "You've torn your sleeve."

"It caught on a nail," Linda said.

"I can see," Mother said. "Come on up to my room and slip it off and I'll tack it back for you."

"It's all right," Linda said. "If you've just got a pin."

"Then you take the needle and do it yourself while I see about dinner," Mother said. "You can sew, can't you?"

"Yessum," Linda said. So they went up to Mother's room and Uncle Gavin and I went to the office so Father could say to Uncle Gavin:

"Somebody been mauling at her before she could even get here? What's the matter, boy? Where's your spear and sword? Where's your white horse?" Because Matt didn't blow the two-toned horn when he passed that first time so none of us knew yet what Linda was listening for, sitting at the dinner table with the shoulder of her dress sewed back all right but looking like somebody about ten years old had done it and her face still looking rigid and scared. Because we didn't realise it then. I mean, that she was having to do so many things at once: having to look like she was enjoying her dinner and having to remember her manners in a strange house and with folks that she didn't have any particular reason to think were going to like her, and still having to wonder what Matt Levitt would do next without letting anybody know that's what was mainly on her mind. I mean, having to expect what was going to happen next and then, even while it was happening, having to look like she was eating and saying Yessum and Nome to what Mother was saying, and that cut-down racer going past in the street again with that two-toned horn blowing this time, blowing all the way past the house, and Father suddenly jerking his head up and making a loud snuffing noise, saying, "What's that I smell?"

"Smell?" Mother said. "Smell what?"

"That," Father said. "Something we haven't smelled around here in . . . how long was it, Gavin?" Because I knew now what Father meant, even if I wasn't born then and Cousin Gowan just told me. And Mother knew too. I mean, she remembered, since she had heard the other one when it was Mr de Spain's cut-out. I mean, even if she didn't know enough to connect that two-toned horn with Matt Levitt, all she had to do was look at Linda and Uncle Gavin. Or maybe just Uncle Gavin's face was enough, which is what you get for being twins with anybody. Because she said,

"Charley," and Father said:

"Maybe Miss Snopes will excuse me this time." He was talking at Linda now. "You see, whenever we have a pretty girl to eat with us, the prettier she is, the harder I try to make jokes so they will want to come back again. This time I just tried too hard. So if Miss Snopes will forgive me for trying too hard to be funny, I'll forgive her for being too pretty."

"Good boy," Uncle Gavin said. "Even if that one wasn't on tiptoe, at least it didn't wear spikes like the joke did. Let's go out to the gallery where it's cool, Maggie."

"Let's," Mother said. Then we were all standing there in the hall, looking at Linda. It wasn't just being scared in her face now, of being a sixteen-year-old girl for the first time in the home of people that probably had already decided not to approve of her. I didn't know what it was. But Mother did, maybe because it was Mother she was looking at it with.

"I think it will be cooler in the parlour," Mother said. "Let's go there." But it was too late. We could hear the horn, not missing a note: da Da da Da da Da getting louder and louder then going past the house still not missing a note as it faded on, and Linda staring at Mother for just another second or two with the desperation. Because it—the desperation—went too; maybe it was something like despair for a moment, but then that was gone too and her face was just rigid again.

"I've got to go," she said. "I . . . excuse me, I've got . . ." Then at least she kind of got herself together. "Thank you for my dinner, Mrs Mallison," she said. "Thank you for my dinner, Mr Mallison. Thank you for my dinner, Mr Gavin," already moving toward the table where she had put the hat and her purse. But then I hadn't expected her to thank me for it.

"Let Gavin drive you home," Mother said. "Gavin—"

"No no," she said. "I don't—he don't—" Then she was gone, out the front door and down the walk toward the gate, almost running again, then through the gate and then she was running, desperate and calm, not looking back. Then she was gone.

"By Cicero, Gavin," Father said. "You're losing ground. Last time you at least picked out a Spanish-American War hero with an E.M.F. sportster. Now the best you can do is a Golden Gloves amateur with a home-made racer. Watch yourself, bud, or next time you'll have a boy scout defying you to mortal combat with a bicycle."

"What?" Mother said.

"What would you do," Father said, "if you were a twenty-one year-old garage mechanic who had to work until six p.m., and a white-headed old grandfather of a libertine was waylaying your girl on her way home from school every afternoon and tolling her into soda dens and plying her with ice cream? Because how could he know that all Gavin wants is just to form her mind?"

Only it wasn't every afternoon any more. It wasn't any afternoon at all. I don't know what happened, how it was done: whether she sent word to Uncle Gavin not to try to meet her after school or whether she came and went the back way where he wouldn't see her, or whether maybe she stopped going to school at all for a while. Because she was in high school and I was in grammar school so there was no reason for me to know whether she was still going to school or not.

Or whether she was still in Jefferson, for that matter. Because now and then I would see Matt Levitt in his racer after the garage closed in the afternoon, when Linda used to be with him, and now and then at night going to and from the picture show. But not any more now. He would be alone in the racer, or with another boy or man. But as far as I knew, Matt never saw her any more than Uncle Gavin did.

And you couldn't tell anything from Uncle Gavin. It used to be that on the way home from school I would see him and Linda inside Christian's drugstore eating ice cream, and when he or they saw me he would beckon me in and we would all have ice cream. But that—the fact that there was no longer any reason to look in Christian's when I passed—was the only difference in him. Then one day—it was Friday—he was sitting at the table inside waiting and watching to beckon me inside, and even though there was no second dish on the table I thought that

Linda had probably just stepped away for a moment, maybe to the perfume counter or the magazine rack, and even when I was inside and he said, "I'm having peach. What do you want?" I still expected Linda to step out from behind whatever for the moment concealed her.

"Strawberry," I said. On the table was the last book—it was John Donne—he had ordered for her.

"It will cost the same dime to mail it to her here in Jefferson that it would cost if she were in Memphis," he said. "Suppose I stand the ice cream and give you the dime and you take it by her house on the way home."

"All right," I said. When Mr Snopes first came to Jefferson he rented the house. Then he must have bought it because since he became vice-president of the bank they had begun to fix it up. It was painted now, and Mrs Snopes I reckon had had the wistaria arbour in the side yard fixed up and when I came through the gate Linda called me and I saw the hammock under the arbour. The wistaria was still in bloom and I remember how she looked with her black hair under it because her eyes were kind of the colour of wistaria and her dress almost exactly was: lying in the hammock reading and I thought *Uncle Gavin didn't need to send this book because she hasn't finished the other one yet.* Then I saw the rest of her school books on the ground beneath the hammock and that the one she was reading was geometry and I wondered if knowing she would rather study geometry than be out with him would make Matt Levitt feel much better than having her eat ice cream with Uncle Gavin.

So I gave her the book and went on home. That was Friday. The next day, Saturday, I went to the baseball game and then I came back to the office to walk home with Uncle Gavin. We heard the feet coming up the outside stairs, more than two of them, making a kind of scuffling sound, and we could hear hard breathing and something like whispering, then the door kind of banged open and Matt Levitt came in, quick and fast, holding something clamped under his arm, and shoved the door back shut against whoever was trying to follow him inside, holding the door shut with his braced knee until he fumbled at the knob until he found how to shoot the bolt and lock it. Then he turned. He was good-looking. He didn't have a humorous or happy look, he had what

Ratliff called a merry look, the merry look of a fellow that hadn't heard yet that they had invented doubt. But he didn't even look merry now and he took the book—it was the John Donne I had taken to Linda yesterday—and kind of shot it on to the desk so that the ripped and torn pages came scuttering and scattering out across the desk and some of them even on down to the floor.

"How do you like that?" Matt said, coming on around the desk where Uncle Gavin had stood up. "Don't you want to put up your dukes?" he said. "But that's right, you ain't much of a fighter, are you? But that's O.K.; I ain't going to hurt you much anyway: just mark you up a little to freshen up your memory." He didn't, he didn't seem to hit hard, his fists not travelling more than four or five inches it looked like, so that it didn't even look like they were drawing blood from Uncle Gavin's lips and nose but just instead wiping the blood on to them; two or maybe three blows before I could seem to move and grab up Grandfather's heavy walking stick where it still swayed in the umbrella stand behind the door and raise it to swing at the back of Matt's head as hard as I could.

"You, Chick!" Uncle Gavin said. "Stop! Hold it!" Though even with that, I wouldn't have thought Matt could have moved that fast. Maybe it was the Golden Gloves that did it. Anyway he turned and caught the stick and jerked it away from me almost before I knew it and naturally I thought he was going to hit me or Uncle Gavin or maybe both of us with it so I had already crouched to dive at his legs when he dropped the point of the stick like a bayoneted rifle, the point touching my chest just below the throat as if it were not holding me up but had really picked me up with the stick like you would a rag or a scrap of paper.

"Tough luck, kid," he said. "Nice going almost; too bad your uncle telegraphed it for you," and threw the stick into the corner and stepped around me toward the door, which was the first time I reckon that any of us realised that whoever it was he had locked out was still banging on it, and shot the bolt back and opened it, then stepped back himself as Linda came in, blazing; yes, that's exactly the word for it: blazing: and without even looking at Uncle Gavin or me, whirled on to her tiptoes and slapped Matt twice, first with her left hand and then the right, panting and crying at the same time:

"You fool! You ox! You clumsy ignorant ox! You clumsy ignorant stupid son of a bitch!" Which was the first time I ever heard a sixteen-year-old girl say that. No: the first time I ever heard any woman say that, standing there facing Matt and crying hard now, like she was too mad to even know what to do next, whether to slap him again or curse him again, until Uncle Gavin came around the desk and touched her and said,

"Stop it. Stop it now," and she turned and grabbed him, her face against his shirt where he had bled on to it, still crying hard, saying,

"Mister Gavin, Mister Gavin, Mister Gavin."

"Open the door, Chick," Uncle Gavin said. I opened it. "Get out of here, boy," Uncle Gavin said to Matt. "Go on." Then Matt was gone. I started to close the door. "You too," Uncle Gavin said.

"Sir?" I said.

"You get out too," Uncle Gavin said, still holding Linda where she was shaking and crying against him, his nose bleeding on to her too now.

13

GAVIN STEVENS

"Go on," I said. "You get out too." So he did, and I stood there holding her. Or rather, she was gripping me, quite hard, shuddering and gasping, crying quite hard now, burrowing her face into my shirt so that I could feel my shirt front getting wet. Which was what Ratliff would have called tit for tat, since what Victorians would have called the claret from my nose had already stained the shoulder of her dress. So I could free one hand long enough to reach around and over her other shoulder to the handkerchief in my breast pocket and do a little emergency work with it until I could separate us long enough to reach the cold-water tap.

"Stop it," I said. "Stop it now." But she only cried the harder, clutching me, saying,

"Mister Gavin. Mister Gavin. Oh, Mister Gavin."

"Linda," I said. "Can you hear me?" She didn't answer, just clutching me; I could feel her nodding her head against my chest. "Do you want to marry me?" I said.

"Yes!" she said. "Yes! All right! All right!"

This time I got one hand under her chin and lifted her face by force until she would have to look at me. Ratliff had told me that McCarron's eyes were grey, probably the same hard grey as Hub Hampton's. Hers were not grey at all. They were darkest hyacinth, what I have always imagined that Homer's hyacinthine sea must have had to look like.

"Listen to me," I said. "Do you want to get married?" Yes, they don't need minds at all, except for conversation, social intercourse. And I have known some who had charm and tact without minds even then. Because when they deal with men, with human beings, all they need is the instinct, the intuition before it became battered and dulled, the infinite capacity for devotion untroubled and unconfused by cold moralities and colder facts.

"You mean I don't have to?" she said.

"Of course not," I said. "Never if you like."

"I don't want to marry anybody!" she said, cried; she was clinging to me again, her face buried again in the damp mixture of blood and tears which seemed now to compose the front of my shirt and tie. "Not anybody!" she said. "You're all I have, all I can trust. I love you! I love you!"

14

CHARLES MALLISON

WHEN he got home, his face was clean. But his nose and his lip still showed, and there wasn't anything he could have done about his shirt and tie. Except he could have bought new ones, since on Saturday the stores were still open. But he didn't. Maybe even that wouldn't have made any difference with Mother; maybe that's one of the other things you have to accept in being a twin. And yes sir, if dentist's drills could talk, that's exactly what Mother would have sounded like after she got done laughing and crying both and saying Damn you, Gavin, damn you, damn you, and Uncle Gavin had gone upstairs to put on a clean shirt and tie for supper.

"Forming her mind," Mother said.

It was like he could stand just anything except getting knocked down or getting his nose bloodied. Like if Mr de Spain hadn't knocked him down in the alley behind that Christmas dance, he could have got over Mrs Snopes without having to form Linda's mind. And like if Matt Levitt hadn't come into the office that afternoon and bloodied his nose again, he could have stopped there with Linda's mind without having to do any more to it.

So he didn't stop because he couldn't. But at least he got rid of Matt Levitt. That was in the spring. It was her last year in high school; she would graduate in May and any school afternoon I could see her walking along the street from school with a few books under her arm. But if any of them was poetry now I didn't know it, because when she came to Christian's drugstore now she wouldn't even look toward the door, just walking on past with her face straight in front and her head up a little like the pointer just a step or two from freezing on the game; walking on like she saw people, saw Jefferson, saw the Square all right because at the moment, at any moment she had to walk on and among and through something and it might as well be Jefferson and Jefferson people and the Jefferson square as anything else, but that was all.

Because Uncle Gavin wasn't there somewhere around like an accident any more now. But then, if Uncle Gavin wasn't sitting on the opposite side of that marble-topped table in Christian's watching her eating something out of a tall glass that cost every bit of fifteen or twenty cents, Matt Levitt wasn't there either. Him and his cut-down racer both because the racer was empty now except for Matt himself after the garage closed on week-days, creeping along the streets and across the Square in low gear, parallelling but a little behind where she would be walking to the picture show now with another girl or maybe two or three of them, her head still high and not once looking at him while the racer crept along at her elbow almost, the cut-out going chuckle-chuckle-chuckle, right up to the picture show and the two or three or four girls had gone into it. Then the racer would dash off at full speed around the block, to come rushing back with the cut-out as loud as he could make it, up the alley beside the picture show and then across in front of it and around the block and up the alley again, this time with Otis Harker, who had succeeded Grover Cleveland Winbush as night marshal after Grover Cleveland retired after what Ratliff called his eye trouble, waiting at the corner yelling at Matt at the same time he was jumping far enough back not to be run over.

And on Sunday through the Square, the cut-out going full blast and Mr Buck Connors, the day marshal, hollering after him. And now he—Matt—had a girl with him, a country girl he had found somewhere, the racer rushing and roaring through the back streets into the last one, to rush slow and loud past Linda's house, as if the sole single symbol of frustrated love or anyway desire or maybe just frustration possible in Jefferson was an automobile cut-out; the sole single manifestation which love or anyway desire was capable of assuming in Jefferson, was rushing slow past the specific house with the cut-out wide open, so that he or she would have to know who was passing no matter how hard they worked at not looking out the window.

Though by that time Mr Connors had sent for the sheriff himself. He—Mr Connors—said his first idea was to wake up Otis Harker to come back to town and help him, but when Otis heard that what Mr Connors wanted was to stop that racer, Otis wouldn't even get out of bed. Later, afterward, somebody asked Matt if he would have run over Mr Hampton too and Matt said— he was crying then, he was so mad—"Hit him? Hub Hampton? Have all them god-damn guts splashed over my paint job?" Though by then even Mr Hampton wasn't needed for the cut-out because Matt went right on out of town, maybe taking the girl back home; anyway about midnight that night they telephoned in for Mr Hampton to send somebody out to Caledonia where Matt had had a bad fight with Anse McCallum, one of Mr Buddy McCallum's boys, until Anse snatched up a fence rail or something and would have killed Matt except that folks caught and held them both while they telephoned for the sheriff and brought them both in to town and locked them in the jail and the next morning Mr Buddy McCallum came in on his cork leg and paid them both out and took them down to the lot behind I.O. Snopes's mule barn and told Anse:

"All right. If you can't be licked fair without picking up a fence rail, I'm going to take my leg off and whip you with it myself."

So they fought again, without the fence rail this time, with Mr Buddy and a few more men watching them now, and Anse still wasn't as good as Matt's Golden Gloves, but he never quit until at last Mr Buddy himself said, "All right. That's enough," and told Anse to wash his face at the trough and then go and get in the car and then said to Matt: "And I reckon the time has come for you to be moving on too." Except that wasn't necessary now either; the garage said Matt was already fired and Matt said,

"Fired, hell. I quit. Tell that bastard to come down here and say that to my face." And Mr Hampton was there too by then, tall, with his big belly and his little hard eyes looking down at Matt. "Where the hell is my car?" Matt said.

"It's at my house," Mr Hampton said, "I had it brought in this morning."

"Well well," Matt said. "Too bad, ain't it? McCallum came in and sprung me before you had time to sell it and stick the money in your pocket, huh? What are you going to say when I walk over there and get in it and start the engine?"

"Nothing, son," Mr Hampton said. "Whenever you want to leave."

"Which is right now," Matt said. "And when I leave your ——ing town, my foot'll be right down to the floor board on that cut-out too. And you can stick that too, but not in your pocket. What do you think of that?"

"Nothing, son," Mr Hampton said. "I'll make a trade with you. Run that cut-out wide open all the way to the county line and then ten feet past it, and I won't let anybody bother you if you'll promise never to cross it again."

And that was all. That was Monday, trade day; it was like the whole county was there, had come to town just to stand quiet around the Square and watch Matt cross it for the last time, the paper suitcase he had come to Jefferson with on the seat by him and the cut-out clattering and popping; nobody waving good-bye to him and Matt not looking at any of us: just that quiet and silent suspension for the little gaudy car to rush slowly and loudly through, blatant and noisy and defiant yet at the same time looking as ephemeral and innocent and fragile as a child's toy, a birthday favour, so that looking at it you knew it would probably never get as far as Memphis, let alone Ohio; on across the Square and into the street which would become the Memphis highway at the edge of town, the sound of the cut-out banging and clattering and echoing between the walls, magnified a thousand times now beyond the mere size and bulk of the frail little machine which produced it; and we—some of us—thinking how surely now he would rush slow and roaring for the last time at least past Linda Snopes's house. But he didn't. He just went on, the little car going faster and faster up the broad street empty too for the moment as if it too had vacated itself for his passing, on past where the last houses of town would give way to country, the vernal space of woods and fields where even the defiant uproar of the cut-out would become puny and fade and be at last absorbed.

So that was what Father called—said to Uncle Gavin—one down. And now it was May and already everybody knew that Linda Snopes was going to be the year's number-one student, the class's valedictorian; Uncle Gavin slowed us as we approached Wildermark's and nudged us in to the window, saying, "That one. Just behind the green one."

It was a lady's fitted travelling-case.

"That's for travelling," Mother said.

"All right," Uncle Gavin said.

"For travelling," Mother said. "For going away."

"Yes," Uncle Gavin said. "She's got to get away from here. Get out of Jefferson."

"What's wrong with Jefferson?" Mother said. The three of us stood there. I could see our three reflections in the plate glass, standing there looking at the fitted feminine case. She didn't talk low or loud: just quiet. "All right," she said. "What's wrong with Linda then?"

Uncle Gavin didn't either. "I don't like waste," he said. "Everybody should have his chance not to waste."

"Or his chance to the right not to waste a young girl?" Mother said.

"All right," Uncle Gavin said. "I want her to be happy. Everybody should have the chance to be happy."

"Which she can't possibly do of course just standing still in Jefferson," Mother said.

"All right," Uncle Gavin said. They were not looking at one another. It was like they were not even talking to one another but simply at the two empty reflections in the plate glass, like when you put the written idea into the anonymous and even interchangeable empty envelope, or maybe into the sealed empty bottle to be cast into the sea, or maybe two written thoughts sealed forever at the same moment into two bottles and cast into the sea to float and drift with the tides and the currents on to the cooling world's end itself, still immune, still intact and inviolate, still ideas and still true and even still facts whether any eye ever saw them again or any other idea ever responded and sprang to them, to be elated or validated or grieved.

"The chance and duty and right to see that everybody is happy, whether they deserve it or not or even want it or not," Mother said.

"All right," Uncle Gavin said. "Sorry I bothered you. Come on. Let's go home. Mrs Rouncewell can send her a dozen sunflowers."

"Why not?" Mother said, taking his arm, already turning him, our three reflections turning in the plate glass, back toward the entrance and into the store, Mother in front now across to the luggage department.

"I think the blue one will suit her colouring, match her eyes," Mother said. "It's for Linda Snopes—her graduation," Mother told Miss Eunice Gant, the clerk.

"How nice," Miss Eunice said. "Is Linda going on a trip?"

"Oh yes," Mother said. "Very likely. At least probably to one of the Eastern girls' schools next year perhaps. Or so I heard."

"How nice," Miss Eunice said. "I always say that every young boy and girl should go away from home for at least one year of school in order to learn how the other half lives."

"How true," Mother said. "Until you do go and see, all you do is hope. Until you actually see for yourself, you never do give up and settle down, do you?"

"Maggie," Uncle Gavin said.

"Give up?" Miss Eunice said. "Give up hope? Young people should never give up hope."

"Of course not," Mother said. "They don't have to. All they have to do is stay young, no matter how long it takes."

"Maggie," Uncle Gavin said.

"Oh," Mother said, "you want to pay cash for it instead of charge? All right; I'm sure Mr Wildermark won't mind." So Uncle Gavin took two twenty-dollar bills from his wallet and took out one of his cards and gave it to Mother.

"Thank you," she said. "But Miss Eunice probably has a big one, that will hold all four names." So Miss Eunice gave her the big card and Mother held out her hand until Uncle Gavin uncapped his pen and gave it to her and we watched her write in the big sprawly hand that still looked like somebody thirteen years old in the ninth grade:

> Mr and Mrs Charles Mallison
> Charles Mallison, Jr
> Mr Gavin Stevens

and capped the pen and handed it back to Uncle Gavin and took the card between the thumb and finger of one hand and waved it dry and gave it to Miss Eunice.

"I'll send it out tonight," Miss Eunice said. "Even if the graduation isn't until next week. It's such a handsome gift, why shouldn't Linda have that much more time to enjoy it?"

"Yes," Mother said. "Why shouldn't she?" Then we were

outside again, our three reflections jumbled into one walking now across the plate glass; Mother had Uncle Gavin's arm again.

"All four of our names," Uncle Gavin said. "At least her father won't know a white-headed bachelor sent his seventeen-year-old daughter a fitted travelling-case."

"Yes," Mother said. "One of them won't know it."

15

GAVIN STEVENS

THE difficulty was, how to tell her, explain to her. I mean, why. Not the deed, the act itself, but the reason for it, the *why* behind it—say point blank to her over one of the monstrous synthetic paradoxes which were her passion or anyway choice in Christian's drugstore, or perhaps out on the street itself: "We won't meet any more from now on because after Jefferson assimilates all the details of how your boy-friend tracked you down in my office and bloodied my nose one Saturday, and eight days later, having spent his last night in Jefferson in the county jail, shook our dust forever from his feet with the turbulent uproar of his racer's cut-out—after that, for you to be seen still meeting me in ice-cream dens will completely destroy what little was left of your good name."

You see? That was it: the very words *reputation* and *good name.* Merely to say them, speak them aloud, give their existence vocal recognition, would irrevocably soil and besmirch them, would destroy the immunity of the very things they represented, leaving them not just vulnerable but already doomed; from the inviolable and proud integrity of principles they would become, reduce to, the ephemeral and already doomed and damned fragility of human conditions; innocence and virginity become symbol and postulant of loss and grief, evermore to be mourned, existing only in the past tense *was* and *now is not, no more no more.*

That was the problem. Because the act, the deed itself, was simple enough. Luckily the affair happened late on a Saturday afternoon, which would give my face thirty-six hours anyway before it would have to make a public appearance. (It wouldn't have needed that long except for the ring he wore—a thing not quite as large as a brass knuckle and not really noticeably unlike gold if you didn't get too close probably, of a tiger's head gripping between its jaws what had been—advisedly—a ruby; advisedly because the fact that the stone was missing at the moment was a loss only to my lip.)

Besides, the drugstore meetings were not even a weekly affair, let alone daily, so even a whole week could pass before (1) it would occur to someone that we had not met in over a week, who (2) would immediately assume that we had something to conceal was why we had not met in over a week, and (3) the fact that we had met again after waiting over a week only proved it.

By which time I was even able to shave past my cut lip. So it was very simple; simple indeed in fact, and I the simple one. I had planned it like this: the carefully timed accident which would bring me out the drugstore door, the (say) tin of pipe tobacco still in plain sight on its way to the pocket, at the exact moment when she would pass on her way to school: "Good-morning, Linda—" already stepping on past her and then already pausing: "I have another book for you. Meet me here after school this afternoon and we'll have a Coke over it."

Which would be all necessary. Because I was the simple one, to whom it had never once occurred that the blow of that ruby-vacant reasonably almost-gold tiger's head might have marked her too even if it didn't leave a visible cut; that innocence is innocent not because it rejects but because it accepts; is innocent not because it is impervious and invulnerable to everything, but because it is capable of accepting anything and still remaining innocent; innocent because it foreknows all and therefore doesn't have to fear and be afraid; the tin of tobacco now in my coat pocket because by this time even it had become noticeable, the last book-burdened stragglers now trotting toward the sound of the first strokes of the school bell and still she had not passed; obviously I had missed her somehow: either taken my post not soon enough or she had taken another route to school or perhaps would not leave home for school at all today, for whatever reasons no part of which were the middle-aged bachelor's pandering her to Jonson and Herrick and Thomas Campion; crossing—I— the now-unchildrened street at last, mounting the outside stairs since tomorrow was always tomorrow; indeed, I could even use the tobacco tin again, provided I didn't break the blue stamp for verity, and opened the screen door and entered the office.

She was sitting neither in the revolving chair behind the desk nor in the leather client's one before it, but in a straight hard armless one against the bookcase as though she had fled, been driven until the wall stopped her, and turned then, her back against it, not quite sitting in the chair nor quite huddled in it because although her legs, knees were close and rigid and her hands were clasped tight in her lap, her head was still up watching the door and then me with the eyes the McCarron boy had marked her with which at a distance looked as black as her hair until you saw they were that blue so dark as to be almost violet.

"I thought . . ." she said. "They—somebody said Matt quit his job and left—went yesterday. I thought you might . . ."

"Of course," I said. "I always want to see you," stopping myself in time from *I've been waiting over there on the corner until the last bell rang, for you to pass* though this is what I really stopped from: *Get up. Get out of here quick. Why did you come here anyway? Don't you see this is the very thing I have been lying awake at night with ever since Saturday?* So I merely said what I had bought the can of tobacco which I must now find someone capable or anyway willing to smoke, to give it to, to create the chance to say: "I have another book for you. I forgot to bring it this morning, but I'll bring it at noon. I'll wait for you at Christian's after school and stand you a soda too. Now you'll have to hurry; you're already late."

I had not even released the screen door and so had only to open it again, having also in that time in which she crossed the room, space to discard a thousand frantic indecisions: to remain concealed in the office as though I had not been there at all this morning, and let her leave alone; to follow to the top of the stairs and see her down them, avuncular and fond; to walk her to the school itself and wait to see her through the actual door: the family friend snatching the neighbour's child from the rife midst of truancy and restoring it to duty—family friend to Flem Snopes who had no more friends than Blackbeard or Pistol, to Eula Varner who no more had friends than man or woman either would have called them that Messalina and Helen had.

So I did all three: waited in the office too long, so that I had to follow down the stairs too fast, and then along the street beside her not far enough either to be unnoticed or forgotten. Then there remained only to suborn my nephew with the dollar bill and the book; I don't remember which one; I don't believe I even noticed.

"Sir?" Chick said. "I meet her in Christian's drugstore after

school and give her the book and tell her you'll try to get there
but not to wait. And buy her a soda. Why don't I just give her the
book at school and save time?"

"Certainly," I said. "Why don't you just give me back the
dollar?"

"And buy her a soda," he said. "Do I have to pay for that out
of the dollar?"

"All right," I said. "Twenty-five cents then. If she takes a
banana split you can drink water and make a nickel more."

"Maybe she'll take a Coke," he said. "Then I can have one
too and still make fifteen cents."

"All right," I said.

"Or suppose she don't want anything."

"Didn't I say all right?" I said. "Just don't let your mother
hear you say 'She don't.' "

"Why?" he said. "Father and Ratliff say 'she don't' all the
time, and so do you when you are talking to them. And Ratliff
says 'taken' for 'took' and 'drug' for 'dragged' and so do you
when you are talking to country people like Ratliff."

"How do you know?" I said.

"I've heard you. So has Ratliff."

"Why? Did you tell him to?"

"No sir," he said. "Ratliff told me."

My rejoinder may have been Wait until you get as old as
Ratliff and your father and me and you can too, though I don't
remember. But then, inside the next few months I was to discover
myself doing lots of things he wasn't old enough yet for the
privilege. Which was beside the point anyway now; now only the
afternoon remained: the interminable time until a few minutes
after half-past three filled with a thousand indecisions which each
fierce succeeding harassment would revise. You see? She had not
only abetted me in making that date with which I would break,
wreck, shatter, destroy, slay something, she had even forestalled
me in it by the simplicity of directness.

So I had only to pass that time. That is, get it passed, live it
down; the office window as good as any for that and better than
most since it looked down on the drugstore entrance, so I had
only to lurk there. Not to hear the dismissal bell of course this far
away but rather to see them first: the little ones, the infantile

inflow and scatter of primer- and first-graders, then the middle-graders boisterous and horsing as to the boys, then the mature ones, juniors and seniors grave with weight and alien with puberty; and there she was, tall (no: not for a girl that tall but all right then: tall, like a heron out of a moil of frogs and tadpoles), pausing for just one quick second at the drugstore entrance for one quick glance, perhaps at the empty stairway. Then she entered, carrying three books any one of which might have been that book and I thought *He gave it to her at school; the damned little devil has foxed me for that odd quarter.*

But then I saw Chick; he entered too, carrying the book, and then I thought how if I had only thought to fill a glass with water, to count off slowly sixty seconds, say, to cover the time Skeets McGowan, the soda squirt, would need to tear his fascinations from whatever other female junior or senior and fill the order, then drink the water slowly to simulate the Coke; thinking *But maybe she did take the banana split; maybe there is still time,* already across the office, the screen door already in my hand before I caught myself: at least the County Attorney must not be actually *seen* running down his office stairs and across the street into a drugstore where a sixteen-year-old high-school junior waited.

And I was in time, but just in time. They had not even sat down, or if they had she had already risen, the two of them only standing beside the table, she carrying four books now and looking at me for only that one last instant and then no more with the eyes you thought were just dark grey or blue until you knew better.

"I'm sorry I'm late," I said. "I hope Chick told you."

"It's all right," she said. "I have to go on home anyway."

"Without a Coke even?" I said.

"I have to go home," she said.

"Another time then," I said. "What they call a rain check."

"Yes," she said. "I have to go home now." So I moved so she could move, making the move first to let her go ahead, toward the door.

"Remember what you said about that quarter," Chick said.

And made the next move first too, opening the screen for her then stopping in it and so establishing severance and separation by that little space before she even knew it, not even needing to pause and half-glance back to prove herself intact and safe, intact and secure and unthreatened still, not needing to say Mister Stevens nor even Mister Gavin nor Good-bye nor even anything to need to say Thank you for, nor even to look back then although she did. "Thank you for the book," she said; and gone.

"Remember what you said about that quarter," Chick said.

"Certainly," I said. "Why the bejesus don't you go somewhere and spend it?"

Oh yes, doing a lot of things Chick wasn't old enough yet himself to do. Because dodging situations which might force me to use even that base shabby lash again was fun, excitement. Because she didn't know (Must not know, at least not now, not yet: else why the need for that base and shabby lash?), could not be certainly sure about that afternoon, that one or two or three (whatever it was) minutes in the drugstore; never sure whether what Chick told her was the truth: that I actually was going to be late and had simply sent my nephew as the handiest messenger to keep her company until or when or if I did show up, I so aged and fatuous as not even to realise the insult either standing her up would be, or sending a ten-year-old boy to keep her company and believing that she, a sixteen-year-old high-school junior, would accept him; or if I had done it deliberately: made the date then sent the ten-year-old boy to fill it as a delicate way of saying *Stop bothering me.*

So I must not even give her a chance to demand of me with the temerity of desperation which of these was right. And that was the fun, the excitement. I mean, dodging her. It was adolescence in reverse, turned upside down: the youth, himself virgin and— who knew?—maybe even more so, at once drawn and terrified of what draws him, contriving by clumsy and timorous artifice the accidental encounters in which he still would not and never quite touch, would not even hope to touch, really want to touch, too terrified in fact to touch; but only to breathe the same air, be laved by the same circumambience which laved the mistress's moving limbs; to whom the glove or the handkerchief she didn't even know she had lost, the flower she didn't even know she had crushed, the very ninth- or tenth-grade arithmetic or grammar or geography bearing her name in her own magical hand on the flyleaf, are more terrible and moving than ever will be afterward the gleam of the actual naked shoulder or spread of unbound hair on the pillow's other twin.

That was me: not to encounter; continuously just to miss her yet never be caught at it. You know: in a little town of three thousand people like ours, the only thing that could cause more talk and notice than a middle-aged bachelor meeting a sixteen-year-old maiden two or three times a week would be a sixteen-year-old maiden and a middle-aged bachelor just missing each other two or three times a week by darting into stores or up alleys. You know: a middle-aged lawyer, certainly the one who was County Attorney too, could always find enough to do even in a town of just three thousand to miss being on the one street between her home and the school house at eight-thirty and twelve and one and three-thirty o'clock when the town's whole infant roster must come and go, sometimes, a few times even, but not forever.

Yet that's what I had to do. I had no help, you see; I couldn't stop her suddenly on the street one day and say, "Answer quickly now. Exactly how much were you fooled or not fooled that afternoon in the drugstore? Say in one word exactly what you believed about that episode." All I could do was leave well enough alone, even when the only well enough I had wasn't anywhere that well.

So I had to dodge her. I had to plan not just mine but Yokna-patawpha County's business too ahead in order to dodge a six-teen-year-old girl. That was during the spring. So until school was out in May it would be comparatively simple, at least for five days of the week. But in time vacation would arrive, with no claims of regimen or discipline on her; and observation even if not personal experience had long since taught me that anyone sixteen years old not nursing a child or supporting a family or in jail could be almost anywhere at any time during the twenty-four hours.

So when the time came, which was that last summer before her final year in high school when she would graduate, I didn't even have the catalogues and brochures from the alien and out-land schools sent first to me in person, to be handed by me to her, but sent direct to her, to Miss Linda Snopes, Jefferson, Mississippi, the Mississippi to be carefully spelt out in full else the envelope would go: first, to Jefferson, Missouri; second, to every other

state in the forty-eight which had a Jefferson in it, before: third,
it would finally occur to somebody somewhere that there might
be someone in Mississippi capable of thinking vaguely of attending an Eastern or Northern school or capable of having heard of
such or anyway capable of enjoying the pictures in the catalogues
or even deciphering the one-syllable words, provided they were
accompanied by photographs.

So I had them sent direct to her—the shrewd suave snob-
enticements from the Virginia schools at which Southern mothers
seemed to aim their daughters by simple instinct, I don't know
why, unless because the mothers themselves did not attend them,
and thus accomplishing by proxy what had been denied them in
person since they had not had mothers driven to accomplish
vicariously what they in their turn had been denied.

And not just the Virginia ones first but the ones from the smart
"finishing" schools north of Mason's and Dixon's too. I was being
fair. No: we were being fair, she and I both, the two of us who
never met any more now for the sake of her good name, in
federation and cahoots for the sake of her soul; the two of us
together saying *in absentia* to her mother: *There they all are: the
smart ones, the snob ones. We have been fair, we gave you your chance.
Now, here is where we want to go, where you can help us go, if not by
approval, at least by not saying no;* arranging for the other catalogues
to reach her only then: the schools which would not even notice
what she wore and how she walked and used her fork and all the
rest of how she looked and acted in public because by this time
all that would be too old and fixed to change, but mainly because
it had not mattered anyway, since what did matter was what she
did and how she acted in the spirit's inviolable solitude.

So now—these last began to reach her about Christmas time
of that last year in high school—she would have to see me, need
to see me, not to help her decide which one of them but simply
to discuss, canvass the decision before it became final. I waited,
in fact quite patiently, while it finally dawned on me that she
was not going to make the first gesture to see me again. I had
avoided her for over six months now and she not only knew I had
been dodging her since in a town the size of ours a male can no
more avoid a female consistently for that long by mere accident
than they can meet for that long by what they believed or thought

was discretion and surreptition, even she realised by this time that that business in Christian's drugstore that afternoon last April had been no clumsy accident. (Oh yes, it had already occurred to me also that she had no reason whatever to assume I knew she had received the catalogues, let alone had instigated them. But I dismissed that as immediately as you will too if we are to get on with this.)

So I must make that first gesture. It would not be quite as simple now as it had used to be. A little after half-past three on any weekend afternoon I could see her from the office window (if I happened to be there) pass along the Square in the schools' scattering exodus. Last year, in fact during all the time before, she would be alone, or seemed to be. But now, during this past one, particularly since the Levitt troglodyte's departure, she would be with another girl who lived on the same street. Then suddenly (it began in the late winter, about St Valentine's Day) instead of two there would be four of them: two boys, Chick said the Rouncewell boy and the youngest Bishop one, the year's high-school athletic stars. And now, after spring began, the four of them would be on almost any afternoon in Christian's drug-store (at least there harboured apparently there no ghosts to make her blush and squirm, and I was glad of that), with Coca-Colas and the other fearsome (I was acquainted there) messes which young people, young women in particular, consume with terrifying equanimity not only in the afternoon but at nine and ten in the morning too: which—the four of them—I had taken to be two pairs, two couples in the steadfast almost uxorious fashion of high-school juniors and seniors, until one evening I saw (by chance) her going toward the picture show squired by both of them.

Which would make it a little difficult now. But not too much. In fact, it would be quite simple (not to mention the fact that it was already May and I couldn't much longer afford to wait): merely to wait for some afternoon when she would be without her convoy, when the Bishop and the Rouncewell would have to practice their dedications or maybe simply be kept in by a teacher after school. Which I did, already seeing her about a block away but just in time to see her turn suddenly into a street which would by-pass the Square itself: obviously a new route home she had adopted to use on the afternoons when she was alone, was already or (perhaps) wanted to be.

But that was simple too: merely to back-track one block then turn myself one block more to the corner where the street she was in must intercept. But quicker than she, faster than she, so that I saw her first walking fast along the purlieus of rubbish and ashcans and loading platforms until she saw me at the corner and stopped in dead midstride and one quick fleeing half-raised motion of the hand. So that, who knows? At that sudden distance I might not have even stopped, being already in motion again, raising my hand and arm in return and on, across the alley, striding on as you would naturally expect a county attorney to be striding along a side street at forty-two minutes past three in the afternoon; one whole block more for safety and then safe, inviolate still the intactness, unthreatened again.

There was the telephone of course. But that would be too close, too near the alley and the raised hand. And *grüss Gott* they had invented the typewriter; the Board of Supervisors could subtract the letterhead from my next pay check or who knows they might not even miss it; the typewriter and the time of course were already mine:

Dear Linda:

When you decide which one you like the best, let's have a talk. I've seen some of them myself and can tell you more than the catalogue may have. We should have a banana split too; they may not have heard of them yet at Bennington and Bard and Swarthmore and you'll have to be a missionary as well as a student.

Then in pencil, in my hand:

Saw you in the alley the other afternoon but didn't have time to stop. Incidentally, what were you doing in an alley?

You see? *The other afternoon,* so that it wouldn't matter when I mailed it: two days from now or two weeks from now; two whole weeks in which to tear it up, and even addressed the stamped envelope, knowing as I did so that I was deliberately wasting two —no, three, bought singly—whole cents, then tore them neatly across once and matched the torn edges and tore them across again and built a careful small tepee on the cold hearth and struck a match and watched the burn and uncreaked mine ancient knees and shook my trousers down.

Because it was May now; in two weeks she would graduate. But then Miss Eunice Gant had promised to send the dressing-case yesterday afternoon and *grüss Gott* they had invented the telephone too. So once more (this would be the last one, the last lurk) to wait until half-past eight o'clock (the bank would not open until nine, but then even though Flem was not president of it you simply declined to imagine him hanging around the house until the last moment for the chance to leap to the ringing telephone) and then picked it up:

"Good-morning, Mrs Snopes. Gavin Stevens. May I speak to Linda if she hasn't already . . . I see, I must have missed her. But then I was late myself this morning. . . . Thank you. We are all happy to know the dressing-case pleased her. Maggie will be pleased to have the note. . . . If you'll give her the message when she comes home to dinner. I have some information about a Radcliffe scholarship which might interest her. That's practically Harvard too and I can tell her about Cambridge. . . . Yes, if you will: that I'll be waiting for her in the drugstore after school this afternoon. Thank you."

And good-bye. The sad word, even over the telephone. I mean, not the word is sad nor the meaning of it, but that you really can say it, that the time comes always in time when you can say it without grief and anguish now but without even the memory of grief and anguish, remembering that night in this same office here (when was it? ten years ago? twelve years?) when I had said not just Good-bye but Get the hell out of here to Eula Varner, and no hair bleached, no bead of anguished sweat or tear sprang out, and what regret still stirred a little was regret that even if I had been brave enough not to say No then, even that courage would not matter now since even the cowardice was only thin regret.

At first I thought I would go inside and be already sitting at the table waiting. Then I thought better: it must be casual but not taken-for-granted casual. So I stood at the entrance, but back, not to impede the juvenile flood or perhaps rather not to be trampled by it. Because she must not see me from a block away waiting, but casual, by accident outwardly and chance: first the little ones, first- and second- and third-grade; and now already the larger ones, the big grades and the high school; it would be soon now, any time now. Except that it was Chick, with a folded note.

"Here," he said. "It seems to be stuck."

"Stuck?" I said.

"The record. The victrola. This is the same tune it was playing before, ain't it? Just backward this time." Because she probably had insisted he read it first before she released it to him. So I was the second, not counting her:

> *Dear Mr Stevens*
> *I will have to be a little late if you can wait for me*
> *Linda*

"Not quite the same," I said. "I don't hear any dollar now."

"Okay," he said. "Neither did I. I reckon you ain't coming home now."

"So do I," I said. So I went inside then and sat down at the table; I owed her that much anyway; the least I could give her was revenge, so let it be full revenge; full satisfaction of watching from wherever she would be watching while I sat still waiting for her long after even I knew she would not come; let it be the full whole hour then since "finis" is not "good-bye" and has no cause to grieve the spring of grief.

So when she passed rapidly across the plate-glass window, I didn't know her. Because she was approaching not from the direction of the school but from the opposite one, as though she were on her way to school, not from it. No: that was not the reason. She was already in the store now, rapidly, the screen clapping behind her, at the same instant and in the same physical sense both running and poised motionless, wearing not the blouse and skirt or print cotton dress above the flat-heeled shoes of school; but dressed, I mean "dressed," in a hat and high heels and silk stockings and makeup who needed none and already I could smell the scent: one poised split-second of immobilised and utter flight in bizarre and paradox panoply of allure, like a hawk caught by a speed lens.

"It's all right," I said. Because at least I still had that much presence.

"I can't," she said. At least that much presence. There were not many people in the store, but even one could have been too many, so I was already up now, moving toward her.

"How nice you look," I said. "Come on; I'll walk a way with you," and turned her that way, not even touching her arm, on and out, on to the pavement, talking (I presume I was; I usually am), speaking: which was perhaps why I did not even realise that she had chosen the direction, not in fact until I realised that she had actually turned toward the foot of the office stairs, only then touching her: her elbow, holding it a little, on past the stairs so that none (one hoped intended must believe) had marked that falter, on along the late spring storefronts—the hardware and farm-furnish stores cluttered with garden and farm tools and rolls of uncut plough-line and sample sacks of slag and fertiliser and even the grocery ones exposing neat cases of seed packets stencilled with gaudy and incredible vegetables and flowers—talking (oh ay, trust me always) sedate and decorous: the young girl decked and scented to go wherever a young woman would be going at four o'clock on a May afternoon, and the grey-headed bachelor, avuncular and what old Negroes called "settled", incapable now of harm, slowed the blood and untroubled now the flesh by turn of wrist or ankle, faint and dusty-dry as memory now the hopes and anguishes of youth—until we could turn a corner into privacy or at least room or anyway so long as we did not actually stop.

"I can't," she said.

"You said that before," I said. "You can't what?"

"The schools," she said. "The ones you . . . the catalogues. From outside Jefferson, outside Mississippi."

"I'm glad you can't," I said. "I didn't expect you to decide alone. That's why I wanted to see you: to help you pick the right one."

"But I can't," she said. "Don't you understand? I can't."

Then I—yes, I—stopped talking. "All right," I said. "Tell me."

"I can't go to any of them. I'm going to stay in Jefferson. I'm going to the Academy next year." Oh yes, I stopped talking now. It wasn't what the Academy was that mattered. It wasn't even that the Academy was in Jefferson that mattered. It was Jefferson itself which was the mortal foe since Jefferson was Snopes.

"I see," I said. "All right. I'll talk to her myself."

"No," she said. "No. I don't want to go away."

"Yes," I said. "We must. It's too important. It's too important for even you to see now. Come on. We'll go home now and talk to mother—" already turning. But already she had caught at me, grasping my wrist and forearm with both hands, until I stopped. Then she let go and just stood there in the high heels and the silk stockings and the hat was a little too old for her or maybe I was not used to her in a hat or maybe the hat just reminded me of the only other time I ever saw her in a hat which was that fiasco of a Sunday dinner at home two years ago which was the first time I compelled, forced her to do something because she didn't know how to refuse; whereupon I said suddenly: "Of course I don't really need to ask you this, but maybe we'd better just for the record. You don't really want to stay in Jefferson, do you? You really do want to go up East to school?" then almost immediately said: "All right, I take that back. I can't ask you that; I can't ask you to say outright you want to go against your mother.—All right," I said, "you don't want to be there yourself when I talk to her: is that It?" Then I said: "Look at me," and she did, with the eyes that were not blue or grey either but hyacinthine, the two of us standing there in the middle of that quiet block in full view of at least twenty discreet window-shades; looking at me even while she said, breathed, again:

"No. No."

"Come on," I said. "Let's walk again," and she did so, docile enough. "She knows you came to meet me this afternoon because of course she gave you my telephone message.—All right," I said. "I'll come to your house in the morning then, after you've left for school. But it's all right; you don't need to tell her. You don't need to tell her anything—say anything—" Not even No No again, since she had said nothing else since I saw her and was still saying it even in the way she walked and said nothing. Because now I knew why the clothes, the scent, the makeup which belonged on her no more than the hat did. It was desperation, not to defend the ingratitude but at least to palliate the rudeness of it: the mother who said *Certainly, meet him by all means. Tell him I am quite competent to plan my daughter's education, and we'll both thank him to keep his nose out of it;* the poor desperate child herself covering, trying to hide the baseness of the one and the shame of the other behind the placentae of worms and the urine and vomit of cats and cancerous whales. "I'll come tomorrow morning, after you've gone to school," I said. "I know. I know. But it's got too important now for either of us to stop."

So the next morning, who—I—had thought yesterday to have seen the last of lurking. But I had to be sure. And there was Ratliff.

"What?" he said. "You're going to see Eula because Eula won't let her leave Jefferson to go to school? You're wrong."

"All right," I said. "I'm wrong. I don't want to do it either. I'm not that brave—offering to tell anybody, let alone a woman, how to raise her child. But somebody's got to. She's got to get away from here. Away for good from all the very air that ever heard or felt breathed the name of Snopes—"

"But wait, I tell you! Wait!" he said. "Because you're wrong—"

But I couldn't wait. Anyway, I didn't. I mean, I just deferred, marked time until at least nine o'clock. Because even on a hot Mississippi May morning, when people begin to get up more or less with the sun, not so much in self-defence as to balance off as much as possible of the day against the hours between noon and four, a housewife would demand a little time to prepare (her house and herself or perhaps most of all and simply, her soul) for a male caller not only uninvited but already unwelcome.

But she was prepared, self, house and soul too; if her soul was ever in her life unready for anything that just wore pants or maybe if any woman's soul ever needed pre-readying and pre-arming against anything in pants just named Gavin Stevens, passing through the little rented (still looking rented even though the owner or somebody had painted it) gate up the short rented walk toward the little rented veranda and on to it, my hand already lifted to knock before I saw her through the screen, standing there quite still in the little hallway watching me.

"Good-morning," she said. "Come in," and now with no screen between us still watching me. No: just looking at me, not brazenly, not with welcome, not with anything. Then she turned, the hair, where all the other women in Jefferson, even Maggie, had bobbed theirs now, still one heavy careless yellow bun at the back of her head, the dress which was not a morning gown nor a hostess gown nor even a house dress but just a simple cotton dress that was simply a dress and which, although she was thirty-five now—

yes: thirty-six now by Ratliff's counting from that splendid fall—
like that one when she first crossed the Square that day sixteen
years ago, appeared not so much as snatching in desperate haste
to hide them but rather to spring in suppliance and adulation to
the moving limbs, the very flowing of the fabric's laving folds
crying *Evoe! Evoe!*

Oh yes, it was a sitting-room, exactly like the hall, and both of
them exactly like something else I had seen somewhere but
didn't have time to remember. Because she said, "Will you have
some coffee?" and I saw that too: the service (not silver but the
stuff the advertisements don't tell you is better than silver but
simply newer. New: implying that silver is quite all right and even
proper for people still thrall to gaslight and the horse-and-buggy)
on a low table, with two chairs already drawn up and I thought *I
have lost* even if she had met me wearing a barrel or a feed sack.
Then I thought *So it really is serious*, since this—the coffee, the
low table, the two intimate chairs—was an assault not on the
glands nor even just the stomach but on the civilised soul or at
least the soul which believes it thirsts to be civilised.

"Thank you," I said and waited and then sat too. "Only,
do you mind if I wonder why? We don't need an armistice, since I
have already been disarmed."

"You came to fight then," she said, pouring.

"How can I, without a weapon?" I said, watching: the bent
head with the careless, almost untidy bun of hair, the arm, the
hand which could have rocked a warrior-hero's cradle or even
caught up its father's fallen sword, pouring the trivial (it would
probably not even be very good coffee) fluid from the trivial
spurious synthetic urn—this, in that room, that house; and
suddenly I knew where I had seen the room and hallway before.
In a photograph, the photograph from say *Town and Country*
labelled *American Interior*, reproduced in colour in a wholesale
furniture catalogue, with the added legend: *This is neither a Copy
nor a Reproduction. It is our own Model scaled to your individual Require-
ments.* "Thank you," I said. "No cream. Just sugar.—Only it
doesn't look like you."

"What?" she said.

"This room. Your house." And that was why I didn't even
believe at first that I had heard her.

"It wasn't me. It was my husband."

"I'm sorry," I said.

"My husband chose this furniture."

"Flem?" I said, cried. "Flem Snopes?"—and she looking at me now, not startled, amazed: not anything or if anything, just waiting for my uproar to reach its end: nor was it only from McCarron that Linda got the eyes, but only the hair from him. "Flem Snopes!" I said. "Flem Snopes!"

"Yes. We went to Memphis. He knew exactly what he wanted. No, that's wrong. He didn't know yet. He only knew he wanted, had to have. Or does that make any sense to you?"

"Yes," I said. "Terribly. You went to Memphis."

"Yes," she said. "That was why: to find somebody who could tell him what he had to have. He already knew which store he was going to. The first thing he said was, 'When a man don't intend to buy anything from you, how much do you charge him just to talk?' Because he was not trading now, you see. When you're on a trade, for land or stock or whatever it is, both of you may trade or both of you may not, it all depends; you don't have to buy it or sell it; when you stop trading and part, neither of you may be any different from when you began. But not this time. This was something he had to have and knew he had to have: he just didn't know what it was and so he would not only have to depend on the man who owned it to tell him what he wanted, he would even have to depend on the man selling it not to cheat him on the price or the value of it because he wouldn't know that either: only that he had to have it. Do you understand that too?"

"All right," I said. "Yes. And then?"

"It had to be exactly what it was, for exactly what he was. That was when the man began to say, 'Yes, I think I see. You started out as a clerk in a country store. Then you moved to town and ran a café. Now you're vice-president of your bank. A man who came that far in that short time is not going to stop just there, and why shouldn't everybody that enters his home know it, see it? Yes, I know what you want.' And Flem said No. 'Not expensive,' the man said, 'Successful.' and Flem said No. 'All right,' the man said. 'Antique then,' and took us into a room and showed us what he meant. 'I can take this piece here for instance and make it look still older.' And Flem said, 'Why?' and the man said, 'For back-

G

ground. Your grandfather.' And Flem said, 'I had a grandfather because everybody had. I don't know who he was, but I know that whoever he was he never owned enough furniture for a room, let alone a house. Beside, I don't aim to fool anybody. Only a fool would try to fool smart people, and anybody that needs to fool fools is already one.' And that was when the man said wait while he telephoned. And he did, it was not long before a woman came in. She was his wife. She said to me: 'What are your ideas?' and I said, 'I don't care,' and she said 'What?' and I said it again and then she looked at Flem and I watched them looking at one another, a good while. Then she said, not loud like her husband, quite quiet: 'I know,' and now it was Flem that said, 'Wait. How much will it cost?' and she said, 'You're a trader. I'll make a trade with you. I'll bring the stuff down to Jefferson and put it in your house myself. If you like it, you buy it. If you don't like it, I'll load it back up and move it back here and it won't cost you a cent.' "

"All right," I said. "And then?"

"That's all," she said. "Your coffee's cold. I'll get another cup—" and began to rise until I stopped her.

"When was this?" I said.

"Four years ago," she said. "When he bought this house."

"Bought the house?" I said. "Four years ago? That's when he became vice-president of the bank!"

"Yes," she said. "The day before it was announced. I'll get another cup."

"I don't want coffee," I said, sitting there saying *Flem Snopes Flem Snopes* until I said, cried: "I don't want anything! I'm afraid!" until I finally said "What?" and she repeated:

"Will you have a cigarette?" and I saw that too: a synthetic metal box also and there should have been a synthetic matching lighter, but what she had taken from the same box with the cigarette was a kitchen match. "Linda says you smoke a corncob pipe. Smoke it if you want to."

"No," I said again. "Not anything.—But Flem Snopes," I said. "Flem Snopes."

"Yes," she said. "It's not me that won't let her go away from Jefferson to school."

"But why?" I said. "Why? When she's not even his—he's not

even her—I'm sorry. But you can see how urgent, how we don't even have time for . . ."

"Politeness?" she said. Nor did I make that move either: just sitting there watching while she leaned and scratched the match on the sole of her side-turned slipper and lit the cigarette.

"For anything," I said. "For anything except her. Ratliff tried to tell me this this morning, but I wouldn't listen. So maybe that's what you were telling me a moment ago when I wouldn't or didn't listen? The furniture. That day in the store. Didn't know what he wanted because what he wanted didn't matter, wasn't important: only that he did want it, did need it, must have it, intended to have it no matter what cost or who lost or who anguished or grieved. To be exactly what he needed to exactly fit exactly what he was going to be tomorrow after it was announced: a vice-president's wife and child along with the rest of the vice-president's furniture in the vice-president's house? Is that what you tried to tell me?"

"Something like that," she said.

"Just something like that," I said. "Because that's not enough. It's nowhere near enough. We won't mention the money because everybody who ever saw that bow tie would know he wouldn't pay out his own money to send his own child a sleeper-ticket distance to school, let alone another man's ba—" and stopped. But not she, smoking, watching the burning tip of cigarette.

"Say it," she said. "Bastard."

"I'm sorry," I said.

"Why?" she said.

"I'm trying," I said. "Maybe I could, if only you were. Looked like you were. Or even like you were trying to be."

"Go on," she said. "Not the money."

"Because he—you—could get that from Uncle Will probably, not to mention taking it from me as a scholarship. Or is that it? He can't even bear to see the money of even a mortal enemy like old man Will Varner probably is to him wasted on sending a child out of the state to school when he pays taxes every year to support the Mississippi ones?"

"Go on," she said again. "Not the money."

"So it is that furniture catalogue picture after all, scaled in cheap colour from the Charleston or Richmond or Long Island or

Boston photograph, down to that one which Flem Snopes holds imperative that the people of Yoknapatawpha County must have of him. While he was just owner of a back-alley café it was all right for all Frenchman's Bend (and all Jefferson and the rest of the county too after Ratliff and a few others like him got through with it) to know that the child who bore his name was really a—"

"Bastard," she said again.

"All right," I said. But even then I didn't say it: "—and even when he sold the café for a nice profit and was superintendent of the power-plant, it still wouldn't have mattered. And even after that when he held no public position but was simply a private usurer and property-grabber quietly minding his own business; not to mention the fact that ten or twelve years had now passed, by which time he could even begin to trust Jefferson to have enough tenderness for a twelve- or thirteen-year-old female child not to upset her life with that useless and gratuitous information. But now he is vice-president of a bank and now a meddling outsider is persuading the child to go away to school, to spend at least the three months until the Christmas holidays among people none of whose fathers owe him money and so must keep their mouths shut, any one of whom might reveal the fact which at all costs he must now keep secret. So that's it," I said, and still she wasn't looking at me: just smoking quietly and steadily while she watched the slow curl and rise of the smoke. "So it's you, after all," I said. "He forbade her to leave Jefferson, and blackmailed you into supporting him by threatening you with what he himself is afraid of: that he himself will tell her of her mother's shame and her own illegitimacy. Well, that's a blade with three edges. Ask your father for the money, or take it from me, and get her away from Jefferson or I'll tell her myself who she is—or is not."

"Do you think she will believe you?" she said.

"What?" I said. "Believe me? Believe me? Even without a mirror to look into, nothing to compare with and need to repudiate from, since all she needed was just to live with him for the seventeen years which she has. What more could she want than to believe me, believe anyone, a chance to believe anyone compassionate enough to assure her she's not his child? What are you talking about? What more could she ask than the right to love the mother who by means of love waved her from being a Snopes?

And if that were not enough, what more could anybody want than this, that most never have the chance to be, not one in ten million have the right to be, deserve to be: not just a love child but one of the elect to share cousinhood with the world's immortal love-children—fruit of that brave virgin passion not just capable but doomed to count the earth itself well lost for love, which down all the long record of man the weak and impotent and terrified and sleepless that the rest of the human race calls its poets, have dreamed and anguished and exulted and amazed over—" and she watching me now, not smoking: just holding the poised cigarette while the last blue vapour faded, watching me through it.

"You don't know very much about women, do you?" she said. "Women aren't interested in poets' dreams. They are interested in facts. It doesn't even matter whether the facts are true or not, as long as they match the other facts without leaving a rough seam. She wouldn't even believe you. She wouldn't even believe him if he were to tell her. She would just hate you both—you most of all because you started it."

"You mean she will take . . . this—him—in preference to nothing? Will throw away the chance for school and everything else? I don't believe you."

"To her, this isn't nothing. She will take it before a lot of things. Before most things."

"I don't believe you!" I said, cried, or thought I did. But only thought it, until I said: "So there's nothing I can do."

"Yes," she said. And now she was watching me, the cigarette motionless, not even seeming to burn. "Marry her."

"What?" I said, cried. "A grey-headed man more than twice her age? Don't you see, that's what I'm after: to set her free of Jefferson, not tie her down to it still more, still further, still worse, but to set her free? And you talk about the reality of facts."

"The marriage is the only fact. The rest of it is still the poet's romantic dream. Marry her. She'll have you. Right now, in the middle of all this, she won't know how to say No. Marry her."

"Good-bye," I said. "Good-bye."

And Ratliff again, still in the client's chair where I had left him an hour ago.

"I tried to tell you," he said. "Of course it's Flem. What

reason would Eula and that gal have not to jump at a chance to be
shut of each other for nine or ten months for a change?"

"I can tell you that now myself," I said. "Flem Snopes is vice-
president of a bank now with a vice-president's house with vice-
president's furniture in it and some of that vice-president's
furniture has got to be a vice-president's wife and child."

"No," he said.

"All right," I said. "The vice-president of a bank don't dare
have it remembered that his wife was already carrying somebody
else's bastard when he married her, so if she goes off to school
some stranger that don't owe him money will tell her who she is
and the whole playhouse will blow up."

"No," Ratliff said.

"All right," I said. "Then you tell a while."

"He's afraid she'll get married," he said.

"What?" I said.

"That's right," he said. "When Jody was born, Uncle Billy
Varner made a will leaving half of his property to Miz Varner
and half to Jody. When Eula was born, he made a new will leaving
that same first half to Miz Varner and the other half split in two
equal parts, one for Jody and one for Eula. That's the will he
showed Flem that day him and Eula was married, and he ain't
changed it since. That is, Flem Snopes believed him when he said
he wasn't going to change it, whether anybody else believed him
or not—especially after Flem beat him on that Old Frenchman
place trade."

"What?" I said. "He gave that place to them as Eula's dowry."

"Sho," Ratliff said. "It was told around so because Uncle
Billy was the last man of all that would have corrected it. He
offered Flem the place, but Flem said he would rather have the
price of it in cash money. Which was why Flem and Eula was a
day late leaving for Texas: him and Uncle Billy was trading, with
Uncle Billy beating Flem down to where he never even thought
about it when Flem finally said all right, he would take that
figger provided Uncle Billy would give him a option to buy the
place at the same amount when he come back from Texas. So
they agreed, and Flem come back from Texas with them paint
ponies, and when the dust finally settled, me and Henry Armstid
had done bought that Old Frenchman place from Flem for my

half of that restaurant and enough of Henry's cash money to pay off Uncle Billy's option, which he had done forgot about. And that's why Flem Snopes at least knows that Uncle Billy ain't going to change that will. So he don't dare risk letting that girl leave Jefferson and get married, because he knows that Eula will leave him too then. It was Flem started it by saying No, but you got all three of them against you, Eula and that girl too until that girl finds the one she wants to marry. Because women ain't interested—"

"Wait," I said, "wait. It's my time now. Because I don't know anything about women because things like love and morality and jumping at any chance you can find that will keep you from being a Snopes are just a poet's romantic dream and women aren't interested in the romance of dreams; they are interested in the reality of facts, they don't care what facts, let alone whether they are true or not if they just dovetail with all the other facts without leaving a saw-tooth edge. Right?"

"Well," he said, "I might not a put it jest exactly that way."

"Because I don't know anything about women," I said. "So would you mind telling me how the hell you learned?"

"Maybe by listening," he said. Which we all knew, since what Yoknapatawphian had not seen at some time during the past ten or fifteen years the tin box shaped and painted to resemble a house and containing the demonstrator machine, in the old days attached to the back of a horse-drawn buckboard and since then to the rear of a converted automobile, hitched or parked beside the gate to a thousand yards on a hundred back-country roads, while, surrounded by a group of four or five or six ladies come in sunbonnets or straw hats from anywhere up to a mile along the road, Ratliff himself with his smooth brown bland inscrutable face and his neat faded tieless blue shirt, sitting in a kitchen chair in the shady yard or on the gallery, listening. Oh yes, we all knew that.

"So I didn't listen to the right ones," I said.

"Or the wrong ones neither," he said. "You never listened to nobody because by that time you were already talking again."

Oh yes, easy. All I had to do was stand there on the street at the right time, until she saw me and turned, ducked with that semblance of flight, into the side street which would by-pass the ambush. Nor even then to back-track that one block but merely to go straight through the drugstore itself, out the back door, so that no matter how fast she went I was in the alley first, ambushed again behind the wall's angle in ample time to hear her rapid feet and then step out and grasp her arm just above the wrist almost before it began to rise in that reflex of flight and repudiation, holding the wrist, not hard, while she wrenched, jerked faintly at it, saying, "Please. Please."

"All right," I said. "All right. Just tell me this. When you went home first and changed before you met me in the drugstore that afternoon. It was your idea to go home first and change to the other dress. But it was your mother who insisted on the lipstick and the perfume and the silk stockings and the high heels. Isn't that right?" And she still wrenching and jerking faintly at the arm I held, whispering:

"Please. Please."

16

CHARLES MALLISON

THIS is what Ratliff said happened up to where Uncle Gavin could see it.

It was January, a grey day though not cold because of the fog. Old Het ran in Mrs Hait's front door and down the hall into the kitchen, already hollering in her strong bright happy voice, with strong and childlike pleasure:

"Miss Mannie! Mule in the yard!"

Nobody knew just exactly how old old Het really was. Nobody in Jefferson even remembered just how long she had been in the poorhouse. The old people said she was about seventy, though by her own counting, calculated from the ages of various Jefferson ladies from brides to grandmothers that she claimed to have nursed from infancy, she would be around a hundred and, as Ratliff said, at least triplets.

That is, she used the poorhouse to sleep in or anyway pass most or at least part of the night in. Because the rest of the time she was either on the Square or the streets of Jefferson or somewhere on the mile-and-a-half dirt road between town and the poorhouse; for twenty-five years at least ladies, seeing her through the front window or maybe even just hearing her strong loud cheerful voice from the house next door, had been locking themselves in the bathroom. But even this did no good unless they had remembered first to lock the front and back doors of the house itself. Because sooner or later they would have to come out and there she would be, tall, lean, of a dark chocolate colour, voluble, cheerful, in tennis shoes and the long rat-coloured coat trimmed with what forty or fifty years ago had been fur, and the purple toque that old Mrs Compson had given her fifty years ago while General Compson himself was still alive, set on the exact top of her headrag (at first she had carried a carpetbag of the same colour and apparently as bottomless as a coal-mine, though since the ten-cent store came to Jefferson the carpetbag had given place to a succession of the paper shopping-bags which it gave away), already settled in a chair in the kitchen, having established already upon

G*

the begging visitation a tone blandly and incorrigibly social.

She passed that way from house to house, travelling in a kind of moving island of alarm and consternation as she levied her weekly toll of food scraps and cast-off garments and an occasional coin for snuff, moving in an urbane uproar and as inescapable as a tax-gatherer. Though for the last year or two since Mrs Hait's widowing, Jefferson had gained a sort of temporary respite from her because of Mrs Hait. But even this was not complete. Rather, old Het had merely established a kind of local headquarters or advanced foraging post in Mrs Hait's kitchen soon after Mr Hait and five mules belonging to Mr I. O. Snopes died on a sharp curve below town under the fast northbound through freight one night and even the folks at the poorhouse heard that Mrs Hait had got eight thousand dollars for him. She would come straight to Mrs Hait's as soon as she reached town, sometimes spending the entire forenoon there, so that only after noon would she begin her implacable rounds. Now and then when the weather was bad she spent the whole day with Mrs Hait. On these days her regular clients or victims, freed temporarily, would wonder if in the house of the man-charactered and man-tongued woman who as Ratliff put it had sold her husband to the railroad company for eight thousand per cent profit, who chopped her own firewood and milked her cow and ploughed and worked her own vegetable garden—they wondered if maybe old Het helped with the work in return for her entertainment or if even now she still kept the relationship at its social level of a guest come to divert and be diverted.

She was wearing the hat and coat and was carrying the shopping-bag when she ran into Mrs Hait's kitchen, already hollering: "Miss Mannie! Mule in the yard!"

Mrs Hait was squatting in front of the stove, raking live ashes from it into a scuttle. She was childless, living alone now in the little wooden house painted the same colour that the railroad company used on its stations and boxcars—out of respect to and in memory of, we all said, that morning three years ago when what remained of Mr Hait had finally been sorted from what remained of the five mules and several feet of new manila rope scattered along the right-of-way. In time the railroad claims adjuster called on her, and in time she cashed a check for eight thousand five hundred dollars, since (as Uncle Gavin said, these were the halcyon days when even the railroad companies considered their Southern branches and divisions the rightful legitimate prey of all who dwelt beside them) although for several years before Mr Hait's death single mules and pairs (by coincidence belonging often to Mr Snopes too; you could always tell his because every time the railroad killed his mules they always had new strong rope on them) had been in the habit of getting themselves killed on that same blind curve at night, this was the first time a human being had—as Uncle Gavin put it—joined them in mutual apotheosis.

Mrs Hait took the money in cash; she stood in a calico wrapper and her late husband's coat sweater and the actual felt hat he had been wearing (it had been found intact) on that fatal morning and listened in cold and grim silence while the bank teller then the cashier then the president (Mr de Spain himself) tried to explain to her about bonds, then about savings accounts, then about a simple checking account, and put the money into a salt sack under her apron and departed; that summer she painted her house that serviceable and time-defying colour which matched the depot and the boxcars, as though out of sentiment or (as Ratliff said) gratitude, and now she still lived in it, alone, in the calico wrapper and the sweater coat and the same felt hat which her husband had owned and worn until he no longer needed them; though her shoes by this time were her own: men's shoes which buttoned, with toes like small tulip bulbs, of an archaic and obsolete pattern which Mr Wildermark himself ordered especially for her once a year.

She jerked up and around, still clutching the scuttle, and glared at old Het and said—her voice was a good strong one too, immediate too—

"That son of a bitch," and, still carrying the scuttle and with old Het still carrying the shopping-bag and following, ran out of the kitchen into the fog. That's why it wasn't cold: the fog: as if all the sleeping and breathing of Jefferson during that whole long January night was still lying there imprisoned between the ground and the mist, keeping it from quite freezing, lying like a scum of grease on the wooden steps at the back door and on the brick coping and the wooden lid of the cellar stairs beside the kitchen

door and on the wooden planks which led from the steps to the
wooden shed in the corner of the back yard where Mrs Hait's
cow lived; when she stepped down on to the planks, still carrying
the scuttle of live ashes, Mrs Hait skated violently before she
caught her balance. Old Het in her rubber soles didn't slip.

"Watch out!" she shouted happily. "They in the front!" One
of them wasn't. Because Mrs Hait didn't fall either. She didn't
even pause, whirling and already running toward the corner of
the house where, with silent and apparition-like suddenness, the
mule appeared. It belonged to Mr I.O. Snopes too. I mean, until
they finally unravelled Mr Hait from the five mules on the railroad
track that morning three years ago, nobody had connected him
with Mr Snopes's mule business, even though now and then
somebody did wonder how Mr Hait didn't seem to need to do anything steady to make a living. Ratliff said the reason was that
everybody was wondering too hard about what in the world I.O.
Snopes was doing in the livestock business. Though Ratliff said
that on second thought maybe it was natural: that back in Frenchman's Bend I.O. had been a blacksmith without having any
business at that, hating horses and mules both since he was deathly
afraid of them, so maybe it was natural for him to take up the next
thing he wouldn't have any business in or sympathy or aptitude
for, not to mention being six or eight or a dozen times as scared
since now, instead of just one horse or mule tied to a post and
with its owner handy, he would have to deal alone with eight or
a dozen of them running loose until he could manage to put a rope
on them.

That's what he did though—bought his mules at the Memphis
market and brought them to Jefferson and sold them to farmers
and widows and orphans, black and white, for whatever he could
get, down to some last irreducible figure, after which (up to the
night when the freight train caught Mr Hait too and Jefferson
made the first connection between Mr Hait and Mr Snopes's
livestock business) single mules and pairs and gangs (always tied
together with that new strong manila rope which Snopes always
itemised and listed in his claim) would be killed by night freight
trains on that same blind curve of Mr Hait's exit; somebody
(Ratliff swore it wasn't him but the depot agent) finally sent
Snopes through the mail a printed train schedule for the division.

Though after Mr Hait's misfortune (miscalculation, Ratliff said; he said it was Mr Hait the agent should have sent the train schedule to, along with a watch) Snopes's mules stopped dying of sudden death on the railroad track. When the adjuster came to adjust Mrs Hait, Snopes was there too, which Ratliff said was probably the most terrible decision Snopes ever faced in his whole life: between the simple prudence which told him to stay completely clear of the railroad company's investigation, and his knowledge of Mrs Hait which had already told him that his only chance to get any part of that indemnity would be by having the railroad company for his ally.

Because he failed. Mrs Hait stated calmly that her husband had been the sole owner of the five mules; she didn't even have to dare Snopes out loud to dispute it; all he ever saw of that money (oh yes, he was there in the bank, as close as he dared get, watching) was when she crammed it into the salt bag and folded the bag into her apron. For five or six years before that, at regular intervals, he had passed across the peaceful and somnolent Jefferson scene in dust and uproar, his approach heralded by forlorn shouts and cries, his passing marked by a yellow cloud of dust filled with the tossing jug-shaped heads and the clattering hooves, then last of all Snopes himself at a panting trot, his face gaped with forlorn shouting and wrung with concern and terror and dismay.

When he emerged from his conference with the adjuster he still wore the concern and the dismay, but the terror was now blended into an incredulous, a despairing, a shocked and passionate disbelief which still showed through the new overlay of hungry hope it wore during the next three years (again, Ratliff said, such a decision and problem as no man should be faced with: who—Snopes—heretofore had only to unload the mules into the receiving pen at the depot and then pay a Negro to ride the old bell mare which would lead them across town to his sales stable-lot, while now and single-handed he had to let them out of the depot pen and then force, herd them into the narrow street blocked at the end by Mrs Hait's small unfenced yard) when the uproar—the dust-cloud filled with plunging demonic shapes—would seem to be translated in one single burst across the peaceful edge of Jefferson and into Mrs Hait's yard, where the two of them, Mrs Hait and Snopes—Mrs Hait clutching a broom or a mop or whatever weapon she was able to snatch up as she ran out of the house cursing like a man, and Snopes, vengeance for the moment sated or at least the unbearable top of the unbearable sense of impotence and injustice and wrong taken off (Ratliff said he had probably long since given up any real belief of actually extorting even one cent of that money from Mrs Hait and all that remained now was the raging and baseless hope) who would now have to catch the animals somehow and get them back inside a fence—ducked and dodged among the thundering shapes in a kind of passionate and choreographic pantomime against the backdrop of that house whose very impervious paint Snopes believed he had paid for and within which its very occupant and chatelaine led a life of queenly and sybaritic luxury on his money (which according to Ratliff was exactly why Mrs Hait refused to appeal to the law to abate Snopes as a nuisance: this too was just a part of the price she owed for the amazing opportunity to swap her husband for eight thousand dollars)—this, while that whole section of town learned to gather—the ladies in the peignoirs and boudoir caps of morning, the children playing in the yards, and the people, Negro and white, who happened to be passing at the moment—and watch from behind neighbouring shades or the security of adjacent fences.

When they saw it, the mule was running too, its head high too in a strange place it had never seen before, so that coming suddenly out of the fog and all, it probably looked taller than a giraffe rushing down at Mrs Hait and old Het with the halter-rope whipping about its ears.

"Dar hit!" old Het shouted, waving the shopping-bag, "Hoo! Scat!" She told Ratliff how Mrs Hait whirled and skidded again on the grassy planks as she and the mule now ran parallel with one another toward the cowshed from whose open door the static and astonished face of the cow now looked out. To the cow, until a second ago standing peacefully in the door chewing and looking at the fog, the mule must have looked taller and more incredible than any giraffe, let alone looking like it aimed to run right through the shed as if it were straw or maybe even pure and simple mirage. Anyway, old Het said the cow snatched her face back inside the shed like a match going out and made a sound inside the shed, old Het didn't know what sound, just a sound of

pure shock and alarm like when you pluck a single string on a
harp or a banjo, Mrs Hait running toward the sound old Het said
in a kind of pure reflex, in automatic compact of female with
female against the world of mules and men, she and the mule
converging on the shed at top speed, Mrs Hait already swinging
the scuttle of live ashes to throw at the mule. Of course it didn't
take this long; old Het said she was still hollering "Dar hit! Dar
hit!" when the mule swerved and ran at her until she swung the
shopping-bag and turned it past her and on around the next corner
of the house and back into the fog like a match going out too.

That was when Mrs Hait set the scuttle down on the edge of the
brick coping of the cellar entrance and she and old Het turned the
corner of the house in time to see the mule coincide with a rooster
and eight white-leghorn hens coming out from under the house.
Old Het said it looked just like something out of the Bible, or
maybe out of some kind of hoodoo witches' Bible: the mule that
came out of the fog to begin with like a hant or a goblin, now kind
of soaring back into the fog again borne on a cloud of little
winged ones. She and Mrs Hait were still running; she said Mrs
Hait was now carrying the worn-out stub of a broom though old
Het didn't remember when she had picked it up.

"There's more in the front!" old Het hollered.

"That son of a bitch," Mrs Hait said. There were more of them.
Old Het said that little handkerchief-sized yard was full of mules
and I. O. Snopes. It was so small that any creature with a stride of
three feet could have crossed it in two paces, yet when they came
in sight of it it must have looked like watching a drop of water
through a microscope. Except that this time it was like being in
the middle of the drop of water yourself. That is, old Het said that
Mrs Hait and I. O. Snopes were in the middle of it because she
stopped against the house where she would be more or less out of
the way even though nowhere in that little yard was going to be
safe, and watched Mrs Hait still clutching the broom and with a
kind of sublime faith in something somewhere, maybe in just her
own invulnerability, though old Het said Mrs Hait was just too
mad to notice, rush right into the middle of the drove, after the
one with the flying halter-rein that was still vanishing into the fog
still in that cloud of whirling loose feathers like confetti or the
wake behind a speed boat.

And Mr Snopes too, the mules running all over him too, he and Mrs Hait glaring at each other while he panted:

"Where's my money? Where's my half of it?"

"Catch that big son of a bitch with the halter," Mrs Hait said. "Get that big son of a bitch out of here," both of them, old Het and Mrs Hait both, running on so that Snopes's panting voice was behind them now:

"Pay me my money! Pay me my part of it!"

"Watch out!" old Het said she hollered. "He heading for the back again!"

"Get a rope!" Mrs Hait hollered back at Snopes.

"'Fore God, where is ere rope?" Snopes hollered.

"In the cellar, 'fore God!" old Het hollered. She didn't wait either. "Go round the other way and head him!" she said. And she said that when she and Mrs Hait turned that corner, there was the mule with the flying halter once more seeming to float lightly onward on a cloud of chickens with which, since the chickens had been able to go under the house and so along the chord while the mule had to go around on the arc, it had once more coincided. When they turned the next corner, they were in the back yard again.

"'Fore God!" Het hollered. "He fixing to misuse the cow!" She said it was like a tableau. The cow had come out of the shed into the middle of the back yard; it and the mule were now facing each other about a yard apart, motionless, with lowered heads and braced legs like two mismatched book-ends, and Snopes was half in and half out of the now-open cellar door on the coping of which the scuttle of ashes still sat, where he had obviously gone seeking the rope; afterward old Het said she thought at the time an open cellar door wasn't a very good place for a scuttle of live ashes, and maybe she did. I mean, if she hadn't said she thought that, somebody else would, since there's always somebody handy afterward to prove their foresight by your hindsight. Though if things were going as fast as she said they were, I don't see how anybody there had time to think anything much.

Because everything was already moving again; when they went around the next corner this time, I.O. was leading, carrying the rope (he had found it), then the cow, her tail raised and rigid and raked slightly like the flagpole on a boat, and then the mule,

Mrs Hait and old Het coming last and old Het told again how she noticed the scuttle of live ashes sitting on the curb of the now-open cellar with its accumulation of human refuse and Mrs Hait's widowhood—empty boxes for kindling, old papers, broken furniture—and thought again that wasn't a very good place for the scuttle.

Then the next corner. Snopes and the cow and the mule were all three just vanishing on the cloud of frantic chickens which had once more crossed beneath the house just in time. Though when they reached the front yard there was nobody there but Snopes. He was lying flat on his face, the tail of his coat flung forward over his head by the impetus of his fall, and old Het swore there was the print of the cow's split foot and the mule's hoof too in the middle of his white shirt.

"Where'd they go?" she shouted at him. He didn't answer. "They tightening on the curves!" she hollered at Mrs Hait. "They already in the back again!" They were. She said maybe the cow had aimed to run back into the shed but decided she had too much speed and instead whirled in a kind of desperation of valour and despair on the mule itself. Though she said that she and Mrs Hait didn't quite get there in time to see it: only to hear a crash and clash and clatter as the mule swerved and blundered over the cellar entrance. Because when they got there the mule was gone. The scuttle was gone from the cellar coping too but old Het said she never noticed it then: only the cow in the middle of the yard where she had been standing before, her fore legs braced and her head lowered like somebody had passed and snatched away the other book-end. Because she and Mrs Hait didn't stop either, Mrs Hait running heavily now, old Het said, with her mouth open and her face the colour of putty and one hand against her side. In fact she said they were both run out now, going so slow this time that the mule overtook them from behind and she said it jumped clean over them both: a brief demon thunder rank with the ammonia-reek of sweat, and went on (either the chickens had finally realised to stay under the house or maybe they were worn out too and just couldn't make it this time); when they reached the next corner the mule had finally succeeded in vanishing into the fog; they heard its hooves, brief, staccato and derisive on the hard street, dying away.

Old Het said she stopped. She said, "Well, Gentlemen, hush," she said. "Ain't we had—" Then she smelled it. She said she stood right still, smelling, and it was like she was actually looking at that open cellar as it was when they passed it last time without any coal scuttle setting on the coping. "'Fore God," she hollered at Mrs Hait, "I smell smoke! Child, run in the house and get your money!"

That was about nine o'clock. By noon the house had burned to the ground. Ratliff said that when the fire engine and the crowd got there, Mrs Hait, followed by old Het carrying her shopping-bag in one hand and a framed crayon portrait of Mr Hait in the other, was just coming out of the house carrying an umbrella and wearing an army overcoat which Mr Hait had used to wear, in one pocket of which was a quart fruit jar packed with what remained of the eighty-five hundred dollars (which would be most of it, according to how the neighbours said Mrs Hait lived) and in the other a heavy nickel-plated revolver, and crossed the street to a neighbour's house, where with old Het beside her in a second rocker, she had been sitting ever since on the gallery, the two of them rocking steadily while they watched the volunteer fire-fighters flinging her dishes and furniture up and down the street. By that time Ratliff said there were plenty of them interested enough to go back to the Square and hunt up I.O. and keep him posted.

"What you telling me for?" I.O. said. "It wasn't me that set that-ere scuttle of live fire where the first thing that passed would knock it into the cellar."

"It was you that opened the cellar door though," Ratliff said.

"Sho," Snopes said. "And why? To get that rope, her own rope, right where she sent me to get it."

"To catch your mule, that was trespassing on her yard," Ratliff said. "You can't get out of it this time. There ain't a jury in the county that won't find for her."

"Yes," Snopes said. "I reckon not. And just because she's a woman. That's why. Because she is a durned woman. All right. Let her go to her durned jury with it. I can talk too; I reckon it's a few things I could tell a jury myself about—" Then Ratliff said he stopped. Ratliff said he didn't sound like I.O. Snopes anyway because whenever I.O. talked what he said was so full of mixed-up proverbs that you stayed so busy trying to unravel just which of

two or three proverbs he had jumbled together that you couldn't
even tell just exactly what lie he had told you until it was already
too late. But right now Ratliff said he was too busy to have time for
even proverbs, let alone lies. Ratliff said they were all watching him.

"What?" somebody said. "Tell the jury about what?"

"Nothing," he said. "Because why, because there ain't going to
be no jury. Me and Miz Mannie Hait? You boys don't know her
if you think she's going to make trouble over a pure acci-dent
couldn't me nor nobody else help. Why, ain't a fairer, finer
woman in Yoknapatawpha County than Mannie Hait. I just wish
I had a opportunity to tell her so." Ratliff said he had it right
away. He said Mrs Hait was right behind them, with old Het
right behind her, carrying the shopping-bag. He said she just
looked once at all of them generally. After that she looked at I.O.

"I come to buy that mule," she said.

"What mule?" I.O. said. He answered that quick, almost automatic, Ratliff said. Because he didn't mean it either. Then Ratliff
said they looked at one another for about a half a minute. "You'd
like to own that mule?" he said. "It'll cost you a hundred and
fifty, Miz Mannie."

"You mean dollars?" Mrs Hait said.

"I don't mean dimes nor nickels neither, Miz Mannie,"
Snopes said.

"Dollars," Mrs Hait said. "Mules wasn't that high in Hait's
time."

"Lots of things is different since Hait's time," Snopes said.
"Including you and me, Miz Mannie."

"I reckon so," she said. Then she went away. Ratliff said she
turned without a word and left, old Het following.

"If I'd a been you," Ratliff said, "I don't believe I'd a said
that last to her."

And now Ratliff said the mean harried little face actually
blazed, even frothing a little. "I just wisht she would," Snopes
said. "Her or anybody else, I don't care who, to bring a court suit
about anything, jest so it had the name mule and the name Hait
in it—" and stopped, the face smooth again. "How's that?" he
said. "What was you saying?"

"That you don't seem to be afraid she might sue you for
burning down her house," Ratliff said.

"Sue me?" Snopes said. "Miz Hait? If she was fixing to try to law something out of me about that fire, do you reckon she would a hunted me up and offered to pay me for it?"

That was about one o'clock. Then it was four o'clock; Aleck Sander and I had gone out to Sartoris Station to shoot quail over the dogs that Miss Jenny Du Pre still kept, I reckon until Benbow Sartoris got big enough to hold a gun. So Uncle Gavin was alone in the office to hear the tennis shoes on the outside stairs. Then old Het came in; the shopping-bag was bulging now and she was eating bananas from a paper sack which she clamped under one arm, the half-eaten banana in that hand while with the other she dug out a crumpled ten-dollar bill and gave it to Uncle Gavin.

"It's for you," old Het said. "From Miss Mannie. I done already give him hisn"—telling it: waiting on the corner of the Square until it looked like sure to God night would come first, before Snopes finally came along, and she handed the banana she was working on then to a woman beside her and got out the first crumpled ten-dollar bill. Snopes took it.

"What?" he said. "Miz Hait told you to give it to me?"

"For that mule," old Het said. "You don't need to give me no receipt. I can be the witness I give it to you."

"Ten dollars?" Snopes said. "For that mule? I told her a hundred and fifty dollars."

"You'll have to contrack that with her yourself," old Het said. "She just give me this to hand to you when she left to get the mule."

"To get the—she went out there herself and taken that mule out of my lot?" Snopes said.

"Lord, child," old Het said. "Miss Mannie ain't skeered of no mule. Ain't you done found that out?—And now here's yourn," she said to Uncle Gavin.

"For what?" Uncle Gavin said. "I don't have a mule to sell."

"For a lawyer," old Het said. "She fixing to need a lawyer. She say for you to be out there at her house about sundown, when she had time to get settled down again."

"Her house?" Uncle Gavin said.

"Where it use to be, honey," old Het said. "Would you keer for a banana? I done et about all I can hold."

"No, much obliged," Uncle Gavin said.

"You're welcome," she said. "Go on. Take some. If I et one more, I'd be wishing the good Lord hadn't never thought banana one in all His life."

"No, much obliged," Uncle Gavin said.

"You're welcome," she said. "I don't reckon you'd have nothing like a extra dime for a little snuff."

"No," Uncle Gavin said, producing it. "All I have is a quarter."

"That's quality," she said. "You talk about change to quality, what you gets back is a quarter or a half a dollar or sometimes even a whole dollar. It's just trash that can't think no higher than a nickel or ten cents." She took the quarter; it vanished somewhere. "There's some folks thinks all I does, I tromps this town all day long from can-see to can't, with a hand full of gimme and a mouth full of much oblige. They're wrong. I serves Jefferson too. If it's more blessed to give than to receive like the Book say, this town is blessed to a fare-you-well because it's steady full of folks willing to give anything from a nickel up to a old hat. But I'm the onliest one I knows that steady receives. So how is Jefferson going to be steady blessed without me steady willing from dust-dawn to dust-dark, rain or snow or sun, to say much oblige? I can tell Miss Mannie you be there?"

"Yes," Uncle Gavin said. Then she was gone. Uncle Gavin sat there looking at the crumpled bill on the desk in front of him. Then he heard the other feet on the stairs and he sat watching the door until Mr Flem Snopes came in and shut it behind him.

"Evening," Mr Snopes said. "Can you take a case for me?"

"Now?" Uncle Gavin said. "Tonight?"

"Yes," Mr Snopes said.

"Tonight," Uncle Gavin said again. "Would it have anything to do with a mule and Mrs Hait's house?"

And he said how Mr Snopes didn't say What house? or What mule? or How did you know? He just said, "Yes."

"Why did you come to me?" Uncle Gavin said.

"For the same reason I would hunt up the best carpenter if I wanted to build a house, or the best farmer if I wanted to share-crop some land," Mr Snopes said.

"Thanks," Uncle Gavin said. "Sorry," he said. He didn't even have to touch the crumpled bill. He said that Mr Snopes had not only seen it the minute he entered, but he believed he even knew

at that same moment where it came from. "As you already
noticed, I'm already on the other side."

"You going out there now?" Mr Snopes said.

"Yes," Uncle Gavin said.

"Then that's all right." He began to reach into his pocket. At
first Uncle Gavin didn't know why; he just watched him dig out
an old-fashioned snap-mouth wallet and open it and separate a
ten-dollar bill and close the wallet and lay the bill on the desk
beside the other crumpled one and put the wallet back into the
pocket and stand looking at Uncle Gavin.

"I just told you I'm already on the other side," Uncle Gavin
said.

"And I just said that's all right," Mr Snopes said. "I don't
want a lawyer because I already know what I'm going to do. I
just want a witness."

"And why me for that?" Uncle Gavin said.

"That's right," Mr Snopes said. "The best witness too."

So they went out there. The fog had burned away by noon and
Mrs Hait's two blackened chimneys now stood against what re-
mained of the winter sunset; at the same moment Mr Snopes said,
"Wait."

"What?" Uncle Gavin said. But Mr Snopes didn't answer,
so they stood, not approaching yet; Uncle Gavin said he could
already smell the ham broiling over the little fire in front of the
still-intact cowshed, with old Het sitting on a brand-new kitchen
chair beside the fire turning the ham in the skillet with a fork,
and beyond the fire Mrs Hait squatting at the cow's flank, milking
into a new tin bucket.

"All right," Mr Snopes said, and again Uncle Gavin said
What? because he had not seen I.O. at all: he was just suddenly
there as though he had materialised, stepped suddenly out of the
dusk itself into the light of the fire (there was a brand-new
galvanised-iron coffee-pot sitting in the ashes near the blaze and
now Uncle Gavin said he could smell that too), to stand looking
down at the back of Mrs Hait's head, not having seen Uncle
Gavin and Mr Flem yet. But old Het had, already talking to
Uncle Gavin while they were approaching:

"So this coffee and ham brought you even if them ten dollars
couldn't," she said. "I'm like that, myself. I ain't had no appetite

in years it seems like now. A bird couldn't live on what I eats. But just let me get a whiff of coffee and ham together, now.—Leave that milk go for a minute, honey," she said to Mrs Hait. "Here's your lawyer."

Then I.O. saw them too, jerking quickly around over his shoulder his little mean harassed snarling face; and now Uncle Gavin could see inside the cowshed. It had been cleaned and raked and even swept; the floor was spread with fresh hay. A clean new kerosene stable lantern burned on a wooden box beside a pallet bed spread neatly on the straw and turned back for the night and now Uncle Gavin saw a second wooden box set out for a table beside the fire, with a new plate and knife and fork and spoon and cup and saucer and a still-sealed loaf of machine-made bread.

But Uncle Gavin said there was no alarm in I.O.'s face at the sight of Mr Flem though he said the reason for that was that he, Uncle Gavin, hadn't realised yet that I.O. had simply reached that stage where utter hopelessness wears the mantle of temerity. "So here you are," I.O. said. "And brung your lawyer too. I reckon you come now to get that-ere lantern and them new dishes and chair and that milk bucket and maybe the milk in too soon as she's done, hey? That's jest fine. It's even downright almost honest, coming right out in the open here where it ain't even full dark yet. Because of course your lawyer knows all the rest of these here recent mulery and arsonery circumstances; likely the only one here that ain't up to date is old Aunt Het there, and sholy she should be learned how to reco-nise a circumstance that even if she was to get up and run this minute, likely she would find she never had no shirt nor britches left neither by the time she got home, since a stitch in time saves nine lives for even a cat, as the feller says. Not to mention the fact that when you dines in Rome you durn sho better watch your overcoat.

"All right then. Now, jest exactly how much of them eight thousand and five hundred dollars the railroad company paid Miz Hait here for that husband of hern and them five mules of mine, do you reckon Miz Hait actively" (Uncle Gavin said he said actively for actually too, just like Ratliff. And Uncle Gavin said they were both right) "got? Well, in that case you will be jest as wrong as everybody else was. She got half of it. The reason being that the vice-presi-dent here handled it for her. Of course, without a fi-nancial expert like the vice-presi-dent to handle it for her, she wouldn't a got no more than that half nohow, if as much, so by rights she ain't got nothing to complain of, not to mention the fact that jest half of even that half was rightfully hern, since jest Lonzo Hait was hern because them five mules was mine.

"All right. Now, what do you reckon become of the other half of them eight thousand and five hundred dollars? Then you'll be jest as wrong this time as you were that other one. Because the vice-presi-dent here taken them. Oh, it was done all open and legal; he explained it: if Miz Hait sued the railroad, a lone lorn widder by herself, likely she wouldn't get more than five thousand at the most, and half of that she would have to give to me for owning the mules. And if me and her brought the suit together, with a active man on her side to compel them cold hard million-aire railroad magnits to do a lone woman justice, once I claimed any part of them mules, due to the previous bad luck mules belonging to me had been having on that-ere curve, the railroad would smell a rat right away and wouldn't nobody get nothing. While with him, the vice-presi-dent, handling it, it would be seventy-five hundred or maybe a even ten thousand, of which he would not only guarantee her a full half, he would even take out of his half the hundred dollars he would give me. All legal and open: I could keep my mouth shut and get a hundred dollars, where if I objected, the vice-presi-dent his-self might accidently let out who them mules actively belonged to, and wouldn't nobody get nothing, which would be all right with the vice-presi-dent since he would be right where he started out, being as he never owned Lonzo Hait nor the five mules neither.

"A pure and simple easy choice, you see: either a feller wants a hundred dollars, or either he don't want a hundred dollars. Not to mention, as the vice-presi-dent his-self pointed out, that me and Miz Hait was fellow townsmen and you might say business acquaintances and Miz Hait a woman with a woman's natural tender gentle heart, so who would say that maybe in time it wouldn't melt a little more to where she might want to share a little of her half of them eight thousand and five hundred dollars. Which never proved much except that the vice-presi-dent might know all there was to know about railroad companies and eight thousand and five hundred dollars but he never knowed much about what Miz Hait toted around where other folks totes their hearts. Which is neither here nor there; water that's still under a bridge don't fill no oceans, as the feller says, and I was simply out-voted two to one, or maybe eight thousand and five hundred dollars to one hundred dollars; or maybe it didn't even take that much: jest Miz Hait's half of them eight thousand and five hundred, against my one hundred, since the only way I could a outvoted Miz Hait would a been with four thousand and two hundred and fifty-one dollars of my own, and even then I'd a had to split that odd dollar with her.

"But never mind. I done forget all that now; that spilt milk ain't going to help no ocean neither." Now Uncle Gavin said he turned rapidly to Mrs Hait with no break in the snarling and outraged babble: "What I come back for was to have a little talk with you. I got something that belongs to you, and I hear you got something that belongs to me. Though naturally I expected to a-just it in private."

"Lord, honey," old Het said. "If you talking at me. Don't you mind me. I done already had so much troubles myself that listening to other folks even kind of rests me. You gawn talk what you wants to talk; I'll just set here and mind this ham."

"Come on," I.O. said to Mrs Hait. "Run them all away for a minute."

Mrs Hait had turned now, still squatting, watching him. "What for?" she said. "I reckon she ain't the first critter that ever come in this yard when it wanted and went or stayed when it liked." Now Uncle Gavin said I.O. made a gesture, brief, fretted, and restrained.

"All right," he said. "All right. Let's get started then. So you taken the mule."

"I paid you for it," Mrs Hait said. "Het brought you the money."

"Ten dollars," I.O. said. "For a hundred-and-fifty-dollar mule."

"I don't know anything about hundred-and-fifty-dollar mules," Mrs Hait said. "All I know about mules is what the railroad pays for them. Sixty dollars a head the railroad paid that other time before that fool Hait finally lost all his senses and tied himself to that track too—"

"Hush!" I.O. said. "Hush!"

"What for?" Mrs Hait said. "What secret am I telling that ain't already blabbed to anybody within listening?"

"All right," I.O. said. "But you just sent me ten."

"I sent you the difference," Mrs Hait said. "The difference between that mule and what you owed Hait."

"What I owed Hait?" I.O. said.

"Hait said you paid him fifty dollars a trip, each time he got in front of the train in time, and the railroad had paid you sixty dollars a head for the mules. That last time, you never paid him because you never would pay him until afterward and this time there wasn't no afterward. So I taken a mule instead and sent you the ten dollars difference with Het here for the witness." Uncle Gavin said that actually stopped him. He actually hushed; he and Mrs Hait, the one standing and the other still squatting, just stared at one another while again old Het turned the hissing ham in the skillet. He said they were so still that Mr Flem himself spoke twice before they even noticed him.

"You through now?" he said to I.O.

"What?" I.O. said.

"Are you through now?" Mr Flem said. And now Uncle Gavin said they all saw the canvas sack—one of the canvas sacks stamped with the name of the bank which the bank itself used to store money in the vault—in his hands.

"Yes," I.O. said. "I'm through. At least I got one ten dollars out of the mule business you ain't going to touch." But Mr Flem wasn't even talking to him now. He had already turned toward Mrs Hait when he drew a folded paper out of the sack.

"This is the mortgage on your house," he said. "Whatever the insurance company pays you now will be clear money; you can build it back again. Here," he said. "Take it."

But Mrs Hait didn't move. "Why?" she said.

"I bought it from the bank myself this afternoon," Mr Flem said. "You can drop it in the fire if you want to. But I want you to put your hand on it first." So she took the paper then, and now Uncle Gavin said they all watched Mr Flem reach into the sack again and this time draw out a roll of bills, I.O. watching too now, not even blinking.

" 'Fore God," old Het said. "You could choke a shoat with it."

"How many mules have you got in that lot?" Mr Flem said to I.O. Still I.O. just watched him. Then he blinked, rapid and hard.

"Seven," he said.

"You've got six," Mr Flem said. "You just finished selling one of them to Mrs Hait. The railroad says the kind of mules you deal in are worth sixty dollars a head. You claim they are worth a hundred and fifty. All right. We won't argue. Six times a hundred and fifty is—"

"Seven!" I.O. said, loud and harsh. "I ain't sold Mrs Hait nor nobody else that mule. Watch." He faced Mrs Hait. "We ain't traded. We ain't never traded. I defy you to produce ara man or woman that seen or heard more than you tried to hand me this here same ten-dollar bill that I'm a handing right back to you. Here," he said, extending the crumpled bill, then jerking it at her so that it struck against her skirt and fell to the ground. She picked it up.

"You giving this back to me," she said, "before these witnesses?"

"You durn right I am," he said. "I jest wish we had ten times this many witnesses." Now he was talking to Mr Flem. "So I ain't sold nobody no mule. And seven times a hundred and fifty dollars is ten hundred and fifty dollars—"

"Nine hundred dollars," Mr Flem said.

"Ten hundred and fifty," I.O. said.

"When you bring me the mule," Mr Flem said. "And on the main condition."

"What main condition?" I.O. said.

"That you move back to Frenchman's Bend and never own a business in Jefferson again as long as you live."

"And if I don't?" I.O. said.

"I sold the hotel this evening too," Mr Flem said. And now even I.O. just watched him while he turned toward the light of the fire and began to count bills—they were mostly fives and ones, with an occasional ten—from the roll. I.O. made one last effort.

"Ten hundred and fifty," he said.

"When you bring me the mule," Mr Flem said. So it was still only nine hundred dollars which I.O. took and counted for himself and folded away into his hip pocket and buttoned the pocket and turned to Mrs Hait.

"All right," he said, "where's Mister Vice-Presi-dent Snopes's other mule?"

"Tied to a tree in the ravine ditch behind Mr Spilmer's house," Mrs Hait said.

"What made you stop there?" I.O. said. "Why didn't you take it right on up to Mottstown? Then you could a really enjoyed my time and trouble getting it back." He looked around again, snarling, sneering, indomitably intractable. "You're right fixed up here, ain't you? You and the vice-presi-dent could both save money if he jest kept that mortgage which ain't on nothing now noway, and you didn't build no house a-tall. Well, good-night, all. Soon as I get this-here missing extry mule into the lot with the vice-presi-dent's other six, I'll do myself the honour and privilege of calling at his residence for them other hundred and fifty dollars since cash on the barrelhead is the courtesy of kings, as the feller says, not to mention the fact that beggars' choices ain't even choices when he ain't even got a roof to lay his head in no more. And if Lawyer Stevens has got ara thing loose about him, the vice-presi-dent might a taken a notion to, he better hold on to it since as the feller says even a fool won't tread where he jest got through watching somebody else get bit. Again, good-night, all." Then he was gone. And this time Uncle Gavin said that Mr Flem had to speak to him twice before he heard him.

"What?" Uncle Gavin said.

"I said, how much do I owe you?" Mr Flem said. And Uncle Gavin said he started to say one dollar, so that Mr Flem would say One dollar? Is that all? And then Uncle Gavin could say Yes, or your knife or pencil or just anything so that when I wake up tomorrow I'll know I didn't dream this. But he didn't. He just said:

"Nothing. Mrs Hait is my client." And he said how again Mr Flem had to speak twice. "What?" Uncle Gavin said.

"You can send me your bill."

"For what?" Uncle Gavin said.

"For being the witness," Mr Snopes said.

"Oh," Uncle Gavin said. And now Mr Snopes was going and Uncle Gavin said how he expected he might even have said Are you going back to town now? or maybe even Shall we walk together? or maybe at last Good-bye. But he didn't. He didn't say anything at all. He simply turned and left and was gone too. Then Mrs Hait said:

"Get the box."

"That's what I been aiming to do soon as you can turn loose all this business and steady this skillet," old Het said. So Mrs Hait came and took the chair and the fork and old Het went into the shed and set the lantern on the ground and brought the box and set it at the fire. "Now, honey," she said to Uncle Gavin, "set down and rest."

"You take it," Uncle Gavin said. "I've been sitting down all day. You haven't." Though old Het had already begun to sit down on the box before he declined it; she had already forgotten him, watching now the skillet containing the still hissing ham which Mrs Hait had lifted from the fire.

"Was it you mentioned something about a piece of that ham," she said, "or was it me?" So Mrs Hait divided the ham and Uncle Gavin watched them eat, Mrs Hait in the chair with the new plate and knife and fork, and old Het on the box eating from the skillet itself since Mrs Hait had apparently purchased only one of each new article, eating the ham and sopping the bread into the greasy residue of its frying, and old Het had filled the coffee-cup from the pot and produced from somewhere an empty can for her own use when I.O. came back, coming up quietly out of the darkness (it was full dark now), to stand holding his hands to the blaze as though he were cold.

"I reckon I'll take that ten dollars," he said.

"What ten dollars?" Mrs Hait said. And now Uncle Gavin expected him to roar, or at least snarl. But he did neither, just standing there with his hands to the blaze; and Uncle Gavin said he did look cold, small, forlorn somehow since he was so calm, so quiet.

"You ain't going to give it back to me?" he said.

"Give what back to you?" Mrs Hait said. Uncle Gavin said he didn't seem to expect an answer nor even to hear her: just standing at the fire in a kind of quiet and unbelieving amazement.

"I bear the worry and the risk and the agoment for years and years, and I get sixty dollars a head for them. While you, one time, without no trouble and risk a-tall, sell Lonzo Hait and five of my mules that never even belonged to him for eighty-five hundred dollars. Of course most of that-ere eighty-five hundred was for Lonzo, which I never begrudged you. Can't nere a man living say I did, even if it did seem a little strange that you should get it all, even my sixty standard price a head for them five mules, when he wasn't working for you and you never even knowed where he was, let alone even owned the mules; that all you done to get half of that money was jest to be married to him. And now, after all them years of not actively begrudging you it, you taken the last mule I had, not didn't jest beat me out of another hundred and forty dollars, but out of a entire another hundred and fifty."

"You got your mule back, and you ain't satisfied yet?" old Het said. "What does you want?"

"Justice," I.O. said. "That's what I want. That's all I want: justice. For the last time," he said. "Are you going to give me my ten dollars back?"

"What ten dollars?" Mrs Hait said. Then he turned. He stumbled over something—Uncle Gavin said it was old Het's shopping-bag—and recovered and went on. Uncle Gavin said he could see him for a moment—he could because neither Mrs Hait nor old Het was watching him any longer—as though framed between the two blackened chimneys, flinging both clenched hands up against the sky. Then he was gone; this time it was for good. That is, Uncle Gavin watched him. Mrs Hait and old Het had not even looked up.

"Honey," old Het said to Mrs Hait, "what did you do with that mule?" Uncle Gavin said there was one slice of bread left. Mrs Hait took it and sopped the last of the gravy from her plate.

"I shot it," she said.

"You which?" old Het said. Mrs Hait began to eat the slice of bread. "Well," old Het said, "the mule burnt the house and you shot the mule. That's what I calls more than justice: that's what I calls tit for tat." It was full dark now, and ahead of her was still the mile-and-a-half walk to the poorhouse with the heavy shopping-bag. But the dark would last a long time on a winter night, and Uncle Gavin said the poorhouse too wasn't likely to move any time soon. So he said that old Het sat back on the box with the empty skillet in her hand and sighed with peaceful and happy relaxation. "Gentlemen, hush," she said. "Ain't we had a day."

And there, as Uncle Gavin would say, was Ratliff again, sitting in the client's chair with his blue shirt neat and faded and quite clean and still no necktie even though he was wearing the imitation leather jacket and carrying the heavy black policeman's slicker which were his winter overcoat; it was Monday and Uncle Gavin had gone that morning over to New Market to the supervisors' meeting on some more of the drainage-canal business and I thought he would have told Ratliff that when Ratliff came to see him yesterday afternoon at home.

"He might a mentioned it," Ratliff said. "But it don't matter. I didn't want nothing. I jest stopped in here where it's quiet to laugh a little."

"Oh," I said. "About I.O. Snopes's mule that burned down Mrs Hait's house. I thought you and Uncle Gavin laughed at that enough yesterday."

"That's right," he said. "Because soon as you set down to laugh at it, you find out it ain't funny a-tall." He looked at me. "When will your uncle be back?"

"I thought he would be back now."

"Oh well," he said. "It don't matter." He looked at me again. "So that's two down and jest one more to go."

"One more what?" I said. "One more Snopes for Mr Flem to run out of Jefferson, and the only Snopes left will be him; or—"

"That's right," he said. "—one more uncivic ditch to jump like Montgomery Ward's photygraph studio and I.O.'s railroad mules, and there won't be nothing a-tall left in Jefferson but Flem Snopes." He looked at me. "Because your uncle missed it."

"Missed what?" I said.

"Even when he was looking right at it when Flem his—himself come in here the morning after them—those federals raided that studio and give your uncle that studio key that had been missing from the sheriff's office ever since your uncle and Hub found them—those pictures; and even when it was staring him in the face out yonder at Miz Hait's chimbley Saturday night when Flem give—gave her that mortgage and paid I.O. for the mules, he still missed it. And I can't tell him."

"Why can't you tell him?" I said.

"Because he wouldn't believe me. This here is the kind of a thing you—a man has got to know his—himself. He has got to

learn it out of his own hard dread and skeer. Because what somebody else jest tells you, you jest half believe, unless it was something you already wanted to hear. And in that case, you don't
even listen to it because you had done already agreed, and so all
it does is make you think what a sensible feller it was that told you.
But something you don't want to hear is something you had done
already made up your mind against, whether you knowed—knew
it or not; and now you can even insulate against having to believe
it by resisting or maybe even getting even with that-ere scoundrel
that meddled in and told you."

"So he wouldn't hear you because he wouldn't believe it
because it is something he don't want to be true. Is that it?"

"That's right," Ratliff said. "So I got to wait. I got to wait for
him to learn it his—himself, the hard way, the sure way, the only
sure way. Then he will believe it, enough anyhow to be afraid."

"He is afraid," I said. "He's been afraid a long time."

"That's good," Ratliff said. "Because he had purely better be.
All of us better be. Because a feller that jest wants money for the
sake of money, or even for power, there's a few things right at the
last that he won't do, will stop at. But a feller that come—came
up from where he did, that soon as he got big enough to count it
he thought he discovered that money would buy anything he
could or would ever want, and shaped all the rest of his life and
actions on that, trompling when and where he had to but without
no—any hard feelings because he knowed—knew that he
wouldn't ask nor expect no—any quarter his—himself if it had
been him—to do all this and then find out at last, when he was a
man growed—grown and it was maybe already too late, that the
one thing he would have to have if there was to be any meaning
to his life or even peace in it was not only something that jest
money couldn't buy, it was something that not having money to
begin with or even getting a holt of all he could count or imagine
or even dream about and then losing it, couldn't even hurt or
harm or grieve or change or alter—to find out when it was
almost too late that what he had to have was something that any
child was born having for free until one day he growed—grew up
and found out when it was maybe too late that he had throwed
—thrown it away."

"What?" I said. "What is it he's got to have?"

"Respectability," Ratliff said.

"Respectability?"

"That's right," Ratliff said. "When it's jest money and power a man wants, there is usually some place where he will stop; there's always one thing at least that ever—every man won't do jest for money. But when it's respectability he finds out he wants and has got to have, there ain't nothing he won't do to get it and then keep it. And when it's almost too late when he finds out that's what he's got to have, and that even after he gets it he can't jest lock it up and set—sit down on top of it and quit, but instead he has got to keep on working with ever—every breath to keep it, there ain't nothing he will stop at, ain't nobody or nothing within his scope and reach that may not anguish and grieve and suffer."

"Respectability," I said.

"That's right," Ratliff said. "Vice-president of that bank ain't enough any more. He's got to be president of it."

"*Got* to be?" I said.

"I mean soon, that he don't dare risk waiting, putting it off. That girl of Miz Snopes's—Linda. She's going on—"

"She'll be nineteen the twelfth of April," I said.

"—nineteen now, over there—How do you know it's the twelfth?"

"That's what Uncle Gavin says," I said.

"Sho, now," Ratliff said. Then he was talking again. "—at the University at Oxford where there's a thousand extry young fellers all new and strange and interesting and male and nobody a-tall to watch her except a hired dormitory matron that ain't got no wife expecting to heir half of one half of Uncle Billy Varner's money, when it was risky enough at the Academy right here in Jefferson last year before your uncle or her maw or whichever it was or maybe both of them together, finally persuaded Flem to let her quit at the Academy and go to the University after Christmas where he couldn't his—himself supervise her masculine acquaintance down to the same boys she had growed—grown up with all her life so at least their folks might have kinfolks that owed him money to help handle them; not to mention having her home ever—every night where he could reach out and put his hand on her ever—every time the clock struck you might say. So he can't, he dassent, risk it; any time now the telegram or the telephone might come saying

H

she had jest finished running off to the next nearest town with a
J.P. in it that never give a hoot who Flem Snopes was, and got
married. And even if he located them ten minutes later and
dragged her—"

"Drug," I said.

"—back, the—what?" he said.

"Drug," I said. "You said 'dragged'."

Ratliff looked at me a while. "For ten years now, whenever he
would stop talking his-self long enough that is, and for five of
them I been listening to you too, trying to learn—teach myself to
say words right. And, jest when I call myself about to learn and I
begin to feel a little good over it, here you come, of all people,
correcting me back to what I been trying for ten years to forget."

"I'm sorry," I said. "I didn't mean it that way. It's because I
like the way you say it. When you say it, 'taken' sounds a heap
more took than just 'took', just like 'drug' sounds a heap more
dragged than just 'dragged'."

"And not jest you neither," Ratliff said. "Your uncle too: me
saying 'dragged' and him saying 'drug' and me saying 'dragged'
and him saying 'drug' again, until at last he would say, 'In a free
country like this, why ain't I got as much right to use your *drug* for
my *dragged* as you got to use my *dragged* for your *drug*?' "

"All right," I said. " 'Even if he drug her back.' "

"—even if he drug—dragged—drug—You see?" he said.
"Now you done get me so mixed up until even I don't know
which one I don't want to say?"

" '—it would be too late and the damage—' " I said.

"Yes," Ratliff said. "And at least even your Uncle Gavin knows
this; even a feller as high- and delicate-minded as him must know
that the damage would be done then and Miz Snopes would quit
Flem too and he could kiss good-bye not jest to her share of Uncle
Billy's money but even to the voting weight of his bank stock too.
So Flem's got to strike now, and quick. He's not only got to be
president of that bank to at least keep that much of a holt on that
Varner money by at least being president of where Uncle Billy
keeps it at, he's got to make his lick before the message comes that
Linda's done got married or he'll lose the weight of Uncle Billy's
voting stock."

GAVIN STEVENS

AT last we knew why he had moved his money. It was as a bait. Not putting it into the other bank, the old Bank of Jefferson, as the bait, but for the people of Jefferson and Yoknapatawpha County to find out that he had withdrawn his own money from the bank of which he himself was vice-president, and put it somewhere else.

But that wasn't first. At first he was simply trying to save it. Because he knew no better then. His association with banks had been too brief and humble for the idea even to have occurred to him that there was a morality to banking, an inevictable ethics in it, else not only the individual bank but banking as an institution, a form of social behaviour, could not endure.

His idea and concept of a bank was that of the Elizabethan tavern or a frontier inn in the time of the opening of the American wilderness: you stopped there before dark for shelter from the wilderness; you were offered food and lodging for yourself and horse, and a bed (of sorts) to sleep in; if you waked the next morning with your purse rifled or your horse stolen or even your throat cut, you had none to blame but yourself since nobody had compelled you to pass that way nor insisted on your stopping. So when he realised that the very circumstances which had made him vice-president of a bank had been born of the fact that the bank had been looted by an oaf with no more courage or imagination than he knew his cousin Byron to possess, his decision to remove his money from it as soon as he could was no more irrational than the traveller who, unsaddling in the inn yard, sees a naked body with its throat cut being flung from an upstairs window and recinches his saddle with no loss of time and remounts and rides on again, to find another inn perhaps, or if not, to pass the night in the woods, which, after all, Indians and bears and highwaymen to the contrary, would not be a great deal more unsafe.

It was simply to save his money—that money he had worked so hard to accumulate, too hard to accumulate, sacrificed all his life to gather together from whatever day it had been on whatever worn-out tenant farm his father had moved from, on to that other worn-out one of old Will Varner's at Frenchman's Bend which nobody else except a man who had nothing would undertake, let alone hope, to wrest a living from—from that very first day when he realised that he himself had nothing and would never have more than nothing unless he wrested it himself from his environment and time, and that the only weapon he would ever have to do it with would be just money.

Oh yes, sacrificed all his life for, sacrificed all the other rights and passions and hopes which make up the sum of a man and his life. Perhaps he would never, could never, have fallen in love himself and knew it: himself constitutionally and generically unfated ever to match his own innocence and capacity for virginity against the innocence and virginity of who would be his first love. But, since he was a man, to do that was his inalienable right and hope. Instead, his was to father another man's bastard on the wife who would not even repay him with the passion of gratitude, let alone the passion of passion since he was obviously incapable of that passion, but merely with her dowry.

Too hard for it, all his life for it, knowing at the same time that as long as life lasted he could never for one second relax his vigilance, not just to add to it but simply to keep, hang on to, what he already had, had so far accumulated. Amassing it by terrible and picayune nickel by nickel, having learned soon, almost simultaneously probably, that he would never have any other method of gaining it save simple ruthless antlike industry, since (and this was the first time he ever experienced humility) he knew now that he not only had not the education with which to cope with those who did have education, whom he must outguess and outfigure and despoil, but that he never would have that education now, since there was no time now, since his was the fate to have first the need for the money before he had opportunity to acquire the means to get it. And, even having acquired some of the money, he still had no place to put it down in safety while he did acquire the education which would enable him to defend it from those with the education who would despoil him of it in their turn.

Humility, and maybe a little even of regret—what little time there was to regret in—but without despair, who had nothing save the will and the need and the ruthlessness and the industry and what talent he had been born with, to serve them; who never in his life had been given anything by any man yet and expected no more as long as life should last; who had no evidence yet that he could cope with and fend off that enemy which the word Education represented to him, yet had neither qualm nor doubt that he was going to try.

So at first his only thought was to save that money which had cost him so dear, had in fact cost him everything, since he had sacrificed his whole life to gain it and so it was his life, from the bank which his cousin had already proved vulnerable. That was it: a bank so vulnerable that someone like the one he himself knew his cousin Byron to be could have robbed it—an oaf without courage or even vision in brigandage to see further than the simple temptation of a few temporarily unguarded nickels and dimes and dollar bills of the moment, a feller, as Ratliff would have said, hardly bright enough to be named Snopes even, not even bright enough to steal the money without having to run immediately all the way to Texas before he could stop long enough to count it; having in fact managed to steal just about enough to buy the railroad ticket with.

Because remember, he didn't merely know that banks could be looted (*vide* his cousin Byron which he had witnessed himself), he believed, it was a tenet of his very being, that they were constantly looted; that the normal condition of a bank was a steady and decorous embezzlement, its solvency an impregnable illusion like the reputation of a woman who everybody knows has none yet which is intact and invulnerable because of the known (maybe proven) fact that every one of her male connections will spring as one man, not just to repudiate but to avenge with actual gunfire the slightest whisper of a slur on it. Because that—the looting of them—was the reason for banks, the only reason why anybody would go to the trouble and expense of organising one and keeping it running.

That was what Colonel Sartoris had done (he didn't know how yet, that was the innocence, but give him time) while he was president, and what Manfred de Spain would do as long as he in his turn could or did remain on top. But decently, with decorum, as they had done and would do: not rieved like a boy snatching a handful of loose peanuts while the vendor's back was turned, as his cousin Byron had done. Decently and peacefully and even more: cleverly, intelligently; so cleverly and quietly that the very people whose money had been stolen would not even discover it until after the looter was dead and safe. Nor even then actually, since by that time the looter's successor would have already shouldered the burden of that yet-intact disaster which was a natural part of his own heritage. Because, to repeat, what other reason was there to establish a bank, go to all the work and trouble to start one to be president of, as Colonel Sartoris had done; and to line up enough voting stock, figure and connive and finagle and swap and trade (not to mention digging into his own pocket— Ratliff always said De Spain borrowed some if not all of it on his personal note from old Will Varner—to replace the sum which Byron Snopes had stolen) to get himself elected president after the Colonel's death, as Manfred de Spain had done: who—De Spain—would have to be more clever even than the Colonel had been, since he—De Spain—must also contrive to cover up the Colonel's thievery in order to have any bank to loot himself.

He didn't—to repeat again—know how Colonel Sartoris had done it and how De Spain would continue to do it of course—how Colonel Sartoris had robbed it for twelve years yet still contrived to die and be buried in the odour of unimpugnable rectitude; and how De Spain would carry on in his turn and then quit his tenure (whenever that would be) not only with his reputation unimpaired but somehow even leaving intact that bubble of the bank's outward solvency. Or not yet, anyway. Which may have been when he first really tasted that which he had never tasted before— the humility of not knowing, of never having had any chance to learn the rules and methods of the deadly game in which he had gauged his life; whose fate was to have the dreadful need and the will and the ruthlessness, and then to have the opportunity itself thrust upon him before he had had any chance to learn how to use it.

So all he knew to do was to move his money out of the bank of which he was only vice-president: not high enough in rank to rob it himself in one fell swoop which would net him enough to make it worth while fleeing beyond extradition for the rest of his life, nor even high enough in its hierarchy to defend himself from the inevitable next Byron Snopes who would appear at the book-keeper's desk, let alone from the greater hereditary predator who already ranked him.

And then he had nowhere to put it. If he could withdraw it from his own bank in utter secrecy, with no one ever to know it, he could have risked hiding it in his house or burying it in the back yard. But it would be impossible to keep it a secret; if no one else, the very book-keeper who recorded the transaction would be an automatic threat. And if word did spread that he had withdrawn his money from the bank in cash, every man and his cousin in the county would be his threat and enemy until every one of them was incontrovertibly convinced that the actual money actually was somewhere else, and exactly where that somewhere else was.

So he had no choice. It would have to be another bank, and done publicly. Of course he thought at once of the best bank he could find, the strongest and safest one: a big Memphis bank for instance. And here he had a new thought: a big bank where his (comparative) widow's mite would be safe because of its very minuscularity; but, believing as he did that money itself, cash dollars, possessed an inherent life of its mutual own like cells or disease, his minuscule sum would increment itself by simple parasitic osmosis like a leech or a goitre or cancer.

And even when he answered that thought immediately with *No. That won't do. The specific whereabouts of the money must be in-dubitably and incontrovertibly known. All Jefferson and Yoknapatawpha County must know by incontrovertible evidence that the money still is and will remain in Jefferson and Yoknapatawpha County, or I won't even dare leave my home long enough to go to the post-office, for my neighbours and fellow citizens waiting to climb in the kitchen window to hunt for the sock inside the mattress or the coffee-can beneath the hearth*, he did not yet realise what his true reason for moving the money was going to be. And even when he thought how by transferring it to the other Jefferson bank, he would simply be moving it from the frying-pan into the fire itself by laying it vulnerable to whatever Byron Snopes the Bank of Jefferson contained, not to mention that one's own Colonel Sartoris or Manfred de Spain, and immediately rejected that by reminding himself that the Bank of Jefferson was

older, had had a whole century since 1830 or so to adjust itself
to the natural and normal thieving of its officers and employees
which was the sole reason for a bank, and so by now its very unbroken longevity was a protection, its very unaltered walls themselves a guarantee, as the simple edifice of the longtime-standing
church contains, diffuses and even compels a sanctity invulnerable to the human frailties and vices of parson or vestry or choir—
even when he told himself this, his eyes had still not seen the
dazzling vista composed not only of civic rectitude but of personal
and private triumph and revenge too which the simple withdrawing of that first dollar had opened before him.

He was too busy; his own activity blinded him. Not just getting
the money from one bank to the other, but seeing to it, making
sure, that everyone in the town and the county knew that he was
doing so, labouring under his preconception that the one universal
reaction of every man in the county to the news that he had withdrawn his money from the Sartoris bank would be determined the
intention of stealing it as soon as he put it down and turned his
back; not for the county to know he had withdrawn it from a
bank, but that he had put every cent of it into a bank.

It was probably days afterward, the money safe again or at
least still again or at least for the moment still again; and I like
to imagine it: one still in the overalls and the tieless shirt and still
thrall, attached irrevocably by the lean umbilicus of bare liveli-
hood which if it ever broke he would, solvently speaking, die,
to the worn-out tenant farm which—the farm and the tieless shirt
and the overalls—he had not wrenched free of yet as Snopes himself had, nor ever would probably and who for that very reason
had watched the rise of one exactly like himself, from the overalls
and the grinding landlord to a white shirt and a tie and the vice-
presidency of a bank; watched this not with admiration but simply
with envy and respect (ay, hatred too), stopping Snopes on the
street one day, calling him mister, servile and cringing because
of the white shirt and the tie but hating them also because they
were not his:

"Likely hit ain't a thing to it, but I heerd tell you taken your
money outen your bank."

"That's right," Snopes said. "Into the Bank of Jefferson."

"Outen the bank that you yourself are vice-president of."

"That's right," Snopes said. "Into the Bank of Jefferson."

"You mean, the other one ain't safe?" Which to Snopes was to laugh, to whom no bank was safe; to whom any bank was that clump of bushes at the forest's edge behind the one-room frontier cabin, which the pioneer had to use for outhouse since he had no other: the whole land, the whole dark wilderness (which meant the clump of bushes too) infested with Indians and brigands, not to mention bears and wolves and snakes. Of course it was not safe. But he had to go there. Because not until then did that vista, prospect containing the true reason why he moved his money, open before him. "Then you advise me to move mine too."

"No," Snopes said. "I just moved mine."

"Outen the bank that you yourself air vice-president of."

"That's right," Snopes said. "That I myself am vice-president of."

"I see," the other said. "Well, much oblige."

Because he saw it then, whose civic jealousy and pride four years later would evict and eliminate from Jefferson one of his own kinsmen who had set up a pay-as-you-enter peep show with a set of imported pornographic photographs, by planting in his place of business several gallons of untaxed home-made whiskey and then notifying the federal revenue people; the same civic jealousy and pride which six years later would evict and eliminate from Jefferson another (and the last) objectionable member of his tribe who had elevated into a profession the simple occupation of hitching mules between the rails at a strategic curve of the railroad where engine drivers couldn't see them in time, by the direct expedient of buying the kinsman's remaining mules at his —the kinsman's—own figure on condition that the kinsman never show his face in Jefferson again.

Civic jealousy and pride which you might say only discovered civic jealousy and pride at the same moment he realised that, in the simple process of saving his own private money from rapine and ravagement, he could with that same stroke evict and eliminate from his chosen community its arch-fiend among sinners too, its supremely damned among the lost infernal seraphim: a creature who was a living mockery of virtue and morality because he was a paradox: lately mayor of the town and now president of one of its two banks and a warden of the Episcopal church, who was not content to be a normal natural Saturday-night whore-monger or woman chaser whom the town could have forgiven for the simple reason that he was natural and human and understand-able and censurable, but instead must set up a kind of outrageous morality of adultery, a kind of flaunted uxoriousness in *paramours* based on an unimpugnable fidelity which had already lasted flagrant and unimpugnable ever since the moment the innocent cuckolded husband brought the female partner of it into town twelve years ago and which promised, bade or boded, whichever side you are on, to last another twelve unless the husband found some way to stop it, and twice twelve probably if he—the husband —waited for the town itself to do anything about it.

Civic virtue which, like all virtue, was its own reward also. Because in that same blinding flash he saw his own vengeance and revenge too, as if not just virtue loved virtue, but so did God since here He was actually offering to share with virtue that quality which He had jealously reserved solely to Himself: the husband's vengeance and revenge on the man who had presented him with the badge of his championship; vengeance and revenge on the man who had not merely violated his home but outraged it—the home which in all good faith he had tried to establish around a woman already irrevocably soiled and damaged in the world's (Frenchman's Bend's, which was synonymous enough then) sight, and so give her bastard infant a name. He had been paid for it, of course. That is, he had received her dowry: a planta-tion of barely accessible worn-out land containing the weed-choked ruins of a formal garden and the remains (what the neighbours had not pulled down plank by plank for firewood) of a columned colonial house—a property so worthless that Will Varner gave it away, since even as ruthless an old pirate as Will Varner had failed in a whole quarter-century of ownership to evolve any way to turn a penny out of it; so worthless in fact that even he, Snopes, had been reduced to one of the oldest and hoariest expedients man ever invented: the salted gold-mine: in order to sell the place to Henry Armstid and V. K. Ratliff, one of whom, Ratliff anyhow, should certainly have known better, for which reason he, Snopes, had no pity on him.

So in return for that worthless dowry (worthless since what value it had he had not found in it but himself had brought there) he had assumed the burden not only of his wife's moral fall and shame, but of the nameless child too; giving his name to it. Not much of a name maybe, since like what remained of the Old Frenchman's plantation, what value he found in it he himself had brought there. But it was the only name he had, and even if it had been Varner (ay, or Sartoris or De Spain or Compson or Grenier or Habersham or McCaslin or any of the other cognomens long and splendid in the annals of Yoknapatawpha County) he would have done the same.

Anyway, he gave the child a name and then moved the mother herself completely away from that old stage and scene and milieu of her shame, on to, into a new one, where at least no man could say *I saw that fall* but only *This is what gossip said*. Not that he expected gratitude from her, any more than he did from old Will Varner, who by his (Varner's) lights had already paid him. But he did expect from her the simple sense and discretion taught by hard experience: not gratitude toward him but simple sensibleness toward herself, as you neither expect nor care that the person you save from burning is grateful for being saved but at least you expect that from now on that person will stay away from fire.

But that was not the point, that maybe women are no more capable of sensibleness than they are of gratitude. Maybe women are capable only of gratitude, capable of nothing else but gratitude. Only, since the past no more exists for them than morality does, they have nothing which might have taught them sensibility with which to deal with the future and gratitude toward what or who saved them from the past; gratitude in them is a quality like electricity: it has to be produced, projected and consumed all in the same instant to exist at all.

Which was simply saying what any and every man whose fate —doom, destiny, call it whatever you will—finally led him into marriage, long since and soon learned the hard way: his home had been violated not because his wife was ungrateful and a fool, but simply because she was a woman. She had no more been seduced from the chastity of wifehood by the incorrigible bachelor flash and swagger of Manfred de Spain than she had been seduced from that of maidenhood by that same quality in that boy— youth—man—McCarron—back there in her virginity which he was convinced she no longer even remembered. She was seduced

simply by herself: by a nymphomania not of the uterus: the hot
unbearable otherwise unreachable itch and burn of the mare or
heifer or sow or bitch in season, but by a nymphomania of a gland
whose only ease was in creating a situation containing a recipient
for gratitude, then supplying the gratitude.

Which still didn't exculpate Manfred de Spain. He didn't
expect Manfred de Spain to have such high moral standards that
they would forbid him seducing somebody else's wife. But he did
expect him to have enough sense not to, since he wasn't a woman;
to have too much sense this time, enough sense to look a little
ahead into the future and refrain from seducing this wife anyway.
But he hadn't. Worse: De Spain had even tried to recompense
him for the privilege of that violation and defilement; out of base
fear to pay him in base and niggling coin for what he, De Spain,
juxtaposing De Spain against Snopes, considered his natural and
normal *droit de seigneur*. True, old Will Varner had paid him for
marrying his damaged daughter, but that was not the same. Old
Will wasn't even trying to cover up, let alone liquidate, his
daughter's shame. The very fact of what he offered for it—that
ruined and valueless plantation of which even he, with a quarter
of a century to do it in, had been able to make nothing, revealed
what value he held that honour at; and as for liquidating the
shame, he—old Will—would have done that himself with his
pistol, either in his hand or in that of his oafish troglodyte son Jody
if he had ever caught McCarron. He—old Will—had simply used
that forthrightness to offer what he considered a fair price to get
out of his house the daughter who had already once outraged his
fireside peace and in time would very likely do it again.

But not De Spain, who without courage at all had tried to
barter and haggle, using his position as mayor of the town to offer
the base coinage of its power-plant superintendency and its implied privileges of petty larceny, not only to pay for the gratifica-
tion of his appetite but to cover his reputation, trying to buy at
the same time the right to the wife's bed and the security of his
good name from the husband who owned them both—this, for
the privilege of misappropriating a handful of brass which he—
Snopes—had availed himself of not for the petty profit it brought
him but rather to see what depth De Spain's base and timorous
fear would actually descend to.

He saw. They both did. It was not his—Snopes's—shame any more than it was De Spain's pride that when the final crisis of the brass came which could have destroyed him, De Spain found for ally his accuser himself. The accuser, the city official sworn and —so he thought until that moment—dedicated too, until he too proved to be vulnerable (not competent: merely vulnerable) to that same passion from which derived what should have been his —De Spain's—ruin and desolation; the sworn and heretofore dedicated city official who found too dangerous for breathing too that same air simply because she had breathed it, walked in it while it laved and ached; the accuser, the community's civic champion likewise blasted and stricken by that same lightning-bolt out of the old passion and the old anguish. But for him (the accuser) only the grieving without even the loss; for him not even ruin to crown the grieving: only the desolation, who was not competent for but merely vulnerable to, since it was not even for him to hold her hand.

So De Spain brazened that through too, abrogating to courage what had merely been his luck. And as if that were not temerity enough, effrontery enough: Colonel Sartoris barely dead of his heart attack in his grandson's racing automobile (almost as though he—De Spain—had suborned the car and so contrived the accident) and the presidency of the bank barely vacant, when here he—De Spain—was again not requesting or suggesting but with that crass and brazen gall assuming, taking it for granted that he, Snopes, was downright panting for the next new chance not merely to re-compound but publicly affirm again his own cuckolding, that mutual co-violating of his wife's bed—ay, publicly affirming her whoredom; the last clod still echoing as it were on Colonel Sartoris's coffin when De Spain approaches, figuratively rubbing his hands, already saying, "All right, let's get going. That little shirt-tail full of stock you own will help some of course. But we need a big block of it. You step out to Frenchman's Bend tomorrow—tonight if possible—and sew up Uncle Billy before somebody else gets to him. Get moving now." Or maybe even the true explicit words: *Your kinsman—cousin—has destroyed this bank by removing a link, no matter how small or large, in the chain of its cash integrity. Which means not just the value of the stock you own in it, but the actual dollars and cents which you worked so hard to acquire and deposit in*

it, and which until last night were available to you on demand, were still
yours. The only way to anneal that chain is to restore that link to the last
penny which your cousin stole. I will do that, but in return for it I must be
president of the bank; anyone who restores that money will insist on being
president in return, just as anyone to become president will have to restore
that money first. That's your choice: keep the par of your stock and the full
value of your deposit through a president that you know exactly how far you
can trust him, or take your chance with a stranger to whom the value of
your stock and deposit may possibly mean no more than they did to your
cousin Byron.

He obeyed. He had no choice. Because there was the innocence;
ignorance, if you like. He had naturally taught himself all he
could about banking, since he had to use them or something
equivalent to keep his money in. But so far his only opportunities
had been while waiting in line at a window, to peer through the
grilled barricade which separated the money and the methods
of handling it from the people to whom it belonged, who brought
it in and relinquished it on that simple trust of one human being
in another, since there was no alternative between that baseless
trust and a vulnerable coffee-can buried under a bush in the back
yard.

Nor was it only to save his own money that he obeyed. In going
out to Frenchman's Bend to solicit the vote of old Will Varner's
stock for Manfred de Spain, he not only affirmed the fact that
simple baseless unguaranteed unguaranteeable trust between man
and man was solvent, he defended the fact that it not only could
endure: it must endure, since the robustness of a nation was in
the solvency of its economy, and the solvency of an economy
depended on the rectitude of its banks and the sacredness of the
individual dollars they contained, no matter to whom the dollars
individually belonged, and that rectitude and sanctity must in the
last analysis depend on the will of man to trust and the capacity
of man to be trusted; in sacrificing the sanctity of his home to the
welfare of Jefferson, he immolated the chastity of his wife on the
altar of mankind.

And at what added price: not just humbling his pride but
throwing it completely away to go out there and try to persuade,
perhaps even plead and beg with that old pirate in his dingy
country store at Varner's Crossroads—that tall lean choleric out-

rageous old brigand with his grim wife herself not church-ridden
but herself running the local church she belonged to with the cold
high-handedness of a ward-boss, and his mulatto concubines
(Ratliff said he had three: the first Negroes in that section of the
county and for a time the only ones he would permit there, by
whom he now had grandchildren, this—the second—generation
already darkening back but carrying intact still the worst of the
new White Varner traits grafted on to the worst of their fatherless
or two-fathered grandmothers' combined original ones), who was
anything in the world but unmoral since his were the strictest of
simple moral standards: that whatever Will Varner decided to
do was right, and anybody in the way had damned well better
beware.

Yet he went, to deal with the old man who despised him for
having accepted an already-dishonoured wife for a price no
greater than what he, Varner, considered the Old Frenchman
place to be worth; and who feared him because he, Snopes, had
been smart enough to realise from it what he, Varner, had not
been able to in twenty-five years; who feared him for what that
smartness threatened and implied and therefore hated him because he had to fear.

And dealt with him too, persuaded or tricked or forced. Even
Ratliff, whose Yoknapatawpha County reputation and good name
demanded that he have an answer to everything, did not have
that one, Ratliff himself knowing no more than the rest of us did,
which was, one day there was a rumoured coalition De Spain-
Varner-Snopes; on the second day De Spain's own personal hand
restored the money which Byron Snopes had absconded to Texas
with; on the third day the stockholders elected De Spain president
of the Bank and Flem Snopes vice-president.

That was all. Because there was the innocence. Not ignorance;
he didn't know the inner workings of banks not because of ignorance but simply because he had not had opportunity and time
yet to teach himself. Now he had only the need, the desperate
necessity of having to save the entire bank in order to free his own
deposit in it long enough to get the money out and into safety
somewhere. And now that he was privileged, the actual vice-
president of it, from whom all the most secret mechanisms and
ramifications of banking and the institution of banks, not only the

terror and threat of them but the golden perquisites too, could no longer be hidden, he had less than ever of time. He had in fact time only to discover how simple and easy it was to steal from a bank since even a courageless unimaginative clod like his cousin Byron, who probably could not even conceive of a sum larger than a thousand or two dollars, had been able to do it with impunity; and to begin to get his own money out of it before all the rest of the employees, right on down to the Negro janitor who swept the floor every morning, would decide that the dust and alarm had settled enough to risk (or perhaps simply that the supply of loose money had built up enough again to make it worth while) emulating him.

That was it: the rush, the hurry, the harassment; it was prob-ably with something very like shame that he remembered how it was not his own perspicuity at all but the chance meeting with an ignorant country man alarmed over his own (probably) two-figure bank balance, which opened to him that vista, that dazzling opportunity to combine in one single stroke security for himself and revenge on his enemy—that vengeance which had apparently been afoot for days and even weeks since a well-nigh nameless tenant farmer who probably never came to town four times a year had been his first notice of its existence; that revenge which he was not only unaware of, which he himself had not even planned and instigated, as if the gods or fates—circumstance—something—had taken up the cudgel in his behalf without even asking his permission, and naturally would some day send him a bill for it.

But he saw it now. Not to destroy the bank itself, wreck it, bring it down about De Spain's ears like Samson's temple; but simply to move it still intact out from under De Spain. Because the bank stood for money. A bank was money, and as Ratliff said, he would never injure money, cause to totter for even one second the parity and immunity of money; he had too much veneration for it. He would simply move the bank and the money it represented and stood for, out from under De Spain, intact and uninjured and not even knowing it had been moved, into a new physical niche in the hegemony and economy of the town, leaving De Spain high and dry with nothing remaining save the mortgage on his house which (according to Ratliff) he had given old Will Varner for the money with which to restore what Byron Snopes had stolen.

Only, how to do it. How to evict De Spain from the bank or remove the bank from under De Spain without damaging it—snatch it intact from under De Spain by persuading or frightening enough more of the depositors into withdrawing their money; how to start the avalanche of dollars which would suck it dry; persuade enough of the depositors and stockholders to move their stock and funds bodily out of this one and into a new set of walls across the Square, or perhaps even (who knew) into the set of walls right next door to De Spain's now empty ones without even breaking the slumber of the bank's solvency.

Because even if every other one-gallused share-cropper in the county whose sole cash value was the October or November sale of the single bale of cotton which was his tithe of this year's work, withdrew his balance also, it would not be enough. Nor did he have nature, biology, nepotism, for his weapon. Although there were probably more people named Snopes or married to a Snopes or who owed sums ranging from twenty-five cents to five dollars to a Snopes, than any other name in that section of Mississippi, with one exception not one of them represented the equity of even one bale of share-crop cotton, and that exception—Wallstreet Panic, the grocer—already banked with the other bank and so could not have been used even if he—Flem—could have found any way to cope with the fierce implacable enmity of his—Wallstreet's wife.

And less than any did he possess that weapon which could have served him best of all: friendship, a roster of people whom he could have approached without fear or alarm and suggested or formed a cabal against De Spain. He had no friends. I mean, he knew he didn't have any friends because he had never (and never would) intended to have them, be cluttered with them, be constantly vulnerable or anyway liable to the creeping sentimental parasitic importunity which his observation had shown him friendship meant. I mean, this was probably when he discovered, for the first time in his life, that you needed friends for the simple reason that at any time a situation could—and in time would, no matter who you were—arise when you could use them; could not only use them but would have to, since nothing else save friendship, someone to whom you could say "Don't ask why; just take this mortgage or lien or warrant or distrainer or pistol and point it where I tell you, and pull the trigger," would do. Which was the innocence again: having had to scratch and scrabble and clutch and fight so soon and so hard and so unflaggingly long to get the money which he had to have, that he had had no time to teach himself how to hold on to it, defend and keep it (and this too with no regret either, since he still had no time to spend regretting). Yes, no regret for lack of that quantity which his life had denied him the opportunity to teach himself that he would need, not because he had no time for regret at this specific moment, but because that desperate crisis had not yet risen where even friendship would not have been enough. Even Time was on his side now; it would be five years yet before he would be forced to the last desperate win-all lose-all by the maturation of a female child.

Though he did have his one tool, weapon, implement—that nethermost stratum of unfutured, barely solvent one-bale tenant farmers which pervaded, covered thinly the whole county and on which in fact the entire cotton economy of the county was founded and supported; he had that at least, with running through his head probably all the worn platitudinous saws about the incrementation of the mere enoughs: enough grains of sand and single drops of water and pennies saved. And working underground now. He had always worked submerged each time until the mine was set and then blew up in the unsuspecting face. But this time he actually consorted with the moles and termites—not with Sartorises and Benbows and Edmondses and Habershams and the other names long in the county annals, which (who) owned the bank stock and the ponderable deposits, but with the other nameless tenants and croppers like his first interlocutor who as that one would have put it: "Knowed a rat when he smelt one."

He didn't proselytise among them. He was simply visible, depending on that first one to have spread the word, the idea, letting himself be seen going and coming out of the other bank, the Bank of Jefferson, himself biding until they themselves would contrive the accidental encounter for corroboration, in pairs or even groups, like a committee, straight man and clown, like this:

"Mawnin, Mister Snopes. Ain't you strayed off the range a little, over here at this bank?"

"Maybe Mister Flem has done got so much money now that jest one bank won't hold it."

"No, boys, it's like my old pappy used to say: Two traps will hold twice as many coons as one trap."

"Did your pappy ever ask that smart old coon which trap he would ruther be in, Mister Snopes?"

"No, boys. All that old coon ever said was, Just so it ain't the wrong trap."

That would be all. They would guffaw; one might even slap the faded blue of his overall knee. But that afternoon (or maybe they would even wait a day or two days or even a week) they would appear singly at the teller's window of the old long-established Bank of Jefferson, the gnarled warped sunburned hands relinquishing almost regretfully the meagre clutch of bank-notes; never to transfer the account by a simple check at the counter but going in person first to the bank which because of a whispered word supported by a clumsy parable they were repudi-ating, and withdraw the thin laborious sum in its actual cash and carry it across the Square to the other bank which at that same cryptic anonymous sourceless breath they would repudiate in its turn.

Because they were really neither moles nor termites. Moles can undermine foundations and the termites can reduce the entire house to one little pile of brown dust. But these had neither the individual determination of moles nor the communal determina-tion of the termites even though they did resemble ants in num-bers. Because like him, Snopes, they simply were trying to save their meagre individual dollars, and he—Flem—knew it: that another breath, word, would alarm them back into the other bank; that if De Spain himself only wanted to, with the judicious planting of that single word he could recover not merely his own old one-bale clients, but the Bank of Jefferson's entire roster too. Which he nor any other sane broker would want, since it would mean merely that many more Noes to say to the offers of galled mules and worn-out farm and household gear as security to make down payments on second-hand and worn-out automobiles.

It was not enough. It would be nowhere near enough. He

recast his mind, again down the diminishing vain roster of names which he had already exhausted, as though he had never before weighed them and found them all of no avail: his nephew or cousin Wallstreet Panic the grocer, who less than ten years ago, by simple industry and honesty and hard work, plus the thousand-dollar compensation for his father's violent death, had gained an interest in a small side-street grocery store and now, in that ten years, owned a small chain of them scattered about north Mississippi, with his own wholesale warehouse to supply them; who— Wallstreet—would alone have been enough to remove De Spain's bank from under him except for two insurmountable obstacles: the fact that he already banked and owned stock in the other bank, and the implacable enmity of his wife toward the very word Snopes, who, it was said in Jefferson, was even trying to persuade her husband to change his own by law. Then the rest of his tribe of Snopes, and the other Snopeses about the county who were not Snopeses nor tenant farmers either, who had been paying him the usury on five- or ten- or twenty-dollar loans for that many years, who, even if he could have enrolled them at the price of individual or maybe lump remission, would have added no weight to his cause for the simple reason that anyone with any amount of money in a public institution anywhere would never have dared put his signature on any piece of paper to remain in his, Flem's, possession.

Which brought him back to where he had started, once more to rack and cast his mind down the vain and diminishing list, knowing that he had known all the while that one name to which he would finally be reduced, and had been dodging it. Old man Will Varner, his father-in-law, knowing all the time that in the end he would have to eat that crow: go back to the choleric irascible old man who never had and never would forgive him for having tricked him into selling him the Old Frenchman place for five hundred dollars, which he, Flem, sold within two weeks for a profit of three or four hundred per cent; go back again to the old man whom only five years ago he had swallowed his pride and approached and persuaded to use the weight of his stock and money to make president of the bank the same man he must now persuade Varner to dispossess.

You see? That was his problem. Probably, except for the really incredible mischance that the bastard child he had given his name to happened to be female, he would never have needed to surmount it. He may have contented himself with the drowsy dream of his revenge, himself but half awake in the long-familiar embrace of his cuckoldry as you recline in a familiar chair with a familiar book, if his wife's bastard had not been a girl.

But she was. Which fact (oh yes, men are interested in facts too, even ones named Flem Snopes) must have struck him at last, whatever the day, moment, was, with an incredible unanticipated shock. Here was this thing, creature, which he had almost seen born you might say, and had seen, watched, every day of its life since. Yet in all innocence, unsuspecting, unforewarned. Oh, he knew it was female, and, continuing to remain alive, it must inevitably mature; and, being a human creature, on maturing it would have to be a woman. But he had been too busy making money, having to start from scratch (scratch? scratch was euphemism indeed for where he started from) to make money without owning or even hoping for anything to make it with, to have had time to learn or even to discover that he might need to learn anything about women. You see? A little thing, creature, is born; you say: It will be a horse or a cow, and in time it does become that horse or that cow and fits, merges, fades into environment with no seam, juncture, suture. But not that female thing or creature which becomes (you cannot stop it; not even Flem Snopes could) a woman—woman who shapes, fits herself to no environment, scorns the fixitude of environment and all the behaviour patterns which had been mutually agreed on as being best for the greatest number; but on the contrary just by breathing, just by the mere presence of that fragile and delicate flesh, warps and wrenches milieu itself to those soft unangled rounds and curves and planes.

That's what he had. That's what happened to him. Because by that time he had probably resigned himself to no more than the vain and hopeless dream of vengeance and revenge on his enemy. I mean, to canvass and canvass, cast and recast, only to come always back to that one-gallused one-bale residuum which if all their resources, including the price of the second-hand overalls too, could have been pooled, the result would not have shaken the economy of a country church, let alone a county-seat bank.

So he probably gave up, not to the acceptance of his horns, but at least to living with them.

Then the bastard child to whom in what you might call all innocence he had given his name, not satisfied with becoming just *a* woman, must become or threaten to become this particular and specific woman. Being female, she had to become a woman, which he had expected of her and indeed would not have held against her, provided she was content to become merely an ordinary woman. If he had had choice, he naturally would have plumped for a homely one, not really insisting on actual deformity, but one merely homely and frightened from birth and hence doomed to spinsterhood to that extent that her coeval young men would as one have taken one glance at her and then forgot they had ever seen her; and the one who would finally ask for her hand would have one eye, probably both, on her (purported) father's money and so would be malleable to his hand.

But not this one, who was obviously not only doomed for marriage from the moment she entered puberty, but as obviously doomed for marriage with someone beyond his control, either because of geography or age or, worst, most outrageous of all: simply because the husband already had money and would neither need nor want his. *Vide* the gorilla-sized bravo drawn from as far away as Ohio while she was still only fifteen years old, who with his Golden Gloves fists or maybe merely his Golden Gloves reputation intimidated into a male desert except for himself her very surrounding atmosphere; until he was dispossessed by a fact which even his Golden Gloves could not cope with: that she was a woman and hence not just unpredictable: incorrigible.

You see? The gorilla already destined to own at least a Ford agency if not an entire labour union, not dispossessed by nor even superseded by, because they overlapped: the crown prince of the motor age merely on the way out because his successor was already in: the bachelor lawyer twice her age who, although apparently now fixed fast and incapable of harm in the matrix of the small town, bringing into her life and her imagination that same deadly whiff of outland, meeting her in the afternoon at soft-drink stands, not just to entice and corrupt her female body but far worse: corrupting her mind, inserting into her mind and her imagination not just the impractical and dreamy folly in poetry books but the fatal poison of dissatisfaction's hopes and dreams.

You see? The middle-aged (whiteheaded too even) small-town lawyer you would have thought incapable and therefore safe, who had actually served as his, Flem's champion in the ejection of that first, the Ohio gorilla, threat, had now himself become even more of a danger, since he was persuading the girl herself to escape beyond the range of his control, not only making her dissatisfied with where she was and should be, but even showing her where she could go to seek images and shapes she didn't know she had until he put them in her mind.

That was his problem. He couldn't even solve it by choosing, buying for her a husband whom he could handle and control. Because he dared not let her marry anybody at all until God or the devil or justice or maybe simple nature herself, wearied to death of him, removed old Will Varner from the surface at least of the earth. Because the moment she married, the wife who had taken him for her husband for the single reason of providing her unborn child with a name (a little perhaps because of old Will's moral outrage and fury, a good deal maybe just to escape the noise he was probably making at the moment, but mostly, almost all, for the child) would quit him too, either with her present lover or without; in any case, with her father's will drawn eighteen years before she married Flem Snopes and ten or twelve before she ever heard of him, still unchanged.

She must not marry at all yet. Which was difficult enough to prevent even while she was at home in Jefferson, what with half the football and baseball teams escorting her home from school in the afternoon and squiring her in gangs to the picture show during her junior and senior high-school years. Because at least she was living at home where her father could more or less control things either by being her father (oh yes, her father; she knew no different and in fact would have denied, repudiated the truth if anyone had tried to tell her it, since women are not interested in truth or romance but only in facts whether they are true or not, just so they fit all the other facts, and to her the fact was that he was her father for the simple fact that all the other girls, boys too of course, had fathers unless they were dead beneath locatable tombstones) or by threatening to call in or foreclose a usurious note

or mortgage bearing the signature of the father or kin of the
would-be bridegroom, or—if he, Flem, were lucky—that of the
groom himself.

Then who must appear but this meddling whiteheaded outsider plying her with ice-cream sodas and out-of-state college
catalogues and at last convincing her that not only her pleasure
and interest but her duty too lay in leaving Jefferson, getting out
of it the moment she graduated from high school. Upon which,
she would carry that rich female provocation which had already
drawn blood (ay, real blood once anyway) a dozen times in
Jefferson, out into a world rifely teeming with young single men
vulnerable to marriage whether they knew it or not before they
saw her. Which he forestalled or rather stalled off for still another
year which he compelled, persuaded (I don't know what he used;
tears even perhaps; certainly tears if he could have found any to
use) her to waste at the Academy (one of the last of those gentle
and stubbornly fading anachronisms called Miss So-and-So's or
The So-and-So Female Academy or Institute whose curriculum
included deportment and china-painting, which continue to dot
the South though the rest of the United States knows them no
more); this, while he racked his brain for how to eliminate this
menace and threat to his wife's inheritance which was the middle-
aged country lawyer with his constant seduction of out-of-state
school brochures. The same middle-aged lawyer in fact who had
evicted the preceding menace of the Ohio garage mechanic.
But none appeared to eliminate the lawyer save him, the embattled father, and the only tool he knew was money. So I can
imagine this: Flem Snopes during all that year, having to remain
on constant guard against any casual stranger like a drummer
with a line of soap or hardware stopping off the train overnight,
and at the same time wring and wrack his harassed imagination
for some means of compelling me to accept a loan of enough
money at usurious enough interest to be under his control.

Which was what I expected of course. I had even reached the
point of planning, dreaming what I would do with the money,
what buy with the money for which I would continue to betray
him. But he didn't do that. He fooled me. Or perhaps he did me
that honour too: not just to save my honour for me by with-
holding the temptation to sully it, but assuming that I would

even sell honour before I would sully it and so temptation to do the one would be automatically refused because of the other. Anyway, he didn't offer me the bribe. And I know why now. He had given up. I mean, he realised at last that he couldn't possibly keep her from marriage even though he kept her in Jefferson, and that the moment that happened, he could kiss good-bye forever to old Will Varner's money.

Because some time during that last summer—this last summer or fall rather, since school had opened again and she had even begun her second year at the Academy, wasting another year within the fading walls where Miss Melissa Hogganbeck still taught stubbornly to the dwindling few who were present, that not just American history but all history had not yet reached Christmas Day, 1865, since although General Lee (and other soldiers too, including her own grandfather) had surrendered, the war itself was not done and in fact the next ten years would show that even those token surrenders were mistakes—he sat back long enough to take stock. Indeed, he—or any other male—had only to look at her to know that this couldn't go on much longer, even if he never let her out of the front yard—that girl (woman now; she will be nineteen this month) who simply by moving, being, promised and demanded and would have not just passion, not her mother's fierce awkward surrender in a roadside thicket at night with a lover still bleeding from a gang fight; but love, something worthy to match not just today's innocent and terrified and terrifying passion, but tomorrow's strength and capacity for serenity and growth and accomplishment and the realisation of hope and at last the contentment of one mutual peace and one mutual conjoined old age. It—the worst, disaster, catastrophe, ruin, the last irrevocable chance to get his hands on any part of old Will Varner's money—could happen at any time now; and who knows what relief there might have been in the simple realisation that at any moment now he could stop worrying not only about the loss of the money but having to hope for it, like when the receptionist opens the door to the dentist's torture-chamber and looks at you and says "Next" and it's too late now, simple face will not let you leap up and flee.

You see? Peace. No longer to have to waste time hoping or even regretting, having canvassed all the means and rejected all, since who knows too if during that same summer while he racked his harassed and outraged brain for some means to compel me to accept a loan at a hundred per cent interest he had not also toyed with the possibility of finding some dedicated enthusiast panting for martyrdom in the simple name of Man who would shoot old Will some night through his kitchen window and then rejected that too, relinquishing not hope so much as just worry.

And not just peace, but joy too since, now that he could relinquish forever that will-o'-the wisp of his father-in-law's money, he could go back to his original hope and dream of vengeance and revenge on the man responsible for the situation because of which he must give over all hope of his wife's inheritance. In fact he knew now why he had deferred that vengeance so long, dodged like a coward the actual facing of old Will's name in the canvass of possibilities. It was because he had known instinctively all the time that only Will could serve him, and once he had employed Will for his vengeance, by that same stroke he himself would have destroyed forever any chance of participating in that legacy.

But now that was all done, finished, behind him. He was free. Now there remained only the method to compel, force, cajole, persuade, trick—whichever was handiest or quickest or most efficient—the voting power of old Will's stock, plus the weight of that owned by others who were too afraid of old Will to resist him, in addition to his—Flem's—own stock and his corps of one-gallused depositors and their whispering campaign, to remove De Spain's bank from under him by voting him out of its presidency.

All that remained was how, how to handle—in a word, lick— Will Varner. And who to dispute that he already knew that too, that plan already tested and retested back in the very time while he was still dodging the facing of old Will's name. Because apparently once his mind was made up and he had finally brought himself to cut out and cauterise with his own hand that old vain hope of his wife's inheritance, he didn't hesitate. Here was the girl, the one pawn which could wreck his hopes of the Varner money, whom he had kept at home where he could delay to that extent at least the inevitable marriage which would ruin him, keeping her at home not only against her own wishes but against those of her mother too (not to mention the meddling neighbour);

keeping her at home even when to him too probably it meant she
was wasting her time in that anachronistic vacuum which was the
Female Academy. This for one entire year and up to the Christmas holidays in the second one; then suddenly, without warning,
overnight, he gives his permission for her to go, leave Jefferson and
enter the State University; only fifty miles away to be sure, yet
they were fifty miles, where it would be impossible for her to
report back home every night and where she would pass all her
waking hours among a thousand young men, all bachelors and
all male.

Why? It's obvious. Why did he ever do any of the things he did?
Because he got something in return more valuable to him than
what he gave. So you don't really need to imagine this: he and
his wife talking together (of course they talked sometimes; they
were married, and you have to talk sometime to someone even
when you're not married)—or four of them that is since there
would be two witnesses waiting in the synthetic hall until she
should take up the pen: *Sign this document guaranteeing me one half
of whatever you will inherit under your father's will, regardless of whatever your and my status in respect to one another may be at that time, and I
will give my permission for Linda to go away from Jefferson to school.*
All right, granted it could be broken, abrogated, set aside, would
not hold. She would not know that. And even if she had never
doubted it would hold, had the actual inheritance in her hand
at the moment, would she have refused to give him half of it for
that in return? Besides, it wasn't her it was to alarm, spook out
of the realm of cool judgment.

That was the "how". Now remained only the "when"; the rest
of the winter and she away at the University now and he still
about town, placid, inscrutable, unchanged, in the broad black
planter's hat and the minute bow tie seen somewhere about the
Square at least once during the day as regular as the courthouse
clock itself; on through the winter and into the spring, until
yesterday morning.

That's right. Just gone. So you will have to imagine this too
since there would be no witnesses even waiting in a synthetic hall
this time: once more the long, already summer-dusty gravel road
(it had been simple dirt when he traversed it that first time
eighteen years ago) out to Varner's store. And in an automobile

this time, it was that urgent, "how" and "when" having at last
coincided. And secret; the automobile was a hired one. I mean,
an imported hired one. Although most of the prominent people in
Jefferson and the county too owned automobiles now, he was not
one of them. And not just because of the cost, of what more men
than he in Yoknapatawpha County considered the foolish, the
almost criminal immobilisation of that many dollars and cents
in something which, even though you ran it for hire, would not
pay for itself before it wore out, but because he was not only not
a prominent man in Jefferson yet, he didn't even want to be: who
would have defended as he did his life the secret even of exactly
how solvent he really was.

But this was so urgent that he must use one for speed, and so
secret that he would have hired one, paid money for the use of
one, even if he had owned one, so as not to be seen going out
there in his own; too secret even to have ridden out with the mail
carrier, which he could have done for a dollar; too secret even
to have commandeered from one of his clients a machine which
he actually did own since it had been purchased with his money
secured by one of his myriad usurious notes. Instead, he hired one.
We would never know which one nor where: only that it would
not bear Yoknapatawpha County licence plates, and drove out
there in it, out to Varner's Crossroads once more and for the last
time, dragging, towing a fading cloud of yellow dust along the
road which eighteen years ago he had travelled in the mule-
drawn wagon containing all he owned: the wife and her bastard
daughter, the few sticks of furniture Mrs Varner had given them,
the deed to Ratliff's half of the little back-street Jefferson restaurant and the few dollars remaining from what Henry Armstid
(now locked up for life in a Jackson asylum) and his wife had
scrimped and hoarded for ten years, which Ratliff and Armstid
had paid him for the Old Frenchman place where he had buried
the twenty-five silver dollars where they would find them with
their spades.

For the last time, completing that ellipsis which would contain
those entire eighteen years of his life, since Frenchman's Bend and
Varner's Crossroads and Varner's store would be one, perhaps
the one, place to which he would never go again as long as he
lived, since win or lose he would not need to, and win or lose he

certainly would not dare to. And who knows, thinking even then
what a shame that he must go to the store and old Will instead of
to Varner's house where at this hour in the forenoon there would
be nobody but Mrs Varner and the Negro cook,—must go to the
store and beard and beat down by simple immobility and a
scrap of signed and witnessed paper that violent and choleric old
brigand instead. Because women are not interested in romance or
morals or sin and its punishment, but only in facts, the immutable
facts necessary to the living of life while you are in it and which
they are going to damned well see themselves don't fiddle and fool
and back and fill and mutate. How simple to have gone straight
to her, a woman (the big hard cold grey woman who never came
to town any more now, spending all her time between her home
and her church, both of which she ran exactly alike: herself self-
appointed treasurer of the collections she browbeat out of the
terrified congregation, herself selecting and choosing and hiring
the ministers and firing them too when they didn't suit her; legend
was that she chose one of them out of a cotton field while passing
in her buggy, hoicked him from between his plough-handles and
ordered him to go home and bathe and change his clothes and
followed herself thirty minutes later and ordained him).

How simple to ride up to the gate and say to the hired driver:
"Wait here. I won't be long," and go up the walk and enter his
ancestral halls (all right, his wife's; he was on his way now to
dynamite his own equity in them) and on through them until
he found Mrs Varner wherever she was, and say to her: Good-
morning, Ma-in-law. I just found out last night that for eighteen
years now our Eula's been sleeping with a feller in Jefferson named
Manfred de Spain. I packed up and moved out before I left town,
but I ain't filed the divorce yet because the judge was still asleep
when I passed his house. I'll tend to that when I get back tonight," and turn and go back to the car and say to the driver:
"All right, son. Back to town," and leave Mrs Varner to finish it,
herself to enter the lair where old Will sat among the symbolical
gnawed bones—the racks of hames and plough-handles, the rank
side meat and flour and cheap molasses and cheese and shoes and
coal oil and work gloves and snuff and chewing tobacco and fly-
specked candy and the liens and mortgages on crops and plough-
tools and mules and horses and land—of his fortune. There would

be a few loungers though not many since this was planting time and even the ones there should have been in the field, which they would realise, already starting in an alarmed surge of guilt when they saw her, though not fast enough.

"Get out of here," she would say while they were already moving. "I want to talk to Will.—Wait. One of you go to the sawmill and tell Jody I want his automobile and hurry." And they would say "Yessum, Miz Varner," which she would not hear either, standing over old Will now in his rawhide-bottomed chair. "Get up from there. Flem has finally caught Eula, or says he has. He hasn't filed the suit yet so you will have time before the word gets all over the county. I don't know what he's after, but you go in there and stop it. I won't have it. We had enough trouble with Eula twenty years ago. I ain't going to have her back in my house worrying me now."

But he couldn't do that. It wasn't that simple. Because men, especially one like old Will Varner, were interested in facts too, especially a man like old Will in a fact like the one he, Flem, had signed and witnessed and folded inside his coat pocket. So he had to go, walk himself into that den and reach his own hand and jerk the unsuspecting beard and then stand while the uproar beat and thundered about his head until it spent itself temporarily to where his voice could be heard: "That's her signature. If you don't know it, them two witnesses do. All you got to do is help me take that bank away from Manfred de Spain—transfer your stock to my name, take my post-dated check if you want, the stock to be yourn again as soon as Manfred de Spain is out, or you to vote the stock yourself if you had druther—and you can have this paper. I'll even hold the match while you burn it."

That was all. And here was Ratliff again (oh yes, Jefferson could do without Ratliff, but not I—we—us; not I nor the whole damned tribe of Snopes could do without him), all neat and clean and tieless in his blue shirt, blinking a little at me. "Uncle Billy rid into town in Jody's car about four o'clock this morning and went straight to Flem's. And Flem ain't been to town today. What you reckon is fixing to pop now?" He blinked at me. "What do you reckon it was?"

"What what was?" I said.

"That he taken out there to Miz Varner yesterday that was

important enough to have Uncle Billy on the road to town at four o'clock this morning?"

"To *Mrs* Varner?" I said. "He gave it to Will."

"No no," Ratliff said. "He never seen Will. I know. I taken him out there. I had a machine to deliver to Miz Ledbetter at Rockyford and he suh-jested would I mind going by Frenchman's Bend while he spoke to Miz Varner a minute and we did, he was in the house about a minute and come back out and we went on and et dinner with Miz Ledbetter and set up the machine and come on back to town." He blinked at me. "Jest about a minute. What do you reckon he could a said or handed to Miz Varner in one minute that would put Uncle Billy on the road to Jefferson that soon after midnight?"

18

V. K. RATLIFF

No no, no no, no no. He was wrong. He's a lawyer, and to a lawyer, if it ain't complicated it don't matter whether it works or not because if it ain't complicated up enough it ain't right and so even if it works, you don't believe it. So it wasn't that —a paper phonied up on the spur of the moment, that I don't care how many witnesses signed it, a lawyer not nowhere near as smart as Lawyer Stevens would a been willing to pay the client for the fun he would have breaking it wide open.

It wasn't that. I don't know what it was, coming up to me on the Square that evening and saying, "I hear Miz Ledbetter's sewing machine come in this morning. When you take it out to her, I'll make the run out and back with you if you won't mind going by Frenchman's Bend a minute." Sho. You never even wondered how he heard about things because when the time come around to wonder how he managed to hear about it, it was already too late because he had done already made his profit by that time. So I says,

"Well, a feller going to Rockyford could go by Frenchman's Bend. But then, a feller going to Memphis could go by Birmingham too. He wouldn't have to, but he could."—You know: jest to hear him dicker. But he fooled me.

"That's right," he says. "It's a good six miles out of your way. Would four bits a mile pay for it?"

"It would more than pay for it," I says. "To ride up them extra three dollars, me and you wouldn't get back to town before sunup Wednesday. So I'll tell you what I'll do. You buy two cigars, and if you'll smoke one of them yourself, I'll carry you by Frenchman's Bend for one minute jest for your company and conversation."

"I'll give them both to you," he says. So we done that. Oh sho, he beat me out of my half of that little café me and Grover Winbush owned, but who can say jest who lost then? If he hadn't a got it, Grover might a turned it into a French postcard peepshow too, and then I'd be out there where Grover is now: night watchman at that brick yard.

So I druv him by Frenchman's Bend. And we had the conversation too, provided you can call the monologue you have
with Flem Snopes a conversation. But you keep on trying. It's
because you hope to learn. You know silence is valuable because
it must be, there's so little of it. So each time you think *Here's my
chance to find out how a expert uses it.* Of course you won't this time
and never will the next neither, that's how come he's a expert.
But you can always hope you will. So we druv on, talking about
this and that, mostly this of course, with him stopping chewing
ever three or four miles to spit out the window and say "Yep" or
"That's right" or "Sounds like it" until finally—there was
Varner's Crossroads jest over the next rise—he says, "Not the
store. The house," and I says,

"What? Uncle Billy won't be home now. He'll be at the store
this time of morning."

"I know it," he says. "Take this road here." So we taken that
road; we never even seen the store, let alone passed it, on to the
house, the gate.

"You said one minute," I says. "If it's longer than that, you'll
owe me two more cigars."

"All right," he says. And he got out and went on, up the walk
and into the house, and I switched off the engine and set there
thinking *What? What? Miz Varner. Not Uncle Billy: MIZ Varner.*
That Uncle Billy jest hated him because Flem beat him fair and
square, at Uncle Billy's own figger, out of that Old Frenchman
place, while Miz Varner hated him like he was a Holy Roller or
even a Baptist because he had not only condoned sin by marrying
her daughter after somebody else had knocked her up, he had
even made sin pay by getting the start from it that wound him up
vice-president of a bank. Yet it was *Miz* Varner he had come all
the way out here to see, was willing to pay me three extra dollars
for it. (I mean, offered. I know now I could a asked him ten.)

No, not thinking *What? What?* because what I was thinking was
Who, who ought to know about this, trying to think in the little
time I would have, since he his-self had volunteered that-ere
one minute, so one minute it was going to be, jest which who
that was. Not me, because there wasn't no more loose dangling
Ratliff-ends he could need; and not Lawyer Stevens and Linda
and Eula and that going-off-to-school business that had been the

last what you might call Snopes uproar to draw attention on the local scene, because that was ended too now, with Linda at least off at the University over at Oxford even if it wasn't one of them Virginia or New England colleges Lawyer was panting for. I didn't count Manfred de Spain because I wasn't on Manfred de Spain's side. I wasn't against him neither; it was jest like Lawyer Stevens his-self would a said: the feller that already had as much on his side as Manfred de Spain already had or anyway as ever body in Jefferson whose business it wasn't neither, believed he had, didn't need no more. Let alone deserve it.

Only there wasn't time. It wasn't one minute quite but it wasn't two neither when he come out the door in that-ere black hat and his bow tie, still chewing because I doubt if he ever quit chewing any more than he probably taken off that hat while he was inside, back to the car and spit and got in and I started the engine and says, "It wasn't quite a full two, so I'll let you off for one," and he says,

"All right," and I put her in low and set with my foot on the clutch and says,

"In case she was out, you want to run by the store and tell Uncle Billy you left a message on the hatrack for her?" and he chewed a lick or two more and balled up the ambeer and leaned to the window and spit again and set back and we went on to Rockyford and I set up the machine for Miz Ledbetter and she invited us to dinner and we et and come home and at four o'clock this morning Uncle Billy druv up to Flem's house in Jody's car with his Negro driver and I know why four o'clock because that was Miz Varner.

I mean Uncle Billy would go to bed soon as he et his supper, which would be before sundown this time of year, so he would wake up anywhere about one or two o'clock in the morning. Of course he had done already broke the cook into getting up then to cook his breakfast, but jest one Negro woman rattling pans in the kitchen wasn't nowhere near enough for Uncle Billy, ever body else hadn't jest to wake up then but to get up too: stomping around and banging doors and hollering for this and that until Miz Varner was up and dressed too. Only Uncle Billy could eat his breakfast then set in a chair until he smoked his pipe out and then he would go back to sleep until daylight. Only Miz

Varner couldn't never go back to sleep again, once he had done woke her up good.

So this was her chance. I don't know what it was Flem told her or handed her that was important enough to make Uncle Billy light out for town at two o'clock in the morning. But it wasn't no more important to Miz Varner than her chance to go back to bed in peace and quiet and sleep until a decent Christian hour. So she jest never told him or give it to him until he woke up at his usual two a.m.; if it was something Flem jest handed her that she never needed to repeat, likely she never had to get up a-tall but jest have it leaning against the lamp when Uncle Billy struck a match to light it so he could see to wake up the rest of the house and the neighbours.

So I don't know what it was. But it wasn't no joked-up piece of paper jest in the hopes of skeering Uncle Billy into doing something that until now he hadn't aimed to do. Because Uncle Billy don't skeer, and Flem Snopes knows it. It had something to do with folks, people, and the only people connected with Jefferson that would make Uncle Billy do something he hadn't suspected until this moment he would do are Eula and Linda. Not Flem; Uncle Billy has knowed for twenty years now exactly what he will do to Flem the first time Flem's eye falters or his hand slips or his attention wanders.

Let alone going to Uncle Billy his-self with it. Because anything in reference to that bank that Flem would know in advance that jest by handing it or saying it to Miz Varner would be stout enough to move Uncle Billy from Frenchman's Bend to Jefferson as soon as he heard about it, would sooner or later have to scratch or leastways touch Eula. And maybe Uncle Billy Varner don't skeer and Flem Snopes knows it, but Flem Snopes don't skeer neither and most folks knows that too. And it don't take no especial coward to not want to walk into that store and up to old man Will Varner and tell him his daughter ain't reformed even yet, that she'd been sleeping around again for eighteen years now with a feller she ain't married to, and that her husband ain't got guts enough to know what to do about it.

19

CHARLES MALLISON

IT was like a circus day or the county fair. Or more: it was like the District or even the whole State field meet because we even had a holiday for it. Only it was more than just a fair or a field day because this one was going to have death in it too, though of course we didn't know that then.

It even began with a school holiday that we didn't even know we were going to have. It was as if time, circumstance, geography, contained something which must, anyway was going to, happen and now was the moment and Jefferson, Mississippi, was the place, and so the stage was cleared and set for it.

The school holiday began on Tuesday morning. Last week some new people moved to Jefferson, a highway engineer, and their little boy entered the second grade. He must have been already sick when his mother brought him, because he had to go home; they sent for her and she came and got him that same afternoon and that night they took him to Memphis. That was Thursday, but it wasn't until Monday afternoon that they got the word back that what he had was polio and they sent word around that the school would be closed while they found out what to do next or what to not do or whatever it was while they tried to learn more about polio or about the engineer's little boy or whatever it was. Anyhow it was a holiday we hadn't expected or even hoped for, in April; that April morning when you woke up and you would think how April was the best, the very best time of all not to have to go to school, until you would think *Except in the fall* with the weather brisk and not cold at the same time and the trees all yellow and red and you could go hunting all day long; and then you would think *Except in the winter* with the Christmas holidays over and now nothing to look forward to until summer; and you would think how no time is the best time to not have to go to school and so school is a good thing after all because without it there wouldn't be any holidays or vacations.

Anyhow we had the holiday, we didn't know how long; and that was fine too because now you never had to say *Only two days left* or *Only one day left* since all you had to do was just be holiday, breathe holiday, today and tomorrow too and who knows? tomorrow after that and, who knows? still tomorrow after that. So on Wednesday, when even the children who would have been in school except for the highway engineer's little boy began to know that something was happening, going on inside the president's office of the bank—not the old one, the Bank of Jefferson, but the other, the one we still called the new bank or even Colonel Sartoris's bank although he had been dead seven years now and Mr de Spain was president of it—it was no more than we expected, since this was just another part of whatever it was time or circumstance or whatever it was had cleared the stage and emptied the school so it could happen.

No, to say that the stage was limited to just one bank; to say that time, circumstance, geography, whatever it was, had turned school out in the middle of April in honour of something it wanted to happen inside just one set of walls was wrong. It was all of Jefferson. It was all the walls of Jefferson, the ground they stood on, the air they rose up in; all the walls and air in Jefferson that people moved and breathed and talked in; we were already at dinner except Uncle Gavin, who was never late unless he was out of town on county business, and when he did come in something was already wrong. I mean, I didn't always notice when something was wrong with him and it wasn't because I was only twelve yet, it was because you didn't have to notice Uncle Gavin because you could always tell from Mother since she was his twin; it was like when you said "What's the matter?" to Mother, you and she and everybody else knew you were saying What's wrong with Uncle Gavin?

But we could always depend on Father. Uncle Gavin came in at last and sat down and unfolded his napkin and said something wrong and Father glanced at him and then went back to eating and then looked at Uncle Gavin again.

"Well," he said, "I hear they got old Will Varner out of bed at two this morning and brought him all the way in to town to promote Manfred de Spain. Promote him where?"

"What?" Uncle Gavin said.

"Where do you promote a man that's already president of the bank?" Father said.

"Charley," Mother said.

"Or maybe promote ain't the word I want," Father said. "The one I want is when you promote a man quick out of bed—"

"Charley!" Mother said.

"—especially a bed he never had any business in, not to mention having to send all the way out to Frenchman's Bend for your pa-in-law to pronounce that word—"

"Charles!" Mother said. That's how it was. It was like we had had something in Jefferson for eighteen years, and whether it had been right or whether it had been wrong to begin with didn't matter any more now because it was ours, we had lived with it and now it didn't even show a scar, like the nail driven into the tree years ago that violated and outraged and anguished that tree. Except that the tree hasn't got much choice either: either to put principle above sap and refuse the outrage and next year's sap both, or accept the outrage and the sap for the privilege of going on being a tree as long as it can, until in time the nail disappears. It don't go away; it just stops being so glaring in sight, barked over; there is a lump, a bump of course, but after a while the other trees forgive that and everything else accepts that tree and that bump too until one day the saw or the axe goes into it and hits that old nail.

Because I was twelve then. I had reached for the second time that point in the looping circles children—boys anyway—make growing up when for a little while they enter, live in, the same civilisation that grown people use, when it occurs to you that maybe the sensible and harmless things they won't let you do really seem as silly to them as the thing they seem either to want to do or have to do seem to you. No: it's when they laugh at you and suddenly you say, *Why, maybe I am funny*, and so the things they do are not outrageous and silly or shocking at all: they're just funny; and more than that, it's the same funny. So now I could ask. A few more years and I would know more than I knew then. But the loop, the circle, would be swinging on away out into space again where you can't ask grown people because you can't talk to anybody, not even the others your age because they too are rushing on out into space where you can't touch anybody, you don't dare try, you are too busy just hanging on; and you know that all the others out there are just as afraid of asking as you are, nobody to ask, nothing to do but make noise, the louder the better, then at least the other scared ones won't know how scared you are.

But I could still ask now, for a little while. I asked Mother. "Why don't you ask Uncle Gavin?" she said.

She wanted to tell me. Maybe she even tried. But she couldn't. It wasn't because I was only twelve. It was because I was her child, created by her and Father because they wanted to be in bed together and nothing else would do, nobody else would do. You see? If Mrs Snopes and Mr de Spain had been anything else but people, she could have told me. But they were people too, exactly like her and Father; and it's not that the child mustn't know that the same magic which made him was the same thing that sent an old man like Mr Will Varner into town at four o'clock in the morning just to take something as sorry and shabby as a bank full of money away from another man named Manfred de Spain: it's because the child couldn't believe that. Because to the child, he was not created by his mother's and his father's passion or capacity for it. He couldn't have been because he was there first, he came first, before the passion; he created the passion, not only it but the man and the woman who served it; his father is not his father but his son-in-law, his mother not his mother but his daughter-in-law if he is a girl.

So she couldn't tell me because she could not. And Uncle Gavin couldn't tell me because he wasn't able to, he couldn't have stopped talking in time. That is, that's what I thought then. I mean, that's what I thought then was the reason why they— Mother—didn't tell me: that the reason was just my innocence and not Uncle Gavin's too and she had to guard both, since maybe she was my mother but she was Uncle Gavin's twin, and if a boy or a girl really is his father's and her mother's father-in-law or mother-in-law, which would make the girl her brother's mother no matter how much younger she was, then a girl with just one brother and him a twin at that, would maybe be his wife and mother too.

So maybe that was why: not that I wasn't old enough to accept biology, but that everyone should be, deserves to be, must be, defended and protected from the spectators of his own passion save in the most general and unspecific and impersonal terms of

the literary and dramatic lay-figures of the protagonists of passion
in their bloodless and griefless posturings of triumph or anguish;
that no man deserves love since nature did not equip us to bear
it but merely to endure and survive it, and so Uncle Gavin's must
not be watched where she could help and fend him, while it
anguished on his own unarmoured bones.

Though even if they had tried to tell me, it would have been
several years yet, not from innocence but from ignorance, before
I would know, understand, what I had actually been looking at
during the rest of that Wednesday afternoon while all of Jefferson
waited for the saw to touch that buried nail. No: not buried, not
healed or annealed into the tree but just cysted into it, alien and
poison; not healed over but scabbed over with a scab which
merely renewed itself, incapable of healing, like a signpost.

Because ours was a town founded by Aryan Baptists and
Methodists, for Aryan Baptists and Methodists. We had a Chinese
laundryman and two Jews, brothers with their families, who ran
two clothing stores. But one of them had been trained in Russia
to be a rabbi and spoke seven languages including classic Greek
and Latin and worked geometry problems for relaxation and he
was absolved, lumped in the same absolution with old Doctor
Wyott, president emeritus of the Academy (his grandfather had
founded it), who could read not only Greek and Hebrew but
Sanskrit too, who wore two foreign decorations for (we, Jefferson,
believed) having been not just a professing but a militant and
even boasting atheist for at least sixty of his eighty years and who
had even beaten the senior Mr Wildermark at chess; and the
other Jewish brother and his family and the Chinese all attended,
were members of, the Methodist church and so they didn't count
either, being in our eyes merely non-white people, not actually
coloured. And although the Chinese was definitely a coloured
man even if not a Negro, he was only he, single peculiar and
barren; not just kinless but even kindless, half the world or anyway half the continent (we all knew about San Francisco's China-
town) sundered from his like and therefore as threatless as a mule.

There is a small Episcopal church in Jefferson, the oldest
extant building in town (it was built by slaves and called the best,
the finest too, I mean by the Northern tourists who passed through
Jefferson now with cameras, expecting—we don't know why since

they themselves had burned it and blown it up with dynamite in
1863—to find Jefferson much older or anyway older looking than
it is and faulting us a little because it isn't) and a Presbyterian
congregation too, the two oldest congregations in the county,
going back to the old days of Issetibbeha, the Chickasaw chief,
and his sister's son Ikkemotubbe whom they called Doom, before
the county was a County and Jefferson was Jefferson. But nowa-
days there wasn't much difference between the Episcopal and
Presbyterian churches and Issetibbeha's old mounds in the low
creek bottoms about the county because the Baptists and Methodists had heired from them, usurped and dispossessed; ours a town
established and decreed by people neither Catholics nor Protest-
ants nor even atheists but incorrigible nonconformists, nonconformists not just to everybody else but to each other in mutual
accord; a nonconformism defended and preserved by descendants
whose ancestors hadn't quitted home and security for a wilderness in which to find freedom of thought as they claimed and oh
yes, believed, but to find freedom in which to be incorrigible and
unreconstructible Baptists and Methodists; not to escape from
tyranny as they claimed and believed, but to establish one.

And now, after eighteen years, the saw of retribution, which we
of course called that of righteousness and simple justice, was about
to touch that secret hidden unhealed nail buried in the moral tree
of our community—that nail not only corrupted and unhealed but
unhealable because it was not just sin but mortal sin—a thing
which should not exist at all, whose very conception should be
self-annihilative, yet a sin which people seemed constantly and
almost universally to commit with complete impunity; as witness
these two for eighteen years, not only flouting decency and
morality but even compelling decency and morality to accept
them simply by being discreet: nobody had actually caught them
yet; outraging morality itself by allying economics on their side
since the very rectitude and solvency of a bank would be involved
in their exposure.

In fact, the town itself was divided into two camps, each split
in turn into what you might call a hundred individual noncon-
forming bivouacs: the women who hated Mrs Snopes for having
grabbed Mr de Spain first or hated Mr de Spain for having
preferred Mrs Snopes to them, and the men who were jealous of

1*

De Spain because they were not him or hated him for being younger than they or braver than they (they called it luckier of course); and those of both sexes—no: the same sour genderless sex—who hated them both for having found or made together something which they themselves had failed to make, whatever the reason; and in consequence of which that splendour must not only not exist, it must never have existed—the females of it who must abhor the splendour because it was, had to be, barren; the males of it who must hate the splendour because they had set the cold stability of currency above the wild glory of blood: they who had not only abetted the sin but had kept alive the anguish of their own secret regret by supporting the sinners' security for the sake of De Spain's bank. Two camps: the one that said the sin must be exposed now, it had already lasted eighteen years too long; the other which said it dare not be exposed now and so reveal our own baseness in helping to keep it hidden all this long time.

Because the saw was not just seeking that nail. As far as Jefferson was concerned it had already touched it; we were merely waiting now to see in what direction the fragments of that particular tree in our wood (not the saw itself, never the saw: if that righteous and invincible moral blade flew to pieces at the contact, we all might as well give up, since the very fabric of Baptist and Methodist life is delusion, nothing) would scatter and disintegrate.

That was that whole afternoon while old Mr Varner still stayed hidden or anyway invisible in Mr Snopes's house. We didn't even know definitely that he was actually in town, nobody had seen him; we only had Ratliff's word that he had come in in his son's automobile at four o'clock this morning, and we didn't know that for sure unless Ratliff had sat up all night watching the Snopes's front door. But then Mr Varner was there, he had to be or there wouldn't be any use for the rest of it. And Mr de Spain's bank continued its ordinary sober busy prosperous gold-auraed course to the closing hour at three o'clock, when almost at once the delivery boy from Christian's drugstore knocked at the side door and was admitted with his ritual tray of four Coca-Colas for the two girl book-keepers and Miss Killebrew the teller and Mr Hovis the cashier. And presently, at his ordinary hour, Mr de Spain came out and got in his car as usual and drove away to look at one of the farms which he now owned or on which the bank held a mortgage, as he always did: no rush, no panic to burst upon the ordered financial day. And sometime during the day, either forenoon or afternoon, somebody claimed to have seen Mr Snopes himself, unchanged too, unhurried and unalarmed, the wide black planter's hat still looking brand new (the tiny bow tie which he had worn for eighteen years now always did), going about his inscrutable noncommunicable affairs.

Then it was five o'clock and nothing had happened; soon now people would begin to go home to eat supper and then it would be too late and at first I thought of going up to the office to wait for Uncle Gavin to walk home, only I would have to climb the stairs and then turn around right away and come back down again and I thought what a good name spring fever was to excuse not doing something you didn't want to do, then I thought maybe spring fever wasn't an excuse at all because maybe spring fever actually was.

So I just stood on the corner where he would have to pass, to wait for him. Then I saw Mrs Snopes. She had just come out of the beauty parlour and as soon as you looked at her you could tell that's where she had been and I remembered how Mother said once she was the only woman in Jefferson that never went to one because she didn't need to since there was nothing in a beauty shop that she could have lacked. But she had this time, standing there for a minute and she really did look both ways along the street before she turned and started toward me and then she saw me and came on and said, "Hello, Chick," and I tipped my cap, only she came up and stopped and I took my cap off; she had a bag on her arm like ladies do, already opening it to reach inside.

"I was looking for you," she said. "Will you give this to your uncle when you go home?"

"Yessum," I said. It was an envelope.

"Thank you," she said. "Have they heard any more about the little Riddell boy?"

"I don't know'm," I said. It wasn't sealed. It didn't have any name on the front either.

"Let's hope they got him to Memphis in time," she said. Then she said Thank you again and went on, walking like she does, not like a pointer about to make game like Linda, but like water

moves somehow. And she could have telephoned him at home
and I almost said *You don't want me to let Mother see it* before I
caught myself. Because it wasn't sealed. But then, I wouldn't have
anyway. Besides, I didn't have to. Mother wasn't even at home
yet and then I remembered: Wednesday, she would be out at
Sartoris at the meeting of the Byron Society though Mother said
it had been a long time now since anybody listened to anybody
read anything because they played bridge now but at least she
said that when it met with Miss Jenny Du Pre they had toddies
or juleps instead of just coffee or Coca-Colas.

So nothing had happened and now it was already too late, the
sun going down though the pear tree in the side yard had
bloomed and gone a month ago and now the mocking-bird had
moved over to the pink dogwood, already beginning where he had
sung all night long all week until you would begin to wonder why
in the world he didn't go somewhere else and let people sleep.
And nobody at home at all yet except Aleck Sander sitting on the
front steps with the ball and bat. "Come on," he said. "I'll knock
you out some flies." Then he said, "All right, you knock out and
I'll chase um."

So it was almost dark inside the house; I could already smell
supper cooking and it was too late now, finished now: Mr de
Spain gone out in his new Buick to watch how much money his
cotton was making, and Mrs Snopes coming out of the beauty
shop with her hair even waved or something or whatever it was,
maybe for a party at her house tonight so maybe it hadn't even
begun; maybe old Mr Varner wasn't even in town at all, not
only wasn't coming but never had aimed to and so all the Riddell
boy did by catching polio was just to give us a holiday we didn't
expect and didn't know what to do with; until I heard Uncle
Gavin come in and come up the stairs and I met him in the upstairs hall with the envelope in my hand: just the shape of him
coming up the stairs and along the hall until even in that light
I saw his face all of a sudden and all of a sudden I said:

"You're not going to be here for supper."

"No," he said. "Will you tell your mother?"

"Here," I said and held out the envelope and he took it.

20

GAVIN STEVENS

Though you have to eat. So after I went back and unlocked the office and left the door on the latch, I drove out to Seminary Hill, to eat cheese and crackers and listen to old Mr Garraway curse Calvin Coolidge while he ran the last loafing Negroes out of the store and closed it for the night.

Or so I thought. Because you simply cannot go against a community. You can stand singly against any temporary unanimity of even a city full of human behaviour, even a mob. But you cannot stand against the cold inflexible abstraction of a long-suffering community's moral point of view. Mr Garraway had been one of the first—no: the first—to move his account from Colonel Sartoris's bank to the Bank of Jefferson, even before Flem Snopes ever thought or had reason to think of his tenant-farmer panic. He had moved it in fact as soon as we—the town and county—knew that Manfred de Spain was definitely to be president of it. Because he—Mr Garraway—had been one of that original small inflexible unreconstructible Puritan group, both Baptists and Methodist, in the county who would have moved their fiscal allegiance also from Jefferson while De Spain was mayor of it, to escape the moral contamination and express their opinion of that liaison which he represented, if there had been another fiscal town in the county to have moved it to. Though later, a year or two afterward, he moved the account back, perhaps because he was just old or maybe he could stay in his small dingy store out at Seminary Hill and not have to come to town, have to see with his own eyes and so be reminded of his county's shame and disgrace and sin if he didn't want to be. Or maybe once you accept something, it doesn't really matter any more whether you like it or not. Or so I thought.

The note said ten o'clock. That was all, *Please meet me at your office at ten tonight.* Not *if convenient*, let alone *when could you see me at your office?* but simply *at ten tonight please.* You see. Because in the first place, Why me? *Me?* To say that to all of them, all three of them—no, all four, taking De Spain with me: *Why can't you let me*

alone? What more can you want of me than I have already failed to do?
But there would be plenty of time for that; I would have plenty
of time to eat the sardines and crackers and say What a shame
to the account of whatever the recent outrage the President and
his party had contrived against Mr Garraway, when he—Mr
Garraway—said suddenly (an old man with an old man's dim
cloudy eyes magnified and enormous behind the thick lenses of
his iron-framed spectacles): "Is it so that Will Varner came in to
town this morning?"

"Yes," I said.

"So he caught them." Now he was trembling, shaking, standing
there behind the worn counter which he had inherited from his
father, racked with tins of meat and spools of thread and combs
and needles and bottles of cooking extract and malaria tonic and
female compound some of which he had probably inherited too,
saying in a shaking voice: "Not the husband! The father himself
had to come in and catch them after eighteen years!"

"But you put your money back," I said. "You took it out at
first, when you just heard at second hand about the sin and shame
and outrage. Then you put it back. Was it because you saw her
too at last? She came out here one day, into your store, and you
saw her yourself, got to know her, to believe that she at least was
innocent? Was that it?"

"I knew the husband," he said, cried almost, holding his voice
down so the Negroes couldn't hear what we—he was talking
about. "I knew the husband! He deserved it!"

Then I remembered. "Yes," I said. "I thought I saw you in
town this afternoon." Then I knew. "You moved it again today,
didn't you? You drew it out again and put it back into the Bank of
Jefferson today, didn't you?" and he standing there, shaking even
while he tried to hold himself from it. "Why?" I said. "Why again
today?"

"She must go," he said. "They must both go—she and De
Spain too."

"But why?" I said, muttered too, not to be overheard: two
white men discussing in a store full of Negroes a white woman's
adultery. More: adultery in the very top stratum of a white man's
town and bank. "Why only now? It was one thing as long as the
husband accepted it; it became another when somebody—how

did you put it?—catches them, blows the gaff? They become
merely sinners then, criminals then, lepers then? Nothing for
constancy, nothing for fidelity, nothing for devotion, unpoliced
devotion, eighteen years of devotion?"

"Is that all you want?" he said. "I'm tired. I want to go home."
Then we were on the gallery where a few of the Negroes still
lingered, the arms and faces already fading back into the darkness
behind the lighter shades of shirts and hats and pants as if they
were slowly vacating them, while his shaking hands fumbled the
heavy padlock, through the hasp and fumbled it shut; until
suddenly I said, quite loud:

"Though if anything the next one will be worse because the
next president will probably be Governor Smith and you know
who Governor Smith is of course: a Catholic," and would have
stopped that in time in very shame but could not, or maybe
should have stopped it in time in very shame but would not.
Since who was I, what anguish's missionary I that I must compound it blindly right and left like some blind unrational minor
force of nature? Who had already spoiled supper and ruined sleep
both for the old man standing there fumbling with his clumsy lock
as if I had actually struck him—the old man who in his fashion, in
a lot of people's fashion, really was a kindly old man who never
in his life wittingly or unwittingly harmed anyone black or white,
not serious harm: not more than adding a few extra cents to what
it would have been for cash, when the article went on credit; or
selling to a Negro for half-price or often less (oh yes, at times even
giving it to him) the tainted meat or rancid lard or weevilled
flour or meal he would not have permitted a white man—a
Protestant gentile white man of course—to eat at all out of his
store; standing there with his back turned fumbling at the giant
padlock as though I had actually struck him, saying,

"They must go. They must go, both of them."

There is a ridge; you drive on beyond Seminary Hill and in
time you come upon it: a mild unhurried farm road presently
mounting to cross the ridge and on to join the main highway leading from Jefferson to the world. And now, looking back and down,
you see all Yoknapatawpha in the dying last of day beneath you.
There are stars now, just pricking out as you watch them among
the others already coldly and softly burning; the end of day is one

vast green soundless murmur up the north-west toward the zenith. Yet it is as though light were not being subtracted from earth, drained from earth backward and upward into that cooling green, but rather had gathered, pooling for an unmoving moment yet, among the low places of the ground so that ground, earth itself is luminous and only the dense clumps of trees are dark, standing darkly and immobile out of it.

Then, as though at signal, the fireflies—lightning-bugs of the Mississippi child's vernacular—myriad and frenetic, random and frantic, pulsing; not questing, not quiring, but choiring as if they were tiny incessant appeaseless voices, cries, words. And you stand suzerain and solitary above the whole sum of your life beneath that incessant ephemeral spangling. First is Jefferson, the centre, radiating weakly its puny glow into space; beyond it, enclosing it, spreads the County, tied by the diverging roads to that centre as is the rim to the hub by its spokes, yourself detached as God Himself for this moment above the cradle of your nativity and of the men and women who made you, the record and chronicle of your native land proffered for your perusal in ring by concentric ring like the ripples on living water above the dreamless slumber of your past; you to preside unanguished and immune above this miniature of man's passions and hopes and disasters—ambition and fear and lust and courage and abnegation and pity and honour and sin and pride—all bound, precarious and ramshackle, held together by the web, the iron-thin warp and woof of his rapacity but withal yet dedicated to his dreams.

They are all here, supine beneath you, stratified and superposed, osseous and durable with the frail dust and the phantoms —the rich alluvial river-bottom land of old Issetibbeha, the wild Chickasaw king, with his Negro slaves and his sister's son called Doom who murdered his way to the throne and, legend said (record itself said since there were old men in the county in my own childhood who had actually seen it), stole an entire steamboat and had it dragged intact eleven miles overland to convert into a palace proper to aggrandise his state; the same fat black rich plantation earth still synonymous of the proud fading white plantation names whether we—I mean of course they—ever actually owned a plantation or not: Sutpen and Sartoris and

Compson and Edmonds and McCaslin and Beauchamp and Grenier and Habersham and Holston and Stevens and De Spain, generals and governors and judges, soldiers (even if only Cuban lieutenants) and statesmen failed or not, and simple politicians and over-reachers and just simple failures, who snatched and grabbed and passed and vanished, name and face and all. Then the roadless, almost pathless perpendicular hill-country of McCallum and Gowrie and Frazier and Muir translated intact with their pot stills and speaking only the Gaelic and not much of that, from Culloden to Carolina, then from Carolina to Yoknapatawpha still intact and not speaking much of anything except that they now called the pots "kettles" though the drink (even I can remember this) was still usquebaugh; then and last on to where Frenchman's Bend lay beyond the south-eastern horizon, cradle of Varners and ant-heap for the north-east crawl of Snopes.

And you stand there—you, the old man, already white-headed (because it doesn't matter if they call your grey hairs premature because life itself is always premature which is why it aches and anguishes) and pushing forty, only a few years from forty—while there rises up to you, proffered up to you, the spring darkness, the unsleeping darkness which, although it is the dark itself, declines the dark since dark is of the little death called sleeping. Because look how, even though the last of west is no longer green and all of firmament is now one unlidded studded slow-wheeling arc and the last of earth-pooled visibility has drained away, there still remains one faint diffusion, since everywhere you look about the dark panorama you still see them, faint as whispers: the faint and shapeless lambence of blooming dogwood returning loaned light to light as the phantoms of candles would.

And you, the old man, standing there while there rises to you, about you, suffocating you, the spring dark peopled and myriad, two and two seeking never at all solitude but simply privacy, the privacy decreed and created for them by the spring darkness, the spring weather, the spring which an American poet, a fine one, a woman and so she knows, called girls' weather and boys' luck. Which was not the first day at all, not Eden morning at all because girls' weather and boys' luck is the sum of all the days: the cup, the bowl proffered once to the lips in youth and then no more; proffered to quench or sip or drain that lone one time and even that sometimes premature, too soon. Because the tragedy of life is, it must be premature, inconclusive and inconcludable, in order to be life; it must be before itself, in advance of itself, to have been at all.

And now for truth was the one last chance to choose, decide: whether or not to say *Why me? Why bother me? Why can't you let me alone? Why must it be my problem whether I was right and your husband just wants your lover's scalp, or Ratliff is right and your husband doesn't care a damn about you or his honour either and just wants De Spain's bank?*—the Square empty beneath the four identical faces of the courthouse clock saying ten minutes to ten to the north and east and south and west, vacant now beneath the arclight-stippled shadows of fledged leaves like small bites taken out of the concrete paving, the drugstores closed and all still moving now were the late last homeward stragglers from the second running of picture show. Or better still, what she herself should have thought without my needing to say it: *Take Manfred de Spain in whatever your new crisis is, since you didn't hesitate to quench with him your other conflagration eighteen years ago. Or do you already know in advance he will be no good this time, since a bank is not a female but neuter?*

And of course Otis Harker. "Evening, Mr Stevens," he said. "When you drove up I almost hoped maybe it was a gang come to rob the post-office or the bank or something to bring us a little excitement for a change."

"But it was just another lawyer," I said, "and lawyers don't bring excitement: only misery?"

"I don't believe I quite said that, did I?" he said. "But leastways lawyers stays awake, so if you're going to be around a while, maybe I'll jest mosey back to the station and maybe take a nap while you watch them racing clockhands a spell for me." Except that he was looking at me. No: he wasn't looking at me at all: he was watching me, deferent to my white hairs as a "well-raised" Mississippian should be, but not my representative position as his employer; not quite servile, not quite inpudent, waiting maybe or calculating maybe.

"Say it," I said "Except that—"

"Except that Mr Flem Snopes and Mr Manfred de Spain might cross the Square any time now with old Will Varner chasing them both out of town with that pistol."

"Good-night," I said. "If I don't see you again."

"Good-night," he said. "I'll be somewhere around. I mean around awake. I wouldn't want Mr Buck himself to have to get up out of bed and come all the way to town to catch me asleep."

You see? You can't beat it. Otis Harker too, who, assuming he does keep awake all night as he is paid to do, should have been at home all day in bed asleep. But of course, he was there; he actually saw old Varner cross the Square at four this morning on his way to Flem's house. Yes. You can't beat it: the town itself officially on record now in the voice of its night marshal; the county itself had spoken through one of its minor clowns; eighteen years ago when Manfred de Spain thought he was just bedding another loose-girdled bucolic Lilith, he was actually creating a piece of buffoon's folklore.

Though there were still ten minutes, and it would take Otis Harker at least twenty-five to "round up" the gin and compress and their purlieus and get back to the Square. And I know now that I already smelled tobacco smoke even before I put my hand on what I thought was an unlocked door for the reason that I myself had made a special trip back to leave it unlocked, still smelling the tobacco while I still tried to turn the knob, until the latch clicked back from inside and the door opened, she standing there against the dark interior in what little there was of light. Though it was enough to see her hair, that she had been to the beauty parlour: who according to Maggie had never been to one, the hair not bobbed of course, not waved, but something, I don't know what it was except that she had been to the beauty parlour that afternoon.

"Good for you for locking it," I said. "We won't need to risk a light either. Only I think that Otis Harker already—"

"That's all right," she said. So I closed the door and locked it again and turned on the desk lamp. "Turn them all on if you want to," she said. "I wasn't trying to hide. I just didn't want to have to talk to somebody."

"Yes," I said, and sat behind the desk. She had been in the client's chair, sitting in the dark, smoking; the cigarette was still burning in the little tray with two other stubs. Now she was sitting again in the client's chair at the end of the desk where the light fell upon her from the shoulder down but mostly on her hands lying quite still on the bag on her lap. Though I could still see her hair—no makeup, lips or nails either: just her hair that had been to the beauty shop. "You've been to the beauty shop," I said.

"Yes," she said. "That's where I met Chick."

"But not inside," I said, already trying to stop. "Not where water and soap are coeval, conjunctive," still trying to stop. "Not for a few years yet," and did. "All right," I said. "Tell me. What was it he took out there to your mother yesterday that had old Will on the road to town at two o'clock this morning?"

"There's your cob pipe," she said. They were in the brass bowl beside the tobacco jar. "You've got three of them. I've never seen you smoke one. When do you smoke them?"

"All right," I said. "Yes. What was it he took out there?"

"The will," she said.

"No no," I said. "I know about the will; Ratliff told me. I mean, what was it Flem took out there to your mother yesterday morning—"

"I told you. The will."

"Will?" I said.

"Linda's will. Giving her share of whatever she would inherit from me, to her fa— him." And I sat there and she too, opposite one another across the desk, the lamp between us low on the desk so that all we could really see of either probably was just the hands: mine on the desk and hers quite still, almost as if two things asleep, on the bag in her lap, her voice almost as if it was asleep too so that there was no anguish, no alarm, no outrage anywhere in the little quiet dingy mausoleum of human passions, high and secure, secure even from any random exigency of what had been impressed on Otis Harker as his duty for which he was paid his salary, since he already knew it would be me in it: "The will. It was her idea. She did it herself. I mean, she believes she thought of it, wanted to do it, did it, herself. Nobody can tell her otherwise. Nobody will. Nobody. That's why I wrote the note."

"You'll have to tell me," I said. "You'll have to."

"It was the . . . school business. When you told her she wanted to go, get away from here; all the different schools to choose among that she hadn't even known about before, that it was perfectly natural for a young girl—young people to want to go to them and to go to one of them, that until then she hadn't even thought about, let alone known that she wanted to go to one of them. Like all she needed to do to go to one of them was just to pick out the one she liked the best and go to it, especially after I said Yes. Then her—he said No.

"As if that was the first time she ever thought of No, ever heard of No. There was a . . . scene. I don't like scenes. You don't have to have scenes. Nobody needs to have a scene to get what you want. You just get it. But she didn't know that, you see. She hadn't had time to learn it maybe, since she was just seventeen then. But then you know that yourself. Or maybe it was more than not knowing better. Maybe she knew too much. Maybe she already knew, felt even then that he had already beat her. She said: 'I will go! I will! You can't stop me! Damn your money; if Mama won't give it to me, Grandpa will—Mr Stevens' (oh yes, she said that too) 'will—' While he just sat there—we were sitting then, still at the table; only Linda was standing up—just sat there saying, 'That's right. I can't stop you.' Then she said, 'Please.' Oh yes, she knew she was beaten as well as he did. 'No,' he said. 'I want you to stay at home and go to the Academy.'

"And that was all. I mean . . . nothing. That was just all. Because you—a girl anyway—don't really hate your father no matter how much you think you do or should or should want to because people expect you to or that it would look well to because it would be romantic to—"

"Yes," I said, "—because girls, women, are not interested in romance but only facts. Oh yes, you were not the only one: Ratliff told me that too, that same day in fact."

"Vladimir too?" she said.

"No: Ratliff," I said. Then I said, "Wait." Then I said: "Vladimir? Did you say Vladimir? V.K. Is his name Vladimir?" And now she did sit still, even the hands on the bag that had been like things asleep and breathing their own life apart, seemed to become still now.

"I didn't intend to do that," she said.

"Yes," I said. "I know: nobody else on earth knows his name is Vladimir because how could anybody named Vladimir hope to make a living selling sewing machines or anything else in rural Mississippi? But he told you: the secret he would have defended like that of insanity in his family or illegitimacy. Why?—No, don't answer that. Why shouldn't I know why he told you; didn't I breathe one blinding whiff of that same liquor too? Tell me. I won't either. Vladimir K. What K.?"

"Vladimir Kyrilytch."

"Vladimir Kyrilytch what? Not Ratliff. Kyrilytch is only his middle name; all Russian middle names are itch or ovna. That's just son or daughter of. What was his last name before it became Ratliff?"

"He doesn't know. His . . . six or eight or ten times grandfather was . . . not lieutenant—"

"Ensign."

"—in a British army that surrendered in the Revolution—"

"Yes," I said. "Burgoyne. Saratoga."

"—and was sent to Virginia and forgotten and Vla—his grandfather escaped. It was a woman of course, a girl, that hid him and fed him. Except that she spelled it R-a-t-c-l-i-f-f-e and they married and had a son or had the son and then married. Anyway he learned to speak English and became a Virginia farmer. And his grandson, still spelling it with a c and an e at the end but with his name still Vladimir Kyrilytch though nobody knew it, came to Mississippi with old Doctor Habersham and Alexander Holston and Louis Grenier and started Jefferson. Only they forgot how to spell it Ratcliffe and just spelled it like it sounds but one son is always named Vladimir Kyrilytch. Except that like you said, nobody named Vladimir Kyrilytch could make a living as a Mississippi country man—"

"No," I said, cried. "Wait. That's wrong. We're both wrong. We're completely backward. If only everybody had known his name was really Vladimir Kyrilytch, he would be a millionaire by now, since any woman anywhere would have bought anything or everything he had to sell or trade or swap. Or maybe they already do?" I said, cried. "Maybe they already do?—All right," I said. "Go on."

"But one in each generation still has to have the name because Vla—V.K. says the name is their luck."

"Except that it didn't work against Flem Snopes," I said. "Not when he tangled with Flem Snopes that night in that Old French-man's garden after you come back from Texas.—All right," I

said. " 'So that was all because you don't really hate your
father—' "

"He did things for her. That she didn't expect, hadn't even
thought about asking for. That young girls like, almost as
though he had put himself inside a young girl's mind even before
she thought of them. He gave me the money and sent us both to
Memphis to buy things for her graduation from high school—not
just a graduating dress but one for dancing too, and other things
for the summer; almost a trousseau. He even tried—offered, anyway told her he was going to—to have a picnic for her whole
graduating class but she refused that. You see? He was her father
even if he did have to be her enemy. You know: the one that said
'Please' accepting the clothes, while the one that defied him to
stop her refused the picnic.

"And that summer he gave me the money and even made the
hotel reservations himself for us to go down to the coast—you
may remember that—"

"I remember," I said.

"—to spend a month so she could swim in the ocean and meet
people, meet young men; he said that himself: meet young men.
And we came back and that fall she entered the Academy and he
started giving her a weekly allowance. Would you believe that?"

"I do now," I said. "Tell me."

"It was too much, more than she could need, had any business
with, too much for a seventeen-year-old girl to have every week
just in Jefferson. Yet she took that too that she didn't really need
just like she took the Academy that she didn't want. Because he
was her father, you see. You've got to remember that. Can you?"

"Tell me," I said.

"That was the fall, the winter. He still gave her things—clothes
she didn't need, had no business with, seventeen years old in
Jefferson; you may have noticed that too; even a fur coat until
she refused to let him, said No in time. Because you see, that was
the You can't stop me again; she had to remind him now and then
that she had defied him; she could accept the daughter's due but
not the enemy's bribe.

"Then it was summer, last summer. That was when it happened. I saw it, we were all at the table again and he said,
'Where do you want to go this summer? The coast again? Or

maybe the mountains this time? How would you like to take your mother and go to New York?' And he had her; she was already beat; she said, 'Won't that cost a lot of money?' and he said, 'That doesn't matter. When would you like to go?' and she said, 'No. It will cost too much money. Why don't we just stay here?' Because he had her, he had beat her. And the . . . terrible thing was, she didn't know it, didn't even know there had been a battle and she had surrendered. Before, she had defied him and at least she knew she was defying him even if she didn't know what to do with it, how to use it, what to do next. Now she had come over to his side and she didn't even know it.

"And that's all. Then it was fall, last October, she was at the Academy again and this time we had finished supper, we were in the living-room before the fire and she was reading, sitting on one of her feet I remember and I remember the book too, the John Donne you gave her—I mean, the new one, the second one, to replace the one that boy—what was his name? the garage mechanic, Matt Something, Levitt—tore up that day in your office—when he said, 'Linda,' and she looked up, still holding the book (that's when I remember seeing what it was) and he said, 'I was wrong. I thought the Academy ought to be good enough, because I never went to school and didn't know any better. But I know better now, and the Academy's not good enough any more. Will you give up the Yankee schools and take the University at Oxford?'

"And she still sat there, letting the book come down slow on to her lap, just looking at him. Then she said, 'What?'

" 'Will you forget about Virginia and the Northern schools for this year, and enter the University after Christmas?' She threw the book, she didn't put it down at all: she just threw it, flung it as she stood up out of the chair and said:

" 'Daddy.' I had never seen her touch him. He was her father, she never refused to speak to him or to speak any way except respectfully. But he was her enemy; she had to keep him reminded always that although he had beaten her about the schools, she still hadn't surrendered. But I had never seen her touch him until now, sprawled, flung across his lap, clutching him around the shoulders, her face against his collar, crying, saying, 'Daddy! Daddy! Daddy! Daddy!' "

"Go on," I said.

"That's all. Oh, that was enough; what more did he need to do than that? have that thing—that piece of paper—drawn up himself and then twist her arm until she signed her name to it? He didn't have to mention any paper. He probably didn't even need to see her again and even if he did, all he would have needed —she already knew about the will, I mean Papa's will leaving my share to just Eula Varner without even mentioning the word Snopes—all he would need would be just to say something like 'Oh yes, your grandfather's a fine old gentleman but he just never did like me. But that's all right; your mother will be taken care of no matter what happens to me myself; he just fixed things so I nor nobody else can take her money away from her before you inherit it'—something like that. Or maybe he didn't even need to do that much, knew he didn't have to. Not with her. He was her father, and if he wouldn't let her go off to school it was because he loved her, since that was the reason all parents seemed to have for the things they won't let their children do; then for him to suddenly turn completely around and almost order her to do the thing she wanted, which he had forbidden her for almost two years to do, what reason could that be except that he loved her still more: loved her enough to let her do the one thing in her life he had ever forbidden her?

"Or I don't know. He may have suggested it, even told her how to word it; what does it matter now? It's done, there: Papa storming into the house at four this morning and flinging it down on my bed before I was even awake—Wait," she said, "I know all that too; I've already done all that myself. It was legal, all regular— What do they call it?"

"Drawn up," I said.

"—drawn up by a lawyer in Oxford, Mr Stone—not the old one: the young one. I telephoned him this morning. He was very nice. He—"

"I know him," I said. "Even if he did go to New Haven."

"—said he had wanted to talk to me about it, but there was the . . ."

"Inviolacy," I said.

"Inviolacy—between client and lawyer. He said she came to him, it must have been right after she reached Oxford—Wait," she said. "I asked him that too: why she came to him and he said—He said she was a delightful young lady who would go far in life even after she ran out of—of—"

"Contingencies," I said.

"—contingencies to bequeath people—she said that she had just asked someone who was the nicest lawyer for her to go to and they told her him. So she told him what she wanted and he wrote it that way; oh yes, I saw it: 'my share of whatever I might inherit from my mother, Eula Varner Snopes, as distinct and separate from whatever her husband shall share in her property, to my father Flem Snopes.' Oh yes, all regular and legal though he said he tried to explain to her that she was not bequeathing a quantity but merely devising a—what was it? contingency, and that nobody would take it very seriously probably since she might die before she had any inheritance or get married or even change her mind without a husband to help her or her mother might not have any inheritance beyond the one specified or might spend it or her father might die and she would inherit half of his inheritance from herself plus the other half which her mother would inherit as her father's relict, which she would heir in turn back to her father's estate to pass to her mother as his relict to be inherited once more by her; but she was eighteen years old and competent and he, Mr Stone, was a competent lawyer or at least he had a licence saying so, and so it was at least in legal language and on the right kind of paper. He—Mr Stone— even asked her why she felt she must make the will and she told him: Because my father has been good to me and I love and admire and respect him—do you hear that? Love and admire and respect him. Oh yes, legal. As if that mattered, legal or illegal, contingency or incontingency—"

Nor did she need to tell me that either: that old man seething out there in his country store for eighteen years now over the way his son-in-law had tricked him out of that old ruined plantation and then made a profit out of it, now wild with rage and frustration at the same man who had not only out-briganded him in brigand-age but since then had even out-usury-ed him in sedentary usury, and who now had used the innocence of a young girl, his own granddaughter, who could repay what she thought was love with gratitude and generosity at least, to disarm him of the one re-

maining weapon which he still held over his enemy. Oh yes, of
course it was worth nothing except its paper, but what did that
matter, legal or valid either. It didn't even matter now if he
destroyed it (which of course was why Flem ever let it out of his
hand in the first place); only that he saw it, read it, comprehended
it: took one outraged incredulous glance at it, then came storming
into town—

"I couldn't make him hush," she said. "I couldn't make him
stop, be quiet. He didn't even want to wait until daylight to get
hold of Manfred."

"De Spain?" I said. "Then? At four in the morning?"

"Didn't I tell you I couldn't stop him, make him stop or hush?
Oh yes, he got Manfred there right away. And Manfred attended
to everything. It was quite simple to him. That is, when I finally
made him and Papa both believe that in another minute they
would wake up, rouse the whole neighbourhood and before that
happened I would take Papa's—Jody's—car and drive to Oxford
and get Linda and none of them would ever see us again. So he
and Papa hushed then—"

"But Flem," I said.

"He was there—for a little while, long enough—"

"But what was he doing?" I said.

"Nothing," she said. "What was he supposed to do? What did
he need to do now?"

"Oh," I said. " 'long enough' to—"

"—enought for Manfred to settle everything: we would simply
leave, go away together, he and I, which was what we should
have done eighteen years ago—"

"What?" I said, cried. "Leave—elope?"

"Oh yes, it was all fixed; he stopped right there with Papa still
standing over him and cursing him—cursing him or cursing
Flem; you couldn't tell now which one he was talking to or about
or at—and wrote out the bill of sale. Papa was—what's that word?
—neutral. He wanted both of them out of the bank, intended to
have both of them out of it, came all the way in from home at
four o'clock in the morning to fling both of them out of Jefferson
and Yoknapatawpha County and Mississippi all three—Manfred
for having been my lover for eighteen years, and Flem for waiting
eighteen years to do anything about it. Papa didn't know about

Manfred until this morning. That is, he acted like he didn't. I think Mamma knew. I think she has known all the time. But maybe she didn't. Because people are really kind, you know. All the people in Yoknapatawpha County that might have made sure Mamma knew about us, for her own good, so she could tell Papa for his own good. For everybody's own good. But I don't think Papa knew. He's like you. I mean, you can do that too."

"Do what?" I said.

"Be able to not have to believe something just because it might be so or somebody says it is so or maybe even it is so."

"Wait," I said. "Wait. What bill of sale?"

"For his bank stock. Manfred's bank stock. Made out to Flem. To give Flem the bank, since that was what all the trouble and up-roar was about.—And then the check for Flem to sign to buy it with, dated a week from now to give Flem time to have the money ready when we cashed the check in Texas—when people are not married, or should have been married but aren't yet, why do they still think Texas is far enough? or is it just big enough?—or California or Mexico or wherever we would go."

"But Linda," I said. "Linda."

"All right," she said. "Linda."

"Don't you see? Either way, she is lost? Either to go with you, if that were possible, while you desert her father for another man; or stay here in all the stink without you to protect her from it and learn at last that he is not her father at all and so she has nobody, nobody?"

"That's why I sent the note. Marry her."

"No. I told you that before. Besides, that won't save her. Only Manfred can save her. Let him sell Flem his stock, give Flem the damned bank; is that too high a price to pay for what—what he—he—"

"I tried that," she said. "No."

"I'll talk to him," I said. "I'll tell him. He must. He'll have to; there's no other—"

"No," she said. "Not Manfred." Then I watched her hands, not fast, open the bag and take out the pack of cigarettes and the single kitchen match and extract the cigarette and put the pack back into the bag and close it and (no, I didn't move) strike the match on the turned sole of her shoe and light the cigarette and put the match into the tray and put her hands again on the bag. "Not Manfred. You don't know Manfred. And so maybe I don't either. Maybe I don't know about men either. Maybe I was completely wrong that morning when I said how women are only interested in facts because maybe men are just interested in facts too and the only difference is, women don't care whether they are facts or not just so they fit, and men don't care whether they fit or not just so they are facts. If you are a man, you can lie unconscious in the gutter bleeding and with most of your teeth knocked out and somebody can take your pocketbook and you can wake up and wash the blood off and it's all right; you can always get some more teeth and even another pocketbook sooner or later. But you can't just stand meekly with your head bowed and no blood and all your teeth too while somebody takes your pocketbook, because even though you might face the friends who love you afterward, you never can face the strangers that never heard of you before. Not Manfred. If I don't go with him, he'll have to fight. He may go down fighting and wreck everything and everybody else, but he'll have to fight. Because he's a man. I mean, he's a man first. I mean he's got to be a man first. He can swap Flem Snopes his bank for Flem Snopes's wife, but he can't just stand there and let Flem Snopes take the bank away from him."

"So Linda's sunk," I said. "Finished. Done. Sunk." I said, cried: "But you anyway will save something! To get away yourself at least, out of here, never again to . . . never again Flem Snopes, never again, never—"

"Oh, that," she said. "You mean that. That doesn't matter. That's never been any trouble. He . . . can't. He's— what's the word?—impotent. He's always been. Maybe that's why, one of the reasons. You see? You've got to be careful or you'll have to pity him. You'll have to. He couldn't bear that, and it's no use to hurt people if you don't get anything for it. Because he couldn't bear being pitied. It's like V.K.'s Vladimir. Ratliff can live with Ratliff's Vladimir, and you can live with Ratliff's Vladimir. But you mustn't ever have the chance to, the right to, the choice to. Like he can live with his impotence, but you mustn't have the chance to help him with pity. You promised about the Vladimir, but I want you to promise again about this."

"I promise," I said. Then I said: "Yes. You're going tonight.

That's why the beauty parlour this afternoon: not for me but for Manfred. No: not even for Manfred after eighteen years: just to elope with, get on the train with. To show your best back to Jefferson. That's right, isn't it? You're leaving tonight."

"Marry her, Gavin," she said. I had known her by sight for eighteen years, with time out of course for the war; I had dreamed about her at night for eighteen years including the war. We had talked to one another twice: here in the office one night fourteen years ago, and in her living-room one morning two years back. But not once had she ever called me even Mister Stevens. Now she said Gavin. "Marry her, Gavin."

"Change her name by marriage, then she won't miss the name she will lose when you abandon her."

"Marry her, Gavin," she said.

"Put it that I'm not too old so much as simply discrepant; that having been her husband once, I would never relinquish even her widowhood to another. Put it that way then."

"Marry her, Gavin," she said. And now I stopped, she sitting beyond the desk, the cigarette burning on the tray, balancing its muted narrow windless feather where she had not touched it once since she lit it and put it down, the hands still quiet on the bag and the face now turned to look at me out of the half-shadow above the rim of light from the lamp—the big broad simple still unpainted beautiful mouth, the eyes not the hard and dusty blue of fall but the blue of spring blooms, all one inextricable mixture of wistaria cornflowers larkspur bluebells weeds and all, all the lost girls' weather and boys' luck and too late the grief, too late.

"Then this way. After you're gone, if or when I become convinced that conditions are going to become such that something will have to be done, and nothing else but marrying me can help her, and she will have me, but have me, take me. Not just give up, surrender."

"Swear it then," she said.

"I promise. I have promised. I promise again."

"No," she said. "Swear."

"I swear," I said.

"And even if she won't have you. Even after that. Even if she w— you can't marry her."

"How can she need me then?" I said. "Flem—unless your

father really does get shut of the whole damned boiling of you, runs Flem out of Jefferson too—will have his bank and won't need to swap, sell, trade her any more; maybe he will even prefer to have her in a New England school or even further than that if he can manage it."

"Swear," she said.

"All right," I said. "At any time. Anywhere. No matter what happens."

"Swear," she said.

"I swear," I said.

"I'm going now," she said and rose and picked up the burning cigarette and crushed it carefully out into the tray and I rose too.

"Of course," I said. "You have some packing to do even for an elopment, don't you? I'll drive you home."

"You don't need to," she said.

"A lady, walking home alone at—it's after midnight. What will Otis Harker say? You see, I've got to be a man too; I can't face Otis Harker otherwise since you won't stop being a lady to him until after tomorrow's southbound train; I believe you did say Texas, didn't you?" Though Otis was not in sight this time, though with pencil, paper and a watch I could have calculated about where he would be now. Though the figures could have been wrong and only Otis was not in sight, not we, crossing the shadow-bitten Square behind the flat rapid sabre-sweep of the headlights across the plate-glass store-fronts, then into the true spring darkness where the sparse street lights were less than stars. And we could have talked if there had been more to talk about or maybe there had been more to talk about if we had talked. Then the small gate before the short walk to the small dark house not rented now of course and of course not vacant yet with a little space yet for decent decorum, and I wondered, thought *Will Manfred sell him his house along with his bank or just abandon both to him—provided of course old Will Varner leaves him time to collect either one?* and stopped.

"Don't get out," she said and got out and shut the door and said, stooping a little to look at me beneath the top: "Swear again."

"I swear," I said.

"Thank you," she said. "Good-night," and turned and I

watched her, through the gate and up the walk, losing dimension now, on to or rather into the shadow of the little gallery and losing even substance now. And then I heard the door and it was as if she had not been. No, not that; not *not been*, but rather no more *is*, since *was* remains always and forever, inexplicable and immune, which is its grief. That's what I mean: a dimension less, then a substance less, then the sound of a door and then, not *never been* but simply *no more is* since always and forever that *was* remains, as if what is going to happen to one tomorrow already gleams faintly visible now if the watcher were only wise enough to discern it or maybe just brave enough.

The spring night, cooler now, as if for a little while, until tomorrow's dusk and the new beginning, somewhere had suspired into sleep at last the amazed hushed burning of hope and dream two-and-two engendered. It would even be quite cold by dawn, daybreak. But even then not cold enough to chill, make hush for sleep the damned mocking-bird for three nights now keeping his constant racket in Maggie's pink dogwood just under my bedroom window. So the trick of course would be to divide, not him but his racket, the having to listen to him: one Gavin Stevens to cross his dark gallery too and into the house and up the stairs to cover his head in the bedclothes, losing in his turn a dimension of Gavin Stevens, an ectoplasm of Gavin Stevens impervious to cold and hearing too to bear its half of both, bear its half or all of any other burdens anyone wanted to shed and shuck, having only this moment assumed that one of a young abandoned girl's responsibility.

Because who would miss a dimension? Who indeed but would be better off for having lost it, who had nothing in the first place to offer but just devotion, eighteen years of devotion, the ectoplasm of devotion too thin to be crowned by scorn, warned by hatred, annealed by grief. That's it: unpin, shed, cast off the last clumsy and anguished dimension, and so be free. Unpin: that's the trick, remembering Vladimir Kyrilytch's "He ain't unpinned it yet"—the twenty-dollar gold piece pinned to the undershirt of the country boy on his first trip to Memphis, who even if he has never been there before, has as much right as any to hope he can be, may be, will be tricked or trapped into a whorehouse before he has to go back home again. *He has unpinned it now* I thought.

21

CHARLES MALLISON

You know how it is, you wake in the morning and you know at once that it has already happened and you are already too late. You didn't know what it was going to be, which was why you had to watch so hard for it, trying to watch in all directions at once. Then you let go for a second, closed your eyes for just one second, and bang! it happened and it was too late, not even time to wake up and still hold off a minute, just to stretch and think *What is it that makes today such a good one?* then to let it come in, flow in: *Oh yes, there's not any school today.* More: *Thursday and in April and still there's not any school today.*

But not this morning. And halfway down the stairs I heard the swish of the pantry door shutting and I could almost hear Mother telling Guster: "Here he comes. Quick. Get out," and I went into the dining-room and Father had already had breakfast, I mean even when Guster has moved the plate and cup and saucer you can always tell where Father has eaten something; and by the look of his place Uncle Gavin hadn't been to the table at all and Mother was sitting at her place just drinking coffee, with her hat already on and her coat over Uncle Gavin's chair and her bag and gloves by her plate and the dark glasses she wore in the car whenever she went beyond the city limits as if light didn't have any glare in it except one mile from town. And I reckon she wished for a minute that I was about three or four because then she could have put one arm around me against her knee and held the back of my head with the other hand. But now she just held my hand and this time she had to look up at me. "Mrs Snopes killed herself last night," she said. "I'm going over to Oxford with Uncle Gavin to bring Linda home."

"Killed herself?" I said. "How?"

"What?" Mother said. Because I was only twelve then, not yet thirteen.

"What did she do it with?" I said. But then Mother remembered that too by that time. She was already getting up.

"With a pistol," she said. "I'm sorry, I didn't think to ask

K

whose." She almost had the coat on too. Then she came and got the gloves and bag and the glasses. "We may be back by dinner, but I don't know. Will you try to stay at home, at least stay away from the Square, find something to do with Aleck Sander in the back yard? Guster's not going to let him leave the place today, so why don't you stay with him?"

"Yessum," I said. Because I was just twelve; to me that great big crêpe knot dangling from the front door of Mr de Spain's bank signified only waste: another holiday when school was suspended for an indefinite time; another holiday piled on top of one we already had, when the best, the hardest holiday user in the world couldn't possibly use two of them at once, when it could have been saved and added on to the end of the one we already had when the little Riddell boy either died or got well or anyway they started school again. Or better still: just to save it for one of those hopeless days when Christmas is so long past you have forgotten it ever was, and it looks like summer itself has died somewhere and will never come again.

Because I was just twelve; I would have to be reminded that the longest school holiday in the world could mean nothing to the people which that wreath on the bank door freed for one day from work. And I would have to be a lot older than twelve before I realised that that wreath was not the myrtle of grief, it was the laurel of victory; that in that dangling chunk of black tulle and artificial flowers and purple ribbons was the eternal and deathless public triumph of virtue itself proved once more supreme and invincible.

I couldn't even know now what I was looking at. Oh yes, I went to town, not quite as soon as Mother and Uncle Gavin were out of sight, but close enough. So did Aleck Sander. We could hear Guster calling us both a good while after we had turned the corner, both of us going to look at the wreath on the closed bank door and seeing a lot of other people too, grown people, come to look at it for what I know now was no braver reason than the one Aleck Sander and I had. And when Mr de Spain came to town as he always did just before nine o'clock and got his mail from the post-office like he always did and let himself into the back door of the bank with his key like he always did because the back door always stayed locked, we—I—couldn't know that the reason he looked exactly like nothing had happened was because that was exactly the way he had to come to town that morning to have to look. That he had to get up this morning and shave and dress and maybe practise in front of the mirror a while in order to come to the Square at the time he always did so everybody in Jefferson could see him doing exactly as he always did, like if there was grief and trouble anywhere in Jefferson that morning, it was not his grief and trouble, being an orphan and unmarried; even to going on into the closed bank by the back door as if still he had the right to.

Because I know now that we—Jefferson—all knew that he had lost the bank. I mean, whether old Mr Will Varner ran Mr Flem Snopes out of Jefferson too after this, Mr de Spain himself wouldn't stay. In a way he owed that not just to the memory of his dead love, his dead mistress; he owed that to Jefferson too. Because he had outraged us. He had not only flouted the morality of marriage which decreed that a man and a woman can't sleep together without a certificate from the police, he had outraged the economy of marriage which is the production of children, by making public display of the fact that you can be barren by choice with impunity; he had outraged the institution of marriage twice: not just his own but the Flem Snopes's too. So they already hated him twice: once for doing it, once for not getting caught at it for eighteen years. But that would be nothing to the hatred he would get if, after his guilty partner had paid with her life for her share of the crime, he didn't even lose that key to the back door of the bank to pay for his.

We all knew that. So did he. And he knew we knew. And we in our turn knew he knew we did. So that was all right. He was finished, I mean, he was fixed. His part was set. No: I was right the first time; and now I know that too. He was done, ended. That shot had finished him too, and now what he did or didn't do either didn't matter any more. It was just Linda now; and when I was old enough I knew why none of us expected that day that old Mr Varner would come charging out of Mr Snopes's house with the same pistol maybe seeking more blood, if for no other reason than that there would have been no use in it. Nor were we surprised when (after a discreet interval of course, for decorum, the decorum of bereavement and mourning) we learned that "for business reasons and health" Mr de Spain had resigned from the bank and was moving out West (he actually left the afternoon of the funeral, appeared at the grave—alone and nobody to speak to him except to nod—with a crêpe armband which was of course all right since the deceased was the wife of his vice-president, and then turned from the grave when we all did except that he was the first one and an hour later that afternoon his Buick went fast across the Square and into the Memphis highway with him in it and the back full of baggage) and that his bank stock—not his house; Ratliff said that even Flem Snopes didn't have that much nerve; to buy the house too the same day he bought the bank stock—was offered for sale, and even less surprised that (even more discreetly) Mr Snopes had bought it.

It was Linda now. And now I know that the other people, the grown people, who had come to look at that wreath on the bank door for exactly the same reason that Aleck Sander and I had come to look at it, had come only incidentally to look at the wreath since they had really come for exactly the same reason Aleck Sander and I had really come: to see Linda Snopes when Mother and Uncle Gavin brought her home, even if mine and Aleck Sander's reason was to see how much Mrs Snopes's killing herself would change the way Linda looked so that we would know how we would look if Mother and Guster ever shot themselves. It was Linda because I know now what Uncle Gavin believed then (not knew: believed: because he couldn't have known because the only one that could have told him would have been Mrs Snopes herself and if she had told him in that note she gave me that afternoon before she was going to commit suicide, he would have stopped her or tried to because Mother anyway would have known it if he had tried to stop her and failed), and not just Uncle Gavin but other people in Jefferson too. So now they even forgave Mrs Snopes for the eighteen years of carnal sin, and now they could even forgive themselves for condoning adultery by forgiving it, by reminding themselves (one another too I reckon) that if she had not been an abomination before God for eighteen years, she wouldn't have reached the point where she would have to choose death in order to leave her child a mere suicide for a mother instead of a whore.

Oh yes, it was Linda. She had the whole town on her side now, the town and the county and everybody who ever heard of her and Mr de Spain or knew or even suspected or just guessed anything about the eighteen years, to keep any part of the guessing or suspecting or actual knowing (if there was any, ever was any) from ever reaching her. Because I know now that people really are kind, they really are; there are lots of times when they stop hurting one another not just when they want to keep on hurting but even when they have to; even the most Methodist and Baptist of the Baptists and Methodists and Presbyterians—all right, Episcopals too—the car coming at last with Linda in the front seat between Mother and Uncle Gavin; across the Square and on to Linda's house so that Aleck Saunder and I had plenty of time to be waiting at the corner to flag Uncle Gavin when he came back.

"I thought Guster and your mother told both of you to stay home this morning," he said.

"Yes sir," we said. We went home. And he didn't eat any dinner either: just trying to make me eat, I don't know why. I mean, I don't know why all grown people in sight believe they have to try to persuade you to eat whether you want to or not or even whether they really want to try to persuade you or not, until at last even Father noticed what was going on.

"Come on," he told me. "Either eat it or leave the table. I don't want to lie to your mother when she comes home and asks me why you didn't eat it and I can always say you left suddenly for Texas." Then he said, "What's the matter, you too?" because Uncle Gavin had got up, right quick, and said,

"Excuse me," and went out; yes, Uncle Gavin too; Mr de Spain was finished now so far as Jefferson was concerned and now we—Jefferson—could put all our mind on who was next in sight, what else the flash of that pistol had showed up like when you set off a flashlight powder in a cave; and one of them was Uncle Gavin. Because I know now there were people in Jefferson then who believed that Uncle Gavin had been her lover too, or if he hadn't he should have been or else not just the whole Jefferson masculine race but the whole masculine race anywhere that called itself a man ought to be ashamed.

Because they knew about that old Christmas Ball older than I was then, and the whole town had seen and then heard about it

so they could come, pass by accident and see for themselves
Uncle Gavin and Linda drinking ice-cream sodas in Christian's
with a book of poetry on the table between them. Except that
they knew he really hadn't been Mrs Snopes's lover too, that
not only if he had really wanted her, tried for her, he would have
failed there too for simple consistency, but that even if by some
incredible chance or accident he had beat Mr de Spain's time, it
would have showed on the outside of him for the reason that
Uncle Gavin was incapable of having a secret life which remained
secret; he was, Ratliff said, "a feller that even his in-growed
toenails was on the outside of his shoes".

So, since Uncle Gavin had failed, he was the pure one, the only
pure one; not Mr Snopes, the husband, who if he had been a man,
would have got a pistol even if he, Flem Snopes, had to buy one
and blown them both, his wife and her fancy banker both, clean
out of Jefferson. It was Uncle Gavin. He was the bereaved, the
betrayed husband forgiving for the sake of the half-orphan child.
It was that same afternoon, he had left right after he went out of
the dining-room, then Mother came back alone in the car, then
about three o'clock Uncle Gavin came back in a taxi and said
(Oh yes, Aleck Sander and I stayed at home after Guster got hold
of us, let alone Mother):

"Four gentlemen are coming to see me. They're preachers so
you'd better show them into the parlour." And I did: the
Methodist, the Baptist, the Presbyterian and ours, the Episcopal,
all looking like any other bankers or doctors or storekeepers except
Mr Thorndyke and the only thing against him was his hind-part-
before dog collar; all very grave and long in the face, like horses;
I mean, not looking unhappy: just looking long in the face like
horses, each one shaking hands with me and kind of bumbling
with each other while they were getting through the door, into the
parlour where Uncle Gavin was standing too, speaking to each of
them by name while they all shook hands with him too, calling
them all Doctor, the four of them bumbling again until the oldest
one, the Presbyterian, did the talking: they had come to offer
themselves singly or jointly to conduct the service; that Mr Snopes
was a Baptist and Mrs Snopes had been born a Methodist but
neither of them had attended, been a communicant of, any church
in Jefferson; that Mr Stevens had assumed—offered his—that is,

they had been directed to call on Mr Stevens in regard to the matter, until Uncle Gavin said:

"That is, you were sent. Sent by a damned lot of damned old women of both sexes, including none. Not to bury her: to forgive her. Thank you, gentlemen. I plan to conduct this service myself." But that was just until Father came home for supper and Mother could sic him on Uncle Gavin too. Because we had all thought, taken it for granted, that the Varners (maybe Mr Flem too) would naturally want her buried in Frenchman's Bend; that Mr Varner would pack her up too when he went back home along with whatever else he had brought to town with him (Ratliff said it wouldn't be much since the only thing that travelled lighter than Uncle Billy Varner was a crow) and take her back with him. But Uncle Gavin said No, speaking for Linda—and there were people enough to say Gavin Stevens said No speaking *to* the daughter. Anyway, it was No, the funeral to be tomorrow after Jody Varner's car could get back in from Frenchman's Bend with Jody and Mrs Varner; and now Uncle Gavin had Father at him too.

"Dammit, Gavin," he said. "You can't do it. We all admit you're a lot of things but one of them ain't an ordained minister."

"So what?" Uncle Gavin said. "Do you believe that this town believes that any preacher that ever breathed could get her into heaven without having to pass through Jefferson, and that even Christ Himself could get her through on that route?"

"Wait," Mother said. "Both of you hush." She was looking at Uncle Gavin. "Gavin, at first I thought I would never understand why Eula did it. But now I'm beginning to believe that maybe I do. Do you want Linda to have to say afterward that another bachelor had to bury her?"

And that was all. And the next day Mrs Varner and Jody came in and brought with them the old Methodist minister who had christened her thirty-eight years ago—an old man who had been a preacher all his adult life but would have for the rest of it the warped back and the wrenched bitter hands of a dirt farmer—and we—the town—gathered at their little house, the women inside and the men standing around the little front yard and along the street, all neat and clean and wearing coats and not quite looking at each other while they talked quietly about crops

and weather; then to the graveyard and the new lot empty except
for the one raw excavation and even that not long, hidden quickly,
rapidly beneath the massed flowers, themselves already doomed
in the emblem-shapes—wreaths and harps and urns—of the
mortality which they de-stingered, euphemised; and Mr de Spain
standing there not apart: just solitary, with his crêpe armband
and his face looking like it must have when he was a lieutenant in
Cuba back in that time, day, moment after he had just led the
men that trusted him or anyway followed him because they were
supposed to, into the place where they all knew some of them
wouldn't come back for the reason that all of them were not
supposed to come back which was all right too if the lieutenant
said it was.

Then we came home and Father said, "Dammit, Gavin, why
don't you get drunk?" and Uncle Gavin said,

"Certainly, why not?"—not even looking up from the paper.
Then it was supper time and I wondered why Mother didn't nag
at him about not eating. But at least as long as she didn't think
about eating, her mind wouldn't hunt around and light on me.
Then we—Uncle Gavin and Mother and I—went to the office.
I mean that for a while after Grandfather died Mother still tried
to make us all call it the library but now even she called it the
office just like Grandfather did, and Uncle Gavin sitting beside the
lamp with a book and even turning a page now and then, until
the door bell rang.

"I'll go," Mother said. But then, nobody else seemed to intend
to or be even curious. Then she came back down the hall to the
office door and said, "It's Linda. Come in, honey," and stood to
one side and beckoned her head at me as Linda came in and
Uncle Gavin got up and Mother jerked her head at me again and
said, "Chick," and Linda stopped just inside the door and this
time Mother said, "Charles!" so I got up and went out and she
closed the door after us. But it was all right. I was used to it by
this time. As soon as I saw who it was, I even expected it.

GAVIN STEVENS

THEN Maggie finally got Chick out and closed the door.
I said, "Sit down, Linda." But she just stood there. "Cry," I
said. "Let yourself go and cry."

"I can't," she said. "I tried." She looked at me. "He's not my
father," she said.

"Of course he's your father," I said. "Certainly he is. What in
the world are you talking about?"

"No," she said.

"Yes," I said. "Do you want me to swear? All right. I swear he's
your father."

"You were not there. You don't know. You never even saw her
until she—we came to Jefferson."

"Ratliff did. Ratliff was there. He knows. He knows who your
father is. And I know from Ratliff. I am sure. Have I ever lied to
you?"

"No," she said. "You are the one person in the world I know
will never lie to me."

"All right," I said. "I swear to you then. Flem Snopes is your
father." And now she didn't move: it was just the tears, the water,
not springing, just running quietly and quite fast down her face. I
moved toward her.

"No," she said, "don't touch me yet," catching, grasping both
my wrists and gripping, pressing my hands hard in hers against
her breast. "When I thought he wasn't my father, I hated her and
Manfred both. Oh yes, I knew about Manfred: I have . . . seen
them look at each other, their voices when they would talk to
each other, speak one another's name, and I couldn't bear it, I
hated them both. But now that I know he is my father, it's all
right. I'm glad. I want her to have loved, to have been happy.—
I can cry now," she said.

V. K. RATLIFF

IT was like a contest, like Lawyer had stuck a stick of dynamite in his hind pocket and lit a long fuse to it and was interested now would or wouldn't somebody step in in time and tromple the fire out. Or a race, like would he finally get Linda out of Jefferson and at least get his-self shut forever of the whole tribe of Snopes first, or would he jest blow up his-self beforehand first and take ever body and ever thing in the neighbourhood along with him.

No, not a contest. Not a contest with Flem Snopes anyway, because it takes two to make a contest and Flem Snopes wasn't the other one. He was a umpire, if he was anything in it. No, he wasn't even a umpire. It was like he was running a little mild game against his-self, for his own amusement, like solitaire. He had ever thing now that he had come to Jefferson to get. He had more. He had things he didn't even know he was going to want until he reached Jefferson, because he didn't even know what they was until then. He had his bank and his money in it and his-self to be president of it so he could not only watch his money from ever being stole by another twenty-two-calibre rogue like his cousin Byron, but nobody could ever steal from him the respectability that being president of one of the two Yoknapatawpha County banks toted along with it. And he was going to have one of the biggest residences in the county or maybe Mississippi too when his carpenters got through with Manfred de Spain's old home. And he had got rid of the only two downright arrant outrageous Snopeses when he run Montgomery Ward and I.O. finally out of town so that now, for the time being at least, the only other Snopes actively inside the city limits was a wholesale grocer not only as respectable but maybe even more solvent than jest a banker. So you would think he would a been satisfied now. But he wasn't. He had to make a young girl (woman now) that wasn't even his child, say "I humbly thank you, Papa, for being so good to me."

That's right, a contest. Not even against Linda, and last of all against Lawyer Stevens, since he had already milked out of

Lawyer Stevens all he needed from him, which was to get his wife
buried all right and proper and decorous and respectable, without no uproarious elements making a unseemly spectacle in the
business. His game of solitaire was against Jefferson. It was like
he was trying to see jest exactly how much Jefferson would stand,
put up with. It was like he knowed that his respectability depended completely on Jefferson not jest accepting but finally
getting used to the fact that he not only had evicted Manfred de
Spain from his bank but he was remodelling to move into it De
Spain's birthsite likewise, and that the only remaining threat now
was what might happen if that-ere young gal that believed all
right so far that he was her paw, might stumble on to something
that would tell her different. That she might find out by accident
that the man that was leastways mixed up somehow in her
mother's suicide, whether he actively caused it or not, wasn't even
her father, since if somebody's going to be responsible why your
maw killed herself, at least let it be somebody kin to you and not
jest a outright stranger.

So you would a thought that the first thing he would do soon
as the dust settled after that funeral would be to get her clean out
of Jefferson and as far away as he could have suh-jested into her
mind she wanted to go. But not him. And the reason he give was
that monument. And naturally that was Lawyer Stevens too. I
mean, I don't know who delegated Lawyer into the monument
business, who gave it to him or if he jest taken it or if maybe by
this time the relationship between him and anybody named
Snopes, or anyway maybe jest the Flem Snopeses (or no: it was
that for him Eula Varner hadn't never died and never would
because oh yes, I know about that too) was like that one between
a feller out in a big open field and a storm of rain: there ain't no
being give nor accepting to it: he's already got it.

Anyway it was him—Lawyer—that helped Linda hunt through
that house and her mother's things until they found the right
photograph and had it—Lawyer still—enlarged, the face part,
and sent it to Italy to be carved into a . . . yes, medallion to fasten
on to the front of the monument, and him that the practice draw-
ings would come back to to decide and change here and there and
send back. Which would a been his right by his own choice even
if Flem had tried to interfere in and stop him because he wanted

that monument set up where Flem could pass on it more than anybody wanted it because then Flem would let her go. But it was Flem's monument; don't make no mistake about that. It was Flem that paid for it, first thought of it, planned and designed it, picked out what size and what was to be wrote on it—the face and the letters—and never once mentioned price. Don't make no mistake about that. It was Flem. Because this too was a part of what he had come to Jefferson for and went through all he went through afterward to get it.

Oh yes, Lawyer had it all arranged for Linda to leave, get away at last; all they was hung on was the monument, because Flem had give his word he would let her go then. It was to a place named Greenwich Village in New York; Lawyer had it all arranged, friends he knowed in Harvard to meet the train at the depot and take care of her, get her settled and ever thing.

"Is it a college?" I says. "Like out at Seminary Hill?"

"No no," he says. "I mean, yes. But not the kind you are talking about."

"I thought you was set on her going to a college up there."

"That was before," he says. "Too much has happened to her since. Too much, too fast, too quick. She outgrew colleges all in about twenty-four hours two weeks ago. She'll have to grow back down to them again, maybe in a year or two. But right now, Greenwich Village is the place for her."

"What is Greenwich Village?" I says. "You still ain't told me."

"It's a place with a few unimportant boundaries but no limitations where young people of any age go to seek dreams."

"I never knowed before that place had no particular geography," I says. "I thought that-ere was a varmint you hunted anywhere."

"Not always. Not for her, anyway. Sometimes you need a favourable scope of woods to hunt, a place where folks have already successfully hunted and found the same game you want. Sometimes, some people even need help in finding it. The particular quarry they want to catch, they have to make first. That takes two."

"Two what?" I says.

"Yes," he says. "Two."

"You mean a husband," I says.

"All right," he says. "Call him that. It don't matter what you call him."

"Why, Lawyer," I says, "you sound like what a heap, a right smart in fact, jest about all in fact, unanimous in fact of our good God-fearing upright embattled Christian Jeffersons and Yokna-patawphas too that can proudly affirm that never in their life did they ever have one minute's fun that the most innocent little child could a stood right there and watched, would call a de-liberate incitement and pandering to the Devil his-self."

Only Lawyer wasn't laughing. And then I wasn't neither. "Yes," he says, "It will be like that with her. It will be difficult for her. She will have to look at a lot of them, a long time. Because he will face something almost impossible to match himself against. He will have to have courage, because it will be doom, maybe disaster too. That's her fate. She is doomed to anguish and to bear it, doomed to one passion and one anguish and all the rest of her life to bear it, as some people are doomed from birth to be robbed or betrayed or murdered."

Then I said it: "Marry her. Naturally you never thought of that."

"I?" he says. It was right quiet: no surprise, no nothing. "I thought I had just been talking about that for the last ten minutes. She must have the best. It will be impossible even for him."

"Marry her," I says.

"No," he says. "That's my fate: just to miss marriage."

"You mean escape it?"

"No no," he says. "I never escape it. Marriage is constantly in my life. My fate is constantly to just miss it or it to, safely again, once more safe, just miss me."

So it was all fixed, and now all he needed was to get his carved marble face back from Italy, nagging by long-distance telephone and telegraph dispatch ever day or so in the most courteous affable legal manner you could want, at the I-talian consul in New Orleans, so he could get it fastened on to the monument and then (if necessary) take a holt on Flem's coat collar and shove him into the car and take him out to the cemetery and snatch the veil offen it, with Linda's ticket to New York (he would a paid for that too except it wasn't necessary since the last thing Uncle Billy done before he went back home after the funeral was to turn over to the bank—not Flem: the bank, with Lawyer as one of the trustees—a good-size chunk of what would be Eula's inheritance under that will of hisn that he hadn't never changed to read Snopes) in his other hand.

So we had to wait. Which was interesting enough. I mean, Lawyer had enough to keep him occupied worrying the I-talian Government, and all I ever needed was jest something to look at, watch, providing of course it had people in it. They—Flem and Linda—still lived in the same little house that folks believed for years after he bought it that he was still jest renting it. Though pretty soon Flem owned a automobile. I mean, presently, after the polite amount of time after he turned up president of the bank; not to have Santy Claus come all at once you might say. It wasn't a expensive car: just a good one, jest the right unnoticeable size, of a good polite unnoticeable black colour and he even learned to drive it because maybe he had to because now ever afternoon after the bank closed he would have to go and watch how the carpenters was getting along with his new house (it was going to have colyums across the front now, I mean the extry big ones so even a feller that never seen colyums before wouldn't have no doubt a-tall what they was, like in the photographs where the Confedrit sweetheart in a hoop skirt and a magnolia is saying good-bye to her Confedrit beau jest before he rides off to finish tending to General Grant) and Flem would have to drive his-self because, although Linda could drive it right off and done it now and then and never mind if all women are naturally interested in the house-building or -remodeling occupation no matter whose it is the same as a bird is interested in the nesting occupation, although she druv him there the first afternoon to look at the house, she wouldn't go inside to look at it and after that one time she never even druv him back any more.

But like I said we was all busy or anyway occupied or at least interested, so we could wait. And sho enough, even waiting ends if you can jest wait long enough. So finally the medallion came. It was October now, a good time of year, one of the best. Naturally it was Lawyer went to the depot and got it, though I'm sho Flem paid the freight on it for no other reason than Lawyer wouldn't a waited long enough for the agent to add it up, herding the two Negroes toting it all wrapped up in straw and nailed up in a wooden box, across the platform to his waiting car like he was herding two geese. And for the next three days when his office seen him it was on the fly you might say, from a distance when he happened to pass it. Which was a good thing there wasn't no passel of brigands or highwaymen or contractors or jest simple lawyers making a concerted financial attack on Yoknapatawpha County at that time because Yoknapatawpha would a jest had to rock along the best it could without no help from its attorney. Because he had the masons already hired and waiting with likely even the mortar already mixed, even before the medallion come; one morning I even caught him, put my hand on the car door and says,

"I'll ride out to the cemetery with you," and he jest reached across, the car already in gear and the engine already racing, and lifted my hand off and throwed it away and says,

"Get out of the way," and went on and so I went up to the office, the door never was locked nohow even when he was jest normal and jest out of it most of the time, and opened the bottom drawer where he kept the bottle but it never even smelled like he used to keep whiskey in it. So I waited on the street until school let out and finally caught that boy, Chick, and says,

"Hasn't your uncle got some whiskey at home somewhere?" and he says,

"I don't know. I'll look. You want me to pour up a drink in something and bring it?" and I says,

"No. He don't need a drink. He needs a whole bottle, providing it's big enough and full enough. Bring all of it; I'll stay with him and watch."

Then the monument was finished, ready for Flem to pass on it, and he—Lawyer—sent me the word too, brisk and lively as a general jest getting ready to capture a town: "Be at the office at three-thirty so we can pick up Chick. The train leaves Memphis at eight o'clock so we won't have any time to waste."

So I was there. Except it wasn't in the office at all because he was already in the car with the engine already running when I got there. "What train at eight o'clock to where and whose?" I says.

"Linda's," he says. "She'll be in New York Saturday morning. She's all packed and ready to leave. Flem's sending her to Memphis in his car as soon as we are done."

"Flem's sending her?" I says.

"Why not?" he says. "She's his daughter. After all, you owe something to your children even if it ain't your fault. Get in," he says. "Here's Chick."

So we went out to the cemetery and there it was—another colyum not a-tall saying what it had cost Flem Snopes because what it was saying was exactly how much it was worth to Flem Snopes, standing in the middle of that new one-grave lot, at the head of that one grave that hadn't quite healed over yet, looking —the stone, the marble—whiter than white itself in the warm October sun against the bright yellow and red and dark red hickories and sumacs and gums and oaks like splashes of fire itself among the dark green cedars. Then the other car come up with him and Linda in the back seat, and the Negro driver that would drive her to Memphis in the front seat with the baggage (it was all new too) piled on the seat by him; coming up and stopping, and him setting there in that black hat that still looked brand new and like he had borrowed it, and that little bow tie that never had and never would look anything but new, chewing slow and steady at his tobacco; and that gal setting there by him, tight and still and her back not even touching the back of the seat, in a kind of dark suit for travelling and a hat and a little veil and her hands in white gloves still and kind of clenched on her knees and not once not never once ever looking at that stone monument with that marble medallion face that Lawyer had picked out and selected that never looked like Eula a-tall you thought at first, never looked like nobody nowhere you thought at first, until you were wrong because it never looked like all women because what it looked like was one woman that ever man that was lucky enough to have been a man would say, "Yes, that's her. I knowed her five years ago or ten years ago or fifty years ago and you would a thought that by now I would a earned the right not to have to remember her any more," and under it the carved letters that he his-self, and I don't mean Lawyer this time, had picked out:

EULA VARNER SNOPES

1889   1927

A Virtuous Wife Is a Crown to Her Husband
Her Children Rise and Call Her Blessed

and him setting there chewing, faint and steady, and her still and straight as a post by him, not looking at nothing and them two white balls of her fists on her lap. Then he moved. He leant a little and spit out the window and then set back in the seat.

"Now you can go," he says.

CHARLES MALLISON

So the car went on. Then I turned and started walking back to ours when Ratliff said behind me: "Wait. You got a clean handkerchief?" and I turned and saw Uncle Gavin walking on away from us with his back to us, not going anywhere: just walking on, until Ratliff took the handkerchief from me and we caught up with him. But he was all right then, he just said:

"What's the matter?" Then he said, "Well, let's get on back. You boys are free to loaf all day long if you want to, but after all I work for the County so I have to stay close enough to the office so that anybody that wants to commit a crime against it can find me."

So we got in the car and he started it and we drove back to town. Except that he was talking about football now, saying to me: "Why don't you wake up and get out of that kindergarten and into high school so you can go out for the team? I'll need somebody I know on it because I think I know what's wrong with football the way they play it now"; going on from there, talking and even turning loose the wheel with both hands to show us what he meant; how the trouble with football was, only an expert could watch it because nobody else could keep up with what was happening; how in baseball everybody stood still and the ball moved and so you could keep up with what was happening. But in football, the ball and everybody else moved at the same time and not only that but always in a clump, a huddle with the ball hidden in the middle of them so you couldn't even tell who did have it, let alone who was supposed to have it; not to mention the ball being already the colour of dirt and all the players thrashing and rolling around in the mud and dirt until they were all that some colour too; going on like that, waving both hands with Ratliff and me both hollering, "Watch the wheel! Watch the wheel!" and Uncle Gavin saying to Ratliff, "Now you don't think so," or "You claim different of course," or "No matter what you say," and Ratliff saying, "Why, I never," or "No I don't," or "I ain't even mentioned football," until finally he—Ratliff—said to me:

"Did you find that bottle?"

"No sir," I said. "I reckon Father drank it. Mr Gowrie won't bring the next kag until Sunday night."

"Let me out here," Ratliff said to Uncle Gavin. Uncle Gavin stopped talking long enough to say,

"What?"

"I'll get out here,'" Ratliff said. "See you in a minute."

So Uncle Gavin stopped long enough for Ratliff to get out (we had just reached the Square), then we went on, Uncle Gavin talking again or still talking since he had only stopped long enough to say What? to Ratliff, and parked the car and went up to the office and he was still talking that same kind of foolishness that you never could decide whether it didn't make any sense or not, and took one of the pipes from the bowl and begun to look around the desk until I went and shoved the tobacco jar up and he looked at the jar and said, "Oh yes, thanks," and put the pipe down, still talking. Then Ratliff came in and went to the cooler and got a glass and the spoon and sugar-bowl from the cabinet and took a pint bottle of white whiskey from inside of his shirt, Uncle Gavin still talking, and made the toddy and came and held it out.

"Here," he said.

"Why, much obliged," Uncle Gavin said. "That looks fine. That sure looks fine." But he didn't touch it. He didn't even take it while Ratliff set it down on the desk where I reckon it was still sitting when Clefus came in the next morning to sweep the office and found it and probably had already started to throw it out when he caught his hand in time to smell it or recognise it or anyway drink it. And now Uncle Gavin took up the pipe again and filled it and fumbled in his pocket and then Ratliff held out a match and Uncle Gavin stopped talking and looked at it and said, "What?" Then he said, "Thanks," and took the match and scratched it carefully on the underside of the desk and blew it carefully out and put it into the tray and put the pipe into the tray and folded his hands on the desk and said to Ratliff:

"So maybe you can tell me because for the life of me I can't figure it out. Why did she do it? Why? Because as a rule women don't really care about facts just so they fit; it's just men that don't give a damn whether they fit or not, who is hurt, how many are hurt, just so they are hurt bad enough. So I want to ask your opinion. You know women, travelling around the country all day long right in the middle of them, from one parlour to another all day long all high and mighty, as dashing and smooth and welcome as if you were a damned rush—" and stopped and Ratliff said,

"What? What rush? Rush where?"

"Did I say rush?" Uncle Gavin said. "No no, I said Why? A young girl's grief and anguish when young girls like grief and anguish and besides, they can get over it. Will get over it. And just a week from her birthday too of course but after all Flem is the one to get the zero for that: for missing by a whole week anything as big as a young girl's nineteenth birthday. Besides, forget all that; didn't somebody just say that young girls really like grief and anguish? No no, what I said was, Why?" He sat there looking at Ratliff. "Why? Why did she have to? Why did she? The waste. The terrible waste. To waste all that, when it was not hers to waste, not hers to destroy because it is too valuable, belonged to too many, too little of it to waste, destroy, throw away and be no more." He looked at Ratliff. "Tell me, V.K. Why?"

"Maybe she was bored," Ratliff said.

"Bored," Uncle Gavin said. Then he said it again, not loud: "Bored." And that was when he began to cry, sitting there straight in the chair behind the desk with his hands folded together on the desk, not even hiding his face. "Yes," he said. "She was bored. She loved, had a capacity to love, for love, to give and accept love. Only she tried twice and failed twice to find somebody not just strong enough to deserve, earn it, match it, but even brave enough to accept it. Yes," he said, sitting there crying, not even trying to hide his face from us, "of course she was bored."

And one more thing. One morning—it was summer again now, July—the northbound train from New Orleans stopped and the first man off was usually the Negro porter—not the Pullman porters, they were always back down the track at the end; we hardly ever saw them, but the one from the day coaches at the front end—to get down and strut a little while he talked to the section hands and the other Negroes that were always around to meet the passenger trains. But this time it was the conductor himself, almost jumping down before the train stopped, with the white flagman at his heels, almost stepping on them; the porter himself didn't get off at all: just his head sticking out a window about half way down the car.

Then four things got off. I mean, they were children. The tallest was a girl though we never did know whether she was the oldest or just the tallest, then two boys, all three in overalls, and then a little one in a single garment down to its heels like a man's shirt made out of a flour- or meal-sack or maybe a scrap of an old tent. Wired to the front of each one of them was a shipping tag written in pencil:

From: Byron Snopes, El Paso, Texas
To: Mr Flem Snopes, Jefferson, Mississippi

Though Mr Snopes wasn't there. He was busy being a banker now and a deacon in the Baptist church, living in solitary widowerhood in the old De Spain house which he had remodelled into an ante-bellum Southern mansion; he wasn't there to meet them. It was Dink Quistenberry. He had married one of Mr Snopes's sisters or nieces or something out at Frenchman's Bend and when Mr Snopes sent I.O. Snopes back to the country the Quistenberrys came in to buy or rent or anyway run the Snopes Hotel, which wasn't the Snopes Hotel any more now but the Jefferson Hotel, though the people that stayed there were still the stock traders and juries locked up by the Circuit Court. I mean, Dink was old enough to be Mr Snopes's brother-in-law or whatever it was, but he was the kind of man it just didn't occur to you to say Mister to.

He was there; I reckon Mr Snopes sent him. And when he saw them I reckon he felt just like we did when we saw them, and like the conductor and the flagman and the porter all looked like they had been feeling ever since the train left New Orleans, which was evidently where they got on it. Because they didn't look like people. They looked like snakes. Or maybe that's too strong too. Anyway, they didn't look like children; if there was one thing in the world they didn't look like it was children, with kind of dark pasty faces and black hair that looked like somebody had put a

bowl on top of their heads and then cut their hair up to the rim
of the bowl with a dull knife, and perfectly black perfectly still
eyes that nobody in Jefferson (Yoknapatawpha County either)
ever afterward claimed they saw blink.

I don't know how Dink talked to them, because the conductor
had already told everybody listening (there was a good crowd by
that time) that they didn't talk any language or anything else
that he had ever heard of and that to watch them because one of
them had a switch knife with a six-inch blade, he didn't know
which one and he himself wasn't going to try to find out. But
anyway Dink got them into his car and the train went on.

Maybe it was the same thing they used in drugstores or at least
with Skeets McGowan in Christian's because it wasn't a week
before they could go into Christian's, all four of them (it was
always all four of them, as if when the medicine man or whoever
it was separated each succeeding one from the mother, he just
attached the severed cord to the next senior child. Because by that
time we knew who they were: Bryon Snopes's children out of a
Jicarilla Apache squaw in Old Mexico), and come out two
minutes later all eating ice-cream cones.

They were always together and anywhere in town or near it at
any time of day, until we found out it was any time of night too;
one night at two o'clock in the morning when Otis Harker caught
them coming in single file from behind the Coca-Cola bottling
plant; Otis said he didn't know how in the world they got into it
because no door was open nor window broken, but he could smell
warm Coca-Cola syrup spilled down the front of the little one's
nightshirt or dressing-sacque or whatever it was from five or six
feet away. Because that was as close as he got; he said he hollered
at them to go on home to the Snopes, I mean the Jefferson Hotel
but they just stood there looking at him and he said he never
intended anything: just to get them moving, since maybe they
didn't understand what he meant yet. So he sort of flung his arms
out and was just kind of jumping at them, hollering again, when
he stopped himself just in time, the knife already in one of their
hands with the blade open at least six inches long; so fast that he
never even saw where it came from and in the next minute gone
so fast he still didn't even know which one of the three in overalls
—the girl or the two boys—had it; that was when Mr Connors

went to Dink Quistenberry the next morning and told him he
would have to keep them off the streets at night.

"Sure," Dink said. "You try it. You keep them off the streets or off
anywhere else. You got my full permission. You're welcome to it!"

So when the dog business happened, even Mr Hub Hampton
himself didn't get any closer than that to them. This was the dog
business. We were getting paved streets in Jefferson now and so
more new families, engineers and contractors and such like the
little Riddell boy's that gave us that holiday two years ago, had
moved to Jefferson. One of them didn't have any children but
they had a Cadillac and his wife had a dog that they said cost five
hundred dollars the only dog higher than fifty dollars except a
field-trial pointer or setter (and a part Airedale bear dog named
Lion that Major de Spain, Mr de Spain's father, owned once that
hunting people in north Mississippi still talked about) that Jefferson
ever heard of, let alone saw— a Pekinese with a gold name-plate
on its collar that probably didn't even know it was a dog, that rode
in the Cadillac and sneered through the window not just at other
dogs but at people too, and even ate special meat that Mr Wall
Snopes's butcher ordered special from Kansas City because it
cost too much for just people to buy and eat it.

One day it disappeared. Nobody knew how, since the only
time it wasn't sneering out through the Cadillac window, it was
sneering out through a window in the house where it—they—
lived. But it was gone and I don't think anywhere else ever saw a
woman take on over anything like Mrs Widrington did, with
rewards in all the Memphis and north Mississippi and west
Tennessee and east Arkansas papers and Mr Hampton and Mr
Connors neither able to sleep at night for Mrs Widrington ringing
their telephone, and the man from the insurance company (its
life was insured too so maybe there were more people insured in
Jefferson than there were dogs, but then there was more of them
not insured in Jefferson than there was dogs too) and Mrs
Widrington herself likely at almost any time day or night to be
in your back yard calling what Aleck Sander and I thought was
Yow! Yow! Yow! until Uncle Gavin told us it was named Lao
T'se for a Chinese poet. Until one day the four Snopes Indians
came out of Christian's drugstore and somebody passing on the
street pointed his finger and hollered "Look!"

It was the collar with the gold name-plate. The little one was wearing it around its neck above the nightshirt. Mr Connors came quick and sent about as quick for Mr Hampton. And that was when Mr Hampton didn't come any closer either and I reckon we all were thinking about what he was: what a mess that big gut of his would make on the sidewalk if he got too close to that knife before he knew it. And the four Snopes Indians or Indian Snopeses, whichever is right, standing in a row watching him, not looking dangerous, not looking anything; not innocent especially and nobody would have called it affectionate, but not dangerous in the same sense that four shut pocket knives don't look threatening. They look like four shut pocket knives but they don't look lethal. Until Mr Hampton said:

"What do they do when they ain't eating ice cream up here or breaking in or out of that bottling plant at two o'clock in the morning?"

"They got a kind of camp or reservation or whatever you might call it in a cave they dug in the big ditch behind the school house," Mr Connors said.

"Did you look there?" Mr Hampton said.

"Sure," Mr Connors said. "Nothing there but just some trash and bones and stuff they play with."

"Bones?" Mr Hampton said. "What bones?"

"Just bones," Mr Connors said. "Chicken bones, spare ribs, stuff like that they been eating I reckon."

So Mr Hampton went and got in his car and Mr Connors went to his that had the red light and the sireen on it and a few others got in while there was still room, and the two cars went to the school house, the rest of us walking because we wanted to see if Mr Hampton with his belly really would try to climb down into that ditch and if he did how he was going to get out again. But he did it, with Mr Connors showing him where the cave was but letting him go first since he was the sheriff, on to where the little pile of bones was behind the fireplace and turned them over with his toe and then raked a few of them to one side. Because he was a hunter, a woodsman, a good one before his belly got too big to go through a thicket. "There's your dog," he said.

And I remember that time, five years ago now, we were all at the table and Matt Levitt's cut-out passing in the street and

Father said at Uncle Gavin: "What's that sound I smell?" Except that Mr Snopes's brass business at the power-plant was before I was even born: Uncle Gavin's office that morning and Mrs Widrington and the insurance man because the dog's life had been insured only against disease or accident or acts of God, and the insurance man's contention (I reckon he had been in Jefferson long enough to have talked with Ratliff; any stranger in town for just half a day, let alone a week, would find himself doing that) was that four half-Snopeses and half-Jicarilla Apache Indians were none of them and so Jefferson itself was liable and vulnerable to suit. So I had only heard about Mr Snopes and the missing brass from Uncle Gavin, but I thought about what Father said that day because I had been there then: "What's that sound I smell?" when Mr Snopes came in, removing his hat and saying "Morning" to everybody without saying it to anybody; then to the insurance man: "How much on that dog?"

"Full pedigree value, Mr Snopes. Five hundred dollars," the insurance man said and Mr Snopes (the insurance man himself got up and turned his chair around to the desk for him) sat down and took a blank check from his pocket and filled in the amount and pushed it across the desk in front of Uncle Gavin and got up and said "Morning" without saying it to anybody and put his hat on and went out.

Except that he didn't quite stop there. Because the next day Byron Snopes's Indians were gone. Ratliff came in and told us.

"Sho," he said. "Flem sent them out to the Bend. Neither of their grandmaws, I mean I.O.'s wives, would have them, but finally Dee-wit Binford"—Dewitt Binford had married another of the Snopes girls. They lived near Varner's store—"taken them in. On a contract, the Snopeses all clubbing together pro rata and paying Dee-wit a dollar a head a week on them, providing of course he can last a week. Though naturally the first four dollars was in advance, what you might call a retainer you might say."

It was. I mean, just about a week. Ratliff came in again; it was in the morning. "We jest finished using up Frenchman's Bend at noon yesterday, and that jest about cleans up the county. We're down at the dee-po now, all tagged and the waybill paid, waiting for Number Twenty-three south-bound or any other train that will connect more or less or thereabouts for El Paso, Texas"—

telling about that too: "A combination you might say of scientific
interest and what's that word?" until Uncle Gavin told him
anthropological "anthropological coincidence; them four vanishing Americans coming durn nigh taking one white man with them
if Clarence Snopes's maw and a few neighbours hadn't got there
in time."

He told it: how when Dewitt Binford got them home he discovered they wouldn't stay in bed at all, dragging a quilt off on to
the floor and lying in a row on it and the next morning he and his
wife found the bedstead itself dismantled and leaned against the
wall in a corner out of the way; and that they hadn't heard a
sound during the process. He—Dewitt—said that's what got on
his mind even before he began to worry about the little one: you
couldn't hear them; you didn't even know they were in the house
or not, when they had entered it or left it; for all you knew, they
might be right there in your bedroom in the dark, looking at
you.

"So he tried it," Ratliff said. "He went over to Tull's and
borrowed Vernon's flashlight and waited until about midnight
and he said he never moved quieter in his life, across the hall to
the door of the room, trying to not even breathe if he could help
it; he had done already cut out sighting notches in the door-
frame so that when he laid the flashlight into them by feel it
would be aimed straight at where the middle two heads would be
on the pallet; and held his breath again, listening until he was sho
there wasn't a sound, and snapped on the light. And them four
faces and them eight black eyes already laying there wide open
looking straight at him.

"And Dee-wit said he would like to a give up then. But by
that time that least un wouldn't give him no rest a-tall. Only he
didn't know what to do because he had done been warned about
that knife even if he hadn't never seen it. Then he remembered
them pills, that bottle of knock-out opium pills that Doc Peabody
had give Miz Dee-wit that time the brooder lamp blowed up and
burnt most of her front hair off, so he taken eight of them and
bought four bottles of sody pop at the store and put two capsules
into each bottle and druv the caps back on and hid the bottles jest
exactly where he figgered they would have to hunt jest exactly
hard enough to find them. And by dark the four bottles was gone

and he waited again to be sho it had had plenty of time to work and taken Vernon's flashlight and went across the hall and got on his hands and knees and crawled across to the pallet—he knowed by practice now exactly where on the pallet that least un slept or anyway laid—and reached out easy and found the hem of that nightshirt with one hand and the flashlight ready to snap on in the other.

"And when he told about it, he was downright crying, not with jest skeer so much as pure and simple unbelief. 'I wasn't doing nothing,' he says. 'I wasn't going to hurt it. All in the world I wanted was jest to see which it was—' "

"Which is it?" Uncle Gavin said.

"That's what I'm telling you," Ratliff said. "He never even got to snap the flashlight on. He jest felt them two thin quick streaks of fire, one down either cheek of his face; he said that all that time he was already running backward on his hands and knees toward the door he knowed there wouldn't even be time to turn around, let alone get up on his feet to run, not to mention shutting the door behind him; and when he ran back into his and Miz Deewit's room there wouldn't be no time to shut that one neither except he had to, banging it shut and hollering for Miz Dee-wit now, dragging the bureau against it while Miz Dee-wit lit the lamp and then come and holp him until he hollered at her to shut the windows first; almost crying, with them two slashes running from each ear, jest missing his eye on one side, right down to the corners of his mouth like a great big grin that would bust scab and all if he ever let his face go, telling how they would decide that the best thing would be to put the lamp out too and set in the dark until he remembered how they had managed somehow to get inside that locked-up Coca-Cola plant without even touching the patented burglar alarm.

"So they jest shut and locked the windows and left the lamp burning, setting there in that air-tight room on that hot summer night, until it come light enough for Miz Dee-wit to at least jump and dodge on the way back to the kitchen to start a fire in the stove and cook breakfast. Though the house was empty then. Not safe of course: jest empty except for themselves while they tried to decide whether to try to get word in to Flem or Hub Hampton to come out and get them, or jest pack up themselves without even waiting to wash up the breakfast dishes, and move over to Tull's. Anyhow Dee-wit said him and Miz Dee-wit was through and they knowed it, four dollars a week or no four dollars a week; and so, it was about nine o'clock, he was on his way to the store to use the telephone to call Jefferson, when Miz I.O. Snopes, I mean the number-two one that got superseded back before she ever had a chance to move to town, saved him the trouble."

We knew Clarence Snopes ourselves. He would be in town every Saturday, or every other time he could get a ride in, according to Ratliff—a big hulking man now, eighteen or nineteen, who was all a grey colour: a greying tinge to his tow-coloured hair, a greyish pasty look to his flesh, which looked as if it would not flow blood from a wound but instead a pallid fluid like thin oatmeal; he was the only Snopes or resident of Frenchman's Bend or Yoknapatawpha County either, for that matter, who made his Texas cousins welcome. "You might say he adopted them," Ratliff said. "Right from that first day. He even claimed he could talk to them and that he was going to train them to hunt in a pack; they would be better than any jest pack of dogs because sooner or later dogs always quit and went home, while it didn't matter to them where they was.

"So he trained them. The first way he done it was to set a bottle of sody pop on a stump in front of the store with a string running from it to where he would be setting on the gallery, until they would manoeuvre around and finally bushwack up to there one of them could reach for it, when he would snatch it off the stump with the string and drag it out of their reach. Only that never worked but once, so then he would have to drink the bottles empty and fill them again with muddy water or some such, or another good training method was to gather up a few throwed-away candy-bar papers and wrap them up again with mud inside or maybe jest not nothing a-tall because it taken them a good while to give up then, especially if now and then he had a sho enough candy bar or a sho enough bottle of strawberry or orange shuffled into the other ones.

"Anyhow he was always with them, hollering at them and waving his arms to go this way or that way when folks was watching, like dogs; they even had some kind of a play house or cave or something in another ditch about half a mile up the road. That's right. What you think you are laughing at is the notion of a big almost growed man like Clarence, playing, until all of a sudden you find out that what you're laughing at is calling anything playing that them four things would be interested in.

"So Dee-wit had jest reached the store when here come Clarence's maw, down the road hollering 'Them Indians! Them Indians!' jest like that: a pure and simple case of mother love and mother instinct. Because likely she didn't know anything yet, and even if she had, in that state she couldn't a told nobody: jest standing there in the road in front of the store wringing her hands and hollering Them Indians until the men squatting along the gallery begun to get up and then to run because about that time Dee-wit come up. Because he knowed what Miz Snopes was trying to say. Maybe he never had no mother love and mother instinct, but then neither did Miz Snopes have a last-night's knife-slash down both cheeks.

" 'Them Indians?' he says. ''Fore God, men, run. It may already be too late.'

"But it wasn't. They was in time. Pretty soon they could hear Clarence bellowing and screaming and then they could line him out and the fastest ones run on ahead and down into the ditch to where Clarence was tied to a blackjack sapling with something less than a cord of wood stacked around him jest beginning to burn good.

"So they was in time. Jody telephoned Flem right away and in fact all this would a formally took place yesterday evening except that Clarence's hunting pack never reappeared in sight until this morning, when Dee-wit lifted the shade enough to see them waiting on the front gallery for breakfast. But when his house was barred in time because he hadn't never unbarred it from last night. And Jody's car was already standing by on emergency alert as they say and it wasn't much trouble to toll them into it since like Clarence said one place was jest like another to them.

"So they're down at the dee-po now. Would either of you gentlemen like to go down with me and watch what they call the end of a erea, if that's what they call what I'm trying to say? The last and final end of Snopes out-and-out unvarnished behaviour in Jefferson, if that's what I'm trying to say."

So Ratliff and I went to the station while he told me the rest of it. It was Miss Emily Habersham; she had done the telephoning herself: to the Travellers' Aid in New Orleans to meet the Jefferson train and put them on the one for El Paso, and to the El Paso Aid to get them across the border and turn them over to the Mexican police to send them back home, to Byron Snopes or the reservation or wherever it was. Then I noticed the package and said, "What's that?" but he didn't answer. He just parked the pickup and took the cardboard carton and we went around on to the platform where they were: the three in the overalls and what Ratliff called the least un in the nightshirt, each with the new shipping tag wired to the front of its garment, but printed in big block capitals this time, like shouting this time:

From: Flem Snopes, Jefferson, Miss.
To: BYRON SNOPES
EL PASO, TEXAS

There was a considerable crowd around them, at a safe distance, when we came up and Ratliff opened the carton; it contained four of everything: four oranges and apples and candy bars and bags of peanuts and packages of chewing gum. "Watch out, now," Ratliff said. "Maybe we better set it on the ground and shove it up with a stick or something." But he didn't mean that. Anyway, he didn't do it. He just said to me, "Come on; you ain't quite growed so they may not snap at you," and moved near and held out one of the oranges, the eight eyes not once looking at it nor at us nor at anything that we could see; until the girl, the tallest one, said something, something quick and brittle that sounded quite strange in the treble of a child; whereupon the first hand came out and took the orange, then the next and the next, orderly, not furtive: just quick, while Ratliff and I dealt out the fruit and bars and paper bags, the empty hand already extended again, the objects vanishing somewhere faster than we could follow, except the little one in the nightshirt which apparently had no pockets: until the girl herself leaned and relieved the overflow.

Then the train came in and stopped; the day coach vestibule clanged and clashed open, the narrow steps hanging downward from the orifice like a narrow dropped jaw. Evidently, obviously, Miss Habersham had telephoned a trainmaster or a superintendent (maybe a vice-president) somewhere too because the conductor and the porter both got down and the conductor looked rapidly at the four tags and motioned, and we—all of us; we represented Jefferson—watched them mount and vanish one by one into that iron impatient maw: the girl and the two boys in overalls and Ratliff's least un in its ankle-length single garment like a man's discarded shirt made out of flour- or meal-sacking or perhaps the remnant of an old tent. We never did know which it was.

Oxford-Charlottesville-Washington-New York
November 1955-September 1956

Printed in Great Britain
at Hopetoun Street, Edinburgh,
by T. and A. CONSTABLE LTD.
Printers to the University of Edinburgh